Also by Owen King

The
CURATOR

A NOVEL

OWEN KING

SCRIBNER

NEW YORK LONDON TORONTO SYDNEY NEW DELHI

Scribner

An Imprint of Simon & Schuster, Inc.

1230 Avenue of the Americas

New York, NY 10020

First Scribner hardcover edition March 2023

SCRIBNER and design are registered trademarks of The Gale Group, Inc.,
used under license by Simon & Schuster, Inc., the publisher of this work.

For information about special discounts for bulk purchases,
please contact Simon & Schuster Special Sales at 1-866-506-1949
or business@simonandschuster.com.

The Simon & Schuster Speakers Bureau can bring authors to
your live event. For more information or to book an event,
contact the Simon & Schuster Speakers Bureau at 1-866-248-3049
or visit our website at www.simonspeakers.com.

Interior design by Kyle Kabel

Manufactured in the United States of America

1   3   5   7   9   10   8   6   4   2

Library of Congress Cataloging-in-Publication Data has been applied for.

ISBN 978-1-9821-9680-6
ISBN 978-1-9821-9682-0 (ebook)

Illustrations by Kathleen Jennings

The Princess was such a wonderful Princess that she had the power of knowing secrets, and she said to the tiny woman, Why do you keep it there? This showed her directly that the Princess knew why she lived all alone by herself spinning at her wheel, and she kneeled down at the Princess's feet, and asked her never to betray her. So, the Princess said, I never will betray you. Let me see it. So, the tiny woman closed the shutter of the cottage window and fastened the door, and trembling from head to foot for fear that any one should suspect her, opened a very secret place, and showed the Princess a shadow.

—Charles Dickens, *Little Dorrit*

I will go further and say all cats are wicked, though often useful. Who has not seen Satan in their sly faces?

—Charles Portis, *True Grit*

PART I

NEW PEOPLE

The city—nicknamed "the Fairest"

Maybe Especially So

The city—nicknamed "the Fairest" by poets and municipal advocates for its river, the mighty Fair—jutted from the body of the country like a hangnail from its thumb.

Folklore told that it was founded by a stonecutter who built a castle there and kept it empty in tribute to God, and was granted eternal youth as a reward; until, after a few hundred years, a family of beggars sneaked inside and their sudden appearance shocked the stonecutter such that he fell dead. More likely, the initial settlement was established by seafarers of Nordic origin.

In modern times, the city was distinguished by the line of handsome, heavy-browed monarchs who kept seat there; by its congress and its courts; by the efficiency, fortitude, reach, profitability, and diversity of its mercenary army, which was said to include speakers of more than twenty languages; by its river, the Fair, which descended from the country's mountain region to split the metropolis in half, into east and west, and to drown its fresh waters in the ocean; by the peninsula's high bluffs, which diminished seaward in parallel to the Fair; by the bustle and trade of its port; by its two cantilevered bridges; by the modern convenience of its network of electric trams; by its vast urban parkland, the Royal Fields, and the Royal Pond therein, where boaters rowed in vessels whose prows were carved into the likenesses of the nation's heavy-browed monarchs, from Macon I to Zak XXI; by the competition among its luxury hotels as to which establishment had the most luxurious cat as its mascot; by its cultural landmarks, such as the theaters and the museums and the Morgue Ship; by the three towering monolithic stones that dominated the plateau above the Great Highway a few miles beyond the city limits and to which, by tradition, newlyweds from all over the world traveled with hammers and picks in order to chip tokens to signal their shared commitment; by the irony of its stinking gray waterway's name; by its factory fires; by its neighborhood fires; by its teeming lower district, the Lees; by the fecund poor who populated the Lees and gave their new generations to nourish its plagues and armies; by its vestiges of paganism; by its secret societies; by the tartness of the brine used to pickle its oysters; by the bands of industrious delinquents that crowded its streets; by the courage and strength of its men; by the wisdom and perseverance of its women; and, like all cities, but maybe especially so, by its essential unmappability.

New People

*P*rior to the uprising she had labored in domestic service at the National University, but now D contrived to obtain a position at the Society for Psykical Research. Everywhere in the city new people would be needed—would they not?—to fill the places that had been occupied by members of the deposed regime and its supporters. This was true not only with regard to the government and the military, but all across day-to-day life, where every place from schools to shops to gasworks to theaters had been ruled over by the elites for as long as anyone could remember.

Although she had passed inside the Society's walls just once, as a young girl, a picture of it remained in D's mind, of "the Grand Hall" where she had waited one morning for a servant to retrieve her older brother, who had been a junior member. The floor had been covered in a gold and red carpet that looked thick enough to her child's eye to bury a marble in; books filled the high shelving that spanned the walls; at a writing table a woman in a sweeping blue hat bent over an open ledger, marking lines with a compass and a ruler; on a neat little stage was arrayed an exhibit of conjurer's tricks; from the ceiling hung a large mobile of the galaxy, its sun the size of a croquet ball and its eleven planets the size of billiard balls; and in front of the fireplace was a gentleman in tweed breeches, asleep in a leather chair with a smile on his face and his hands tucked under his armpits.

In the difficult years that followed her single visit, D had often retreated to the idea of calm and possibility that the commodious and civilized room seemed to represent. If such a perfect space could quietly exist inside a city like this one, maybe there was something else, something more—another part of life, concealed.

Her visit to the Society and its Grand Hall had taken place roughly fifteen years earlier, at a time when an insurrection against the wealthy and the powerful was unimaginable. It was not long afterward that her brother, Ambrose, died after a short bout of cholera. The two events, the visit and Ambrose's death, were connected in her mind.

D often thought of her brother's final words. They had been awestruck, parched but clear: "Yes, I see you. Your . . . face."

Whose face? Ambrose had been nothing if not secretive, forever slipping off, and he sometimes said things D had not known whether to believe or take seriously. Once, he had told her that there were other worlds. Maybe it was true. D was almost certain that he had seen something in those final moments, not a hallucination, something real and amazing. There had been conviction in his voice.

If there was an afterlife, or other-life—anything else, anything at all—her brother was the one D wanted to find there.

In adulthood, however, this hope had occurred to her only dreamily, on the occasions that errands sent her along Legate Avenue, when she would pause to glimpse, down the byway of Little Heritage, the fine brick building that housed the Society for Psykical Research, tucked away in the shade of twin poplar trees.

Until opportunity presented itself. The revolution had all but thrown open the Society's bright-red door and invited her inside.

Δ

D asked her lover, a lieutenant in the Volunteer Civil Defense named Robert Barnes, if he could help her, and he said he would do anything she'd like, but—"psykical research, Dora?" Was that the kind of club where frivolous rich women went in order to have their palms stroked, and to engage deceased eminences in conversation? Because that was what it sounded like.

"Lieutenant," D replied, "just who is giving the orders around here?"

△

They went to the headquarters of the Provisional Government, which was located at the Magistrates' Court near the mid-east bank of the river.

On the plaza they found an aide to Crossley. While the students and the dockmen's union and other radicals had fomented the unrest, it had been General Crossley's alignment with the opposition leaders that accelerated and solidified the revolution. Without the muscle of Crossley's Auxiliary Garrison, they could never have forced the regime into retreat and out of the city.

The aide, a Sergeant Van Goor, was posted at a small table. He wore large emerald cufflinks, and as he propped his chin on his fist, one of the emeralds reflected a spot of watery green light into the eye of the statue of a rearing tiger that dominated the center of the slated plaza. D suspected that the cufflinks had only recently come into Sergeant Van Goor's possession.

Her lieutenant explained what they wanted and pledged that she was a patriot. "That so?" Van Goor smiled at her. She lowered her eyes and nodded.

"Lovely. I'm convinced," he said. "Go to it."

But Robert wanted her to have something more official; he didn't want any trouble or confusion. He dug a scrap of paper from his pocket and wrote out a declaration. It granted D authority over the Society building and its grounds "in order to preserve the public's rightful property until such time as the freely elected government is established and an assessment undertaken for its future use." He read it aloud to the aide.

Van Goor chuckled, said it was handsome, and carefully made his initials on the bottom of the paper.

The pair walked northeast with their elbows linked.

△

An upright piano, a tattered tablecloth, broken wine bottles, a rubber tree with its root ball exposed amid the shards of its pot, scattered books, and a thousand other things, flotsam of the deposed government and its supporters that had been dumped from wagons and carriages, littered the National Boulevard. D thought, *With all the domestics being promoted, everyone will have to learn to tidy up their own messes.* People were only beginning to emerge after the fighting that had driven the Crown's Home Guard from the city.

Those they passed wore jolted expressions, and stood casting glances here and there, as if to locate themselves amid the scattered wreckage.

"Everything's all right now," the lieutenant assured several of the disoriented strangers without being asked. They blinked and smiled tentatively and tipped their hats in response, and seemed to come back to themselves.

"Are you sure, sir?" one woman blurted. She peered at Robert through the scratched lenses of a pair of tiny spectacles. Her skirt was black and dusty; a nurse, D guessed, or a teacher.

"Yes," he said.

"They've surrendered?"

"They're gone," the lieutenant said, "and they're not coming back."

D saw the woman in the dusty skirt frown, but what Robert had said seemed to satisfy the others nearby, several of whom clapped and hooted. "Come on, then," announced one bystander, inspired, and a group gathered around the carcass of a toppled carriage to muscle it off the tram tracks.

D spied her lieutenant grinning to himself. In profile, he looked his rank: curly black hair hooking the tops of his ears and fringing the nape of his neck, excellent straight nose just ahead of his strong chin. It sneaked up on her every now and again, how much she liked him. When he said that everything was all right and would stay that way, you could believe that it was true.

Other young men wearing the green armbands that designated membership in the Volunteer Civil Defense were stationed on the streets to maintain order. Robert, like many of the Volunteers formerly a student at the university, flashed ironically casual salutes to his fellows and they flashed them back in return.

A little boy, feet stuffed into some rich woman's canary-yellow evening slippers that he must have scavenged, ran up and saluted the lieutenant. Robert halted, froze the boy with a dour squint, and abruptly snapped a salute back at him. The boy dashed off squealing.

One man called to the lieutenant from beneath a shaded second-floor window: "How can a hungry man be of service, Officer?"

Her lieutenant hollered up to him to go to the encampment on the grounds of the Magistrates' Court. He told him where to find the aide who had signed D's declaration. "Tell him Lieutenant Barnes sent you." He would be fed and something would be found for him to do; there was no shortage of work to be done.

"Thank you for your help! I won't shame you! I'll work hard at whatever I'm set to," the man called after them. "Once I'm at it, there's no one can outdo me. May a cat smile on you, sir! And your lady!"

There were several more encounters like this one. Each time, Robert stopped and spoke to the person, offering advice on how to find food or work or whatever sort of help they needed. D was impressed at how he didn't shy away from these people, many of whom were visibly in want, clothed in rags and unkempt. By the way he held his shoulders after each of these consultations, she thought her lieutenant was impressed with himself as well.

They neared the edge of the Government District, where Legate Avenue's embassies bumped against midtown, and turned onto the avenue. Here, signs of the conflict diminished. Along the row of embassies, the flags of other nations still hung, their colors resplendent in the clear morning sunlight, though the ambassadors and diplomats had all departed. In its unprecedented vacancy the avenue seemed to lay itself out just for them—all the way to the iron post bearing the street sign that read **Little Heritage Street**.

Events Leading to the Overthrow of the Crown's Government, Pt. 1

$\mathscr{A}$ man named Joven, the owner of a firm that manufactured fine ceramics, accused the currency minister, Westhover, of gross swindle.

Joven's firm had been contracted to produce more than two hundred plates, bowls, vases, and ashtrays to fill the cabinets and dining room tables in Minister Westhover's home in the city, his lodge in the country, and his estate on the Continent. Each piece was designed to incorporate Westhover's device, an illustration of the currency minister in Roman costume, holding a scale laden with coins on one side and wheat on the other. The set for each residence was inked in a different color: red in the city, green in the country, black on the Continent.

These details became common knowledge when Joven, the offended retailer, printed a venomous pamphlet about the affair entitled

A MAN THAT'S WORD CANNOT BE WEIGHED.

The pamphlet recounted that Westhover had accepted delivery of the order and unilaterally changed the price, offering only a small portion of the agreed-upon amount. Joven, the pamphlet continued, refused the altered terms and demanded his products be returned; the currency minister had ignored him, kept the pieces, and used his influence in the courts to frustrate Joven's attempts at legal recompense:

The Minister is friends of the Magistrate that ruled the case, they are Neighbors, which is Outrageous and Not Proper in a Law Hearing.

Further implied by the manufacturer's *cri de cœur* was that the image of the currency minister was wildly idealized.

I even rendered him according to his Fancy of himself because that was how he liked and Wished although he is Not a trim man.

In retaliation, the currency minister authored his own pamphlet. This paper declared that Joven's factory used inferior materials, which resulted in a thin and unsatisfactory plate, and that everyone knew that Westhover was simply robust. "It is lamentable that individuals of low character and no family are allowed to insult their betters." The minister sued for defamation and swiftly won damages.

The whole matter, to that point, played as comedy, welcome relief from the mood of increasing discontent among the citizenry.

Cholera was even more rampant than usual in the poor neighborhoods of the Lees District at the lower tip of the city—to warn visitors not to drink water or eat food from the area, gloves were pinned under the knockers of the houses where the sickness was present, such that whole streets of tenements "wore the hand." A dockmen's strike had collapsed, its ringleaders debarred. In the countryside of the Northland Provinces an early-summer drought had seared crops, and the cascading effect had raised the price of bread, of beans, of meat, and so on. The army, under Frankish contract on the Continent and commanded by the great Gildersleeve, had been bogged down in the mountains after a series of defeats and suffered heavy casualties. The once-beloved general had become a symbol of doddering weakness; rumors said that, in seedier areas of the city, louts would tear the sleeves from your jacket and force you to burn them right there in the street, or else absorb a beating.

The specifics of the minister's ostentatious plates were delicious confirmation of the profligacy of a Crown and a government that lectured the public on the connection between their flagrant spending on spirits and gaming and idolatry and the conditions of their poverty. The simultaneous comeuppance of the imperious businessman who held these deranged ideas about fairness was even more bitterly satisfying, an ancient play performed with fresh zest. Everyone knew that Joven's mistake had not been the use of inferior materials. His mistake was to forget how things worked. True, Joven had been successful and made money. But men such as Westhover—who was not the first or even the second currency minister in his own family—men like that *were* money.

Newspaper cartoons lampooned Joven's squat stature and nearly bare head. The artists indicated his lunacy by wilding his eyes and drawing four or five hairs in apoplectic jags. In one cartoon he waved around a plate leaking glue from a dozen cracks and yelled, "See? Finest craftsmanship!" In another, he sat atop a giant pile of dish shards and spurted tears, wailing, "I s'pose I don't want them back anymore," while each of his four outraged hairs gushed tears of its own.

Perhaps Joven was mad, or what qualified as mad in those waning days of the previous government; for, obdurately, even after the court ruled against him, he refused to let the matter lie.

Joven had grown up in the impoverished neighborhoods of the Lees, close by the bay. He had never attended any school, but learned his trade from a mudman, and started off using rock kilns to fire crude plates fashioned from Fair River muck. Later, he had developed a special technique, mixing Fair sludge with ground bone to create hand-molded pieces that were smooth enough to pass for factory quality and, gradually, one setting at a time, built his capital.

As a child, Joven had avoided cholera and other diseases. When he was a youth, the army missed him. He never married. All he ever did was work, expanding his business without connection or influence, until he had a factory and a warehouse and a gabled manor in the Hills above the Government District—a manor, in fact, that stood not too far from the ancestral estate of Minister Westhover.

The pads of Joven's fingers were burnt nerveless from his early years, operating close to the fires with makeshift implements. He had a menacing, head-down stride that made people who weren't even in his path jump aside at his approach. No one in his association had ever heard him say that he liked anything. If something—a design, a cup of coffee, a seat in a carriage—met his standards, he would sometimes bark, "Yeah!" but that was as close to praise as he ever came. He did seem to relish destroying flawed plates, hurling them down to shatter at the feet of his foremen, so hard that the shards sometimes rebounded and nicked his hands. At Joven's firm the employees had nicknamed their chief the Charmer, or just the Charm, for his dearth of social graces.

Even as a boy, selling single cups and pots, Joven never gave a penny of credit or cut a bargain. Dozens of saloonkeepers and cookshop owners in the Lees maintained invisible monuments to the Charmer's insolence. Here was the street corner, the doorway, the spot along the bar, where young Joven had stood in his muddy bare feet and stared at them with his lip out, and pointed his numb finger, and said a deal was a deal, make it or not.

Which is to say, not even his own people liked him. It did not matter that he had achieved prosperity of a kind that illiterate river rats never achieved. He was admired for his genius, and envied for his luck, but the Charmer had never been one for making friends.

△

The gates of Minister Westhover's mansion opened on a cool spring morning. Four chestnut horses clomped through an ankle-deep mist and pulled the minister's shining white carriage into the street. Joven, who had been waiting beside the fence, stepped out and whipped a plate sideways through the air. It was a replica that he had made himself of one of the plates in Westhover's set.

Joven still possessed the form he'd honed skipping rocks from the banks of the Fair: the plate spun fast and true. It struck the carriage door and splintered a gash in the glossy white wood.

"There's your thin materials, you chiseling fuck!" He scampered forward and snatched up the plate from where it had clattered to the cobbles. Joven waved the intact plate gleefully about his head to show the passersby—domestics, delivery boys, streetsweepers, carpenters on their way to a site. "Perfect! Not so much as a chip out of his ugly face!"

The driver of the carriage drew his horses to a halt. The currency minister opened the cracked door and peered out. The liveryman descended from the box, followed by the footman.

Joven charged at them with the plate in one hand and his other clenched in a fist but was taken off his feet by a shot from the pistol that the footman had removed from his jacket. The slug struck him in the hip and Joven fell over.

The plate dropped, this time hitting the cobbles just wrong. It broke and flopped into two clean semicircles.

"Hold him," Westhover called from the carriage, and the liveryman and the footman went to where Joven lay and pinned his arms and shoulders to the cobbles.

A small brazier had been built into the carriage to keep the government's chief economist warm on brisk mornings like this one. Using an engineer's mitt, Westhover extracted a hot coal, climbed down, and approached the group.

Joven struggled, but they held him fast. The minister crouched on the street and tried to stuff the red rock into his mouth. Joven clamped his lips shut and swung his head to and fro, receiving burns on his cheeks and nose, but not letting the currency minister push the coal in. He made growling noises as he jerked his head back and forth. In the scuffle, the vapor on the ground stirred and the mist licked over their backs and limbs.

After a minute or two, Minister Westhover grunted, tossed away the coal, and flung off the smoldering mitt. He staggered up from the man prostrate on the ground.

The minister, younger by a decade than the businessman but heavy and unfit, was breathing hard. He appeared flustered. Snot clung to his blond mustache. His blue silk tie had bunched up at his throat. He patted his pockets, blinking and swallowing and dragging in breaths.

The minister's men released Joven's arms, and rose. The mist began to seep back into the little clearing that had been carved out by the struggle.

Joven propped himself up on an elbow and spat at Westhover's shoes. The skin of his cheeks and nose was peeled and raw where the coal had pressed.

He was triumphant. "You can't make me eat your shit! Burn my nose off, but I never will!"

The crowd lingering at a distance, the maids and the men with hand-carts, murmured uneasily. Joven's cry echoed what they were thinking: "You saw it! You saw it! He tried to kill me!"

Joven shoved himself after the minister, pushing crablike with his palms, apparently wanting to get close enough to do more than just spit. Blood from his hip wound smeared onto the stones, the mist dulling it to black paint. He laughed as he scrabbled toward Westhover; no one had ever heard that before, the Charmer laughing. "He thinks it's all for him, the chiseling fuck, anything he wants to take! Break any deal! He thinks he can kill an honest craftsman in the street!"

The currency minister inhaled and pursed his lips. He rubbed his thumb over his fingertips, as if to make sure the nails were even.

Abruptly, Westhover stuck his hand in the pocket of his footman standing beside him, yanked free the pistol, and shot Joven twice in the chest.

The uncouth, uneducated, char-fingered crocker who had risen so far above his station was blown flat, dead, right there in full sight of more than thirty witnesses. A gasp of mist puffed up and slowly settled down on the corpse.

△

Someone in the crowd sobbed. "Murder," someone else said, and several voices agreed. The currency minister shoved the pistol at his footman and the footman took it.

"We saw!" a woman yelled. She was seconded and thirded. A man asked, "Why did you have to do that?"

Westhover didn't answer. He stalked back to his carriage and climbed in, slamming the cracked door shut. His men returned to the box, and they drove the carriage around and back through the open gates of the mansion, and closed them behind.

Constables arrived a few minutes later and ordered the crowd to disperse. Meanwhile, the mist had reduced Joven to a dark mound.

△

An inquest was held the next day and the matter was put to rest with no charges filed. The currency minister, investigators for the magistrate determined, had acted within the bounds of self-defense.

What About That Big Place There?

*B*ut as they turned onto Little Heritage they saw that the Society building had burned.

Whether it was an accident or a case of arson, it was impossible to say. In the midst of their retreat, the Home Guard and the portion of the Constabulary that had remained loyal to the Crown had set fire to parts of the city indiscriminately. The Provisional Government was only beginning to make a survey of the damage. Still, Little Heritage Street was the furthest thing from a main thoroughfare. The cause might just as likely have been a tipped candle or a fireplace spark. Her lieutenant explained these obvious things to D as they stood on the sidewalk and regarded the ruins.

The neighboring structures were undamaged. The effect was like a rotten tooth in an otherwise gleaming smile.

D ventured along the path as far as the poplar trees. The red door had been blasted clean from its hinges, and stuck at a slant in the grass of the lawn. The roof had fallen in. Mounds of scorched timbers and bricks and roof slates were visible through the empty doorway. Beneath the ash stench was a deep, muddy tang, as if the heat had been so powerful that it boiled the surrounding earth. Warmth still radiated from the wreckage, and a mist of blackish particles lingered above the remains of the structure.

The beginnings of the plan she had never allowed herself to fully believe in, that she would discover some record of her brother in the Society, some proof of the meaningfulness of his final words, disintegrated. The model sun and its planets were cinders, the writing desk where the lady in the hat had worked in her ledger reduced to sticks, the drowsy man's place by the hearth buried under layers of debris. The Grand Hall was gone along with the rest of the building—along with Ambrose.

But she couldn't afford to dwell in disappointment, not in her position. You could retain pictures of perfect rooms and memories of dead brothers in your head, but when you were on your own you lived on your feet. You continued forward, always, if you wanted to continue at all.

"Dora?" Her lieutenant had come up beside her. "Are you all right?"

She looped her arm through his and brought them around to start back along the path. "I'm fine. I hope no one was inside."

"None of the spirits were injured," Robert said. "I think we can be sure of that."

D had not gotten the impression that the Society for Psykical Research had much to do with ghosts, but she did not quibble. In truth, she had never understood precisely what the Society was about, just that it was a place where the members undertook certain investigations and studies— and that Ambrose had, briefly, been one of them.

"That is comforting, Lieutenant. I hadn't thought of that. Being a ghost seems melancholy, but at least you can't be incinerated." Since the establishment of the Volunteers she had taken to addressing him by his rank.

To the rest of his circle, the other young revolutionaries from the university, D was the whispery little maid that Bobby had shrewdly taken as a lover, a plain gray dress and bonnet who kept near the walls. They couldn't know how it actually was between them. That was part of the fun for him, she knew.

Robert said, "And even if they were vulnerable to fire, they could have been away at the first whiff of smoke. Spirits can pass through walls or windows, or they can slip under doors. Or they can expel themselves through the mail slots, like letters in reverse. It's up to each individual spirit."

"Where did you learn all this?"

"My nurse."

"She was a drunk?"

"Yes. I liked her very much."

D told him it really didn't matter, she had just admired the building, that was all. She didn't want to explain about Ambrose, or about her family, and that made it easier between them anyway. Robert liked her the way he thought of her.

"I know you wanted to do your part, Dora, but there are countless other places that need looking after. We're not even on the street with the good museums."

They had retraced their steps to the foot of Little Heritage, where the street's first building, a looming edifice with a foundation of pocked stone blocks, dwarfed the corner. Robert gestured to the right, north on Legate, past the embassy of the ousted government's foremost ally. "Let's go over to Great Heritage, and I promise we'll find you—" He paused, and shifted his gaze to the great pile of stone blocks beside them. "Wait, though. What about that big place there?"

Something Is
About to Happen

*S*ome boys had taunted her one day many years ago. D was with
her brother. She was eight. The boys were loitering outside an
apothecary's shop, and they wore smart blue school caps and uniforms
and looked to be a couple of years younger than Ambrose, who was fifteen, no longer a boy at all. Her brother held D's damp hand, while in
her elbow she cradled her baby doll.

"Oh, darling, I can't help but notice what a pretty baby you have
there!" one boy howled. His hair was white-blond and, like a grown man,
he had a gold watch chain that drooped from his vest pocket. In the shop
window behind him, there were boards with painted pictures—a man
with a bandaged head, a woman with a bulging eye, a red swollen toe
shooting black lines of hurt—to communicate the variety of injuries
treated by the apothecary's pills and tonics.

"Oh, *darling!*" one of the others crowed, picking up after him. "It's
a *baby!*"

It happened that her doll was named Baby, and she did think Baby
was very pretty in an ivory nightgown with a lace-trim collar. The abuse
of the older, nicely dressed boys confused and embarrassed D, and she
sniffled as her brother led her away.

They made cat sounds, hisses and growly screeches. Their leader kept on with his sneers. "And that must be your little wife! Well done, sir, well done!"

D wondered why her brother didn't tell them to stop; he was bigger than them. But Ambrose didn't even glance their way.

Instead, without pausing or twisting down to her, he whispered, "Hush now, D. They like when you cry. I would never let anyone harm you. Do you believe that?"

She said she did, but really, she wasn't sure of anything. She had not known that there were boys in the world who would yell at you just because you were small and you had a toy that you loved. D cried harder and the tears dripped on Baby.

"Good. Now, just stay close and pay attention," Ambrose said. "Something is about to happen."

The boys did not follow and their voices receded as the siblings walked around the corner onto the next street. D's brother told her to stop, and to look about herself. "Look as close as you can. See everything."

D saw:

Handsome houses that resembled their own, three-leveled except where they were four, with stone stoops that abutted the sidewalk. The thin parallel bars of the tram tracks, splitting the middle of the cobbled avenue, and within the fenced enclosure of the tram stop, a man who had removed his boot and stood, balancing on his other foot, to use a finial to scrape something off the boot's sole. On the far side of the avenue, a woman in a maid's apron and bonnet walking with a basket of lettuce on her head. Farther down, the neighborhood streetsweeper shoveling horse-droppings into his wheelbarrow; the shovel blade clanged off the stone. Grackles perched on the tram wire that hung above the tracks. The cloudless gray sky.

D returned her gaze to her brother. Like the mean boys, Ambrose wore a school cap, but his was a shade of gray not much darker than the sky, and he pulled it low to the tops of his eyebrows. In the years to come, D would picture him most vividly this way, sharp nose and a clever, jutting, top-teeth smile below a visor of shadow.

"Do you see what's happened?"

"No, I don't think so."

"We made them disappear. It's our special magic, D."

She knew it wasn't true. People couldn't be made to vanish, no matter how much you hated them. She appreciated the fantasy for the gift it was, though, a soothing idea that belonged only to them. The fair-haired boy might have had a fancy watch chain, but he didn't have a brother like D's, and he would never get to see that rabbit's grin her brother reserved just for her; and he didn't have a sister like D he could trust and rely on no matter what.

Maybe in that way, by comparison to what D and Ambrose shared, the boys were made so small it was like they disappeared.

Mother hated it when he called her D instead of Dora, but that was part of their closeness. In her infancy, Ambrose's tongue had tended to tangle itself in the tail of her name, and he'd settled on "D" as an alternative.

Nurse delighted in telling this story. "The young sir announced, 'I'm not going to exhaust myself trying to say the whole thing. Why should I? She's not so big she needs more than a letter anyway!'"

D could not remember thinking of herself any other way. It made her feel special, seen and noticed by him. Perhaps a letter was a little thing, but there were only twenty-six of them, and her brother had given the fourth to her.

"I love you," she said, and he patted her shoulder and said he loved her too.

As they stood there, the maid with the lettuce basket on her head carefully stepped around them.

△

When they got home, Nurse had collapsed to the floor in the doorway between the back hall and the kitchen. Father was at work and Mother was somewhere else. Nurse laughed and flapped a hand at them. Nurse had a puffy, creased, jolly face; it was a face like a happy cloud. D had never heard her speak an unkind word, and if she wasn't laughing, she always seemed to be on the verge of laughing.

"Look at this now: my legs went and sat me down! How do you like that?" Nurse chuckled some more. "Touch of something, I suppose. I'll be all right."

Ambrose helped her stand. "Of course you'll be all right." He guided her to a seat at the kitchen table. D caught a sniff of her odd, sweet smell, like the smell of the apples around the roots of an apple tree, the spoiled leaking ones that no one wanted.

D sat across from Nurse and reached out to pat her soft, damp hand. She said to Nurse what Nurse had always said to her when she didn't feel well: "Don't fret, darling, it's not your Day to Sail."

This caused Nurse to let out a hoot of delight before dropping her head into the crook of her elbow and groaning cheerfully. D patted her hand some more.

Her brother rebuttoned his coat. He'd run and fetch Nurse some tonic to settle her nerves. "Look after the patient while I'm gone, D." The apothecary was right around the corner. He plucked the ash shovel from its hook by the stove and promised to be back soon.

△

A month or two later, a day came when Nurse fell sick again.

Ambrose had warned D this was likely to happen and asked her to accept the extraordinarily important responsibility of fetching him immediately if it did. It was vital that their parents not learn about Nurse's fragile condition. This was because instead of walking directly home after school as their parents supposed, D's brother often arrived only minutes before his mother returned from her day's shopping and appointments. If Nurse was dismissed, her replacement might not be as tolerant of Ambrose's tardiness.

"I'm not the fellow Mother and Father would like me to be, D. I don't want to work in a bank, or be husband to someone who'd want to marry a banker. I'm not like them." Ambrose had winked at her from the shadow beneath his gray cap's bill.

"What are you like?" D asked.

"I'm interesting," he said.

"Am I interesting?" She couldn't imagine being interesting like her brother was interesting, but maybe there were gradations.

"Do you know interesting people?"

"You," she said.

"Well," said her brother, "there you have it. You are. Or you will be, because it rubs off. I made friends with one interesting person, one thing led to another, and now I'm part of a whole set of interesting people, and we're going to save the world. I hope you'll want to join us eventually. Now, what do you say? Can you be my spotter and run quick if Nurse is ill?"

D had said she could. At the same time, she'd wondered, *Save the world from what?*

Before she left the house, D tucked a pillow under Nurse's head where she had gone to sleep on the bathroom floor. Just as Ambrose had told her, she took the tram for two stops, got off, and walked to the corner where the street sign read **Great Heritage Street** in one direction and **Legate Avenue** in the other. From there, she continued along Legate a block farther to the street sign that read **Little Heritage Street**. On Little Heritage, just as her brother had described, the second building from the corner was made of bright brick and had two tall, skinny trees in front.

She hurried across the street and up the path to the red door inlaid with a silver triangle, and knocked.

△

A doorman took her brother's name, welcomed her to the Society for Psykical Research, and ushered her inside. He brought her through a tiled lobby to a curtained entranceway. This led through to what the doorman pronounced "the Grand Hall, miss." He instructed her to abide there while he went to retrieve the young gentleman from his studies, and marched away to a second curtained doorway at the far end of the long room.

D was glad to abide right where she stood. Her family circumstances were more than comfortable and she had never wanted for food or clothes or shelter, but the distinctly adult majesty of the room in which she had been deposited was overwhelming. She felt that her commitment to her brother had brought her as far as could reasonably be expected. She also bitterly regretted neglecting to bring Baby for support.

Bookshelves stretched the Hall's great length, and rose to its high ceiling, where a constellation of colored balls—planets, she realized—was strung, suspended by a spidery apparatus of bent silver wires. In the center of the apparatus was the largest ball, the yellow-painted sun. The whole construction moved slowly clockwise, and as it did, peels of light skimmed the curves of the planets.

Quiet, intent activity was taking place throughout the room. In the middle of what seemed like acres of gold-patterned red carpet, there was a woman at a writing desk with a ledger. A lavish touring hat sewn with pearls and flowers was tilted at her crown, screening her face, and she used a measuring instrument to draw lines in the book. At the top of a ladder attached to the wall perched a man examining the titles on the highest shelf. Off in a corner, a small group stood drinking from cups and saucers and chatting. Two identical women—twins!—in high-collared gowns were in consultation over a globe on a bronze stand.

Not too far from D, in a leather armchair by the marble fireplace, slumped an older man in tweed breeches. Even he, in his slumber, seemed happily occupied: his hands were clamped under his armpits, his sleeping mouth was lifted in a thoughtful smile, and there were blooms on his cheeks from the heat.

The Hall smelled wonderful, like cedar and woodsmoke and leather and polish and wax.

D balanced on the vast rug's lip, the toes of her shoes sunken into the pile of the burgundy-colored carpet—checkered with triangles like the one on the Society's door but gold instead of silver—and her heels on the threshold. The fabric of the curtain grazed her back. How had her brother ever found the courage to move beyond this spot?

She stared up at the planets, strategizing that if she focused all her attention on something, she would blend in, and no one would bother with her. Beneath the breeze of whispered conversation, the gently turning wire apparatus made a high, thin hum.

"Welcome, welcome! It's the blood of the new members that keeps our operation fresh and sprightly." The man from the armchair beside the fireplace had appeared in front of her. He was still smiling now that he was awake and his hands were still tucked under his armpits as if he had chilly fingers. His hair was the white-gray of factory smoke and hung around his face in loose curls. The vest under his tweed jacket was a shimmering gold. D had not known you could have a vest that color. She thought he must be very esteemed.

"I'm not a member, sir. I'm only waiting for my brother, Ambrose," D said. She stepped off the lip of the rug and retreated into the curtain. If she was in trouble, she could duck underneath and make a dash for it through the lobby.

"Ambrose, marvelous. Ah, so you're a guest. And a lovely, lovely girl. Well, I hope you do decide to join. As you can see, we have several female members."

His kind manner, and the way he held back his hands, reassured her. D felt it was safe enough to step forward from the curtain. "I had to leave my nurse on the floor in the bathroom. She's had too much medicine."

"A common problem. You know the solution, don't you?"

D shook her head.

"The solution is more medicine. Remember that."

"I will, sir."

"Good. What do you think of the place?"

"I like it," D said.

"Have you noticed the planets?"

"Yes, sir."

"Do you worry that one might break from the hanger and drop on your skull and kill you on your spot?"

"No, sir."

"Good. It has never happened. The wires are tightly fastened. Has anyone given you a tour?"

"No, sir. I was told to abide here."

"That's no way to treat a potential member. Let's see something. Would you accompany me on a short stroll?" With his hands stored under his armpits for safekeeping, the friendly old fellow indicated the direction across the room he wanted to go by tipping his head.

"Yes, sir."

He guided her on a route between the writing tables and seating areas. D kept her eyes on the heels of his slippers as she trailed him. She resisted a powerful urge to step only on the embroidered gold triangles. No one spared her a glance.

"Now, take a look at this, my dear, a good, good look, and tell me what you make of it."

They had come to a platform that extended from between two of the massive bookshelves. On the platform stood a side table and a deep, tall rectangular box with red velvet sides and a red door—a closet. The door of the closet was covered in smaller versions of the silver triangle that was inlaid on the building's front door. On the table were a black bowler hat, a black baton, a pack of fanned cards, and a silver egg.

"Well?"

He peered at her humorously, one eye held as wide as could be and the other nearly shut. He was such a friendly man; he made D feel confident enough to give an honest answer, instead of just saying that she didn't know.

"Is it to play a story game? You might take all those things there on the table into that closet, put on the hat, and then come out again with the other things and use them to tell a story?" This was exactly how she thought she would use the array on the stage. She used her own closet at home as a dressing room for performances of fairy tales that she put on for Nurse.

"Close enough," the cheerful man said. "What a smart girl!" He snorted a chuckle and rubbed his nose against his shoulder. "This is a conjurer's stage, and these were the instruments of a particular conjurer, a valued member of our little club, in fact. I don't know what you know about conjuring. But it's like storytelling. Is storytelling, really. The conjurer tells you an impossible tale and then gives you proof it's true. Canny, canny business. Like thievery, but what a conjurer steals is faith, and the man who made tricks on this stage was the most wonderful, wonderful criminal you can imagine."

The National Museum
of the Worker

*N*o gardens or ornamental bushes edged the stone block foundation of the massive structure at the corner of Legate and Little Heritage. There was no room for them. The great gray building sat flush to the street. Its walls flew straight and wide, interrupted only by the five belts of scabbed green window shutters that marked each level. D thought it had existed in her childhood, but its enormity was nondescript, and in her memory, by contrast to the cheery Society building with its fresh brick façade, the hulk's presence was faint and uncertain. It didn't appear to have been built; it looked as if it had settled, like a boulder in a field.

Brass letters bolted above the tall front doors announced the building's name and purpose:

THE NATIONAL MUSEUM OF THE WORKER:
"TO HONOR THE NAMELESS BUILDERS"

The metal doors were the height of a horse. A smaller plaque on the wall beside the doors informed visitors that they were cast from melted-down tools. Identifiable fragments of hammerheads and ball-peens and anvil horns bubbled from the doors' surfaces like shapes under a sheet.

Robert pressed the latch on the right-hand door, and it clicked—the museum had been left unlocked. D could tell that her lieutenant didn't like it. There was no way to know if they would be the first to enter since the fall of the Crown's government.

"I can find something else to do. It doesn't matter," D said. It really didn't. There were other places, other tasks.

"But it all matters now," he said, brushing aside the excuse she'd offered. "It's the public's property."

Robert held the door while D found an iron stop on the floor inside and jammed it into the gap.

Daylight spiked from the opening of the propped door and fell across the wide stairs leading to the first-floor gallery. Robert said he ought to go first—"just in case there are any holdouts bunkered down in here"—and trotted up the short flight from the foyer. But D followed him without waiting.

At the head of the stairs a ticket booth stood to one side. Ahead of them the first-floor gallery lay in a hazy brown gloom, the light filtered by the slats of the closed shutters lining the walls. D smelled dust, iron, and the tang of the smoke from the Society's ruins next door.

"Hello! Is anybody here? I'm a lieutenant of the Volunteer Civil Defense and I have documentation from the Provisional Government which grants me entry and command over these premises." Her lieutenant had taken his pistol from its holster. "There won't be any trouble—just put down anything you've taken, come out empty-handed, and I'll let you go on your way." His words echoed, chasing each other before they faded.

Robert looked to her with a twist at the corner of his mouth. She could tell he was anxious, asking with his expression if he should be ready to shoot someone, and more than that, if she believed he could.

Six months earlier, when they met, he had been a student at the university. In the forty-eight hours of skirmishing that had taken place mostly around the Government District, Robert had not seen any action.

He'd been stationed at the west end of the South Fair Bridge with a hand-saw, ready if the order came to cut the telegraph wires. He'd joked to D about the anticlimax of the experience. To pass the time, he'd read graffiti scratched on and around the lamp standards, and split the bread he'd brought with a Lees beggar girl. "I don't want to say that I found the battle relaxing," Robert had said to D, "but I did get some very educational reading done. Were you aware that the beer at the Still Crossing is mostly river water, but mixed with a little piss and vinegar so it's safe to drink?"

D didn't know if Robert was a coward or not. How could she? He didn't know yet himself. She would be glad if he never needed to find out.

She adjusted the green armband knotted above his biceps. "If there were looters here, Lieutenant, I think they've left."

"Agreed," he said. He took a deep breath and carefully holstered the gun, buttoning it down.

D kissed his cheek.

He made a noise in his throat while his hand slid up the side of her dress, pressing against her ribs.

D swiveled away. She walked to the nearest pair of shutters, folded them back, and continued along the hall, briskly opening one after another.

The shutters clattered and the gallery's hardwood floors unrolled in strips of dusty sunshine. The first exhibit to resolve itself was a model of oversized, interlocking gears that stood in the middle of the floor. A placard that dangled from the ceiling read *MACHINES AND THEIR OPERATORS*. Everything on this first floor concerned a mechanical invention: the printing press, the sawmill, the steam engine, the time-piece, the bicycle—and the engineers and operators who worked them. The larger exhibits were interspersed with smaller glass-topped display cases set on wooden podiums.

Opened to the daylight, the windows on the building's left side faced out onto Legate; while the windows on the right side, silted with ash from the fire, looked on the Society building's wreckage. The windows at the rear wall held views of the imperialists' embassy and its rear courtyard.

The museum was not wired for electricity. Tarnished gas lamps were fixed to the walls. D opened the tap on one and heard it hiss. She closed it.

Robert called her to the gears. It was an interactive exhibit. There were three gears, each as tall as the lieutenant. He pushed against the top gear, which turned its brother in the middle, which spun and bit the third gear, which caused the whole, slightly raised circular floor of the exhibit to slowly revolve. The gears clunked against each other and the rotation of the platform produced a gritty mumble. "Needs oil," he said.

Wax-figure workers populated several of the displays. A printer in gartered sleeves examined a long paper that unfurled from the printing press. At the sawmill a woodsman with a pipe in his grimacing mouth stood with his hands on his hips, observing the operation. Two wax men in long leather gloves and leather aprons busied themselves at their steam engine, cheeks painted pink and mottled with whitish drips as they sweated in the combustion heat. A young mechanic poked a screwdriver at a wheel bolt on the bicycle while its full-skirted female rider helpfully held it upright by the handlebars. Every figure was distinct; like the real population of the city itself, these wax figures bore different skin tones, and were formed in a range of body types.

A stairwell at the back of the gallery brought them to the second floor, which was dedicated to **HAND WORK**. Here, D opened the shutters to expose exhibitions on such professions as bricklaying, hunting and skinning, rug making, rope making, sewing, pottery making, vending, and baking.

From her oven the baker lifted a tray with several loaves of wooden bread, touched nearly white from handling. Robert removed one from the tray, weighed it, and set it back with a clunk. "It's stale," he said to the wax woman, who had a pained, drawn face. D thought she might be justifiably tired from holding the tray for however many years, and from hearing people laugh about her wooden bread. Dust coated her eyes.

The ropemaker—immediately familiar-looking somehow—sat in a nest of tangled hemp strands, her lined cheeks puffed in a jolly way. Pieces of white string had been threaded through the bricklayers' belt loops to keep their dungarees from falling down. D guessed that someone must have taken their belts. Dust covered these figures' eyes too. Several of the potter's bowls and vases had clearly been broken and cemented together.

The third floor was titled ***THE RAILS, ROADWAYS, AND OCEANS***. In this gallery, wax conductors manned sections of trains and trams, liverymen drove carriages, and a crew of sailors performed duties on a whaler's half-deck that was braced above the floor with scaffolding.

Throughout the museum, many of the wax figures, though impressively detailed and lifelike, showed bare patches on their scalps where hair had fallen out or been torn out. A few had suffered more severe damage: lost fingers, skin gouged, eyes cracked or missing altogether. Like the bricklayers, other figures seemed to have been robbed of their proper accoutrements—instead of a bucket, for instance, the clamdigger carried a coal scuttle. Most of the demonstration machines were broken. Of the half dozen train whistles set on a table for children to test, only the smallest responded when its button was thumbed, releasing a wounded moan; and no water poured from the pump that was supposed to feed the sawmill's wheel. The jury-rigged attempts at upkeep—the bricklayers' string, the coal scuttle—seemed opportunistic, the vague maintenance of a disinterested hand.

There were plaques to mark the gifts made by museum benefactors on benches and the walls beside some of the exhibits. Tellingly, the most recent of these was dated to twenty years earlier. D doubted that the National Museum of the Worker was in much danger of looting—or, in the case of the belts of the bricklayers and the clamdigger's bucket, further looting. It seemed to have been a long while since it had been of interest to visitors at all, and there were far richer pickings these days.

The fourth floor was home to ***COMMUNICATORS AND CUSTODIANS OF KNOWLEDGE***, and the top floor to ***OF STONE AND SOIL: MINES, FARMS, AND FORESTS***.

△

Near the back right corner of the fifth-floor hall, an ersatz prospector's shack hunched by a stream made of thick glass. Below the stream's transparent surface ceramic minnows hung from loops of wire. The wax prospector was encased up to his ankles in the middle of the glass water, panning. Closer to the shack, his wife draped rags on a clothesline.

Robert seated himself on one of the cane chairs in front of the shack. He put his hands on his knees. "Shall I tell you what I think? I think this is remarkably illustrative, Dora. This entire place."

"Hmm?" D strolled out onto the glass stream. Her shoes left footprints in the surface dust.

"You'll have noted, perhaps, that there were no exhibits for kings or dukes or ministers or mayors or legislators. That's quite strange, isn't it?"

If there had been an exhibit dedicated to domestics, or even a wax maid set out and allowed to discreetly sweep a board, D hadn't noticed that either, but she made an acquiescent murmur.

"The men with all the wealth, the ones who make the great rulings of law and decide whether to go to war, they aren't in the museum for workers. It sends a message, doesn't it? Maybe not the one they intended, though, because it dawns on you that the reason none of them are here is because those people don't do anything. Not anything real, anyway.

"And look at how it's been kept! There's dirt on everything, everything needs paint, the figures' clothes are falling off or coming apart or missing, and nothing works. It's actually a terrifically accurate expression of how the powerful view everyone else, or rather don't view them. . . ." Robert went on, and his lecture expanded to, among other subjects: the committees that were already being formed in the city's various neighborhoods, localized groups that would manage resources fairly and efficiently; his oblivious and sheltered parents, who meant well in their way, but couldn't conceive of the world beyond the acres of their estate and holdings in the Northland Provinces; and the blocks of currency that had been discovered in a wet subbasement of the premier's manor, left on pallets in the dark, blooming with mold and half disintegrated, enough money to feed thousands of people, forgotten, literally to rot. "I'd say it was a metaphor for everything that's not right about this country, but these were real banknotes turning into compost. . . ."

Color filled his cheeks. Sweat sheened his forehead and his eyes went frog-wide. Her lieutenant became the boy that his school friends called Bobby.

As he talked about how they planned to drill into the economic strata and let the wealth drain down to soak all the undernourished roots of the nation, it was easy to picture him the way she'd first seen him, playing in a game on the university quad. D had been about her duties, carrying an armload of folded sheets along the paved path at the field's edge to one of the apartment houses. Robert had burst from a group of players with a leather ball clamped under his arm. In his grass-stained shorts and a ripped striped jersey, he'd laughed, shrieking, "Never, never, never!" at the boys who chased him. It was beautiful, D thought; beautiful and alluring to hear him laugh like that, to take such unselfconscious delight in himself, in the glory of himself.

"But is it any wonder"—her lieutenant had returned, at last, to his original subject—"that the place is covered in dust? What worker would want to come here and see their industry paid such shabby tribute?"

A better question, D might have replied, was what worker would even want to spend their few free hours visiting models about work?

"What are you smiling about?" Robert asked. It would never have occurred to him that she could find him unintentionally amusing, let alone find him attractive because of it.

"I'm smiling, Lieutenant," she said, "because I've just had an idea for a tribute I'd like to pay to the workers." D undid the three dark-gray buttons of her light-gray frock and pushed it down her arms, and down her body, and stepped free of it.

△

They did it first on the surface of the stream and the second time, at the lieutenant's insistence, on top of the long counter on the fourth floor where the wax bank cashiers sat in a row making change from drawers and studying paper strips of numbers that spooled from glass-bulbed typing machines. Robert talked continuously. "What a show you're putting on for them! This is the kind of investment that every accountant dreams of making!"

A tray of variously sized silver washers was set before each cashier. D grasped the sides of the counter and with each thrust the washers rattled and jingled, sometimes jumping out altogether, hitting the floor and rolling away along the planks. The paper strips, meanwhile, which trailed between the wax fingers of their readers to the floor, contributed a shushing, sweeping sound of their own.

D didn't feel excitement or ecstasy; mostly, she just felt jostled. For as much as there was to recommend him, her lieutenant was a poor lover. D found his sexual chatter monotonous. Robert had talked before about fucking her in a desert, pounding her into the sand while wolves watched and howled; he had talked about fucking her on a skiff on a river while the people onshore played with themselves; he had talked about fucking her in the street, fucking her on a tram packed with commuters, fucking her for an audience at the Municipal Opera House, fucking her on the back of the tiger statue in front of the Magistrates' Court for the amusement of tourists. Numerous other scenarios had been proposed that she'd forgotten, or been too disengaged to register at all.

D was not shocked by his fantasies, but they were his fantasies, and they did not actually require her as she understood herself. Her fantasies had more in common with the way she had first seen him, running red-cheeked with the ball from the other players. For someone to want her the way that he had wanted to get away from them—euphorically, gloatingly, relishing—that was arousing to her. Only their very first, impulsive assignation had been like that. All the times since it was more as though Robert were chasing and running away from himself at the same time. Her lieutenant had a good heart, but in this way he had turned out to be more of a boy than she'd hoped.

The counter rocked a final time, and Robert cried out and sank on top of her.

She rolled her head to the side. One of the bankers hovered right above her. A green visor screened his eyes above a full smile.

△

Behind the ticket booth they discovered a door labeled **CURATOR**, in flaking gold letters. It opened on a small, windowless office. The key to the museum hung from a nail on the inside of the door. It was cumbersome, as long as her forearm.

D left her lieutenant in the dismal office and returned to the fifth floor where she had seen the figure of a fruit picker who wore a burlap satchel. She unwound the satchel from his neck and dumped his wooden apples at his feet. Someone had already pried an eye from the picker, who wore only dungarees beneath his limp straw hat. She felt slightly guilty for exacerbating his plight. More than that, if she was going to keep the museum, he was, in some sense, hers—they all were, all the figures.

"I'll get this back to you shortly and I'll see what we can do about the eye," D said to the picker. She assumed that eventually she'd get used to the wax figures. For now, it somehow seemed stranger not to say something. They had the same gravity as corpses in open coffins. Though the figures didn't seem alive, they almost seemed dead.

She went to a window on the wall behind the shack, traversing the boxed-in plot of earth that was being not very convincingly tilled by a wax farmer who held a broom instead of a hoe, while his wax hound looked on. At the window D looked down on the ruins of the Society.

From this vantage, the building was an open stomach. Blackened bricks, blackened beams, blackened slates, all jumbled together in the middle of the still-standing walls. Here and there were small shifts in the mounds of rubble, little leaks of rock and plaster as the wreckage continued to settle. A short section of the second floor jutted from the rear wall and, sheltered beneath it, D recognized the stage where the Society's display of conjurer's tricks had been set up.

The platform still held the magician's closet, but the rich fabric covering its sides had been burned away and the door was gone too. It was just a black box now. There was no sign of the table where the conjurer's paraphernalia—hat, baton, cards, silver egg—had once been arrayed. So far as D could tell, the peninsula of the second floor and the ruined closet were the only distinguishable remains of the Society's interior.

Out on the Society's lawn, a bushy white cat eased through the angled space between the ground and the door stuck corner-first into the turf, rubbing its back against the door edge.

Even on the fifth-floor window, soot from the fire had collected in fine wavelets on the glass. She used the dirty reflection to adjust her bonnet.

Δ

Robert sat in the only chair with his elbows on the desk, chin propped on his crossed fingers, appearing contemplative. The office's sole fixture, besides the nail for the key on the back of the door, was a coat hook on the wall, from which hung a ragged tweedside jacket. The one piece of decoration was a framed tintype of the deposed king's father, to whose reign the tweedside jacket likely dated. In keeping with the absence of electricity, there was neither a roto nor the wiring to connect one.

Yes, D thought, the National Museum of the Worker had not received many visitors. She wondered what had become of the previous curator. It seemed as though it had been some time since he was needed.

Robert asked, "Dora, are you sure about this? There are other museums, libraries. We could find someplace more pleasant. A place with fewer wax people."

She said that wouldn't be necessary. "This will do very well, Lieutenant."

He grinned and slapped the desk. "So be it! You're the new curator!"

D went around the side of the desk and stood over him. "I certainly am. And you're in my chair."

Δ

On the paper that Crossley's aide had signed, Robert struck out *The Society for Psykical Research* and neatly wrote *The National Museum of the Worker*. They exited the building, closing the heavy door and locking it behind them. D toted the giant key in the burlap satchel.

They set off together. Robert had a meeting of the Emergency Justice Committee to attend that evening. D would return to the servants' quarters at the university and start fresh at the museum in the morning.

On the corner of Legate Avenue they noticed that while they had been inside, the imperialist flag that had flown from the embassy had been taken down, and a piece of green cloth signifying the revolutionary movement run up in its place. Robert said for D to wait a moment while he presented himself to whoever had taken charge. This time she did as she was directed.

He knocked, and almost immediately the door opened. The light of the setting sun stung off the windows and tin roofs of the embassies and the tram rails that split the street. D squinted and could only make out an impression—beard, wide shoulders—of the man to whom Robert spoke. The conversation was brief, and the lieutenant came back as the door shut.

"One of Crossley's captains," he reported. "Anthony's his name. Working on security matters."

If D ever had any problems, or if she needed access to a roto, she ought to go straight to the former embassy. Her neighbor, Captain Anthony, would help her.

The Gentle

*S*imon the Gentle was the conjurer's performing title, but he was mostly known as the Gentle. His real name was Scott. Or it was Alain, or Salvador. The people who had raised him were clamdiggers; they had saved him, as an infant, from the clutch of a monstrous clam that had washed up on the strand beneath the South Fair Bridge at low tide. Or they were fishers; they had found him in the bottom of an otherwise empty skiff in the bay. Or he had first appeared as a young boy, a whistling amnesiac of six or seven, who was perched on the rusted railing that guarded the heights of the western bluffs; he noticed a woman, an impoverished housekeeper who had intended to cast herself upon the rocks, and asked her if she was his mother—and she had said yes. Or a professor of education had adopted the boy from the Juvenile Lodgings to prove the excellence of his pedagogical method by developing that most unpromising of specimens, a common Lees orphan. There were many more tales, and while he refused to affirm any speculation, he never denied any either. The most he would ever admit was, "Though I have not always been Simon, I have always been gentle."

Illusion and conjuration were not viewed with much favor by the authorities in the Gentle's era. Sleight-of-hand men were even more infamous for picking pockets than in the present day, and in the hill towns of the Northland Provinces people were occasionally still drowned for consorting with demons in the woods or committing other supernatural offenses. However, the Gentle was a beloved exception, because his illusions were so charming and peaceful.

The silver egg, for example, he passed to the members of his audience so that they could test its weight and solidity. When they were satisfied and the egg was returned to him, the Gentle declared that existence was quicksilver. He used his black baton to spell the word **TODAY** in letters that shone in midair, and in the next instant brushed his arm through them. The dispersed letters quickly reconstituted themselves in a new word: **TOMORROW**. When the Gentle broke this word with his baton, its matter sprinkled to the ground in a dusty gray powder. He cupped the egg in his hand and squeezed. Liquid silver leaked out between his fingers and he caught it in his hat. In summation, he went from person to person with a pair of tweezers and meticulously plucked a single white hair from every head, which he claimed had grown during the performance. He clasped the hairs in his fist, and when he opened it, the silver egg, whole again, rested on his palm; and his hat was empty.

In another performance, he ate his playing cards. Tucked into his table, with a carafe of tea and a cup and saucer, the Gentle ripped each card into dainty bites, and chewed them up. In the course of his meal, he paused every so often to sip his tea and dab his mouth with a napkin. The Gentle described the flavor of certain cards: the three of diamonds tasted like the mossy cool of a cave whose entrance was concealed by thick vines, the six of clubs like salty beer, the seven of hearts like a sweet breeze, the jack of spades like the moment your son knows more than you do and you feel pride and the melancholy joy that comes with the release of duty and the first staggering hint of obsolescence. Once he had devoured the entire deck, the Gentle asked everyone to check their reticules and wallets: each woman discovered a queen of clubs in her likeness and each man a king of hearts in his. The Gentle collected the queens and kings and constructed a house of cards on his table. When he finished, he invited members of the audience to attempt to blow it over with their breath. None ever could.

Simon the Gentle's private life was either circumspect or dull. He lived at the Hotel Metropole without a wife or a mistress. After his death, an anonymous Metropole maid testified that he kept a meticulous toilet, but that his ashtrays needed to be changed every day because he smoked so much. It was also said, by the anonymous maid and others, that the Gentle was too fond of the Metropole's famous cat mascot, Talmadge—in those days Talmadge III—and spoiled it. The conjurer brought the fleecy white animal tidbits from the butcher's, and joked that he'd learned all his skills from a cat that looked just like him.

(At this mention of cats, the expression of the cheerful Society man relating the tale briefly curdled to a grimace. "We mustn't judge the Gentle for his superstitions. Remember, this was in a more primitive time and even the most remarkable individuals sometimes have blind spots, my dear.")

D nodded her understanding. Her parents were not regular church-goers, but they disparaged the lower sort of people who actually believed that cats were blessed, when in fact they were just another breed of dumb, disease-carrying vermin.

D admired cats, though, and would have liked to own one of her own. She didn't think cats spread disease and she didn't think they were dumb. They were always cleaning themselves, and wore such clever, deliberative expressions. You couldn't tell what cats made of anything, only that they took everything seriously.)

The conjurer's time preceded the introduction of the city's tramlines, and he was known to enjoy walking all over town. He was a figure of mystery but not a mysterious figure; people saw him along the avenues, on the paths in the Fields, on the viewing platforms above the Bluffs; and when they did, the Gentle tipped his hat to them. Slender, of medium build, his physical presence was unremarkable. He looked like a person in the background of a painting, his lip marked with the type of thin, neat mustache that men in the backgrounds of paintings tend to wear. He gambled on racehorses in moderation and won no more than anyone else. Once the conjurer was initiated into the Society, he made many friends in the upper echelons of the government and of industry, and even became acquainted with the royal family.

△

The Vestibule, as he called his closet, was the core element of the Gentle's most entrancing fantasy. (How the conjurer obtained the Vestibule, whether he designed it himself or came to possess it some other way, was never determined.)

To begin, the Gentle asked for the assistance of a beautiful woman from the audience. Once the volunteer joined him onstage, he inquired whether or not she was afraid of death. If she confessed that she was, the Gentle reassured her that it was just a change of arrangements, like moving house. If the woman said that she wasn't afraid of death, the Gentle pivoted to the assembly, and said, "She may feel differently before we're finished."

He opened the door of the Vestibule to allow a clear view of the empty, velvet-walled interior. He thumped on the walls inside and out, and the sounds were solid. Next, he invited the volunteer to join him within, promised the audience that they'd return shortly, and shut the door behind them.

During the time that passed, perhaps ten or fifteen minutes, the quartet at the foot of the stage tuned their instruments. Soon they began to play a waltz. In the second or third measure, the door swung wide, and the conjurer and his volunteer assistant smoothly danced out onto the stage. They were altered, however: his head sat atop her neck, and hers atop his. While the crowd roared in terror and delight, the couple swept gracefully around and around. As the waltz neared its conclusion, the Gentle dropped his head to his own shoulder and the woman who wore his body, in the lead, danced them back into the Vestibule. The door clapped shut behind them.

When it reopened a minute or two later, Simon the Gentle and his dance partner stepped out with their heads restored to their own bodies. The conjurer grabbed the other's hand and threw the woman, visibly dazed but otherwise unharmed except for a tiny puncture at the tip of her forefinger, forward in a low bow.

The Gentle's performance thrilled the public, packing theaters, and everyone wondered, what could be next? How could he top the Vestibule?

He couldn't.

△

A jealous husband stabbed the Gentle half a dozen times in the stomach and groin, and left the conjurer to bleed to death on the floor of the Society. The man's wife had volunteered to enter the Vestibule during one of the performances, and he accused the Gentle of having taken liberties with her. For the remainder of her life she insisted that it was not true, testifying of her experience inside the closet in the same hazy terms as those of other volunteers: there had been a window, and on its glass a series of shifting visages; the conjurer had helped her to put on his reflection, and he had put on hers, and suggested they dance. They had waltzed out, back in, and back out again. When the woman emerged, her memory was fragmented, but except for a nick on her fingertip she had suffered no injury.

Her husband didn't believe her, however, and in the wake of the attack he used his knife to ward off the Society members who tried to come close and help the badly wounded man.

"His face . . . ," moaned Simon the Gentle as he wormed on the carpet. "His real face . . ."

△

There was a faded, maplike stain on the burgundy-colored carpet, which spread across a pair of the triangles, muting their gold to brown. "We think this is him, but we're not entirely certain," D's new friend said. "We've remodeled several times since then." It was a few feet from the stage by a potted plant on a stand.

Throughout the telling of the story the cheery man's hands had remained in captivity in his armpits, though D noticed that his sleeve had crept up to reveal a cuff of flaking white skin. "Extraordinary, extraordinary history here."

The end of the story confused her. What had happened inside the closet that made the husband so mad that he had murdered Simon the Gentle? How had the conjurer "taken liberties" with the man's wife? Perhaps most important, from D's point of view, was the matter of the conjurer's pet: What had become of the wonderful spoiled white cat that lived at the fine hotel? She wanted to ask to see the man's hands, but knew that would be impolite. She also wanted to ask if she could step inside the Vestibule—not closing the door, of course—and touch the walls like Simon the Gentle had done, but did not dare risk this question either.

"Thank you for telling me a story," D said instead. "I'm sure I'll understand it more when I'm grown up."

The man chuckled and commended her for being a likable, likable girl.

Ambrose finally arrived from wherever he had been behind the Hall's second curtain, and they were soon outside and by foot and tram retracing the journey that had brought her to the redbrick building.

At home, Nurse had managed to prop herself up. "Oh, my terrible nerves!" D's brother produced a fresh bottle of tonic. This settled Nurse's shaking just in time, a minute or two before Mother came home.

Ambrose came into her room that night and crouched by her bed. She'd done exactly as he expected, and he was proud of her. His bucktoothed grin hovered in the dimness.

"What did you think of the fellow in the gold vest?"

"I thought he was a funny, funny man," D said.

"Quite, quite," said Ambrose, and buried his face in her blankets to muffle his laughter. She had to cover her own mouth as well.

"What do you do in that place?" she whispered.

"I told you, we're trying to save the world," Ambrose said. "And maybe not just this world, either. Who knows, maybe we can do good in some other worlds too. Because there are as many worlds as there are hairs on your head, D. We just have to find the places where the strands cross. What do you think about that?"

D reflexively brushed her fingers through her hair. "It makes my head feel itchy," she said, and that started Ambrose giggling again, and her too.

But her brother died before he could tell her what went on behind the curtain at the far end of the Grand Hall, where only members, like himself and the man in the gold vest, were permitted.

Someone Who Can Take Some Words Down

*A*t the Emergency Justice meeting that night, the three chairmen of the Provisional Government sat shoulder to shoulder at a table situated below the judge's bench in the Superior Courtroom. On the walls behind the bench were bleached squares where the portraits of the king, the queen, and the chief minister had hung. The ground-floor rows of the courtroom were filled primarily with Robert's fellow Volunteers from the university, green armbands knotted tight on their upper arms, but there was a handful of Crossley's auxiliary soldiers too. Most of the union men were clustered in the balcony and, the lieutenant observed, as if according to some code, wore their green cloths not as armbands but as neckerchiefs.

The first of the chairmen was Jonas Mosi, representative of the dockmen and the other workingmen's unions; Robert's peer from the university, Lionel Woodstock, the organizer of the student protests, was the second; and Aloys Lumm, the scattered octogenarian playwright chosen as the acting premier, was the third. Each man seemed fundamentally alien to the other two; it struck Robert as less like a political conference than an encounter between three disparate survivors of a shipwreck on a strange and inhospitable shore. One began to wonder who would be the first to pick up a rock and attempt to brain the others. Robert had hoped for a little more from the transitional leadership, but he told himself that the operation was bound to become smoother and, if nothing else, it was only transitional.

Mosi had declared Lionel's plans to codify a new legal system from whole cloth pointless. "You set up the person in front of a jury, and you say what they've done, and they say what they've done, and the jury decides what it was and what it wasn't." The labor organizer was an enormous, gloomy, irritable man; he slumped hugely over the table, shoulders bunched, forearms flexed, and glowered from amid his muscles. "What's wrong with that?"

"There's nothing wrong with it"—Lionel spoke slowly, blinking behind spectacles, his punctiliousness betraying his experience as a member of the university debate club—"but we need to be sure we know exactly what we're doing."

"I know what I'm doing," Mosi said.

"I never said you didn't," Lionel said.

"Gentlemen, gentlemen," said Aloys Lumm, who spoke only in generalities, platitudes, and platitudinous generalities, "we just need to be clear. The people need to see it and the people need to hear it. The questions have to be able to answer themselves, don't they?"

The playwright, clucking at his own wisdom, nodded his snowy-haired head.

The old man's interjections were always followed by a silence as Mosi and Lionel tried to figure out whose side he was on.

At the university Robert had read one of Lumm's plays, *A Little Wolf Box*. Well, Dora had read it and told him what happened. It was about two men who catch the devil, she said, but actually it's the devil who's caught them. Robert had thought it sounded exasperating and bizarre—not, come to think of it, unlike the proceedings that he was witnessing that evening.

"Even a jury trial has to have rules," Lionel said.

"Trial by jury is a rule," Mosi said.

"Respect desires authority," Aloys Lumm croaked, "but does it need authority? I'm not sure that it does. I'm not sure that it does. Conviction and trust, those are the spine of the thing, like the spine of some tremendous beast. . . ."

It went on like this, and somewhere in the midst of an interminable back-and-forth about the wisdom of Crossley's decision to summarily dissolve the entirety of the remaining Constabulary and lock the precinct buildings pending the recruitment and training of a new police force, despite Robert's best attempts to stay focused on the important matters at hand, his mind tiptoed away to Dora. He adored his little maid, adored the way she said "Lieutenant" in that soft voice of hers, snapping each syllable like a piece of chocolate to share into three pieces: *lieu-ten-ant*. He adored, too, how she'd looked that afternoon, stretched across the model of the bank counter, her body somehow endless in its nakedness. Dora was so easy in the world. It seemed strange to think that she walked on feet. In his mind, she glided from place to place, like a fog. How was it, he wondered, that he was here, when he could be wherever she was, putting his hands on her? How had he let that happen? The revolution was essential to raise the standard of living for the lesser classes and give them dignity and a voice, but there was also Dora, flowing down the counter under the noses of the wax cashiers, and Dora was essential too.

The meeting was gaveled to a close.

The other men in his row, eager to escape the packed, stifling room, abruptly forced Robert to his feet. He shuffled in an awkward hunch. What, if any, legal principles had been agreed upon, or whether the matter of the Constabulary had been sorted out, he did not know—or, for the moment, care. His current concern was to not graze a comrade with his erection.

Someone gripped his elbow and it was like a hand reaching into his stomach; he was sure someone must have noticed his arousal.

"Hell, but they like it specific, don't they? On and on. Listen, sir, I don't suppose you have a free moment, do you? I hate to bother you, but I need someone who can take some words down. For a confidential matter. I'd consider it a great favor." Robert twisted and saw Sergeant Van Goor, the Crossley aide who'd helped them that morning. He was moving along the neighboring aisle. "You're bent a little there. You didn't strain your back, did you?"

"Just a little stiff." Besides being embarrassed, Robert was annoyed by how observant the man was. "You want some words taken down? Just any words? In any particular order?"

Van Goor brayed. He still had Robert's elbow and they moved closely together along their respective aisles. There were several lunches on his breath. "No, no, nothing fancy, sir, I swear! Just need someone with a good hand. I took a note of how quick and handsome you did that paper for your miss this morning."

Most of the soldiers from Crossley's Auxiliary were taciturn, if not outright hostile to the university students and union men who had formed the Volunteer Civil Defense and now held positions of authority in the Provisional Government's committee assignments. Robert didn't blame them. Their first loyalty was to their general. They were uneducated and poorly remunerated; the most valuable item that most of them possessed was the uniform they received as an advance on their wages upon enlisting. Van Goor, though as untaught as his brethren, was a genial exception— which must have been the reason Crossley had chosen him as an aide.

When the assignments had gone around the night they seized the government buildings, it was Van Goor who had brought Robert the handsaw to use if he had to cut the telegraph wires. "You see powder flashes, that's it, time to go. Give her a chop with this, wires'll split clean. Kick off your boots, jump over the side, and swim in the direction that's away from the shooting. That end of the bridge is low. Might sting when you hit, but you'll be all right. It'd take a lucky shot to sink you in the dark," he had said. "Stay close to shore, all right?" Robert had managed to whisper, "Right," and Van Goor thumped his shoulder and told him he was gold.

Small, sallow, and bowlegged, the sergeant had a nose like a staircase from some beating he'd taken. He reminded Robert of the hired men who had worked around his family's estate, with whom he felt a lasting bond. It hadn't been his father, the master, but those hired men who had imparted to Robert how to set a trap and to smoke a pipe, and, with a stallion and a mare for examples, candidly narrated the mechanics of the sexual act.

Robert wasn't, in fact, at all convinced that his father fully grasped this last piece of information—or wished to. Procreation was naked, and there was nothing that men like his father feared more than nakedness of any kind.

The next link in this chain of consideration being his mother and father's activities behind their bedroom door, the lieutenant found that he was no longer erect.

Whatever Van Goor needed, Robert said, of course he'd be happy to write it, and the sergeant could rely on his discretion. He straightened as they emerged into the side aisle where the crowd was looser. Robert supposed the man must be illiterate.

"Oh, that's glorious! Grateful to you, Lieutenant Barnes, sir."

The aide led him to a side door at the rear of the courtroom. Van Goor's spurs jingled in time with his hustling stride.

It occurred to Robert that the confidential matter he was being squired away to write up was probably the dictation of a love letter to Van Goor's sweetheart. Dora would enjoy that. "Did he say anything romantic about her womb, Lieutenant?" he could hear her asking, and pictured how she'd lower her lids. "I insist on a full report. You know how I enjoy romance."

Dora wasn't the way you expected a maid to be. There was her confidence with him, the little game of authority that they played, and there was the way she concealed herself around everyone else. She wasn't illiterate either, like Van Goor and most other men and women of their class. On more than one occasion, as on that time with Lumm's inscrutable play, he'd awoken to find her propped on the pillows beside him, reading one of the books from his classes by lamplight. When he asked what she thought of a particular text, she'd say something like, "Oh, I was just wondering if there was anything filthy," and set the book aside, but Robert suspected she was really interested in bettering herself.

And she would be able to now.

They had done it, the whole bunch of them, literate and illiterate alike: thrown the brakes on the machine and brought it to a halt before it could swallow up any more lives. They'd taken back the nation's wealth for the people who made it. If Dora wanted to join one of the women's committees that would eventually be formed, or take on some other role in support of the new representative government, she would be able to do that.

And if the sergeant wanted his assistance in writing a pornographic letter to his true love? It seemed the least he could do for a comrade in arms.

"Right through here we go." They entered a dark hall of oaken panels. At the far end was a heavy-looking door, and beside it on a bench sat a man in a livery uniform—tailed coat and a scarlet scarf knotted around his top hat. His arms were tightly crossed, his chin tilted and clenched. Robert concluded in a glance that he was thankful not to be the man's horse.

"How did you make out, by the way?" Van Goor paused as they came to the door, ignoring the sulking driver seated on the bench. "With the facility your miss volunteered to see about? Psykic something? Or was it a doctors' club? On Heritage, I recall. Or was it on Little Heritage?"

"We secured the premises," Robert said. He didn't care to explain the Society for Psykical Research to Van Goor; he might find it interesting. For the sake of camaraderie, he would set pen to paper to describe Van Goor's tumescence, but he drew the line at a discussion of whatever superstitions the aide might subscribe to. As for the modification he'd made to Dora's declaration of authority, it wasn't worth mentioning.

"Glorious!" Van Goor rapped the wall with a knuckle. "Lovely girl, your miss."

"She's not my miss." It was all right for some of his friends to know that he was associating with a maid, but the lieutenant didn't care to become the subject of gossip among the rank-and-file soldiers. He told himself this was as much for Dora's sake as his own. "Just an ally of the movement."

"Naturally, sir." The aide said this last in a flat, offhand tone that seemed to rule out sarcasm, and anyway, he had opened the door before Robert could respond.

They entered the chief magistrate's chambers. A freighter of a wooden desk captured one end of the room. It was bracketed on either side by bookshelves with leather-bound books in green and red. The river unspooled in a broad, silvery vein beyond the picture window at the back of the chambers.

Two men sat in chairs before the desk, as lawyers must have done in private sessions with the chief magistrate. The first, dressed in an officer's uniform with braided gold tassels at the shoulders and several badges on his chest, was none other than General Crossley, commander of the Auxiliary Garrison. This took Robert aback, causing him to reset his sense of the situation entirely. He shot a glance at Van Goor; the sergeant grinned, evidently relishing his surprise.

The second figure was a rotund man in a bright white jacket, which made him look as if he had arrived from an afternoon paddling on the Royal Pond; he was evidently a civilian. Both men smoked cigarettes and drank brown liquor from cut crystal glasses. Crossley maintained a ramrod posture and a dour expression, but the man in the holiday suit seemed to be in an excellent mood, blowing his cigarette smoke in long streams.

"—cottage cheese is the only thing he can keep down; he lives on it," the civilian was saying.

He turned at the sound of the opening door and said, "Ah, you found a secretary," and indicated for Robert to go around and have the place behind the desk. Pens, ink, and paper were already laid out.

Once Robert was seated, the man in the white jacket looked expectantly at the general. The general checked a note, then tucked it away in a pocket and started to interview his companion, beginning by asking him to state his name. The other man's wide face and the cliff's edge of fair yellow hair above his forehead were strikingly familiar, but it wasn't until he gave his Christian name as Ronald John Westhover that Robert realized he was the now-deposed currency minister.

After that, the general asked for an overview of the nation's financial situation.

Westhover grunted and nodded at the wisdom of this inquiry; it would take more than one night to explain all the details, he said, but "the cash balance hasn't been in our favor just lately, and that can be a real nuisance. . . ." He pointed the finger at the self-benefiting decision-making of the chief minister and the Crown's advisors, without actually calling it corrupt—"we've been rather generous with loans to certain business interests taken against our financial reserves, and the revenue stream hasn't quite flowed back around the way we anticipated"—and also blamed the decreasing returns on the army's charter with the Franks in light of the recent disastrous campaign: ". . . if you lend your army at the correct rate, you'll make a profit no matter what happens. You can be utterly slaughtered and still make money. But there's no denying that you'll do much better if you don't get slaughtered, because there's expense in recruiting and training up fresh men, and that closes up the margins, you see. . . ."

Here he digressed to offer his opinion of Gildersleeve's state of mind: "Much as I respect the man for his courage and for his ability to hold the loyalty of such a disparate mass of men, he's sickly and he's old, and he's never been the swiftest operator. . . ."

Eventually, Westhover insisted on recounting his side of Joven's shooting: ". . . the madman goaded me again, and unfortunately, my own man had left his pistol right there in his pocket where I could access it when my blood was up. Even once I had the weapon, I didn't intend to shoot him I don't think, but he was staring at me. It gave me a start that he'd even dare meet my eyes. My finger jumped on the trigger. And he's dead!

"I was appalled. Feel badly about it to this day. I know I shouldn't hold myself responsible, he was uncouth and out of control, and who's to say he wouldn't have hopped up and bit me. He probably would have, he was rabid, the river poisons the blood down there where those types breed, but there's a part of me that aches with regret." The minister frowned and made a gesture of bemusement, wiggling his fingers up and away. "Just for a few seconds I caught his madness."

The night outside the window was thinning when the general checked the little paper he'd been referring to all night—it was written in a particular bold red ink, Robert had noticed—and announced that they had better leave off for the time being. The lieutenant organized the papers of the transcript he'd written and left them on the desk. As he was conducted out by Van Goor, the general and the minister were pouring out a last round of drinks.

In the hall the liveryman was curled asleep on the bench.

△

Outside, the two men stopped beside Van Goor's table in the plaza by the stone tiger. It was a warm summer evening, and many of the soldiers' tents arrayed on the grass plots between sections of flagstone stood with their flaps pinned open. Robert heard a dreamer mumble from inside one of the tents, "Margaret, won't you . . . ?"

He fumbled out a cigarette from his case. He was flabbergasted by what he'd heard. "The cavalier way he spoke about killing the potter, Westhover acts like he's done nothing wrong." The currency minister had been acquitted of the homicide on grounds of self-defense, but the truth had circulated by word of mouth, anonymous pamphlets, and graffiti. It was one of the chief incidents that had instigated the secret antigovernment meetings among the students and the dockmen and the other unions. If a rich man could be murdered in the middle of the street in front of a crowd of witnesses, what was the hope of justice for anyone else?

Van Goor bent and struck a match off a slate, and used it to light Robert's cigarette. "It's disgraceful, sir."

"Thank you. I had no idea he was in custody. I assumed he'd escaped."

"That's because if it was on the air, these boys here would hang him. That's why it needed to be confidential."

"Of course. I won't say anything."

"Wouldn't it be handsome, though? Put him real high up, fly him like a flag. Not yet, though. Sick individual. I helped search his manse.

Peculiar habits on display, let's leave it there." The sergeant shook his head ruefully.

Robert was curious at this, but there was no way to pursue it without seeming prurient.

"Anyway," continued Van Goor, "got to find out where all the dirt's been shoveled. Need to squeeze him awhile."

As he always did when the subject of the murdered potter arose, Robert thought of the plates at his parents' manor. They were decorated with a picture of a stallion in a meadow. He reassured himself that they only had one color, simple black; not three colors, like the ostentatious minister. They weren't greedy people, his parents; they just didn't see past themselves. His father had worn the same pair of walking boots for years, paying the wife of one of the hired hands to repair them. In fact, in his boots and heavy coat, when Lord Barnes stood at the foot of the fields to greet his hands, it was only his wordlessness that marked him as different. Instead of saying hello, he would nod shyly at his employees and clear his throat in a rumble of greeting, "Hrrumm," to each man in passing and tip his head low. Robert's father was a good man. It was just that he had been born into ownership, and never known anything else.

He vowed to himself, once again, to write his parents the letter he'd been putting off these last few months, in which he would explain how he felt, and how everything was about to change for the better.

"Oh, but he's worried. That's just a face he puts on." Van Goor had lit a cigarette of his own. He clamped it in one corner of his mouth and puffed smoke from the other. "And Crossley's pleasant to him so he talks more. You can see he thinks he might be able to get out of it. I bet his fake face'll fall off when they rope him. I bet he'll drop through squeaking."

"I look forward to hearing his confession read in public at the trial," Robert said.

"Oh, yes. We'll all enjoy that."

He felt he'd misjudged the sergeant. The whole point of what they'd done was to raise up men like Van Goor, who was crude but not stupid—who was, after all, his brother in a sense. Robert wanted to express this somehow. All he could come up with was, "Just let me know what I can do. I'm always glad to help. I'd write something personally for you if you ever needed. You could tell me what to put down or just give me a sense of what you wanted to say, and I could do the rest."

The sergeant coughed. "Kind of you, Lieutenant," he said.

Van Goor rocked on his bootheels and rubbed his thumb on the emerald set into his cufflink, which wasn't the way to do it. You needed a soft cloth. Robert didn't correct him, though; that wasn't the right tack. He supposed the cufflink had come down to Van Goor from Van Goor's father, and maybe from Van Goor's father's father, a treasured heirloom, and the whole line of them, one ugly man after another, had rubbed it in their turn, making a history of smudges. There was a dignity in it, all that pressure brought to bear by all those simple men's thumbs on that small stone. Despite having said nothing, Robert suddenly felt as though he needed to apologize.

The image of his father at the foot of the fields, nodding at the hands and making that bashful throat-clearing noise, came to Robert.

In a rush to suppress the association, he said, "If you needed your boots repaired, I'm sure Dora—the girl I introduced you to, the one you helped, our sister-in-arms—I'm sure she could take care of you. I'm sure she'd be glad to."

"My boots repaired . . . ?" Van Goor nodded, and smiled, and ground his cigarette out against the tiger's thigh. "Ah . . . That's very kind, sir."

The lieutenant, in the following instant, glimpsed the shape of a miscommunication. Did Van Goor think that he was inviting him to—with Dora? The notion was repellent, but he couldn't be sure if it was correct and he couldn't figure out how to test it without insulting the man.

Hoofbeats clattered on the street and a pair of soldiers rode into the square.

Van Goor ripped off a whistle and strode to meet them. Robert followed, tripping over a man sleeping on the bare ground. By the time he had righted himself and apologized to the half-drunk soldier he'd fallen across, Sergeant Van Goor was already hollering for an attendant to wake the general.

The news was that the remnants of the enemy were rallying in the hills north of the city. They had set up a blockade on the Great Highway and fired on a mail coach. It wasn't much of a force, but they could make themselves difficult.

"Not quite done fighting, are we?" Robert asked the sergeant.

"I hope not, sir, don't you?" Van Goor replied.

He jogged off before Robert, who had decided that, for fraternal reasons, he should lie, could express agreement.

Δ

It was nearly noon when Sergeant Van Goor remembered the liveryman. Through the morning Van Goor had been busy carrying messages hither and yon. A unit of cavalry and several artillery pieces had been dispatched to address the rebel position—if necessary. By the numbers, it was clear that Crossley could overwhelm the deposed government's flimsy rear-guard if it came to it, but with the enemy's position fortified it would be painful. The general had already accepted a message from their side and surrender negotiations were being planned.

The sergeant only wanted a drink and a few hours in his bedroll, except there was still the liveryman to deal with. He had been loading Westhover's carriage when the currency minister was arrested, and the soldiers had brought him in for questioning, but it was obvious he was nobody. Van Goor hoped the man had done the sensible thing and taken off.

But he hadn't.

Van Goor found him, awake again, on the same bench in the hall outside the chief magistrate's office. "I've told you everything I know about Westhover, which is nothing. I just worked for him. Am I to sit here forever?" the liveryman asked.

"You'll sit where I put you," the sergeant said.

The liveryman sniffed. He reached up and stroked the foolish scarf that hung from his foolish hat, but kept his mouth closed.

Van Goor went into the fancy office and sat at the desk to write a message. He read it over, mouthing each word. He put the address on the outside, folded the paper, and sealed it with the magistrate's purple seal. He could write perfectly well, whatever that fucking "lieutenant" thought.

Sergeant Van Goor snorted to himself. Before the previous night, he'd supposed he'd never find anyone who disgusted him as much as the currency minister, singing for his life, acting like he was still in charge of anything, like they didn't know what a fucking degenerate oddity he actually was, those drawers in his bedroom that had been filled with animal bones.

(When they'd been sent to the minister's house to search for papers, ledgers, anything that might hold a record of the Crown's crimes, it had been Van Goor himself who yanked open the first drawer of the bureau in the bedroom. It had been so packed with bones that a handful had jumped out and clattered on the floor, and the sergeant had gone skipping backward. All the men with him had had a good laugh at that.

"Fuck you," he'd said to them. "See how you like finding a drawer of vampire leavings."

All five drawers of the bureau had been stuffed with bones. And it wasn't just the number of bones, it was how clean, white as ivory. How had the minister ever managed to find the time to plunder the country? He must have spent his every spare hour boiling the skin off poor creatures. Sexual depravity of some sort was in play there, Van Goor had no doubt.)

Van Goor returned to the hall. He addressed the liveryman. "Now I want you to tell me something."

"Go ahead," the liveryman said, "I have nothing else to do, do I?"

"Do I look to you like a man who doesn't have his letters?" Van Goor asked.

"What do you mean?"

"What I said. Do I look like a man that can't read or write?"

A squint salted more doubt onto the liveryman's already cynical expression. "No, not especially."

But here was this "Lieutenant" Barnes, this schoolboy whose proper rank in the grand scheme of matters was right under scraped shit—he'd last one day in the actual army—presuming on Van Goor's intelligence, presuming that he couldn't read, which you had to be able to do to become a sergeant, that was regulation. Van Goor guessed he didn't dislike Barnes and his airs quite as much as the minister and his bones, but it burned him nonetheless. Van Goor'd only brought Barnes in to do the writing because it had been supposed that Westhover would be more comfortable talking with a person who looked like his sort taking it down, and because after the foolish business with the building the sergeant had thought that he and the schoolboy were getting along. To be looked down upon after he'd done the schoolboy a favor, signed that paper for his whore to have an entire building! The rudeness astonished Van Goor, and only the more so because it had been so casual. He was not a man you spat on like that. And then the fellow had the balls to offer up his whore for compensation—as if Van Goor needed his permission!

"At the same time, I wouldn't be shocked," the liveryman belatedly added, interrupting the sergeant's thoughts. "No offense, but you don't seem like a bookish sort." The liveryman gave a hoot of amusement. "What do I know, though? I live in a hallway."

With a snap of his wrist, the sergeant flicked out the sealed message.

Instead of taking the paper right away, the liveryman slyly eyed the emerald cufflink at Van Goor's extended wrist. "Pretty cufflinks, Sergeant. What'd those cost you?"

The cufflinks hadn't cost Van Goor anything. Which the liveryman knew perfectly well. It was, on the contrary, another individual who had paid a price for not relinquishing them expeditiously enough. The sergeant had a low threshold for insolence.

But he was tired; he dropped the paper in the liveryman's lap.

"Take this to the address. It's an introduction. Man there takes your particulars in case we want to speak to you again, asks you for a pledge of loyalty, and sends you on your way."

The liveryman sneered. "That's it? You made me wait here for the better part of a day for that?"

But Van Goor wasn't so tired he could let this pass. He'd been pushed to the limit. If he had to attend to the man, there was no one around to see.

"Do you mean to be rude?" he asked.

The liveryman's sneer vanished. "Of course not."

"You don't want to be rude with me." Van Goor tapped the butt of his sidearm.

The other man's eyes drifted to the sergeant's tapping fingers, and away, down the empty hallway. "I wasn't."

The sergeant remained standing over him. "Because I won't have it. And I can be ruder than you, I promise you that."

"Well," the liveryman tested. "I guess I should—"

"—I guess you should. Rude shit." Van Goor flicked the side of the man's tall hat—it gave a hollow *tock*—and didn't move.

To get up, the liveryman had to slide along the bench away from Van Goor. Once he had done this, he walked backward down the hall. He waved the sealed message. "I'll go right there," he reassured. "I know this address. From driving the minister. Corner of Little Heritage. It's an embassy, isn't it?"

"Yeah," said Van Goor. "Was, anyway."

"Uh-huh. I bet you never saw a bell rung."
A bell was what they called a winner—a corpse.

Two for the Maid in Her Bonnet

From a wardrobe in an apartment that had belonged to the son of an assemblyman, D requisitioned two pieces of luggage. While the majority of the other students were agitating and signing on with the Volunteers, the assemblyman's son had stayed loyal to his class and bolted from campus.

She packed her own insubstantial possessions in the bags, as well as the assemblyman's son's linens, some of his clothes, and a few other items that she thought might prove useful. She searched for money in the usual spots but didn't find any. In the drawer of the bedside table, she found a straight razor and, perplexingly and unpleasantly, a loose tooth. D took the razor, left the tooth.

D locked the door to the apartment behind her and returned to the servants' dormitory. From the kitchen she took some dry goods, and from the supply closet some brushes, soap, and polish. D put these things in her new bags as well.

One of the other maids, Bethany, came into the kitchen. She gasped when she saw D ransacking the closet. "Those aren't your cases, Dora."

"They are now," D said. "I found a new place. I won't be back."

Bethany was a tall, jutting girl, chin and elbows and feet. She looked and carried herself like she'd been jumbled and put back together again. Like most of the girls employed in service by the university—like D herself—she was an orphan, a graduate of Juvenile Lodgings. D figured that was where she'd been jumbled.

"What do you mean, you found a new place? What place?"

"Just a place. You have to look after yourself. The university has closed and there's no telling when it will reopen, so there's no point in staying."

"It's dangerous out there. There was cavalry in the street this morning, before it was light," Bethany said.

"I'm sure they were just on patrol, maintaining the peace while everything gets straightened out. My friend in the Volunteers tells me they plan to set up a new government that's fairer. I'm sure you've seen the pamphlets."

"Your friend. Your Mr. Barnes."

Bethany's marriage was her one sad point of pride. Her husband, Gid, was an older man who made a paltry living as the keeper of the university rector's terriers. Bet had once made an offhand confession that, for training purposes, Gid sometimes spent nights in the kennel with his charges. The nasty teasing from the other servants that followed had taken a predictable course. It was D who informed the ringleader that the baiting had to stop.

("Why shouldn't we have some fun with Bet?" the girl had asked.

"Because I'll beat you with an ash shovel if you don't quit," D had said, and that ended it.)

She was disappointed, but not surprised, by the ingratitude of Bethany's tone. When they jumbled you, pieces broke off. You were left with lots of sharp points.

"That's right." D met the other maid's eyes straight-on. "My friend."

Bethany frowned and dropped her eyes to the tiled floor that they'd each washed on their knees countless times. "A couple of those green armbands asked Gid about the rector, but the rector scrammed like all the rest. Gid said not to worry, but it scared me."

"So move along. The both of you. Take a new place. Call yourself something different."

"Gid could never leave his pups," Bet said.

The way the girl stood with her lower lip stuck out made it clear that she wanted D to argue with her, but D had nothing else to say. It was time she was leaving. She went to Bet, kissed her on the cheek, and said good-bye. D heard her sniffling as she departed, but didn't look back.

△

A group of women and men herded a flock of black-faced lambs down University Avenue. The lambs had red marks painted on their coats for the estate to which they'd belonged. None of the herders wore green armbands; they were regular working folk, not students or soldiers. At least one appeared to be a sweeper, for he used his long broom to urge the lambs on. The lambs made worried sounds at each other and left a trail of shit.

"Come to supper, sweetie! There's plenty for all," a herder called to her. D ignored him.

At the tram stop, she waited with a small crowd. A street performer with a rubbery face strummed a guitar and sang a humorous song about Joven, the industrialist who had been killed in the street by a government minister.

He was proud and bald and dead
He was rude and short and dead
He's no pals, Westie said,
So I can spill his red
But the mudman got the last word
Oh, the mudman got the last word

The expressions of the people around D evinced a combination of mortification and amusement, cheeks red, fingers pressed to mouths. They were still getting used to the idea that someone could sing such a song in public.

At the end of the song the citizens threw the government out and Joven ascended to heaven, but refused to eat off the angels' shoddily produced plates. A few people dropped pennies into the street performer's upturned hat, and he had sung two more songs before the tram finally arrived.

The carriages were filled to capacity, however, riders poking out every open window. It rattled past without braking. "Sorry! Shorthanded! Express only!" the driver called. The companionable feeling brought on by the song instantly evaporated. Several of the people who had been waiting at the stop swore after the tram, while a few of the riders who were crammed on board offered parting compliments of their own.

D jerked her heavy bags up and struggled along to the river. The museum was on the east side of the waterway, the university on the west.

She started to cross the North Fair Bridge—the No Fair, more commonly, or just the No—one of the two cantilevered bridges that spanned the Fair River.

Directly ahead, the bridge fed into the Great Highway, which swept in a long hook to the upper precincts in the city's hills. In these hills were the estates of the wealthiest ministers, industrialists, and landowners.

To her left, where the river bent toward the Provinces, the Magistrates' Court edged up to the waterside, its roof prickly with chimneys, flagpoles, and lightning rods.

On D's right, the Fair flowed south as it approached the bay. Two miles in the distance it crossed beneath the South Fair Bridge—the So Fair, or the So—while the land on both banks dipped low alongside it. This was the Lees District. From a distance, the proliferation of dark, tightly packed buildings looked like a pattern of mildew.

A small wind flicked D's bonnet strings and dried the sweat on her neck. The weight of the luggage made her shoulders ache. She put them down for a rest.

The air was unusually clear. To the northeast, past the place where the Great Highway disappeared in the jumble of the heights, there rose a hazy outline of the mountains. South, in the direction of the bay, the green of the Fair cracked apart into the midnight-blue scales of the ocean. All throughout the gridded panorama, glimmers of silver winked, the light reflecting off the spidery lines of the tram wires.

It took D a moment to discern the reason for the unusual visibility. Of the dozens of factories that lined the shoreline in either direction, not one showed activity. No smoke rose from the stacks.

Only a few other pedestrians passed in either direction. In their darting looks she made out the same uncertainty they'd encountered the previous morning. Except today, Robert was not there to tell them everything was going to be all right. D thought of what Bet had said about the cavalry before light, and of the flock of sheep being led away, and of the short-handed tram. It would be important to stay aware, on the off chance that Robert was wrong about things getting straightened out.

"Beat your dust for you," offered a weaving wild man. His black coat was worn white at the seams and he carried a wood pole that might previously have served as the handle of a shovel. "Drapes, rugs, whatever needs it. Beat your dust for anything. Do anything for anything."

The wild man was familiar to D. She had often wondered if anyone had ever taken him up on his offer. He seemed unusually frantic this morning, sclera reddened, chest heaving, whapping his stick on the stones of the bridge. D wasn't afraid of him, but she knew to be careful around the desperate; to be careless with them was a good way to become one of them.

She picked up her luggage and quickened her pace, striding by without meeting his eye.

"I know you got dust!" he hollered after her. "I beat dust for anything, miss!"

Δ

At the crest of the No Fair a quick boy was playing a solitary game of Dribs and Drabs. He was nearly six foot, but there was no hair on his smooth cheeks. D made him somewhere in the range of fifteen to seventeen. On the balustrade by his elbow was a stack of stones. The hat he wore was too big and he styled it like a sport, tilted as far back as it would go without falling off. Lank auburn hair grew to the bottoms of his earlobes, a few strands extending, creeper-like, to his chin.

A delinquent's help might be useful. There was no one more aware than a quick boy.

She walked to where he leaned and set down the bags. D plucked one of his rocks.

"You should help yourself," he said. "That's why I went to the trouble of gathering them and walking out to the middle of this bridge. So a stranger could take them."

The game of Dribs and Drabs was simple: you dropped stones down on the river trash that floated past below in order to earn points. The complex part was the scoring. The game's devotees, primarily street children as well as the disreputable sorts of gamblers who favored the game over more refined competitions like dice and dogfighting, were infamous for their arguments over how many points a particular hit was worth; but in general, the more unusual the strike, the better the score. Each player was apportioned a certain number of stones to drop—three or five, most often. If one of your stones hit, say, a piece of driftwood, that was probably just a single point, whereas if one of your stones hit a boot, that was good for three or four points. If you hit a dead animal, that was nine points; if you hit a human corpse, you won outright.

"What's your score?" she asked him.

"My score is, it may surprise you to find that this bridge has a whole other side to it right over there, and these are my droppers that I carried up here."

"It's all shadows on that side this time of day. I wouldn't be able to see what I was aiming at."

This earned her a glance of reappraisal; she understood something about the game. "I wonder if you need something? I could help you, maybe. New dress? Pretty necklace? Items such as that are affordable at the moment. Paper's no good, though. Have to be coin. Or fair exchange, item for item."

"That's kind of you. And why are items so affordable suddenly, do you suppose?" D knew the answer, but she wanted to hear how the quick boy would butter the subject, if he really was quick at all.

He tapped one of his droppers on the balustrade and shook his head in apology. "I'm not knowledgeable in the particularities and like that. I just know what I'm told. What I can tell you is, that bargains never do last."

She'd tried to turn the subject away from business, and he'd steered it back—smart. She introduced herself as Dora and asked him his name. He said to call him Ike. They agreed to play a three-stoner.

A wagon wheel emerged from under the shadow of the bridge. Filmed in green muck, it glistened in the sun and rode high on the water. They dropped their rocks and they both missed, but D was closer. A broken oar came along, and neither made the strike. A minute after that the current carried a piece of what looked like sacking, and D hit it, *sploosh*.

The young man clapped his hands. "Two for the maid in her bonnet! Well done!" The pleasure on his soft, sunlit face was sincere. He looked as though he'd just tasted sugar for the first time.

"Two points? Are you sure? I would have said one."

"Nah," Ike said. "That was a quality shot. We reward that."

"Lucky," she said.

"Uh-huh, Miss Dora. That's what hustlers always say." He chinned at the bags. "That your loot?"

"Those are my possessions," D said. "Carry them for me, would you? I'm going to Little Heritage. It's off of Legate."

"Yeah." He hoisted her bags. "So you're a dribser posing as a maid. I like that. You play much?"

"No. Only every fifteen years or so."

"Uh-huh. I bet you never saw a bell rung."

A bell was what they called a winner—a corpse.

"I have," said D. "I rang one once myself."

Ike rolled his eyes at her. "Uh-huh. You did, did you."

They descended the opposite slope of the bridge, toward the Court. She asked him what he knew. "A lot, I bet," she said.

"I know you can't be slack. That's how you get got. So what if they fired all the constables. It's like I said about bargains: they don't last. The green armbands are nothing, but those others that are Crossley's? I know they're auxiliary but they're still real soldiers, and if they take an interest, they're liable to be as vicious as constables. Now, it's no great concern to me whoever's out there, because I'm fleet. But amateurs, they see a ripe situation, and they start grabbing. Take it from this Ike, you always want to be careful, especially those times when it seems like you don't need to be."

"I wouldn't dream of taking advice from any other Ike."

"You really rang a bell once, Miss Dora?"

"Yes."

"Honest now."

To indicate that she wouldn't have her word questioned D lifted her nose and did not reply. The quick boy laughed and declared that he thought as much.

At the east end of the bridge a poster was pasted on a pole.

TO THE PUBLIC:
THE EMERGENCY JUSTICE COMMITEE Has Established AUTHORITY.
PILFERING, ASSAULT, and Other CRIMES will be Prosecuted HARSHLY.

Ike lifted one of the bags to poke his finger where it read *The Emergency Justice Committee*. "That's just the green armbands. They're nothing."

They took the walk along the East Strand.

△

Ike told D to look at the burnt foundation of what had been a munitions warehouse—the old government had fired it in their retreat.

And at this crossing here, he'd seen a nag collapsed dead on the tram tracks. While a bunch of folks were trying to decide what to do, a gray tomcat had strolled in through the crowd and jumped right on the side of the dead nag and sat there like it had something to say. Ike had seen it happen with his own eyes. Everyone had just let the cat be. There was nothing official on the subject, but it just seemed like bad luck, to move a live cat off a dead horse. Some Lees people, as she might know, the older ones especially, made tributes to cats and asked them for favors, even believed that cats did miracles. Ike didn't follow any religion, but he respected them all. Thank goodness, the cat eventually left on its own after fifteen or twenty minutes.

"Would you have moved the cat, Miss Dora?"

"No," D said.

"That's right!"

Over there, now, was the office of a lawyer who smoked poppy. If you got that lawyer on the right day, he could talk you out of anything. Wrong day and you'd not get a word out of him. Ike didn't know, people exaggerated, but that was what was said. "You know any opium fiends, Miss Dora?"

"No."

Ike said he wished he could say the same.

Those fellas sleeping on the landing there were dockmen. Very few boats had come upriver since the upheaval, but they were there every day, nonetheless, holding their territory. Men were waiting outside the factories too, sitting in the yards, napping and pitching pebbles, nothing to do until someone came and opened the gates. Individuals enjoyed a free hour, but they also liked to make money so they could eat. It was a shame.

Dora said, "I'm sure that the Provisional Government will have them working again soon."

"If you say so, Miss Dora."

There was no reason to feel sorry for the constables who'd been fired, however. "Constables can go lie on the tram tracks like dead horses." Amazing thieves, Ike said, every one of them, robbing the professional ladies and the gambling parlors for protection.

"But listen." He stopped on the Strand where they had come alongside a woman selling packets of pickled oysters off a board.

"Yes, what is it, Ike?"

D had quickly developed a fondness for the young man. She was amused by his evident compulsion to tell her everything he knew. She also felt a little sorry for him. Ike seemed canny enough to live by his wits, but there wasn't any cruelty about him, and wits without cruelty were like cats without claws.

"You can't buy a properly pickled oyster anywhere above the So. Farther north you go, the more disgraceful the quality. If you want pickled oysters, Miss Dora, take it from this Ike: there's no reason to even consider spending your money until you're past the South Fair walking toward the bay."

"You're a disgrace," the woman with the board said.

"It's the truth," Ike said to D, as if the vendor had just proved his point.

They started walking again, and Ike resumed, "And you never want to eat an oyster that's not pickled. That's a good way to get the cholera. You probably know that."

"Yes," D said. "I know that."

△

Ike could find his way from here to there with the best of them, and he maintained a wide range of associations. From among the ragpickers down in the Lees to the professional ladies who patrolled the So, to the hostlers who managed the livery stables near the Magistrates' Court and the Treasury Dome, to the cobblers and tailors and milliners of Silk Terrace and Sable Street, to the opium dealers who sat on stools behind the letter slots of the buildings in Bracy Square waiting to hear the password from that day's back pages, to the canners in the factories on Tunny, to the dockmen on the Northeast Piers and the Southwest Piers, to the Lodgings girls who sold cinnamon sticks in the Fields for strolling swains to give their sweeties, to the gamblers and bookies who haunted the raceway at the Old Bricks, to the sweepers who patrolled the sidewalks in front of the shops on Tourmaline and Peridot, to the touts who sold nip bottles outside the theaters before shows and handed out saloon vouchers after, to the nightsoil men who shoveled for the great people who lived in the manors of the Hills, carting away their ordure—Ike had many acquaintances, and was treated respectfully.

"Because it's my business to know how it is," he said. "Believe me, Miss Dora."

"I do, Ike," D said, and he gave her a fast look—to make sure that she wasn't smiling, she thought—and when he saw that she wasn't, the young man himself smiled at her, unaware that she could read the naked relief in his expression.

D smiled back at him.

Δ

But the revolution had thrown everyone's routine out of whack, Ike explained as they left the Great Strand and turned onto Legate Avenue, entering the eastern center of the city. The horse races and the bookies and the houses of the professional ladies had been closed for some time even before the revolution, and it was unclear when, or if, they'd reopen. The folks who salted the everyday, as it were, had been swept up with the truly bad people, the politicians and the bankers and the constables. It concerned him.

When D met a new person, she often pictured how they lived, how cleanly they kept their home; how much filth they'd leave behind for someone like her to scrub away, if they suddenly disappeared. It told a lot, where the dirt was allowed to collect. Robert, for example, kept things tidy in his own rooms; but he was indifferent to sanitation beyond his door, freely dropping bits of trash and flicking his cigarette butts wherever he walked. You could tell he came from wealth.

For Ike, she imagined a nook, probably in some boardinghouse basement or attic, the floor strewn with hay and a line strung at the top of his reach draped with his washing, a spare shirt and drawers. It was a spot that looked dirty at a glance, but wasn't; the hay on the floor was fresh and it concealed the loose board where he stored his savings and his special treasures. It was a decent, hopeful room.

"I mean, leisure's the fun of life," Ike said, still speaking of his out-of-work friends.

"That's what they tell me," D said. "Have you got a family, Ike?"

"Somewhere. I expect I'll get to know them better once I've made my fortune and the word gets around. They'll come calling."

"I suspect you spent some time in the Lodgings. How long?"

"Until I couldn't stand it anymore."

"Where do you live now?"

"The Metropole, isn't it obvious? I stay in the penthouse suite. I used to live at the King Macon, but I didn't care for their cat, his moods and—"

"You, there! Stay right there!" A Volunteer, stationed at a corner across the street, waved to them.

An alley angled off a few feet ahead. D clapped her hand on Ike's wrist before he could bolt for it. "You'll outrun him if you have to."

He hissed.

"You said the armbands were nothing," D reminded him as the Volunteer marched up to them.

Middle-aged, hair graying around the ears, the Volunteer wore a baggy, shabby wool suit. The beige patches at the elbow under his green armband and at both knees of his pants looked as if they'd been trimmed from a heavy drapery. He was certainly not from the students' wing of the Volunteers. D pegged him as a radical of some kind, a professor or a journalist. He had a waddling, hustling walk that seemed designed to break through barroom clusters while spilling as many drinks as possible. For the unkempt Volunteer's rooms, D visualized everywhere borrowed books left open and facedown with broken spines, and a table covered in empty wine bottles. Stuck in his belt was a long-barreled pistol.

"Those bags don't belong to you, scavenger." He jabbed a finger at Ike. A whistle was tied around his neck with a piece of string. "Don't you know that their stealing is why we just threw off the old government and freed ourselves? It won't continue. You drop those bags right on the ground."

Ike set the bags on the sidewalk. The ankles of his pants rode up as he bent, and D glimpsed the bone handle of a small knife protruding from the top of a sock; she considered the possibility that she'd underestimated Ike's capacities. He straightened and the handle disappeared inside his pant leg.

D fished the declaration from the pocket of her apron. "They belong to me, sir."

The Volunteer snatched it out of her hand. A frown crossed his face as he read. He refolded the paper and returned it to her.

"I've heard of Van Goor, but there's nothing whatsoever written there that entitles you to fill up bags."

"How can I maintain the property without proper supplies?"

Without answering, the Volunteer redirected his attention to Ike. "There's nothing written about you either."

"That's because I'm not involved. She just told me I had to help her or I'd be reported, and then I'd never be able to fulfill my dreams of joining the Emergency Justice Committee and of getting a green armband like you have, sir." Ike removed his hat, clutched it by the brim with both hands, and blinked at the Volunteer.

The Volunteer studied him, trying, D could tell, to determine if the young man was in earnest. The Volunteer fingered the whistle that hung around his neck. Ike ground his toe around on the stones of the sidewalk. There was a faint bulge where the bone handle was tucked at his ankle.

"Why don't we do this?" D proposed. "What's your name, Officer?"

"Rondeau."

"All right. You take the bags into custody. I'll send a message to Sergeant Van Goor explaining what's happened, that Officer Rondeau confiscated my luggage, and he'll have a soldier come and fetch it from you and bring them to the museum. Or perhaps he'll come and fetch it himself, and he can thank you for your attention to detail. I'm sure that Sergeant Van Goor isn't too busy."

The Volunteer breathed out his nose.

"No." He fluttered a hand. "Get along. Sergeant might not be too busy for such nonsense, but I certainly am."

△

Ike deposited the bags inside the doors of the museum. He was gleeful. "See? The green armbands, they don't know what they're doing. A bunch of fat old men and fancy boys playing dress-up. Did you see his face? Put that in a frame to admire." The quick boy's initial move to take flight had apparently been stricken from the record. D found she liked him even more.

She unsnapped the bags and laid them open, inviting Ike to take something for himself.

He pawed through the clothing and other items from the assembly-man's son's apartment, pinching and rubbing at the fabrics of the trousers and shirts to test the materials. Nothing seemed to strike Ike's fancy, though, and he carefully folded the pieces back up and returned them to the bags.

"High quality," he said. "But that's all right. You can owe Ike a favor."

From her apron, tucked in beside the declaration, D removed the ivory-handled straight razor that she'd requisitioned from the assembly-man's son's bedside drawer. She opened the razor blade.

Ike raised an eyebrow.

"I'd rather Ike owed me a favor." She turned it out handle-first. "This'll fit better in your sock."

Ike accepted it and appreciatively stroked the pearl insets with his thumb.

"Now, I have a clamdigger who needs a bucket," D said. "Could you find me one, Ike?"

Events Leading to the Overthrow of the Crown's Government, Pt. 2

*B*ello, the assemblyman's son, called Lionel over and suggested they take the afternoon and go visit the Morgue Ship. They could inspect the corpse of Joven, the infamous plate-maker who had attempted to murder Minister Westhover.

After the inquest determined that the minister was blameless, the body had gone unclaimed and become the property of the city. The authorities had decided to put him on display at the Morgue Ship. Here, the bodies of notorious criminals and other anomalous individuals were preserved in ice and chemicals, and made available for viewing. The location on the river was thought to preserve hygiene and prevent the spread of disease. Joven had been there for more than a month.

Lionel was suspicious. His opinion of Bello was low. "Why would you want to do that?"

"It's funny, isn't it!" Bello laughed ruefully, then yawned. They were in the university lounge and he was lolling in an armchair with one leg thrown across an arm. "My first thought this morning was, 'Maybe I should go see a rotten criminal's corpse.' Nice head I have, isn't it, giving me that kind of a bright idea? And I decided, 'I'll ask the next person who walks in if he'll come with me,' and Dakin walked in with his fly down, and I said to myself, 'I'll ask the next person who walks in who isn't a fool,' and you walked in, Lionel, and I was pleased, because you're not a fool, I can tell you're always thinking. I want to go with someone who has a mind.

"What do you say? It is interesting, you have to admit it. And it's never a bad idea to chuck the books for an afternoon and get some air. Education in the field."

This was nearly funny, and Lionel was not possessed of an overwhelming sense of humor. To the best of his knowledge, Bello had never had his head in any book or cared the slightest for education, in the field or anywhere else. If he had a major, it was in using his umbrella to flick up the skirts of maids, with perhaps a minor in asking if anyone was in the mood for lunch yet.

Lionel was aware of his own reputation for overseriousness. He bore it without regret, and even some pride. In fact, he would have hoped that he'd be the last person Bello would gravitate toward.

Of course, Bello wasn't particularly popular. If Lionel's studiousness had won him few friends, Bello's habits of waving around his money and boasting about his love of prostitutes had earned him none at all.

Lionel was curious about Joven, though; Bello was right about that.

The reporting in the papers, obviously slanted as it was toward the side of the currency minister and his "self-defense," troubled him. If you subtracted out the particular personalities and the specific circumstances, what you were left with was three men and a pistol set against a single man armed with a dinner plate.

Other contemplations had lately scraped at Lionel's conscience: the waiter he'd spotted behind the university canteen, sitting on a box and with liver-spotted hands picking over the remains of a cooked chicken, carefully setting scraggly bits of meat aside on a cloth to take home; peers like Bello who evidenced no interest in their studies and yet were allowed to absorb space in the university's rolls, for no reason except that their families were in the government; and how inexplicable it was that the nation's Grand Army was at war a thousand miles across the ocean, fighting on behalf of another nation, and yet life seemed exactly the same as Lionel had always known it, because neither he nor any of his acquaintances had a relative, or even a friend, in the military. For days on end, you could forget that it was happening, a whole war fought beneath the nation's flag.

Lionel said he'd go along with Bello to the Morgue Ship.

"Aces! Westhover and my father are musketeers, it so happens," the assemblyman's son went on. "From their days here, actually. Here's a thought for you: maybe someday one of us will shoot a madman to death, and our sons can go and view that corpse! Wouldn't that be a great big chuckle, Lionel?"

△

They took a tram from the University stop in the direction of the lower westside berth of the Morgue Ship. Bello had brought along a flask, and he immediately began to harass an impoverished woman, insisting she join him in a drink.

The woman was on the bench across from them. Her hair was gray brown, her features rumpled with late middle age. She was drenched in patches and rags, and the wrinkled paper flowers pinned to her droopy brown hat trembled with the rattling of the tram.

"Just sniff that, and tell me you don't want some," Bello said. He waved the uncapped flask under the woman's nose. In the seat beside him, Lionel didn't need to smell the liquor in the flask to get a whiff because the smell was pouring off Bello's skin.

The woman hugged the uncovered basket in her lap containing scuffed doorknobs and rusty hinges and other unidentifiable bits of brass, and responded in a trickle of words in a language that Lionel didn't recognize. He assumed she'd foraged the doorknobs and the rest of the junk from tumbledown structures and trash heaps—which, in turn, caused him to think of the waiter with the liver-spotted hands, sitting in the yard and stripping the chewy last meat from the chicken and putting it on the cloth. While his own life went on at the university, people crawled around like ants to survive.

"She can't understand you," Lionel said to Bello, trying to get him to leave her alone.

The assemblyman's son ignored him. He said to the woman, "If you have a swallow of this wonderful juice, I'll buy your best doorknob. Hells, I'll buy your worst doorknob. Now, if we were striking a fair bargain, you would have to give me a doorknob and then I would give you a drink, but that's fine." Bello sipped, belched, and waved the flask. "See: it's yummy on your tongue-y."

The woman smiled anxiously and said something else. "Doesn't mean a thing to me, darling," Bello said. "Are we drinking or not?" The tram ground to a halt at the next stop, and she hurriedly debarked.

Bello chuckled. "The poor can be terrible snobs, can't they?" He offered the flask to Lionel and raised his eyebrow.

He had known Bello was a buffoon, but Lionel had not thought through what it would be like to spend whole hours with him. It was shaming. "No," he said.

Bello chuckled some more. "More for me!"

And as the tram rolled farther south, Lionel's traveling companion felt compelled to narrate the passing scenes:

"Ah, look at that there." Bello pointed to a faded house mended with boards of different colors. A gray glove was trapped under the front door's knocker. "That glove means they're all infected with cholera and dying in there. Disgusting cretins. Ought to know better by now than to drink from the same place they shit and piss, but they never do learn."

Another section of the track was lined with market stalls, the tables piled with pieces of clothing. "If your supply of filthy rags ever runs out, this is where I recommend you go to replenish your stock," Bello said. Women with shawls pulled over their heads were sorting through the piles. Letters bent across one woman's fuzzy brown shawl; **LOUR**, Lionel read. It dawned on him that the shawl had been cut from the sacking of a flour bag.

The tram tracks tilted downward, following the land as it steadily declined from the heights to the lowlands of the Lees.

"Look, look!" Bello gestured frantically at an alley. A wiry old man, bare-armed in a vest, was leading a mule down a set of wooden stairs from a second-level door. With each step of the mule, dirt rained from the stairs and the whole structure shook ominously. The tram passed beyond the scene before Lionel could see if they made it safely to the ground.

"Do you suppose it was an arranged marriage, or for love?" Bello drank from his flask. "You have to marvel at it. Creatures find a way to live, don't they?"

Lionel wanted to say that they were people, but he knew that Bello would just make a joke of it.

Chalked on brick and clapboard walls were announcements:

**FAMILY LODGINGS BY THE NIGHT HERE
DOCKMENS BROTHERHOOD/10/USUAL SPOT
DRIMM'S CHEAP & EXCELLENT POTASH
EXPERT BONE-SETTER—ASK FOR COLL
UPSTAIRS BEHIND**

Smoke oozed from pipes that jutted from walls and roofs. It was pitch black from the garbage that was used for fuel instead of wood, and the noxious smell put a tarry taste in Lionel's mouth. When the tram bent toward the river, the smoke mingled with the river tang of fish and mud, and with other varieties of exhaust. Gray plumes unfurled from the chimneys of the factories below the South Fair Bridge and were ripped into streamers by the bay winds. This lighter-colored smoke had the pungency of fresh paint, tickling up his nostrils and sliding behind his eyes, making him feel unpleasantly buoyant in his seat.

"And so many sweet kitties," Bello said.

Oh, so many: crouched on rooftops, on windowsills, in stairwells. Lionel saw one cat sitting upright atop a cornice's sooty stone cupid. The animal's striped gray tail draped in the shape of a six, and it regarded the dirty sky with sleepy yellow eyes.

Bello went on approvingly, "They keep the vermin in check and, if the winter's deep enough, there's meat for your pot. They say they'd never, 'Cats are holy,' but it's bullshit—they would and they have, you can be sure of it. When things get bad enough, you eat the servants. That's a rule of mankind."

At the line's end, at the South Fair Bridge, they got off. The Morgue Ship was another half mile or so along the West Strand. A group of adolescents was gathered at a railing of the bridge. "Dribbers, I think it's called," Bello said. "They try to hit the garbage in the river with rocks. It's the little cretins' sport, if you can believe it."

The land was flat, rising barely above the river. Diggers with their pants pulled up to their knees were sifting sand in the shallows, and though it was late summer, their lips were blue from the cold water that lapped their naked feet.

"Come on!" Bello slapped the flask into Lionel's chest. This time, he drank.

△

As they waited in the line on the wharf that extended to the Morgue Ship, they traded the flask back and forth, and when it was emptied, Bello produced a second flask, and they started on that one.

Only two people at a time were permitted on board. Most of these visitors seemed amused as they returned down the plank walkway. "Nothing to him! I can't see why Westhover bothered to shoot him when he could have just snapped him like a twig," a man moving past said to his date. By the quality of the clothes and hats, and by the private carriages that were waiting on the cross street, it was clear most of them were of the better classes.

The drink loosened Lionel's tongue. "Only a rich person would think to spend money to see something like this."

Bello barked his agreement. "Ha! We do know how to have fun, don't we!"

In Lionel's drunkenness, he had consciously surrendered to Bello's belligerence. The assemblyman's son didn't matter: old people lived in the same room as their donkeys; children were turning blue. Lionel didn't suppose he mattered much either. As the line dwindled, he trudged forward.

At the wharf-side they each handed the boatman a quarter. He gave them pieces of cotton to stuff in their nostrils.

Bello frowned. "I thought he was kept cold. He's not rotted, is he?"

"He's doing well enough. It's for the chemicals in the bath that keep him that way." The bags under the boatman's eyes hung down to his nostrils. His skin had a grated look, as if he slept facedown in netting. "Don't worry, gentlemen, you'll get your money's worth," he added, and the way he said "gentlemen" made Lionel avert his gaze.

They stuck the cotton in their nostrils.

Lionel went first over the short, loose, chained plank bridge that crossed the water and stepped onto the ship's slippery deck.

"I think that man wanted to kiss me," Bello said, following him. "You're probably jealous, Lionel. You probably wished he wanted to kiss you."

Lionel scowled at Bello. "Don't you ever shut up?"

The sharpness of his tone seemed to surprise Bello. "Just joshing, pally," he said.

Converted from a small cargo vessel, the Morgue Ship had been stationary for so long that a crust of barnacles had formed armor up to the gunwales. Rust had eaten pits through its chimney, and its paddlewheel was coated in dark-green slime. The wood of the deck wept and squished under their boots.

They entered through the cabin door and descended a short flight of stairs into the belowdecks gloom. It was a long, low-ceilinged space, and in the center of the floor, beneath a hanging lamp, a corroded tin tub—coffin-shaped, but wider and slightly deeper—rested on a wooden platform. The air was dank and cold. Blocks of ice sat in buckets against the walls. Despite the cotton in his nose, Lionel inhaled an odor that was medicine-sweet.

Bello moved to the right side of the container, Lionel to the left.

Between them, half sunk in a soup of emerald liquid and chunks of ice, lay Joven's corpse. Despite the smallness of the body, Lionel found he could not, at first, take in the whole of the man. His gaze traveled from the bumpy crest of the skull with its four or five hairs plastered to the skin to the closed, furrowed eyelids; to the sharp spoon of a chin; to the puddles of green liquid collected in the scoop of each collarbone; to the narrow chest with the two bullet holes, bloodless and black, situated just to the heart-side of the sternum, one below the other; to the large hands, turned up and out of proportion to the rest of the dead man, thick with fat knuckles that ended in calloused fingertips.

Lionel fixed on these fingertips, and the little curls of skin peeling loose from the calluses after being soaked for many days. He thought of the waiter excavating the chicken bones, stripping every last bit of meat.

He felt dizzy and stepped away. His eyes took in the dead man in his fullness, lying there naked in the ice and the chemical solution. A half-lid covered the container starting at the level of Joven's waist. He looked tucked in. He looked like some terrible sacrifice.

It was all wrong. Everything. Their whole world. Lionel had suspected, but now he knew.

"Honestly," Bello said, "I don't expect I'd look any better. Circumstance isn't likely to be flattering for anyone."

The expression of sympathy filled Lionel with relief.

"Yes," he said.

Bello removed the second flask from inside his jacket and paused, resting it on the ledge of the tub. The tufts of cotton protruding from his nostrils shivered with his breathing. He grunted and pointed at the green liquid. "I wouldn't drink that juice on a bet. Not for every dollar you had."

"No," Lionel said.

"No." Bello drank.

The hanging lamp glowed on Joven's corpse. The ship creaked. Lionel became aware of the river behind its walls, flowing toward the ocean. He felt himself sobering. "Are you ready to leave?"

"Almost." Bello tucked away his flask. "I just need to ask him something."

The assemblyman's son bent low over the body, bringing his nose near Joven's. "I only want to know one thing: Are you sorry?"

"What are you doing?" Lionel's question came out softly, as if he were frightened that Joven would wake up. "Don't do that."

If Bello heard, he gave no sign. The cotton flared as he breathed harder, and he reached with his free hand and pinched the dead man's lips. He squeezed them, making them bulge, and rubbed them back and forth, and the voice he gave to Joven was pathetically querulous: "Oh, yes, oh, yes. I'm so-oo sorry. So-oo sorry."

Bello lifted his bloodshot eyes to Lionel. "What do you think, Lionel? Should we accept his apology or not?"

"Please," Lionel said. His gorge rose and he retasted the alcohol he'd drunk earlier.

Bello clicked his tongue. "No. Can't do it. Scum like this think having coins makes them something, gives them class, but it doesn't. It just makes them lucky. And you should be grateful for your luck. My father's piss has more class."

He took a straight razor from his pocket and opened the blade. "Let me just get a tooth for a souvenir and we can leave this floating cesspool."

Δ

It was black morning when the last gawker departed and the Morgue Ship's boatman, Zanes, went to draw in the plank. A cat sat on it. The jewels in its collar twinkled in the night. It was black with a white bib and a white chin. The animal sat neatly, expectantly.

Zanes was a believer. He removed his cap and stepped aside. "Bless you, friend."

The cat trotted aboard without sparing him a glance. It crossed the deck to the cabin and disappeared through the doorway.

The boatman trailed the animal belowdecks. He found the cat with Joven: it was crouched on the island of the dead man's chest, kneading the bloodless skin with its claws. It was staring intently at the face of the corpse—and it was purring.

Zanes, pressing his cap to his breast, shuffled closer. He instinctively murmured the daily prayer, "Bless me, friend, and look on me with kind eyes, and show me the way." He understood that he was in the presence of a holy occurrence.

The cat purred and kneaded, and the river murmured against the ribs of the boat, and the ice in the dead man's tub clicked against the tin.

After a while, the animal was contented. It stopped kneading, yawned, stretched, and hopped off Joven's chest down to the floor.

Again ignoring Zanes, the black-and-white cat pattered out and up the stairs, the tag on its collar jingling, and hopped from the Morgue Ship to the wharf a second before the vessel's moorings loosened and dropped away from their cleats.

Zanes returned his gaze to the dead man. Joven's lips parted.

Δ

Lionel woke up in his rooms with a hangover and his shirt speckled with vomit. He washed quickly and dragged himself to a carrel in the deep stacks of the university library. For the rest of the morning he ignored his pounding headache to focus on the composition of an impassioned document that he entitled *A MORAL CALL FOR THE BETTERMENT OF THE POOR AND THE VOICELESS*. When he finished, he let himself into the offices of the campus newspaper, and used the press to make copies.

The Salute

The lieutenant was happy when he visited her that evening. They went inside the engineman's cabin of one of the exhibition trains. Robert sat on the engineman's stool and she rode him. "Wave to the people, you dirty girl! Wave to all the people watching us roll by!"

Over Robert's shoulder, a strapping waxwork fireman leaned forward with an empty shovel to fill the iron belly of the firebox, which was also empty but painted red inside to show its heat. The fireman was stripped to the waist, navy suspenders lolling at his hips. His glass eyes were set at a sidelong angle, so that he would appear to be communicating with the engineman at the front of the cabin, except that D and Robert were in the way, which made it seem as if he were quietly observing what they were doing. She liked that idea and followed it while her lieutenant babbled.

She imagined the waxwork man continuing to shovel, not saying anything, just calmly watching, plunging the blade into the coal, lifting, pitching, plunging, not letting himself be hurried, just lifting, plunging, making his own steady pace, lifting and plunging. . . . The fireman would stink, she thought, not like sweat, but like coal and ash, stink like he'd been rolling in it, like he was made of it. There would be nothing said, just his eyes and her eyes, and the force between them as they tried to break each other apart.

She was close when Robert shuddered, groaned, and pulled the rope for the whistle. It shrieked through the museum's third floor. D was yanked back to herself in a thudding instant.

"Oh, damn." He laughed wheezily. "I think we crashed."

D put her hand into the curls on his bare chest. She wanted to rip them out. "Sad," she said, and withdrew her hand, and lifted herself off him.

"What are you doing? Dora? You're just going to leave me naked on this train going to——? My God, I don't even know where it's going."

D dressed quickly. By the time Robert stepped from the compartment, she had taken a seat on a nearby bench and was jotting in a notebook.

"I don't like the looks of that train's fireman. He's got a sneaky expression. What are you writing down?"

"'Coal or wood for the firebox.'"

"What firebox? For the boiler in the basement? You don't think this barn is cold, do you?"

She glanced up and saw him wiping himself with the checkered handkerchief that had been sticking from the fireman's back pocket. Her ears still rang from the train whistle.

"The firebox on the train is empty. It looks like he's shoveling air."

"Oh. I didn't realize you were planning to take this seriously. Good for you." He cast around, holding the soiled handkerchief out from his body. "You should have been a lady with an estate, Dora. You've got the mind for those little details that men can't appreciate until women show them."

Before he did it, she predicted to herself that he was going to toss the handkerchief into the shadows under the train car—and then he did.

"Too late now," D said. "There won't be any more ladies under the new system. Or lords."

This elicited a frown from Robert as he picked his pants off the floor and shook them out. "No, that's true."

In a framed photographic portrait of his family that he kept in his room, Robert's mother was a sparrow of a woman, small hands clasped at the level of her waist, vividly uncomfortable to be seen by the camera. What did he think would become of her now? What actually would become of her? D had been irritated by the whistle and the handkerchief, but these questions softened her. It was the Bobby in Robert who had done those things, and she suspected it was the Bobby in him who hid from the potential ramifications of the revolution for his landed parents.

Her lieutenant began to tell her about the transcription he'd been called upon to take the previous night, in the office of the chief magistrate. The former currency minister had recounted how, along with renting out the army, the Crown had borrowed vast sums to enrich itself. "Meanwhile, there are people in the Lees who suffocate in the winters because they sleep so close to each other to stay warm."

D had heard talk of worse things even than that happening in the Lees, but she just nodded.

Sundown dimmed the gallery. Inside their train car the engineman and the fireman were now a pair of featureless silhouettes. D led the way upstairs as Robert talked about how the minister claimed that he had only killed Joven because the factory owner's insanity had been briefly contagious.

"It was the most incredible thing I've ever heard. He wasn't ashamed, not in the slightest. Can you believe it, Dora?"

"No," D said, but of course she could. Not all the rich young men at the university had been as enlightened as Robert. There were plenty who she thought would have felt Westhover's actions had been more than justified—ones like the assemblyman's son, who had expected her to hold up the spittoon for him to hock his tobacco juice into. She worried about her lieutenant's capacity for incredulousness. It was extravagant this early in the nation's renewal.

When they arrived at the fifth floor, D brought him to the prospector's shack, which she had chosen for her accommodations, because it contained the only bed in the museum. D had swapped the gritty sheets on the bed for the ones she'd taken from the assemblyman's son's apartment. On the prospector's small table, she had set out a lamp, a pitcher of water, and a pair of glasses. Built for exhibition purposes, the structure had no roof and only three walls—front and sides—so to enclose the space D had strung one of the old sheets across the open side. The solid walls were made of raw timber sealed with daubing.

She lit the lamp.

Robert ceased speaking of the degeneracy of the currency minister and paused at the threshold. "You're actually going to live here? In the tramp's house."

"It's an exhibit for prospecting. The prospector is the one panning for gold out in the glass river. It's my responsibility to look after the museum. I signed an oath. I've got to stay somewhere."

Robert stepped inside. "What if the ghosts who lost their homes in the fire next door at the Sorcery Society or whatever it was move in here and inhabit the wax dummies, and begin to move about? You know, if I was a ghost, Dora, the first thing I would do is inhabit one of these wax men and molest you."

"It hadn't crossed my mind," D said. "Do you think I should be concerned?"

"Probably better to try to put the idea out of your mind altogether. You do understand I won't be able to stay with you every night? I have a detail, commitments."

His droll tone, which she was usually so comfortable with, chafed. D understood more about commitment than Robert would ever learn.

But she kept her tone measured. "Yes, I know. I'll lock the doors."

"We're stretched thin. They've had to dispatch units to deal with some holdouts who have a position on the highway."

This made sense of what Bet had said that morning about the cavalry leaving the city. "Is it serious?"

"No. What's left of the real army is up to its ass in snow a thousand miles away. This is just the dregs. They do have a good position on the highway, though, so the leadership wants to avoid a frontal attack. The two sides are already negotiating. Well, negotiating to negotiate." He traversed the tiny room in three steps and bent to examine the bed. "It slows us down, makes it harder to arrange elections, agree on judicial procedures, but that's all it does."

"Things will be getting back to normal, though? The factories starting up and the river opening to ships?"

"Things will be getting back to better than normal," her lieutenant said. He pinched the sheets of the bed between his thumb and forefinger. "Is it odd that the prospector has silk sheets? That doesn't seem accurate."

"Perhaps he had a gold strike not long ago."

Robert acquiesced to this logic with a shrug and sat on the bed. He rocked forward and back, sighed at the springiness, and lay on his side. He propped his head on his fist. His feet dangled over the edge. "It'll be tight."

"We'll manage." Before she could join him, however, she needed to go through the museum and turn down the lights. "I'll only be a few minutes." She picked the lamp up from the table.

"Dora?"

"Yes, Lieutenant?"

He studied her in a searching way, absently tracing a knuckle along his mustache. In the lamp glow his hair looked polished. "I'm sorry about the way that I go on sometimes. I know it's dull, all the politics."

"Lieutenant—"

"Sometimes I like it when you just call me Robert."

"All right, Robert."

"You know I know how smart you are. Don't you? It doesn't matter to me that you worked. You're as fine as any woman."

There was a strangeness about the way he was attending to her, the tone of contrition. Did it have to do with the sheets? If he asked where they had come from, D would tell him the truth, that she requisitioned them, and moreover—the truth, again—that she had been certain he would approve. But why would he apologize for something that *she* had done? For that was the sense of it, that he was feeling guilty toward her for some reason, which didn't seem to fit either. What could he ever do to harm her? There was no vow between them to break and she had never asked for one. Her family was dead. All she possessed, really, was herself—and, for the moment, the museum.

"Thank you, Robert," she said. "You're very kind to me."

He smiled, and flopped onto his back on the bed. "I'll try not to fall asleep while you're gone. No promises."

She said all right and went to the door.

"Listen." He coughed. "If that Sergeant Van Goor who gave us the paper ever comes around and I'm not here, come find me straightaway. Don't stop to give him a tour or anything. Right away you come and get me. It's nothing serious, nothing to be alarmed about, he's a good man, just unsophisticated. He tends to get confused about things, so it's better that I should handle him. If he shows up, you get me straightaway, do you promise?"

D promised and left, but the exchange nagged at her. There was something he wanted to tell her without actually telling her.

To get to the stairs she first had to walk past the glass river, dark and twinkling with its silver fish. A few steps beyond, D passed through the small orchard of three wooden fruit trees. The one-eyed fruit picker from whom she'd borrowed the satchel—since returned—standing under the central tree, seemed to gaze on her expectantly. "Do you know what that was about?" she asked him, but he didn't, of course, and D moved on.

She descended to ground level. She checked the bolt on the front doors, extinguished the wall lights, and moved to the next gallery. Once she had darkened the second floor, D noticed the way the moonlight altered the faces of the two bricklayers who stood at their waist-high wall frosted in crumbles of ancient cement. The cheerful grins they wore by day warped into pained grimaces, as if they were tired of each other, of each other's jokes and smells and noises. Who could blame them? If immortals don't eventually long for their own deaths, they must surely long for the deaths of fellow immortals.

On the third floor, D went to the dark train car and fished underneath to retrieve the soiled handkerchief, which she stowed in the pocket of her apron to wash later. An owl whooped outside, its strangled, burbling complaint penetrating the museum's thin windows and startling D so that she almost dropped the lamp. The next time it screamed she could ignore it, and she put out the fourth-floor lights, putting to sleep the bank tellers and the telegraph operator and the teacher in the little classroom whose bangs had been vandalized with scissors. Before moving to the stairs, she stopped at a window on the Society-side and looked upon the wreckage. The white cat sat on a pile of rubble, cleaning itself, arrogantly indifferent to the owl's threat.

On the fifth floor she retraced her path to the fruit trees and wished the fruit picker good night, then continued toward the glass river.

"Please!" yelled the fruit picker, but there was something wrong with his voice; it sounded like he had a cold. The *l* rolled into a phlegmatic garble before exploding into the last part of the word. D paused. A gunshot exploded, and the begging man—a real man, not one made of wax—fell silent.

△

A minute or two later the heavy door at the rear of the embassy banged wide. D had gone to the nearest window overlooking the stone court- yard behind the embassy. She flinched but stayed to watch. The soldier who stepped out carried a long object wrapped tight in a covering and hoisted over his shoulder. The wrapped thing might have been a rolled rug, but D knew that it wasn't; by the moons' light she could see vivid stains on the material.

The soldier was shirtless. His full black beard flowed without inter- ruption from his cheeks and jaw down his neck, and into a thick pelt that covered most of his broad upper body. A military stripe ran along the seam of his pants; a holstered pistol hung at his hip; incongruously, atop his head he wore the scarfed top hat of a liveryman. He carried his burden effortlessly.

At the rear of the courtyard was a stable. When he came to the sta- ble gate, he kicked up the latch, and the gate swung free. As he crossed under the eaves of the stable, the thing that wasn't a rug shifted inside its wrapper, and a boot slipped out.

The bare-chested soldier reemerged into the courtyard without the object. He walked to the embassy's rear door, then stopped, cocked his gaze to her museum window. A huge, toothsome grin opened up in the middle of his black beard. He saluted her.

D sent a message to her arm and it raised her hand in reply.

Her neighbor nodded, dropped the salute, and reentered the embassy. A second passed, and the top hat flew out from the dark interior. It skidded across the stones and tipped over. The door slammed shut.

△

In the shack, D turned down the lamp on the table and climbed into the bed beside her lieutenant. When she closed her eyes, the towering soldier was saluting her, smiling, the top hat with the knotted scarf balanced on his head. She opened her eyes and listened to Robert's breathing. D waited for the sun to return.

△

When it did, sparking the motes in the air above her and whitening the hanging sheet, D rose and went to the window to look down on the embassy courtyard.

The top hat still lay on the ground. The tongue of its knotted red scarf lolled on the cobbles. At the stable gate, where the shadows butted up against the new light, a cloud of midges stirred and flexed.

Her lieutenant appeared at her shoulder with a yawn and wished her good morning.

"Good morning," she said. "What do you know about the man next door?"

"Captain Anthony? I don't know anything about him, except that he said he was working on security matters for Crossley—conducting interviews, he said. Why do you ask?"

"Curiosity," D said. "Captains rank above lieutenants, don't they?"

"I'm afraid they do." Robert redirected to the close-by fruit picker. "I hope you're paying attention, my friend. As soon as a man with higher status comes along, her devotion will begin to wane."

That was enough of the subject. She needed to forget it and, more important, so did Robert. It was a door that needed to be bolted, chained, and painted to look like another piece of wall.

D moved into his arms and kissed his neck.

"Ah. That's better. And how did you sleep?" he asked.

"Well enough," she said.

Listen

*I*n the Lodgings, the masters and mistresses told the children to listen, but D quickly determined that what they really wanted was for you to be quiet.

After the cholera had taken Ambrose, it had taken her parents too, and when it was determined that her father's investments were made of sand, the second cousin in Canada who had expressed interest in becoming D's guardian changed his mind. The house and the furniture and even the spinet that D had received for her birthday were sold against the debt.

"If it wasn't for my husband, D, you know I'd take you. My husband says no. You know I would, don't you? Don't you?" Nurse had asked over and over on the way to deliver her to Juvenile Lodgings. Twice on the trip they'd had to stop so Nurse could lean into an alley to vomit.

D reassured her that she did understand, and even rubbed the woman's soft back, and said nothing about knowing that Nurse was a widow.

Nurse delivered D to Lodgings #8 at the ironically named Gammon Courts, for no part of a pig was ever served to the young inmates who resided there.

"You will listen," the head mistress said to D on her induction, "and you will learn useful trades."

"Yes, ma'am," D had said, and the mistress had slapped her across the ear and barked that she wasn't finished speaking.

△

"Do you hear that?" the local councilor had said.

All twenty of them, all the boys and girls of Lodgings #8, had lined up before him in the workroom for inspection. He raised up a gold watch on a chain and swung it back and forth. "Seconds ticking, sir!" an eager girl blurted, and the councilor told her she was a silly fucking liar, it was a perfectly silent Swiss timepiece worth more than her life, and he and the head master on duty had laughed uproariously.

Later, the head master shoved the same eager girl into a tub of dirty water. "See if you can get your ears clear."

△

"Have I made myself clear?" a sewing teacher had demanded once.

Someone farted. This caused someone else to snicker. The sewing teacher screamed in rage and rushed at a boy seated at the worktable nearest, who had made no sound whatsoever, and stabbed him in the arm with a sewing machine needle.

△

Every lesson was essentially the same, repeated endlessly for the seven years D lived in the Lodgings, until she turned fifteen and moved out to take her first position in service at the National University. It was a valuable lesson, too. The lesson was this: don't exist.

The ideal maid, D imagined, would be made of air, and use gently stirring currents to manipulate the brooms and brushes in the dark while the rest of the world slept. The ideal maid was magic.

Quiet and small was not actually the same as invisible, but it could be nearly so.

△

There were windows at either end of the long room where the Lodgings' girls slept in bunks. Sometimes in the nights, after the head master or head mistress had made their last round, they silently coalesced at one of the windows to watch a cat on the cobbles below.

There was always at least one cat to see, and usually more. The moons loved their bodies, shone in their stripes and patches, filled their eyes with silver. The other girls whispered how they wanted this cat, or that, like D had when her parents and Ambrose were alive and she was small; but the more she observed them—how they sank low and crept up on their prey, how they seemed to float from the ground up to a sill, how their eyes glowed in the dark—the less she wanted one.

Instead, D wished she could be a cat, and go wherever she wanted, and slash with claws.

Δ

On her first night alone in the museum, D sat on the bed in the prospector's shack, in the absolute dark, and closed her eyes, and listened:

A stub of chalk dragged across the wooden floor, clicked at the joins, *shhh-tk, shhh-tk, shhh-tk.*

Nurse was out in the street, weeping for her D; she was her girl, she was her girl, and she'd made a terrible mistake to give her up.

The youngest head master, the one with the chapped lips and the twitch at the side of his neck, wandered among the bunks, murmuring about licies. "Do the dirty children bring the licies, or do the licies bring the dirty children? Hah-hah, hah-hah."

The assemblyman's son told her to hold on with that spittoon—"Bring it here first, sweets, so I can give you a present"—and he drew up a rattling ball of phlegm from his chest, and it spattered into the tin bowl.

In the university library, the lightbulbs sizzled while she stared into Robert's eyes, and he stared into hers.

D inhaled, and exhaled; her exhalation expanded into the wide and effusive silence of the museum, its walls and halls, its exhibitions and display cases, its benches and fixtures, its men and women made of wax. All of it belonged to her, the things and, more so, the vast space.

She thought of that time her brother had brought her around the corner, and made the boys disappear, and called it magic. But that wasn't the magic. The magic had been in the way he made her feel significant even though she was little, even though she was a girl and their parents became irritated whenever they noticed her.

"Ambrose?" D listened as her brother's name traveled the height and the length of the fifth-floor hall. "Can you hear me?"

She listened to the echo of her own words until they disappeared. "Look what I did."

D waited. Did he hear? Did he see? ("Yes, I see you. Your . . . face.")

"Why?" someone screamed from the former embassy. "Why?" They kept asking, and D listened the whole while until it was over, but if her neighbor Captain Anthony ever answered, that was something she did not hear.

Events Leading to the Overthrow of the Crown's Government, Pt. 3

For the better part of a day, they toured the Lees—its crumbling, dusty, beshitted lanes and alleys, its poisonous hovels and wobbly firetraps. The group was led by a charity worker, and along with Jonas Mosi it included the leader of the university protests and a few other university boys. The leader of the illegal dockmen's union made a point of observing this university boy Lionel, anticipating that he'd turn tail and run back to his campus.

In one peeling, tilted room there were eleven emaciated children. This didn't shock Mosi in the least. A girl blandly explained to the tour group that there had been twelve until a few days earlier, but Betsy curled up and died. The girl showed them a place on the floor. Another child piped up that it was the Unlucky Spot, "People're always dying on that spot."

In another cramped chamber, they spoke with a woman who lived with her husband and her son, both of whom had been blinded by a batch of bad medicine. Mosi had heard often enough of tragedies like this too. The blind husband sat against the wall and scowled in their direction. "Find this interesting, do you?" he asked them. The son leaned against his father's shoulder, and scratched at a crack in a floorboard, dilated eyes staring off.

They ascended after the shriveled keeper of a halfpenny-a-week board-inghouse as she tottered to the domicile's creaking, feather-coated roof to inspect her pigeon house, where she insisted on demonstrating her throttling technique. One jerk-twist of the neck and the bird she'd chosen expelled a spurt of white shit and sagged limp. Perhaps that shocked Mosi marginally. (It certainly shocked the pigeon.) She plucked and dismantled the bird on a bloodstained board set among the cages while the other pigeons beat their wings and cried in their scrap wood cages.

None of these sights, however, had the effect on Lionel that Mosi had foreseen.

Lionel had a monogrammed and perfumed silk handkerchief—worth, by the dockman's estimate, more than every article on the person of every individual they'd met all day—and he pressed the cloth to his nose after they left each location, but the weedy youth carried on with the rest of the group to the finish, not complaining once. If he was shaken by the poverty they saw, he concealed it well. Mosi had to give that to him.

Then they were taken to view an enormous cesspool that had collapsed and swallowed half of a house, two horses, and a man named Valle with it. Here, Lionel did retreat a few yards and retch, but several of the others did too. Mosi barely restrained his own bile at the smell of the fumes that rose off the surface of the sprawling purple-gray lake.

Their final stop was the Point, the foot of rocky turf that formed the city's southern tip. At the Point, the ocean air tangled with the reek of the smoke and shit and largely won out. Mosi knew this place well: it was the location of the oldest shrine in the city. Set among the tufts of grass that clawed up from the shingle were sundry stone and wooden idols of widely differing ages and verisimilitude, some hardly identifiable as figures, let alone cats. Around the bases of the totems, flowers and fish bones and fish bits were left as offerings. A few wizened believers crouched and prayed. To appease his mother, Mosi had prayed at the Point on countless occasions, though not since she had died.

And, as with almost everywhere in the Lees, several strays were on hand. These living, breathing cats perched on rocks, or sprawled near the idols, or hunkered in the pebbly grass, waiting for the supplicants to finish and leave, so they could have at the fish bits. They were magnificent, in the way of wild cats, with nicked ears and scars on their faces, and coarse, bushy pelts. A few thumped their tails, but mostly they bided, narrow-eyed and still.

Here, once again, Lionel defied Mosi's expectations. He thought the university boy would pull a smug face at seeing the pathetic geezers begging the cats to smile on them. Instead, as a man was straining to lever himself off his knees, Lionel hurried to his side and gave an arm to help him up.

"How are you, sir?" Lionel asked the man, whose frayed and sun-bleached hat was the best of his sad garments, and whose maroon and deeply pored nose leaked two horns of yellow snot.

"I'm right, sir, thank you. Did you know that if we look after them creatures, then they'll look after us? Yes, yes, that's how it is. Do you know the story of the girl who was lost in the desert?"

"No," Lionel said. "How does it go?"

The man's damp, ill face opened with joy. "A girl went out into the dark to see what it was like, but later she couldn't find her way home. Then she wandered for hours an days, growing thirsty, fell down in the sand, an thought she'd die. But what should appear but the most beautiful black cat you've ever seen! Satin black! The girl looked in its eyes, an the cat looked in her eyes, an a message was delivered to her: if she rose, an walked to the naked tree with the marks where the black cat had sharpened its claws, an continued in that direction, she'd find water, an a path."

"And she did?" prompted Lionel.

"Oh, yes, sir!"

In the version Mosi's mother had told him, the girl was locked in a dungeon for an evil king's crime, and the cat put scratches on the floor where a key was hidden beneath, but it was the same idea. She'd taught him all the stories, starting with the founding one, about how the devil exhausted himself doing some mischief and fell asleep, and his wisdom escaped in the form of a cat, and endowed grateful men and women with the wits to prosper. His parents had come to the city from their homeland before he was born, his father one of the Grand Army's many foreign-born recruits, drawn by the promise of mercenary riches. After Mosi's father had died of pneumonia amid Gildersleeve's first Ottoman Campaign, leaving behind neither riches nor a pension, Mosi's mother (pregnant with Mosi) had given up her old ways of worship and embraced the local devotion. What that had got her was debatable: her baby had lived, but she'd died when Mosi was ten, her insides rotted, smiling at him and grinding her teeth at the same time. That was how it went in the Lees, for the grateful and ungrateful alike: death by disease when the best you could get was a room with eleven other people; death by starvation when you hurt yourself working and couldn't keep working; death by fire when someone was so weary from begging that they fell asleep and kicked a lamp into a pile of rags; death from some foreigner's bullet because Gildersleeve ordered you to charge onto the battlefield; and now even death by the actual fucking ground when you were just being in a particular spot and it opened up beneath your feet without warning. If there was a humongous magic cat that looked after the faithful, it was certainly very damned strict about waiting to do it until the faithful had died miserably.

"An when we die, if we've been decent, an if we've been good to the little ones here"—the man gestured at the cats languidly picking their way over the rocky ground—"there's a Big One, the Grand Mother. She comes long an picks us up by our scruff, like we were her own young ones."

"Does She?" Lionel asked sincerely.

"Oh, yes." The devotee showed a black-gummed, toothless mouth and patted the back of his neck. "It don't hurt, I promise you that. She knows just how to get you so it don't hurt. She takes us to where it's soft an warm an the milk runs forever an She protects us."

"I'll look forward to that, sir," Lionel said, and the man said, "An I!" and wished for a cat to smile on the university boy.

And despite himself, Mosi repeated the devotion, irritably mumbling it under his breath.

Lionel shook the penitent's hand and offered him his expensive handkerchief. "Good man, good man. Take this. You can have it."

Guilt afflicted Mosi. He bought a fish head from a vendor and put it at one of the altars. He stepped away, and a pair of mottled cats trotted to the fish head and hunkered over it, tearing and gnashing at the free meal, banging skulls with each other. The dockman tried to think of what to say, but the spasm of guilt had already been subsumed by resentment, and he found that the best he could do was a sour, "Bless you, friends."

A needling bay wind cast minute grains of salt in the dockman's face. One of the cats sauntered away from the fish head with a quivering eyeball in its teeth.

When Mosi turned, he saw that Lionel was observing him. The university boy nodded. Mosi ignored him.

With all of his expectations for young Lionel Woodstock upset, the dockman found himself loathing the young patrician more even than he had assumed he would. Soon afterward they departed to a gathering with other conspirators.

△

Night fell as they traveled uptown to the Metropolitan District for what was supposed to be the largest meeting yet between the various parties of agitators: senior dockmen, tram workers, factory foremen, and some of the other university boys who had helped Lionel spread his pamphlets around the city. Mosi wondered what the tourists and the theatergoers made of the strange parade of men in stained work jackets and smooth-faced, cigarette-smoking university boys in fraternity caps. It was funny until you considered that it would only take one nosy constable and they'd all be got.

They left the street at the alley beside the Lear Hotel. Mosi had never been inside any of the city's three famously opulent hotels—hadn't ever been inside a hotel of any kind, in fact; in the Lees there were only boardinghouses—but he was gratified by the filthiness of the alley. The stink of the rich's garbage seemed indistinguishable from the stink of the garbage below the So Fair.

The men entered the Lear through the delivery hatch to the ice room. They navigated the hanging sides of beef, and proceeded up the bare-walled and uncarpeted servants' stairs. At the third floor, their destination, the hotel's mascot was sitting in front of the door to the hall. It was only a kitten, a black-masked bandit with a white bib.

Lionel was in the lead, Mosi right behind him, when the university boy stopped to scratch the kitten's head. "You must be the newest Celandine." It gave a mournful squeak as they passed by it through the door. Even though his faith was inconstant, Mosi was fond of cats, and this one was particularly pretty.

"Have you seen in the papers?" Lionel twisted back to glance at Mosi. "The Lear has been having bad luck with the Celandines. They keep disappearing. This is the fourth one in less than a year."

Mosi grunted his disinterest. He was quite aware of the stories in the papers about the Lear's trouble with its famous cat, because such nonsense was just about all there was in the papers. Most recently it had been days of articles about the Morgue Ship breaking from its mooring and floating off in the night with Joven's corpse, as if a rusty hulk carrying a dead man made a pinch of difference to the thousands of people who didn't have enough to eat. The cat story was nothing but bullshit to distract the public's attention from the real stories: like the story of the crooked inquest that had rescued Westhover from murder charges; like the story of the true casualty numbers from the Frankish campaign; like the story of the people starving to death because they had no money to buy food. Some slavish factotum to the king was snatching up the Celandines, carrying them off to the hills, and letting them go, Mosi would have put money on it; just another way to keep reporters busy worrying everyone about cats instead of human beings.

They came to the door labeled 3B, trailed by the kitten's plaintive meows, and went inside the residence of a radical old playwright named Aloys Lumm, who had opened his rooms for the meeting of the groups.

Lumm's profession meant nothing to Mosi. The only literature he cared about was the writing on his pay stub, and the state of commerce being what it was with the Crown's government flushing every penny in the nation into Gildersleeve's mercenary adventures among the Franks, the dockman had given that bit of art very poor marks even before he was blacklisted for his organizing. Imports and exports were down by more than half and, as always, the workingman was left holding the bag. They didn't need a playwright; they needed an army.

Which was why this meeting was unique, and why Mosi had warily thrown in his lot with the other groups: the promise of an army. General Crossley, the commander of the Auxiliary Garrison, was among the attendees.

The council was held in Lumm's cramped drawing room. There were not enough chairs, so some of the beardless university boys took seats on the rug in front of the fireplace. Several logs were burning, which combined with the crowd of bodies to make the room uncomfortably hot. Above the fireplace was a painting of a lavishly blond huntswoman holding the severed head of a fox; unaware that, behind her, a wolf was emerging from the dead animal's neck. Mosi was as indifferent to the merits of paintings as he was to stage dramas, but it was plainly ridiculous: wolves were much larger animals than foxes.

Overstuffed bookshelves wrapped the room, packed with volumes and littered with bric-a-brac, figures and rows of pebbles and faded photo portraits in small frames. Dusty potted trees claimed the corners. The lightbulbs were held in glass sconces shaped like acorn shells that jutted from the wall. The few chairs were all huge wingbacks. Mosi found himself up against a wall, sweating, hip jammed against a rolltop desk, bending around one of the acorn-shell sconces. The chamber's smells were of pipe and wood and liniment and oniony breath. He disliked all of this. The potted trees reminded him of a whorehouse parlor.

He was suspicious of the trappings of civility. Look where it had got Joven, doing business with ministers and building a great house in the Hills. Civility wasn't just how they tricked you; it was how you tricked yourself. Mosi wasn't like Lumm with his hotel apartment, or Lionel with his silk hanky, or Crossley with his chest of medals. He was irritated by the need to rely on any of them, and found it difficult to convince himself that he really could. He was a son of the filthy Fair River, and proud of it too, proud that, even as he approached fifty years of age, there was not a man on the docks who could outwork him; and he relished the disgust of the rich scum who looked down on him and wrote in the papers that he ought to be hung for his organizing. They could look down on him all they liked and they could write what they wanted. What they could not do was take away his ability to demand a fair wage; they could not slay men in the street as the mood struck them, and call it progress.

Mosi had not come to laze on the rug like an opium smoker; he had come to find out if there were other serious men willing to put up a fight, because that was the only way to make change. You couldn't embarrass the rich, or harangue them into a fair bargain. The Charmer had tried both tacks.

To soothe himself Mosi envisioned how, if the meeting turned out to be a setup for a government raid, he would grab the shovel from the andiron and start bashing skulls. If they intended to put his corpse on ice as a trophy on some new Morgue Ship, he wanted to be wearing twice as many bullet holes as Joven.

The room quieted as the white-haired old man, Lumm, was helped up onto a box.

"My friends, thank you for coming here. I only just moved into these rooms, you know, and I know it's close, rather close. But it's good to have you close. When you're like I am now, you take great strength from the young." Lumm crossed his arms so tightly across his narrow chest that his hands tucked under his armpits. "I can remember when the northeast of the city was all farmland. This was two Zaks and a Macon ago. There were no trams, the construction of the North Fair had only just begun, and there were still water taxis in a few places. I was so young. I could run and climb and do all the things that the young can do. You would not believe it to look at me now.

"And I lived the way the young live, and ought to live, insensible to anything but the compulsions of youth. The light of the sun filled me to the brim, and I was made strong and powerful and beautiful in its glory. And frankly, I would pull down the moons—pull them down!—to be that young again. I would commit any crime—any crime!—to be that young again." He surveyed his audience with a melancholy expression, the white wings of his eyebrows flaring, and Mosi feared that the sentimental fool might cry. "Who wouldn't?"

Several of the older attendees nodded and murmured their understanding.

"But the world moves forward, ever forward," Lumm continued, rueful now. "No amount of wishing stops it. The people are poorer and hungrier. The government grows richer and the kings fatter. The law is only for the ones who make It. Superstition allows vermin to spread disease unchecked. Our armies fight wars in foreign lands and our sons return maimed.

"And it is horribly, horribly wrong."

Not bad, thought Mosi, clapping with the others. The start had been weak, but he'd got around to spilling some blood at the end. Next they needed to hear from the general, see what Crossley had in mind—

"But even today, there are young ones, living as the young do live. And we mustn't resent them, mustn't resent their freshness, or their receptiveness to the marvels that we have become jaded to. The big-lunged feeling of the race. The sight of the wild skies from the Bluffs. The sweet and ingenuous laughter of kindly women. The *toot-toot* of the tram driver's horn as it approaches an intersection. Swatches of velvet in every color, draped in a row outside a tailor's shop, red and blue and yellow, ruffling in a spring breeze—"

Where the fuck was this going? It seemed as if Lumm had forgotten that they were there to discuss revolution, and was listing off all of his favorite things at random. How long before the old man fondly described the circumstances of his ideal shit? A privy with a bolt, set upwind of a vendor's muffin stand, while a singer strummed his guitar at an open window nearby and sang a lullaby. On the floor, in the firelight, the university boys' faces had a waxy glaze.

"—the strength of one's teeth as they break through the grainy skin to the tender, tender sweetness of the pear." Lumm heaved a shaky breath. "And that's what it's all about, isn't it? The youth of tomorrow. Intrepid youth. We want to get that back, make that possible again. Don't we, General Crossley?"

Crossley, who had been standing off to the side in a shadowy corner as tall and still as a coatrack, stepped forward at this prompt. Mosi was relieved. If Lumm had gone on much longer, the university boys might have fallen asleep and tipped into the fire—

"But I'm reminded of the legend of the lonely stonecutter, the one we are told founded our city—"

"Oh, come on," Mosi mumbled to himself, and heard someone else whisper the very same thing at the very same moment. He bent under the sconce and saw that Lionel, a few feet along the wall, had turned to see his echo. The younger man's cheeks reddened and he covered his mouth with a clean new handkerchief to stifle his laughter.

△

Though the playwright did finally allow General Crossley to speak, the military man's bland delivery did as much to unnerve the dockman as Lumm's babble had to vex him.

"I vouchsafe the complete support of the soldiers in my command," the general said.

"We have the capacity to seize and hold all the major government offices," he said.

"I will submit to the authority of a provisional civilian leadership," he said.

After every other sentence or so, the general paused to refer to a little piece of paper covered in red-inked notes, sigh as if greatly burdened, and continue speaking. The dumb son of a bitch couldn't manage to put two sentences together without checking his notes! Mosi thought he was very likely the least inspiring speaker he'd ever listened to.

Could such a man really guarantee the support of the Auxiliary? Once you'd heard him, it was hard to imagine Crossley ordering a cup of coffee, let alone soldiers in battle. Arriving on top of the old man's confused preaching, it all felt like some elaborate joke.

Every now and then when you were unloading ship, you'd rig up a crate for the hoist and you'd be able to tell right away that it was light. Most likely, the stevedores at the shipping port had decided to help themselves to whatever was being shipped. A load of Griffin's Eggs, some called it, and others, Lovers' Promises. Occasionally you'd pop the crate and find a couple of dried-up shits—the wit of a stevedore could not be underestimated—but usually they were completely empty.

The opportunity was there—the government was blasé about the protests and the pamphlets, indifferent to the anger among the workingmen with empty pockets—such that if Crossley was what he claimed, they really might be able to sweep in and take hold. However, after suffering through the dimwitted old man's and the wooden general's stultifying speeches, Mosi could not shunt off his natural pessimism. It felt like Griffin's Eggs to him, a box of air.

The meeting broke to allow separate discussions among the parties before taking proposals and votes. Mosi avoided the other workingmen, and instead went to the fire. He extracted the poker from the andiron and used it to jab sparks from the burning logs.

Lionel came and stood beside him.

"You probably think I'm reckless, that I'm playing at all this," Lionel said in an undertone.

"I do," Mosi said, surprised by the birdy young man's directness.

"Sir, I want you to know that I hold you in the greatest respect. I believe in the common humanity that we all share. I don't believe that it's right for some people to have to live the way those people we met today live, while others live the way that the king and that ministers and assemblymen do, and their friends who own the great factories and get all the contracts."

"Can I tell you something that I believe?" Mosi slid his gaze to the university boy.

"Of course," Lionel said.

"I believe it hurts to die," Mosi said.

Lionel exhaled through his nose. His Adam's apple jutted from his skinny neck like the heel of a doorstop. "Do you think that's where this ends?"

Mosi said, "I know that's where this ends, but listening to these two, I'm afraid it'll be ending sooner than later."

"I'll take that chance," Lionel said quickly, and bit his lip, as if to keep the words from getting back into his mouth.

The dockman stared at him. Lionel's eyes welled, but he held the gaze. Mosi felt his irritation melt down, leaving only the pessimistic sadness that was as much a part of him as the Fair. The university boy was telling the truth. He was brave.

"It was normal to them," Lionel said. "The ground swallowed most of a building, and a man too, and the people down there treated it as normal. That was the worst part, that they weren't shocked, that they weren't up in arms."

"Because it is normal," Mosi said.

"It mustn't be," Lionel said. "Will you stand beside me for the votes? And join our two followings together?"

On the mantel beneath the painting of the huntswoman were some polished animal skulls, little creatures with sharp teeth and wide, empty eye sockets and pitiful black wells where their ears once lay. The dockman thought if animals were smart, they must be scared all the time.

Mosi nodded once in answer to the boy's proposal. "I will."

"Thank you," Lionel said.

"Don't thank me. If it fails, we'll be lucky to just be hung."

"What do you think of Lumm?"

"His brains are mashed-up eggs and someone hungry snuck in through an ear and ate half."

"Crossley?"

"A stone man. I'd be surprised if he contains any blood at all."

"Do you think he's lying about being on our side?"

"If he wasn't on our side, this meeting would've ended in the first minute. But I don't like putting my life in the hands of other people, especially peculiar ones, and that's what he is."

Lionel frowned as he picked up one of the skulls, turned it over in his hands, set it back on the mantel with a hollow click. "My conclusions were the same. We'll have to rely on each other, Mr. Mosi." He looked at the dockman. Lionel's eyes were dry now.

The sincerity of the gaze caused Mosi to avert his own eyes. "Jonas."

"Lionel."

They shook hands.

The two of them remained standing, facing each other. He was not someone who often felt out of sorts, but the abrupt intimacy with the younger, educated stranger plucked a chord of unease in Mosi. He felt acutely the absence of a mug of beer in his hand that he could drink from and use to shield his face.

Lionel surprised him by breaking into a wry smile. "I've never seen so much junk in a single room, have you?"

Mosi shook his head.

Lionel tilted a hand to indicate the fireplace. "And I can't understand this hearth, can you, Jonas?"

Mosi chuckled and said no, he couldn't either. Never before had he seen a triangular fireplace.

△

The members voted for Jonas Mosi, Lionel Woodstock, and Aloys Lumm to act as leaders of the Provisional Government, and for Lumm to stand as the acting premier. Their term in office would extend until the election of local committees, and the writing and establishment of a national contract of equal laws. General Crossley offered his service to the new government, and it was accepted.

Preparations began in earnest. . . .

△

And on a night a little more than three months later, forces acting on behalf of the people and at the command of the Provisional Government seized control of the gun towers that guarded the bay, the city's telegraph offices, and the two great bridges. In brief street-to-street skirmishes in the Government District, they displaced the Crown and its corrupt ministers, assemblymen, and magistrates from all public buildings, and drove them and their rearguard of loyalist soldiers from the city.

At dawn's arrival the victorious rebels counted fewer than twenty casualties altogether, and only a few burned buildings.

Through Green Glass

The men who removed Ambrose's body folded the bedsheets over him. They slipped ropes beneath her brother and tied them tightly to fasten the sheets. The first man lightly hoisted D's shrouded brother over a shoulder and took him out. The second man followed, dragging the mattress with one hand and carrying Ambrose's pillow in the other.

D observed the operation from the doorway of her bedroom. Nurse, exuding fumes of peppermint, rested a hand on her shoulder as if to comfort her, but really, D knew, to keep herself from falling over. Her parents had retreated to the drawing room and shut the door behind them. The dragged mattress smeared the chalk from the line that Nurse had drawn on the floor of Ambrose's bedroom, and a scattering of powder trailed after the men along the hall.

At the sound of the front door slamming, D ran downstairs to look out the narrow pane of green and yellow stained glass beside the entryway.

The men pitched Ambrose's sheeted body into the rear of a covered wagon and threw the mattress in after. The one with the pillow flipped it in. The second man came back to the house, holding a glove. D met his tired eyes through a warped rhomboid of green glass. He nodded at her. She heard the clunk as he raised the iron doorknocker and pinned the glove beneath that told the neighbors that someone inside had died of cholera, and they should be careful of their water. In a week, if no one else sickened, D's parents could remove the glove and return to life.

The man climbed onto the bench beside his partner, who whistled sharply. The two horses jerked forward and as they clopped down the street, the pillow toppled from the back and onto the cobbles, where it landed in a water-filled crater.

D stared at the fabric as the water darkened it, and thought, *Hold on. Hold on. Whose face?*

If her brother had seen someone, it stood to reason that he was somewhere. Maybe she could find him again.

But how?

She let her forehead rest against the cool green glass. The pillow sank into the water.

PART II

CITY OF CATS

When the Beast rose from his slumber he felt not quite himself. He soon discovered that there was an empty cavity in his chest where he had kept his Wisdom. A little bit of himself had run off while he snored, and in the dirt were its pawprints.

—Oral Tradition

At the bottom of the letter, beneath the currency minister's signature and the signatures of the witnesses, was a series of tiny, red-inked symbols.

General M. W. Gildersleeve, Aboard the Lead Transport Ship

*A*board the army's lead transport ship, four weeks after the revolution and one week's sail from his homeland, General M. W. Gildersleeve met the sunrise huddled in a camp chair at the rail, a blanket wrapped around his shoulders, eating cottage cheese from a tin mug. He was eighty-two years old and his stomach was a piano filled with wasps. When they weren't stabbing him, they were riding the strings, making them vibrate; he'd had a cramp in his left side for months. The cottage cheese muted the discomfort, though only somewhat. No matter how many wasps he drowned in cottage cheese, there were always more. It was strange that he should still be alive, after all this time, and so much killing.

The first man he'd killed was a Russian in Sevastopol in '35. Gildersleeve had been twenty, a private. Unarmed, he'd pursued the Russian into a little farmhouse, and the Russian, running ahead and trying to load a rifle at the same time, spilled gunpowder everywhere. Gildersleeve had slipped in it and pulled the other man down with him. The Russian ended up underneath Gildersleeve with his head resting on a green-and-white-flowered pillow, some farmer's wife's neat handiwork. Gildersleeve had used the ramrod to press on the soldier's throat, to squeeze out his last Russian breath, which stank of beer and stomach juices. Only when it was over, only after the Russian's face was plum-colored and his dead lips frozen in a doltish pucker, did the future general discover the Russian's mess knife buried to the hilt in his own right armpit and the blood spurting along the inside of his arm. The next thing he'd known, it was three weeks later and he was on a hospital ship. There was a piece of the blade still in there somewhere that the surgeons had been unable to remove.

After the Ottoman Campaign in '58, and after the Second Ottoman Campaign in '79, and after his victories in the Balkans in '89, Gildersleeve had ridden his horse down the Great Highway and onto the National Boulevard at the head of the Grand Army, and the nation had celebrated him.

Thousands of men from all over the world had died under his command; some had whispered their final words to him in their languages that he could not understand. On battlefields, he'd seen heads without bodies, spools of intestines in the dirt; once seen a wolf dash through a volley, bullets spattering the earth around it, a ribcage clamped in its jaws—a perfect side of beef, red blood and burnt black skin and white bone—and escape unharmed into the shadows of a German wood.

His most recent campaign had been a failure. They'd fought under the Frankish contract for two years and done nothing but lose ground.

But that was how it went. You put the greatest part of your men against the greatest part of their men, and all the men fought, and it turned out the way it turned out. Afterward, you rallied your survivors and fought some more.

Behind the lead vessel was a trail of other transports, breaking the quiet with their honking and clanking, carving the small gold waves. Altogether, the ships conveyed fifty thousand soldiers. Belowdecks, horses clomped and whinnied.

This thing, this revolt in the city, the news of General Crossley's betrayal, it did not overly concern him. He would handle it. Gildersleeve spooned cottage cheese into his mouth, and thought of slipping over the side of the transport ship and of walking on the water, and hearing his boots tap on the little gold waves.

He thought of the Morgue Ship, where he'd once gone to inspect a criminal's corpse because someone told him it bore a resemblance. Now, in his head, he became the corpse, paralyzed in a tub of water clicking with ice chunks, while two strangers talked above his dead body. "He's too far gone and they've got him. We won't be able use him on our crew," one stranger said, a tired-looking man, and the other man, small with a stubborn expression and five or six hairs plastered across his otherwise bare pate, replied, "We'll get all the crew we need, but we have to find a place to dock this fucking bucket." Gildersleeve thought that someone must have hoodwinked him into this dreadful position, some con artist.

Blurry whitish shapes crowded the edges of his vision.

He blinked them away, and their place was filled, abruptly, by the memory of his mother, of her calling him "Mother's Mat," except he'd forgotten her face. She'd been dead seventy years, after all, had died younger than the smooth-faced Russian soldier. In his mind's eye, there was just a tender, humanlike smudge in a bonnet, saying in a sparkling voice, "Is that Mother's Mat? It is, it is!"

He wondered if it was really her, or if some strange woman had invaded his head, a pretender.

"Oh, Mama," he whispered to himself, clinking his spoon around the bottom of the mug. "I'm feeling a little sideways today."

"Do your duty," the smudge said. She was gentle, but firm. "You can't die yet. Mother's Mat does his duty. Then he gets to die."

"Yes, Mama," Gildersleeve said. Mother's Mat was a good boy.

The dispatch from the currency minister on behalf of the Crown, ordering the army's immediate disengagement from the charter with the Frankish government and rapid return to defend the homeland, was folded up in the front pocket of the general's shirt. At the bottom of the letter, beneath the currency minister's signature, was a series of tiny, red-inked symbols—a code?—that neither Gildersleeve nor any of his command could make heads or tails of. After studying the markings for a while, they'd all agreed to ignore them—not to mention the abnormality of the command's issuer, the currency minister, when it ought to have been the premier—and instantly felt relief. (In fact, when the general was not actively looking at the letter, he entirely forgot the red-inked symbols, and so did the rest of his command.)

The rebels' hold on the city meant that they had the bay guns, which in turn meant an approach over land was the only option. They would disembark in the Northlands and march, ten days if the weather co-operated, south along the Great Highway to reclaim the capital. The rebels would be easily swept away.

A clutch of wasps suddenly formed a fist and punched the inside of his stomach on the right side with a dozen stings. He dropped his mug clattering to the deck and threw himself forward from the camp chair. He hung over the railing and vomited cottage cheese down the side of the ship and into the ocean.

As General M. W. Gildersleeve dangled his head, he considered the possibility that he had gone crazy. Rust streaked the steel hull; the waves slapped against the ship and fell away; the blurry whitish shapes re-appeared and pulsed with his heartbeat. His body felt puppet-loose, everything hanging off his spine by humming piano wires. It even seemed likely that he had gone crazy. Still, if it was only one more minor war that he needed to win for his mother, he thought he could manage.

He flopped back into the chair.

The general's aide appeared. "Are you all right, sir? Shall I help you back to your quarters?"

Gildersleeve said no. He wished to sit and be left alone with his thoughts. "But I need another cup of cottage cheese," he said.

The Reopening

On a morning three weeks prior to the general's musings at sea, D reopened the doors of the National Museum of the Worker. Two days after that, Ike was her first visitor.

He appeared in the late morning, a sheepish expression on his face and, as she'd asked, a clamdigger's bucket under his arm. It was dented and salt-pocked. "Sorry it's not nicer, but it's like they are."

D told him it was perfect.

She brought him to the third floor to see the wax clamdigger on her shoal. D removed the coal scuttle, set it aside, and hooked the handle of the dented bucket over the wax woman's hand, which was whole but webbed in cracks.

"See? It wouldn't look right if her bucket was shining."

"Right," Ike said.

Ike strolled around the shoal, which was a raised wooden hexagon glued with a layer of sand. In places the sandy surface was worn away to show the frame underneath. "Your beach needs more beach," he said.

He sat on a bench and used the wrist of his sleeve to polish the little brass plaque that commemorated the individual who'd donated the money to buy it fifty years earlier. Ike leaned backward to gaze up at the model deck of a whaler, where several wax sailors were gathered at the starboard rail. He laughed to see them.

D asked him what he found funny.

"You half expect them to spit on you, don't you?" He added, complimentarily, "They're as ugly as real sailors, take it from this Ike here. Only difference is you can't smell them."

She gestured to the shoal and the clamdigger. "How about this exhibit here? What do you think of it?"

"It's fine," he said. "Like I said, could use some fresh sand. But our gal's going to dig herself some juicy clams. Good for her as long as she doesn't get tempted and eat them raw, give herself a case of the cholera."

"But you've seen clamdiggers, haven't you, Ike? You've seen them on the shore, I know you have. Does she look complete to you?"

The clamdigger was in fair shape. White hair flowed down to the shoulders of her brown smock, and her mouth stretched in a ferocious smile. She was frozen in midstride, the hand holding the bucket swinging forward. You could almost hear her humming a tune as she went.

(The room D saw for the digger had a hammock made of strung shells, and a warped and gritty floor. A collection of bric-a-brac covered the single shelf, pretty stones and fragments of things she'd mudlarked in the course of her work. The digger dusted these treasures every day but never wasted her time sweeping.)

Ike peered this way and that. "Could use a pair of gloves. The ones that you see out there daily, they wear gloves. Saves the fingers."

D, who had seen plenty of clamdiggers herself, realized immediately that he was correct. "That's smart. It would cover up the cracks on her hands too. Do you think you could get her a pair, Ike? And some sand to cover the bare spots, and some glue to fix it?"

He dispatched these questions with a wave. Gloves, sand, glue; such items would be no challenge for Ike to obtain. "Should have a shawl too. They wrap up. Close by the Fair it can be brisk even in the summers. I'll find her a shawl, but nothing too illustrious or like that. That's not like they are."

△

When she showed Ike outside to the steps, D gave him a list of other items she wanted for the museum, and asked how much he wanted to be paid for the bucket.

Ike shook his head. "It's all right."

"Ike . . ." D knew that nothing was for nothing.

The young man's neck reddened under D's cool, steady gaze, but he held his ground. "Really, I enjoy giving back. Like those people on the benches." Ike backed into the street and touched his cap to her. "Now, you look a little tired, Miss Dora. Don't you use yourself up taking care of those fake people. You get your beauty rest, those are Ike's orders."

Her quick boy trotted off.

D remained at the doors to observe which way he traveled. She'd told him that there were more patrols on the upper end of Legate and she wanted to be sure that the information had taken. Only once she saw him turn left, aimed safely toward the river and in the direction opposite the former embassy, did she return inside.

△

Two days later, when her lieutenant arrived in the early evening, he just wanted to sleep. He dropped into the prospector's bed without taking off his clothes.

In his capacity as the temporary Volunteer Leader of the Health and Welfare Committee, Robert had been busy opening up the greenhouses and gardens and pantries of the large estates in the Hills, and setting up more than a dozen stations to feed the hungry. He was irritated at the behavior of some of the men and women he'd dealt with. "As soon as they get to the front of the line, it's 'Where's the meat? Where's the meat? Don't see any meat!' Before they say anything else. As if they suspect that I have a cow secreted inside my jacket."

"Don't you have?" She bent to the bed and patted his jacket.

Robert pulled the blanket over himself. "No, it's all gone. I'm sorry, Dora. I wanted to save you some, but it was a very small cow. Only a pocket cow. One bite."

D thought of the men leading the sheep away on University Avenue who'd called to her. There might not be any meat now, but there had been.

"They're so accustomed to being stolen from, here we are passing out bushels of greens and fresh bread, and they can't accept that there's not some sort of swindle. Can you believe it, Dora?"

"No," D said, but she could, and in her opinion, it was good sense. While D didn't doubt her lieutenant's sincerity, the greens and the bread they'd given out hadn't come from Robert's family's estate. However common people were, they could recognize the difference between what was taken and passed along, and what was freely given. Robert hadn't sacrificed anything of his own yet. Maybe he would. Maybe he would be able to keep that framed photograph of his family—patriarch, matriarch, and scion, posed together on an embroidered divan with large floor vases of orchids on either side—and release everything else it represented, the manor and horses and fields and men and accounts . . . but he hadn't done it yet.

"If the wax people come to life and begin making demands," he said, curling in the prospector's bed, "tell them that I'm off duty. If it absolutely can't wait, tell them to bother the captain next door."

Before another minute elapsed, Robert was asleep.

The screaming began an hour or so after dark, as it had on the previous nights.

Δ

D lowered the lamp on the table to a faint spark. She sat and looked at Robert while the torture went on. With his face stunned by dreams he was a child, and his sleep was a storybook sleep. There was no other explanation, because only magic could close the ears against the horrible sounds. And if she woke him, the magic would break: he'd hear the screams, and he'd go to stop them, and he'd die; either her neighbor would kill Robert, or the men who were higher up in the Provisional Government and who had put Captain Anthony there would have Robert killed. D saw it all happen, saw her neighbor stopping to salute her on his way inside from taking her lover's corpse to the stable.

"No! No!" one voice howled. "I didn't—" The rest of the plea turned into a teapot's whistle.

A different voice didn't make words, just yelled, throat-ripping yells that made D clasp her hands.

It was a woman; the voice that just screamed, it belonged to a woman.

Eventually, three gunshots rattled the night, and it was quiet.

In his sleep Robert uttered a series of plaintive sighs.

D went to the window.

The rear door of the imperialists' embassy banged wide and a cylindrical object tied with rope was shoved out. Her neighbor emerged with a second similarly canvas-bound object draped over his shoulders, and stepped over the one on the ground, leaving it there to stay the door. He brought the first wrapped object into the stable, and came back out to retrieve the other. D wondered if she perceived the thump of the objects being dropped.

Though the moons were smaller than they had been on the first night and there was less shine to see by, D could still make out the ragged bloom of the man's beard, and the white of his teeth when he paused on his way back indoors and saluted her.

While she lay awake beside Robert, she tried to imagine the room her neighbor might keep, but nothing materialized. It was just dark.

Her lieutenant awoke and dressed at dawn. He kissed her cheek before leaving.

"Back to work, darling," he said.

Gid

*I*f it would satisfy her, Gid said to his wife Bet, he'd go to the soldiers and he'd tell them that the rector had gone. Even though he was pretty sure the soldiers had understood the first time he'd told them when they'd come around looking for the rector. He'd damn well get it in writing, if that was the only way she'd leave off.

"Are you sure that's a good idea?" Bet sounded surprised. "I'm just worried, is all."

The faintest whiff of disagreement demoralized and harried Gid. "If I get a paper says I'm clear, will you leave off about it?"

"Yes," she said, "but you don't have to—"

"No more! I'm doing it!" He pushed up from his chair and stomped to the door. "I hope it's all right with you if I feed the pups first." Before he wasted his time getting a paper he didn't need, that was his first duty, to the rector's pups.

"Of course it's all right," Bet said.

"Pups haven't hands to feed themselves," Gid pointed out.

"Yes, Gid," she conceded.

At the kennel, he let the dogs out to run in the rector's field. They were good pups, young and red, long and lean and low to the ground, born for chasing. When they were worn out from playing, he called them in and fed them each some chicken and some milk. He sat on a stool in the kennel to watch and make sure that no one stole from anyone else.

"There was once four red pups and they couldn't be beat. They ran down the rector's game whenever he wished it, because that was their job. They worked hard and they had their chow. The pups always listened to their old friend Gid, who was the big pup, and they had no problems. Now, what do you think about that?"

Gid told this story to the pups every morning, and if the animals did not, in fact, think all that much about anything, the speech brought the kennel keeper himself great contentment. He loved the red dogs dearly, and he was sentimental about his own role as the "big pup." Often, as they lay in bed at night, he thought of them, and remarked to Bet, with sand in his throat, "You have to understand, Bet, to them, I'm the big pup."

Bet said she understood, but he didn't believe she did. She was a nice girl, loved him, kept him fed, but there was a feeling between a man and a dog, a natural connection, that need to run free out in the open.

When they were done eating, Gid groaned to his knees. He rubbed the dogs' heads and their warm, droopy ears, and let them lick his face. "You're good pups," he said, "and the big pup loves you."

He left and walked to the tram stop, but it was overflowing with people, so he walked across the No Fair. A wild man braced Gid and offered to beat his dust. "No, thank you," he told him.

Gid contemplated dinner. The head cook at the university canteen had given Bet a lamb shank, as well as a stack of plates with artistic pictures of the university grounds on them and a set of carving knives with silver handles. All of it had apparently been about to be replaced and thrown out. That was pure foolishness, things as good as new, but it was his and Bet's gain. Gid was looking forward to a first-class dinner, eating lamb off of one of those plates and cutting his pieces with one of those big knives. Afterward he planned to chop the bones up equal and give them to the rectors' pups.

With this thought, he tripped into a strange and discomfiting question: But since the rector had fled, did the pups still belong to the rector?

Gid left the bridge and walked north along the Strand, and the question circled around him the way that the pups themselves circled a treed fox. He thought of the rector, coming to collect the dogs, rifle slung over his shoulder, smoking one of those cigars that he called "Cubanos," which came from some faraway island.

"What a day for a chase," the rector'd say, grinning, and take the damp, gnawed cigar stub from his mouth and offer it to Gid. "Want the last?"

"No, thank you, sir," Gid always replied.

Well, he decided sharply, what did it matter? It didn't! The pups had to belong to someone eventually, and whenever their owner was sorted out, Gid would see to them for that person, and in the meantime, he'd see to them because it was right. They looked to him. He was the big pup, after all!

The dog man dried his suddenly leaky eyes.

Gid arrived at the Magistrates' Court. Uniformed men rushed about on their duties, loading wagons, checking powder cases, wheeling cannons. He wandered among the throng, humbly asking where he could testify that the rector of the university had bolted and that was all the information he had, on his oath.

"How should I know?" one soldier replied.

"Out of the way, you stinky old fucker," another soldier said, "I don't need any more problems."

It was an overwhelming scene and Gid would have abandoned the project entirely, but he knew that Bet would keep on with the worrying and he'd feel compelled to come back and try again. Gid wanted to eat his dinner, and to love his young wife when he wasn't too tired, and to go to sleep and rise in the morning and care for the pups and get them out for their runs. He couldn't be easy in himself if Bet worried at him.

"Why can't you leave be!" he'd once snapped at her after she'd cut one of the rector's old blankets into a curtain.

Gid had intended the blanket for the pups, so they'd have a soft spot; he'd only given it to Bet to wash in order to get out the cigar smoke because of the pups' sensitive noses. Instead, she'd gone and scissored a perfectly good blanket in half and hung it in a window.

Bet had got tears in her eyes and said, "I just thought it would be good, Gid. To make the place nicer. I thought you'd like it."

He'd thrown up his hands. What did nice have to do with anything? What about the pups?

Gid spied a soldier with an officer's insignia sitting at a little table near a statue of a tiger. He was smoking and fiddling with a pair of smart gem cufflinks, turning them this way and that to catch the light.

The officer noticed Gid's hopeful loitering and asked what he wanted.

"Well, sir," he began, and told the officer about how the rector'd left suddenly, and he didn't know anything more than that, he just cared for the hounds, and he'd keep on with that.

"All right, you're lovely," the officer said, but Gid had taken a deep breath and said, "Sir, you'll pardon me, but I got to have a paper to reassure the wife."

The officer shook his head. "You know being old is no excuse for letting a woman rule you? You should be ashamed to allow it."

"Sir," Gid said, "it's not to cause anyone a problem, it's just for peace of mind."

"Very well, if you insist on being inconvenienced." The officer wrote an address on a slip of paper and handed it to Gid. "Probably you didn't think I knew how to read and write."

Gid didn't know where the officer had got that idea. "No, sir, I never—"

"Talk to the man at that address. Get out of here. You smell."

Gid shuffled off. People were so irritated. There was no need for it.

He soon found himself in front of a building that had burned. On the lawn in front of the wreckage, stuck tilted into the ground, was what must have been the building's front door. What a mess.

A large, bushy white cat slunk around the side of the door, as if from nowhere. It sat and glared at Gid with glassy blue eyes.

"Afternoon," Gid said to the cat. It was his custom to speak with virtually anything that ran on four legs. Earlier on his walk, he'd informed a particularly jittery squirrel on the Strand that it looked like a quick boy with a penny to spend.

Long ago, Gid's gran had schooled him that cats were escaped demons, retainers of the devil who had revolted. "They tain't our friends, but they're His sworn enemy," Gran'd said, and hooked a forefinger at the ground to show who she meant—the Beast of the Underworld. "I'm not sayin you should worship em like some does, though it couldn't hurt, they might help you out, but you mind em well in any case, Gid." He'd followed her advice ever since.

The cat continued to glare at Gid.

"I just need to get squared away and I can go home," he said, taking an apologetic tone in response to the cat's unnervingly steady regard. "Now, where's seventy-six, do you suppose?"

Gid peered about and realized he was on the wrong street entirely, one for museums and such. There was a big museum of some kind right beside the rubble, a box of a place. *Museum* it said right over the door, was how he knew. (He wouldn't have guessed without the label; big as the building was, it was as plain as the air.)

"Bless you, friend," he said, but the cat had silently disappeared while his attention was elsewhere.

He went to the corner and turned right. What did you know, there was the embassy numbered 76.

⚠

The bearded soldier who answered the door brought Gid into a sitting room. He asked him to wait while he fetched sweet coffee.

"I'm sorry," the bearded soldier said, "I was getting ready to put in some work. Give two others their hearing. It might be a while before you get your turn."

These words did not make much of an impression on Gid. He was occupied with the startling sight of the man. The soldier had not been wearing a shirt when he invited Gid inside, and appeared to be in no hurry to put one on; he wore only his striped soldier's pants. Black hair covered the man's chest and spun along his thick arms. He was about as tall and wide as the door stuck in the lawn around the corner.

The enormous half-naked soldier brought him a dainty cup on a saucer, then took a seat, filling an upholstered armchair across from Gid.

The walls of the sitting room were papered in maroon bands and there was a small desk with a roto against the wall. Above the desk hung a painting of an eagle flying across the sky with a ribbon streaming from its beak and a rolled parchment in its talons. In a corner stood an eagle-topped standard with a dangling flag for a foreign country. On the floor, at the soldier's feet, was a leather tool bag.

"Oh," Gid said, putting it all together. The man had been in the stables—the tool bag had a horseshoe brand on the side. Horseshoes were a sweaty business. "I see your tools." Gid sipped from the dainty cup. The coffee was thickly sweet, but he drank to be polite.

"Yes. Besides the pokers for the hearths, there was nothing here in the building to work with. I found these in the stables that are good for up-close." The bearded man bent and opened the tool bag. One at a time, he pulled out a hook, a rasp, and a pair of heavy pliers, and held them up. "See?"

"Yes . . ." Gid had come back to what the soldier had said about two others, about it taking some time before Gid's turn. "Someone else is already here?" He didn't see anyone else. There was just the soldier with no shirt.

"I put them upstairs," the soldier said. "That's where we have our talks. There's more space."

"I'll sign whatever you need real quick if that's all right. I'm just the rector's pups. I mean, dog man. I look after the pups." Gid worked his jaw, which had become sticky. "I just need to make—get a paper for the wife. To stop her worry. It's nervous—she is—don't want that. I'm sure she's making dinner now. Bet—the wife." His throat had become gritty. He sipped the sweet coffee. The eagle on the wall floated inside its frame and the ribbon in its beak fluttered. He blinked, but the eagle stayed aloft. There was no fire in the grate, but the sitting room had grown curiously warm. "The rector left and that's all about—that I know."

The soldier returned the tools, *clink-clink-clink*, into the bag. "That's what you say." He leaned back in his chair and crossed his arms over his hairy chest and regarded Gid. His thin red lips slipped into a mournful grimace. "But we need to sort out the facts, make sure of what's what."

Gid's cup fell from his hand. Distantly he felt hot liquid splash on his ankles. He was perplexed by the man's disbelief. Gid was a dog man. What else would he be? There was nothing to be done, though: he was being buried in soft bricks. Bet would keep his dinner if he was late. It had been Bet's idea to marry—it wouldn't have occurred to Gid.

The rector had told her to bring Gid some wine for the pups. The next thing he knew, Bet had been bringing Gid food, fruit and cheese, and bits of bread for the pups. "If you wanted, I could take care of you," she'd said one time, and kissed him, and Gid had heard himself say, "All right," and so they'd married.

But instead of being home with his bride, here he was, hardly able to keep his eyes open beneath this soft avalanche, and a bare-chested giant was frowning at him with lips full of blood.

Gid dreamed of the pups, of watching them chase a rabbit into a rustling green field: oh, it was beautiful to see them run!

They disappeared and he was alone. A wind cut him and he hugged himself; he hugged himself so tight it was like his arms were ropes. Bet walked through the bending grass on her long, young legs, and held out the curtain she'd cut from the rector's old blanket. He had to admit it was a nice-looking piece of cloth, cleaned up like that. It might be pleasant, too, to be able to shut the world out when you wanted. Gid was about to tell his wife she'd been right and the curtain was good, that he'd been intemperate, unworthy, and he was fonder of her than he knew how to express, but it was just as he was about to speak that he had the misfortune of waking.

Tidying Up

*B*ehind the museum was a grassy plot about fifteen steps deep and fifteen steps wide, fenced off from the former embassy's courtyard on one side by a low stone wall, and on another, from the Society property by a high boxwood hedge. A water pump was sunk at the back of the plot and there was a small garden. This garden was partly overgrown—the previous curator seemed to have attended to it with the same lack of constancy as the rest of the museum—but there were tomatoes and cabbage, and signs of a few other vegetables. With some weeding, D thought, it would produce pretty well. It occurred to her that if the fighting on the Great Highway wore on and supplies thinned, she'd be very glad to have it. D sat on the sill of the back door and, wondering about the man who had worn the old-fashioned tweedside jacket on the hook in the office—her office now—ate a whole cucumber. Wherever he'd gone, she hoped her predecessor was all right.

The tang of smoke from the fire had dissolved to just a faint pepper of burn. It was sunny and fine, birds singing. The things she'd heard the previous night seemed far off and unlikely.

△

D started to clean the galleries.

She drew buckets of water, mixed them with soap flakes that she'd taken from the cleaning closet at the university, and started on the first floor. On hands and knees, she scoured the dark boards with rags until the warmth emerged from the wood. To help the floors dry, she opened the doors and the windows.

When she put her head out of a window on the side of the museum facing the husk of the Society building, D noticed, for the first time, the crust of ash that had blown from the fire and covered the facing wall, staining the concrete blocks in layers of inky soot.

Outside, D threw buckets of soap water against the dirtied blocks and scrubbed at them, but the black ash just smeared and swirled. A significant portion of the Society building had been reduced to smoke—books, rugs, curtains, the leather armchair that the cheery man had sat in, the planets on their wire apparatus, whatever else that the Society for Psykical Research had contained—and the deep filth slapped on this section of the museum's exterior was probably composed of tiny bits of all of it.

The only way to get it off, D thought, would be with a scraper. It was that thick and black.

△

In the rear yard, D detected a new scent, just beneath the fading fire smell. It came from the direction of the former embassy: a whiff of sourness, like turned eggs.

After she had filled her bucket and gone inside the museum this time, D closed the back door behind herself.

△

Wooden donation boxes were bolted at the stairwell landings. What they mostly contained was trash: tickets, cigar wrappers, candy wrappers, a crust of moldy bread, a bloodstained and stiffened handkerchief, pamphlets for other museums, pamphlets for sales, pamphlets for cures, and pebbles of chewing gum wadded in scraps of newsprint. There were also twelve-odd pennies and, from the box outside the fourth floor, half of a ripped ten-lire bill.

D saved the crust and the handkerchief, the pennies and the ripped half-bill, and disposed of everything else. She scrubbed the insides of the donation boxes and left the lids flipped up to dry. The money she put into the bank tellers' drawers, artfully arranging the torn bill so that its ripped edge wasn't visible. She washed the blood out of the handkerchief and hung it to dry. On the first floor at the printing press exhibit, the printer in red sleeve garters held a paper in his stiff wax hands that read *The Legend of the Two Moons* at the top, and the rest was blank except for where a vandal had penciled *thats it?* She soaked the crust in a cup of water until it softened, broke off a piece, and used it to gently erase the vandal's marks from the printer's paper. When the handkerchief dried, she tied it around the neck of the farmer's dog.

△

Triangles abounded: they were on the floors, in the arrangement of the three nails at the foot of every board; they were molded into the iron arm rails of the benches; they were on the signs, as in △ **BAKER** △, and △ **ENGINEMAN AND FIREMAN** △; the iron base that upheld the three interlocking gears was shaped into a triangle; there was even a rusty metal triangle on the end of the chain that flushed the toilet in the basement. D recalled the silver triangle on the door of the Society building—the door that was stuck in the ground now—and wondered at the marker. Her only surmise was that the same individual had endowed both structures. Which was interesting.

△

For the exhibit cases, D used soft dry cloths to shine the layers of old fingerprints off the glass.

She dallied at a few of these cases, opening them and examining the contents. One contained full plaster casts of hands, labeled for the different professions of their modelers: △ **TYPICAL DROVER** △; △ **TYPICAL BREWER** △; △ **TYPICAL LUMBERJACK** △; and so on. D tried shaking a few of the hands. She felt an unevenness in the grip of the huge hand of the △ **TYPICAL FARRIER** △ and turned the mold over to study the palm—it was scribbled with the imprints of scars. Another case displayed drill bits. D ran her fingers along their threads. The biggest bit was as long as a sword and as thick as a lamppost; △ **FOR BORING MINE SHAFTS** △, read the label. The smallest was as thin as a toothpick. It was labeled: △ **FOR TAKING SAMPLES FROM SMALL METEORITES** △. The miniature drill bit was slightly rusted; thinking to find some powder to polish it, D slipped it into her apron pocket and shut the case.

△

She brushed the splayed pelts spread on the ground at the animal skinners' camp; the fur was as stiff as the teeth of a comb. Close by, the skinners, burly waxworks draped in blankets, ate waxwork meat off the waxwork bone and warmed themselves at a circle of stones that were flaking the paint that was supposed to make them look charred. D paused to write *black paint* in her notebook.

△

The exhibition machines, the tables, the benches, and the wax people themselves, all had to be dusted.

"I apologize if this tickles," D said as she cleaned the wrinkled face of the cordeur with the luminous, unguarded expression of happiness that was so recognizable. "Now, tell me, miss, where have we met?"

D sat across from her as the museum dimmed with the day, and unknotted and organized the snarl of hemp rope. Once it was unraveled, she looped it between the glad old ropemaker's hands, so it looked as if she'd just finished her work and was presenting it.

The night's business began: next door, a man voiced his sorrow, crying out, "Oh, my poor wife! Oh, my poor, sweet wife!"

D had decided not even to bother with attempting to sleep. She sat with the ropemaker, whose presence she found comforting. "My brother told me once that there were other worlds. Was that where we met, in another world?" D asked the figure. Shadows turned the ropemaker's lovable expression coy.

The dying man screamed and sobbed that his wife was waiting for him. He just wanted to go home to her, please, home to his poor, sweet wife.

"Do you think they hear that?" D asked, and the ropemaker's glass eyes twinkled prettily in the dark.

△

Her other neighbors, D meant.

In the day she had walked Little Heritage Street and glimpsed flickers of activity in the windows of some of the other buildings. These structures were each of a kind with the National Museum of the Worker—though none were so large or nondescript. Like the museum, they housed organizations dedicated to particular fields of study; like the museum, they showed signs of having fallen into degrees of disrepair. Parallel to the museum was the Horological Institute, a faded yellow building with clockfaces engraved on the flagstones of its weedy front walk. Beside it, and across from the Society ruins, was the navy-blue house that held the Archives for the Study of Nautical Exploration and Oceanic Depth, which had a knot of frayed gold rigging attached to its lacquered black door. There was also the Madame Curtiz Academy of Dance and the Human Shape, which had a rusting iron fence of delicately turned arms and *en pointe* ballet shoes; the Museum of Dollhouses and Exquisite Miniatures with its rooftop crenellation of wooden cutouts of little boys and little girls rendered featureless by years of weather; and the Association of the Brotherhood of Tram Workers Historical Guild, where one section of the building was actually partially collapsed beneath the weight of a fallen oak tree.

Once, glancing up at the Archives for the Study of Nautical Exploration and Oceanic Depth, she had glimpsed a vulturous-looking man frowning at her from a second-floor window. Another time, she had seen curtains rustling in the Museum of Dollhouses and Exquisite Miniatures, and a slouchy shadow behind the damask.

It seemed to D that Little Heritage Street was the most perfectly forgotten street in the city—a street of majestically obscure purpose—so perfect, in fact, that it practically seemed designed to be ignored. She assumed it had been forgotten long before the events of the uprising. It seemed to her, further, that her neighbors must have preferred it this way.

She felt a commonality with them—and she thought that they did know what was going on at the former embassy. She did not believe that, like Robert, they slept beneath some lucky, inexplicable enchantment. D did not bother them and she hoped they would extend her the same courtesy. So long as no one said anything about it, there was always the possibility that it was not happening at all, that it was her imagination.

△

D realized who it was the cordeur reminded her of.

"Are you in there, Nurse?" she asked.

D pressed her face into the wax woman's wax neck. It was sticky like gum against her nose, not warm like skin, and the smell of the wax was candy-sweet, not liquor-sweet. But the figure was solid and D took comfort in the feeling of her shape. "I forgive you," she said into the wax flesh.

A while after that, there were screams, and shots, and the banging of the door. The curator of the National Museum of the Worker pushed to her feet and went to the window to show herself to her neighbor, and receive his salute, as she sensed he expected.

△

Many of the figures she carefully undressed to wash their clothes, untying and unbuttoning the coverings from their hollow, fragile bodies. These were the ones whose garments were in decent enough shape to survive scrubbing. The worst of the clothing, D put aside for rags.

She had not expected the wax workers to have sexual organs, and they did not. Between their legs were featureless knuckles; the chests lacked nipples; denuded of shoes and boots their feet turned out to be only foot-shaped, the toes and anklebones without any delineation. To see them this way, sexless and incompletely formed, gave D the strange idea that, as they plied their various trades, hammering spikes into railroad tracks and chopping sod and picking rope, they were undergoing a long-drawn-out maturation, that if enough years passed—a thousand? two thousand?—they'd finally be born. They were like real workers in that way, in their patience. Someday their fair share might come. . . . D could relate: she had waited—was waiting still.

Would her brother even recognize her now? Would he push back his cap and squint at D, and ask, "Now, whose face is this?"

While D was undressing the surgeon at his station on the museum's fourth level—*COMMUNICATORS AND CUSTODIANS OF KNOWLEDGE*—a small accident occurred. He was posed beside an operating table on which lay a patient covered in a sheet. (His patient, a male figure, stared placidly at the gallery ceiling and, D had discovered, was naked under the sheet. A vandal had helpfully scrawled, *BALS GO HEAR!* on the bulb of his crotch. D erased it with her moldy crust.) The surgeon's scalpel and other implements had long since vanished from the tray that stood at his hip, but he still wore his high-necked white medical gown. As she was pulling the gown off, the fabric got bunched under his chin, and with a squeak and a click, the head popped off, fell to the floor, and rolled under the table. Two springy, rusted clips protruded from the figure's headless neck. D rushed to retrieve the head from beneath the table, as if someone might see and she might get in trouble.

Once she had it, though, D paused. There was no crisis. If someone had seen, they weren't going to inform the housekeeper. The only person they could tattle to was her. She could do whatever she wanted. She was the curator.

She turned the surgeon's head in her hands. He appeared frozen in midswallow, lips turned down, nostrils flaring, eyebrows raised above his pale-gray eyes. But the surgeon's most distinguishable feature was a shining, stately forehead that suggested a fine brain the way that a polished cask suggested a fine vintage.

"I could leave you like this," D told the surgeon. "How would you like that?" She thought of the closet in the ruins of the Society, the one that the conjurer and his dance partner had stepped into, and then out of, wearing each other's heads.

The surgeon held his tongue, so D gently worked the head back onto the clips until it clicked into place.

"And where's the woman who mops up the bloody mess you make of your patients?" No answer to this either.

She washed the white medical gown and other pieces of clothing and laid them out wherever there was a flat surface. When they were dry, D re-dressed her people.

△

In the course of her labor, D discovered an exhibit she'd somehow overlooked, located like the surgeon's operating theater on the fourth floor among the *COMMUNICATORS AND CUSTODIANS OF KNOWLEDGE*. Although it was just a modest display behind the bank tellers, she didn't know how she'd missed it. It was as if it had sprouted up overnight.

The exhibit centered on a cedarwood cabinet that was a little taller than D's waist. It was perfectly square, about three feet on each side, with an eyepiece protruding from the flat top. Beside it stood a trim wax man in a red uniform and a gold-tasseled red fez. He had long, droopy cheeks and a dour gaze that was sleepy and severe at the same time. The middle button of his gold-buttoned jacket was missing, so that the cloth puckered out, which gave him a dissipated quality he might not otherwise have possessed. For him, D saw a tidy second-floor room with a mattress in the corner and a chair by the curtained window; and on the curtain, a discolored mark at the place where his thumb and forefinger gripped the fabric as he sat in the chair and spied on the passersby on the street below, making his private calculations. He gestured a long wax hand at the cabinet: *Be my guest.* D took him for a kind of butler, but she had no idea what the cabinet was supposed to do.

She blew off a long white hair that was lying on the lens and lowered her eye to it. There was nothing to see: it was dark.

She straightened and noticed a small black button high behind the eyepiece. (There were some gouges on the wood here, as if someone had been scraping or scratching at the wood for some reason.) A familiar white triangle was painted on the button. D pressed it. There was a click and a shudder, and the sound of small machinery coming alive, shafts unlocking and little wheels rolling. A soft, fizzy light emanated from the eyepiece.

D tentatively brought her eye down a second time:

At the bottom of the lens there was a picture of a luxuriously fluffy cat. The picture was colorless, but she could tell that it was white. A jeweled collar circled the cat's neck. It perched on the arm of a chair and stared with mild inscrutability. The picture flipped and was replaced by an identical picture, flipped again and in the next picture the cat's tail had ticked to the left, another flip and the tail ticked farther, one flip more and the tail kept ticking, a single continuous movement as the pictures picked up speed. The frame of the scene broadened smoothly to reveal a mustached man sitting in the chair, dressed in a long frock coat that had not been the style for a century. His black hair was molded above his forehead in a shiny bulge and he wore little spectacles tight in the eye sockets. The man passed an ace of diamonds between his hands, rolled his wrists, and the card vanished. He turned his neck to see what the cat made of his stunt, but the animal continued to stare out of the picture at D. He gave a visible sigh and casually stroked the animal between its ears.

A card with a title appeared: "THE CONJURER WAS ARROGANT. HE BELIEVED HIS MASTERY OF ILLUSION PROTECTED HIM. HE WAS BLIND."

A fresh living picture took the place of the previous one: a door opened onto darkness. The man who had performed the trick with the ace of diamonds stepped through, drawing after him a laughing woman in a flowery, tasseled gown.

They stepped out again, into a lit room, but now each was blindfolded; and painted on the blindfolds were triangular eyes. On a table in front of them another woman lay asleep, covered in cobwebs. The man and the woman reached out, and their hands jostled the shrouded woman, awakening her. The woman got up and left the frame, trailing cobwebs. The man and the woman waited, dreamy smiles upon their faces; the triangular eyes on their blindfolds blinked.

When the webby woman returned, she carried a long and imposing saw in one hand and a huge, threaded needle in the other. She stowed the needle between her teeth and raised the saw to the necks of the blindfolded pair.

The next title shuttered into view: "FOR EVERY TRICK IS THE TRICK OF ANOTHER . . ."

A third living picture showed a pair of gnarled hands holding out a huge knife to a man dressed in tails and a cummerbund, as if for a night at the opera. The man in tails was sweaty-faced; he goggled at the knife and yanked at his hair in torment. He reached out to take the blade from the twisted hands, whose owner remained outside the moving picture.

The following title read, "HIS HANDS EXTENDED A KNIFE FOR THE CUCKOLD TO TAKE!"

In the fourth living picture, a man leaned over and whispered to a figure that was also himself. The listener's features slackened; he reached up and gouged his fingernails into his own eye socket, determinedly twisting his wrist back and forth as if trying to remove a frozen lid from a jar, and drawing trickles of blood. The whisperer bent below the picture and, after a second, sat up with a new head, a woman's head, held in place at the neck by a gruesome track of stitches. The changed whisperer swiveled in the other direction, where the same woman also sat in a neighboring chair, and handed herself a note. The twin studied the paper, and as she did so, her expression grew remote. She abruptly stood, climbed onto the seat of her chair, and reached her arm above the picture. She yanked down a noose and put it around her neck.

A new title filled the lens: "BEGUILED BY THE MONSTER'S DECEIT, THEY SACRIFICE THEMSELVES!"

With a thud, the light inside the cabinet went out, and D was left looking into the dark again.

She straightened, blinking. D pressed the button again. The machinery gave no further pulse and the eyepiece failed to light. She tapped the button several more times with no effect. She knocked on the cabinet; that didn't do anything either. D pressed her ear to the wood and listened. She tried to lift the cabinet, to tip it an inch, to see if there was a hole underneath, a window or something, but the cabinet was too heavy. D felt foolish and worried and teased.

Δ

Night came around. "I never—!" a man yelled. "God!" he pleaded. "God!"

D went to put out the lights and close the windows she'd left open to let in fresh air. She concentrated on thinking about angled mirrors and trompe l'oeils, trapdoors and secret walls and concealed panels.

When the rest of the museum was dark, D turned out the lamp on the table in the prospector's shack and got into the bed. More yells now, a chorus of victims, four or maybe five, it was hard to differentiate the octaves of pain. There was the man who wanted God, and a woman who said it wasn't her, she hadn't done anything, but mostly it was just help, help, help, if anyone can hear, help.

Do You Know That I Never Stopped Thinking of You?

The trousers and the jacket came from the closet of a young man's bedroom in a great Hills house. Ike supposed the suit must have been meant for the weekend, fit for a trip to the country, or a carriage ride, or a rowboat jaunt in one of the king boats at the Royal Pond. The pants were finely textured, creased sharp, and the jacket collar had beautiful wide wings. The fabric was the rich baked brown of a horse track before the day's first race.

For his shirt, Ike had a blue silk number that he'd dug out of a drawer in a rich doctor's office. Someone had already been through the place before Ike slipped the latch on the back door, and they'd smashed open and emptied out the medicine cabinets, walked away with every last pill and powder, as well as the physician's implements, which Ike had intended to procure for himself. To judge by the hangers on the bare walls, they'd taken a fancy to the artwork as well—but they'd missed the three spare shirts in the narrow bottom drawer of the doctor's desk. Each was folded into its own neat parcel and tied with a white string that had a card with the tailor's compliments attached. Ike had been delighted to discover that they were a fit—the doctor had apparently been trim of build like Ike—and he'd spent a long time comparing the color of each shirt with his brown suit before deciding that the blue made the best contrast.

After that, as part of a larger swap with a fellow enterpriser—which had centered on a set of ivory chess pieces that Ike had extricated from the velvet-walled dining room of a professional house a few blocks from the No Fair—he'd obtained a reddish-brown belt and matching brogues.

His hat he'd lifted off the street the night after the government fell. It must have fallen off someone's head. The bowler had been sitting there on the cobblestones like a big chocolate-colored mushroom, waiting to be picked. Ike dusted it off and stuck it right on.

Suit, shirt, belt, brogues, bowler. Put that in a frame to admire: the outfit of a man anybody would like to know.

Only the matter of the tie remained. He'd keep searching.

In his low, narrow attic room above the Still Crossing, Ike hooked his good duds (as he thought of them) on a nail that was driven into the central beam. His brogues rested atop the beam and his belt was clasped around it. At night, once he'd eaten and cleaned up, and added whatever he'd made or scavenged that day to the hole in the ceiling that was his personal bank vault, he took off his day clothes and carefully dressed in the splendid apparel.

There was just enough height in the very center of the attic for Ike to stand. He'd make himself straight and practice certain phrases that he'd overheard adult men say to adult ladies. "Right this way, my dear" was one of them, and "After you, darling" was another, and so was "Watch your step." (Ike had observed that men seemed to provide women with a great deal of direction.) "Would you be so kind?" he also ventured, and "Would you give me the honor?" and "Did you know that I never stopped thinking of you?"

This last question seemed particularly meaningful to Ike. He'd heard a grizzly vagrant say it to a tiny old woman on the tram one winter's night. The woman had been dressed in smooth black, coat and bonnet and dress, like she'd just come from church, and she'd obviously been angry at the old bear, her mouth cinched like a knotted bag. The vagabond had worn a suit that seemed to be entirely made of patches, and his matted, tangled black beard looked as if it was home to a thousand fleas. But he'd suddenly cleared his throat and gazed at the old woman, and asked in a soft croak, "Did you know that I never stopped thinking of you?"

Ike had seen how, in the moments after he spoke the question, she sniffed, and her mouth trembled and loosened, and she'd dropped her face into the man's shoulder and cried tears of love onto his dirty jacket.

"Do you know that I never stopped thinking of you, Miss Dora?" Ike whispered to himself in the attic. He made his query to a blue dress, which was also hung from the central beam.

In Dora, he recognized a fellow survivor of the Juvenile Lodgings, and a striver too, a girl who was soft to look at but secret as a face behind a mask. She was canny as well: see the way she had got ahold of that great place; see the way she had told him that she'd rung a bell, so matter-of-fact that he'd nearly believed her.

And Ike wanted her to recognize him back. He wanted her to know that he loved her, and he'd let her thump him in Dribs and Drabs for the rest of their lives if that was what it took to make her happy.

Ike rolled his shoulders in the suit. He swept the side of his hand down the front of his silk shirt, and it made a lush whispering sound. He tapped a polished brogue on the attic floor like a man waiting for his carriage. He held his chin at different angles.

It was against nature, Ike told himself, for someone who looked as sharp as he did to be nervous about anything.

The navy-blue dress that hung on the beam nail with the other clothes was for Dora, of course. It had white ribbons at the waist, and velvet flowers at the shoulders, and a small, neat bustle, and had also come from the great house where he found the brown suit. There had been other grander dresses in the vast dressing room off the house's master bedroom, each shaped on its own wooden torso, swollen with layers of flounces, sashed in scarlets and pinks and silvers, bustled with sweeping trains that would be spoiled by a block's walk in any part of the city. The challenge of choosing one for Dora had overwhelmed him, and he'd hastily retreated. It seemed lucky to him now, though, that he did not grab one of the ostentatious dresses. Dora was not that kind of girl. She didn't want a fuss and she didn't need any help to be lovely. The more modest blue dress suited her far better.

It was from the closet of a chamber that opened off a little girl's room. In this chamber there had been a narrow bed, a chalkboard on the wall with numbers written on it, a piano by the window, some shelves of books, and, disturbingly, a glass box with a shrunken frog lying belly up inside, starved to death. He calculated it must have been the little girl's tutor's room, though what there was to learn about a dead frog he could not surmise. But the dress looked the right size, and as soon as he saw it, he could picture Dora in it, her hair floating down to settle on the velvet flowers, and smiling at him with new recognition, seeing him as the man he was.

There was a gold ring for her too. It was secreted among the valuables in Ike's ceiling hole. It was another treasure from the great house; Ike had found it in the master bedroom itself, on the night table, where the mistress of the house had forgotten it in her rush to flee the city. The band of the ring was plain gold, but on top was a circle of pink diamonds, cut sharp enough to prick a finger.

Ike licked his lips. "Do you ever think of me, Miss Dora?" he asked the empty dress, and the momentousness of the question raised tears in his eyes. Ike was surprised at himself. He was no baby. He had absorbed his share of beatings. It was just that, in asking the question, he realized that probably no one ever had—thought of him, that was, the way a woman thinks of a man—and wouldn't it be awfully sweet if Dora did?

They could lie in the dark and that would be enough. Just so he had her, and she had him, and they were never alone again. . . .

Except: the right tie!

He needed the right tie to finish off his ensemble. Only once he was fully turned out could Ike ask her his question and present her with the beautiful ring.

As he ran through his phrases, he tested various gestures: a flourish of the right hand, a half-bow with both hands extended, a showy tip of his hat. The light of the oil lamp, which was arranged atop the central beam along with most of the young man's possessions, threw his shadow across the space and up the walls, and transformed the doffed bowler into a cauldron.

△

At dawn Ike dropped through the trapdoor to the saloon below and found Rei still at her place behind the bar, presiding over a pair of regulars who were nine-tenths liquid. At this early hour, the cavern of a room was otherwise empty except for her husband, Groat, who sat at the table by the Still Crossing's one dirty window, eating pickled oysters and staring out at the riverside street.

The walls of the Still were of filthy brick and the cracked mirror behind the bar retained only a few clouds of silver, which themselves produced only the foggiest reflections. A couple of oil lamps halfheartedly illuminated the space, but luckily not so much that anyone had to confront the full horror of the floor, where layers of ash, spit, insect husks, and, above all, oyster shells had formed atop the packed earth, and alternately crackled, squeaked, and sucked underfoot.

"The bat flies from its roost," Rei said.

Ike strode over and plucked an oyster from Groat's plate.

"Take another and I swear I'll stuff your mouth with the Deadly, you young shit. I'll see you chew it well and swallow, and if I'm not satisfied of your gratitude, I'll see that you have seconds," Groat said, and jerked his plate away.

In the dank, vinegar-stinking yard behind the Crossing there was a terrible tree stump that Groat urinated on. He had been pissing on it for decades. As an apparent result of his efforts the stump was fuzzed with a soft-looking gray-green mold that resembled shearling. Groat called this stuff the Deadly Salad, and perpetually threatened that he would force anyone who failed to pay their bill, or who otherwise offended him or upset his sense of propriety, to eat some. How Groat, who was older than sand and walked with two crutches, planned to execute this punishment was anyone's guess, but no one ever said it. He was too respected; no other man in the Lees could fairly claim to have pissed a new kind of plant into existence.

Ike pried open the oyster, ate it, drank the juice, and returned it to the plate. "I apologize, Groat."

"He's sorry, Groaty, darling," Rei echoed fondly.

"He should be," Groat said, and turned the collection of wiry eyebrow hairs, wrinkled skin, broken blood vessels, and sties that made up his face to the window's muted sunlight. They said he'd been a boxer once. Ike believed it.

At the bar, Rei poured Ike a beer and set it out.

Ike went over, oyster shells and other bits of the floor's topmost crust popping beneath his steps, and took a seat at the last of the bar's three stools. He sniffed the beer, which he knew to be wary of; it was brown with floating spots of a mustard hue and smelled like sweat.

Some said that, on those rare occasions when the bar was empty, Rei capriciously sneaked into the backyard with a pail and pressed upon the Deadly Salad, squeezed it out like a moist rag to catch Groat's piss, took the full pail, and added it to her barrels to stretch the beer. Residing as he did in the attic, Ike was better situated than anyone else to pursue the veracity of this allegation, and he had never seen or heard the saloonkeeper do it. At the same time, Ike was out all hours and could not always surveil her; and what were those mustardy spots drifting around on the surface of the liquid? Even the smallest risk of drinking beer laced with Groat's piss was too great. He pushed the cup aside.

Ike withdrew a set of silver salt and pepper shakers from his jacket and passed them to the saloonkeeper. They had been tucked in the back of a cabinet in one of the abandoned townhouses off Tourmaline; they weren't even the ones that the people used. Some people, like the revolutionaries, might have been offended, but Ike appreciated it; if that wasn't true luxury and contentment—to have a perfect thing in reserve of your perfect thing—what was? And who didn't want true luxury and contentment? Ike had resolved to someday get two pairs just the same for himself and Dora, one for their table and one that he could just take pleasure in knowing was stored away.

Rei, his fence as well as his landlady, cooed over the shakers—"These are sweet, Ike"—and made them disappear into her apron. "We'll do well with these."

He cleared his throat and nodded at the putrid beer. Rei grumbled as if she hadn't just given her a weight in silver that was worth more than every rotten board and broken oyster shell in the Still, but took the cup and poured it back in its barrel. She picked up her personal bottle of whiskey from the bar, took a swig for herself, then poured a finger into the empty cup and shoved it toward Ike. "Your Majesty."

Rei was a daunting presence. Though she was small, not quite five feet, she was distinguished by a magisterial outpouring of silver-streaked black hair that draped around and past her shoulders, and her habitual pose, hunched forward with her hands flat on the bar, left no illusion as to who was in charge. Ike respected Rei, and admired her devotion to the lunatic set of bones she called her husband, and was fascinated by the way she seemed never to cease drinking or to sleep. It was certainly far better to have her on your side than the alternative. If anyone ever force-fed anyone else the Deadly, he thought it likelier to be Rei, not Groat on his crutches. Beneath the bar, she kept a wooden club with a pair of two-inch nails knocked through the top.

"What's the word, Rei?" he asked, and sipped his drink.

"No word, Ikey," she said. "It's quiet."

"Good." The longer the standoff on the Great Highway held—two weeks now—the better for enterprisers like himself. As long as the soldiers were distracted, he only had to worry about Volunteers like the bum that Dora had frightened off the other morning.

Clearly, these fine times wouldn't last forever. Every day the Provisional Government posted their bulletins promising that movement would resume shortly. Even as news of the revolution was carried by fleeing diplomats to their disapproving governments on the Continent and, subsequently, as fewer foreign ships passed beneath the gun towers of the bay to dock at the ports, and even as the action and trade in the city's various markets slackened as a result of the lack of goods, these bulletins declared the Crown's ragtag force of loyalists was exhausted and the conflict was nearly over. They assured the public that materials and supplies would soon be flowing into the city, and those assurances seemed to be holding; the dockmen were still in their spots on the docks every day and the factory men were still biding in the factory yards every day. Once things were settled, it would all tighten up in a moment. Ike was grateful it hadn't yet.

"I don't like it," Rei said.

"What's not to like?"

"They have a whole army out there on the Highway and those ones they kicked out haven't got anything but their little dicks, so why isn't it over?"

"Who cares? Let them take their time and we can do what we want. Besides, the posters say it's almost over."

"It says on my ass in beautiful curling letters that I'm the Queen of Sky and Sea."

"That's your own business," Ike said.

"You can write anything you care to, Ikey. It doesn't have to be true. This doesn't feel right, everything easy. I'm telling you so you'll keep your senses about you."

This was moderately insulting. "I always have my senses about me, Rei. I'm not some stray. My senses are so sharp I've got tiny cuts up and down."

"And there's the ones being nabbt," the fly at Ike's elbow said. The fly's name was Marl. A large swollen presence with moles on both of his cheeks, he was an institution of the Crossing, as much a part of the place as the splintered bar itself.

Marl's neighbor to the left, Elgin, hunched over a nearly empty glass, eyes half-lidded. Elgin was a gray sack of a personage in ragged gray shirtsleeves and ragged gray pants. He was not so large as his drinking companion but similarly bloated. When Elgin shifted on his stool, Ike thought he heard a faint sloshing.

"*Eh-eh-eh*," Elgin said. "Strue."

"Driver I knowt," picked up Marl, "gardener I knowt, a fella delivert milk. Ant others, lots of others."

Elgin nodded in assent. "*Eh-eh-eh*."

"*Eh-eh-eh* yourself," Rei coughed back at the fly. She slapped him across the back of his skull. "You keep your coughs in your mouth."

"Sickness bounces from him." Marl clapped Elgin on the back and Elgin wobbled precipitously on his stool. "Livet through a case of cholera, din't you, Elgin?"

"Strue," Elgin said, but a little sadly, as if he might have preferred otherwise.

It was imprudent to engage too earnestly with men who took the better part of their sustenance from Rei's beer barrels, but Ike had caught the mood of unease. "What are you flies talking about? It reeks of bullshit. What's this about people being 'nabbed'? What would—"

"The one that comes for me will get a whole tasty mouthful of Deadly Salad!" Groat roared. His skinny knees jumped the table from underneath and made the oyster shells clatter off the plate, escaping to join their predecessors on the saloon's floor. "I'll jab their noses bloody and feed them!"

"Don't get upset, Groaty," Rei called to her husband, shuffling from behind the bar to stand beside him. "There's no need, lover. No one would dare drag you off." She rubbed his bony shoulder.

Groat blinked sullenly at the hazy window. He had exhausted himself. He heaved a few gasps. "They might not like it, but they'll eat," he mumbled.

"Of course they will," Rei said, continuing to rub his shoulder.

"Come on. Are you all having a tease on me, or what?" Ike tried again, speaking softly so as not to arouse Groat's wrath. "Someone kidnapped a milkman? Who wants a milkman?" It made no sense. No milkman, no milk, what was the point of that?

Groat appeared to have settled back into his normal stupor. Rei resumed her position behind the bar. "I've heard the same. I heard quite a few were ones who had been employed in the big houses, and around the government, keeping things up. Maybe gone with . . ." Rather than finish the thought, Rei drank again from her bottle. She gasped and set it down. "Anyhow. That's what's said."

"But they're not just gone," Marl said. "They've been hijackt. And you know it. And you know by who. . . ."

"Do I have to beg here? What is this?" Rei and the flies all had their eyes averted, like people on the street when a funeral parade passed. At the hinge of Rei's jaw Ike saw the muscle flex, but she said no more. This further pricked his sense of disquiet; it was not in the nature of saloon-keepers to withhold gossip.

"My mouth's parcht." Marl rubbed a hand over his lips to emphasize his predicament. The movement caused his gray suspender to pop loose from the back of his waist and fall by his leg. "Maybe you'll buy me a spirt, son, me and my pal Elgin, so we can chat more easily. Some of that fine spirt that you and Rei been enjoying."

He should have guessed that was what it would take to get someone to talk straight. Ike bought the flies a whiskey each, and two more after that, six whole pennies' worth, and they told him of how lately the Morgue Ship had taken to the water, the air, and the in-between.

The Morgue Ship

The previous autumn, almost a year ago now, the Morgue Ship, along with its boatman, Zanes, and the corpse of the criminal Joven, had vanished from its moorings. Presumably, it broke free and only drifted a few yards out before its cheesy hull, unsupported by the wharf and rigging for the first time in who knew how many years, had collapsed in on itself, whereupon the Fair had come gushing in and swallowed the hulk altogether, dragging it to the river bottom—but no one had seen the ship get loose.

All that was certain was that it had been there, and now it wasn't.

△

The Fair was, however, an extraordinarily foggy, extraordinarily dark, deep, and filthy river, especially as it moved below the So Fair to the ocean.

When the news spread of the disappearance of the city landmark, it was greeted with peculiar excitement. Ike remembered all this. It had been in the papers. People came to stand on the wharf and crowds formed on the rocks of the west shoreline; but though they angled this way and that, craning their necks, hoping to catch sight of the boat's shape beneath the lacquered green surface of the water, there was no sign of it. A few fishermen went out and plunged their long oars, but struck nothing.

Gradually the public had lost interest. There were other stories: Celandine cats kept disappearing from the Lear Hotel; with the ranks of the latest foreign recruits suffering deep casualties, the Crown was calling for old soldiers to reenlist to bolster Gildersleeve's forces; the National University had been closed because of student protests. All this almost a year before.

Δ

And then, in the last ten days or so, stories began to circulate.

Δ

In the small hours, two professional ladies, sharing a bottle at the eastern foot of the So Fair, saw a cargo ship pass by. They were surprised; they hadn't seen a night boat since before the fighting. In the full glare of the bridge's electric lights, the women perceived two dark figures moving around on the deck. It was, both ladies insisted, not just any boat. It was the Morgue Ship, and they clearly saw the faces of the men on deck: Zanes, the boatman, and Joven, bald as life, standing at the rail.

Δ

The same night, or one like it: a quick girl stirring in some shoreline ruins, searching for metal to sell, said she'd spied a similar boat and heard splashing. The boat was anchored a few yards out. Two people swam to it, and a man at the boat's railing dropped a line and pulled them aboard. One of the swimmers, she remembered vividly, had a tall, fancy hat with a scarf, such as the livery drivers for the rich wore.

The quick girl alleged to have seen them all embracing each other on the deck.

"Like good old pals they greeted each other," she said.

Δ

Two smugglers aboard a dory, traveling for cover below the Bluffs, were enveloped by a sudden fog. They felt their ship grind against a larger vessel.

The latch of their hold banged open and they heard clattering and smashing. "Cheap!" a voice bellowed somewhere in the fog. "Second-rate trash!"

"Come on, Bartol," the bellowing voice said, naming one of the smugglers' comrades, "you're the one we need."

But Bartol, the third member of their gang, had not shown up that night. "He's not here!" a smuggler cried.

Except Bartol spoke next, in a voice that was all around them. "Perhaps one day I'll see you again at sea, comrades. I've got to go now. This man needs me for his crew."

As the fog cleared, the two smugglers had to squint at the brilliance of the dawn. The dory was run up on the same patch of Fairside sand they'd pushed off from the evening before. In the hold, the merchandise they'd planned to sell on the Continent, gold-flecked plates and bowls from the home of a minister, had been destroyed.

There was no sign of Bartol. He was still missing.

△

In the shadows beneath the South Fair Bridge, a destitute family, a husband and wife with two young children, had made a camp. The wife, because her husband was sick, left in the morning to get help from someone in the Provisional Government, medicine, food, a day's labor, something, anything. The day waned and she did not return.

Her husband awakened from a fevered sleep at the sound of a heavy chain rattling slickly and the *sploosh* of an anchor dropping into water. His hot eyes found a ship rocking in the dark beneath the bridge's closest arch.

"Ginny!" a voice was calling. "We could use a hand!"

"Sir? All right, sir."

His wife, Ginny, was down the bank and wading in the shallows.

The stricken husband tottered up from the mound of rags and paper that was the family bed and croaked for her to stop, come back, the currents were stronger than they appeared.

"Another sort of current already took me, my love," she replied to her husband. "Kiss the little ones for me. Good-bye."

A rope ladder clapped over the ship's railing. Ginny climbed it, and as her husband begged for her to stop, fog smoked up around the ship, and the last he saw was a baldish man reaching out his hand to help her aboard.

△

A gambler and his lawyer, out of work like everyone else who wasn't a soldier or a Volunteer, were sharing a melancholy bowl of opium in the lawyer's study.

The gambler poked the shoulder of his lawyer, rousing him from his stupor: a ship was bobbing in one of the lawyer's many mirrors! They watched it float into the gilt frame—and reappear in the next mirror on the wall.

The addled men followed the ship as it sailed from one mirror to another. They pressed their noses to the glass to see more than a dozen men and women at the vessel's railing. One of these passengers was the spitting image of an operator named Bartol, whom the lawyer had defended on larceny charges more than once, and even helped to get a job in the laundry of one of the great houses.

They pressed their ears to the walls between the mirrors and heard the boat creaking and the rigging grinding and the people on the deck talking amongst themselves. "We need to find a landing," someone aboard the boat in the wall said.

The gambler dug out his pocketknife and slashed the silk wall coverings to find the wood beneath. "We've got to get them out of the wall, Charlie!"

"You idiot," his lawyer said, yanking him back. "Do you want to drown? There's an ocean in the walls too!"

The salt water that leaked from the cut in the wall dried in a long white tear.

△

It could be no other than the Charmer himself, the gathering whispers concluded; it was Joven who captained the Morgue Ship now that it was free. He had risen from his tub of ice, cut the ship's lines, and taken the wheel, with Zanes, the boat's custodian, for his first mate.

The ship sailed only at night, but it sailed everywhere: on the Fair, in the Hills, in the Government District, in the Lees, on the west side of the river and on the east, in cheap watery mirrors, in paintings of the sea, through the woods of the Royal Fields, and down narrow, mucky alleys.

At the Western Bluffs, a birdwatcher tucked in the boughs of a pine tree had also seen the Morgue Ship appear aloft. The ship floated just off the cliff's edge and extended a ramp to one of the viewing decks for a woman who wore the badge of a magistracy official to stride aboard. A ptarmigan was perched on the wheelhouse, the birdwatcher noted, and stayed there as the ship and its new passenger glided into the obscurity of the billowing gray cloud cover.

The university's night librarian reported the ascension of the rector's dog man to the ship as it hovered in the air over the middle of the quad just before dawn. The ship was about twenty feet above the grass, he claimed, and a ladder was lowered and the dog man scampered up it. "After the ship had sailed into the branches of the great linden tree and disappeared amid the leaves," the night librarian said, "I rushed to the spot. Do you know what I smelled? The unmistakable pong of wet dog. That was the rector's man, his stink. It was, it was."

A well-known lunatic dubbed Beat Your Dust was said to have been seen to dive headlong into the fountain in Bracy Square, and fail to come up for air. An observer had gone to peer over the fountain's lip. Far under the water, she glimpsed Beat Your Dust, shrunken to the size of a chess piece, swimming toward a boat, also tiny and far below. In the next second, the wavelets created by his plunge shattered the scene.

△

Those who boarded the Morgue Ship, like Ginny and Bartol and Beat Your Dust, could not again be found in the daylight. These poor folks were dead, surely, and Joven had made their ghosts his crew. It was a curse on the city and its population. The Charmer was sailing away with doomed souls and the capacity of his vessel was without limit.

The Fields, Pt. 1

For the price of the story, Ike insisted on the flies' suspenders too. He thought they'd do nicely for Dora's bricklayers, who couldn't be expected to get along with twine for belts.

Since bringing the former maid her clamdigger's bucket, he'd contributed several additional items to the National Museum of the Worker: a thick pair of gloves and a shawl for the wax clamdigger, for which he'd traded with an actual clamdigger; several small cans of paint (white, black, red, and blue) to spruce up any number of exhibits; oil (for hinges, for the great gears, for the train whistles, for the spokes of the demonstration industrial loom that wound the demonstration threads, and for the mechanisms of a dozen other gummed-up devices); a piece of copper and a hammer for the tinker on the museum's second floor who had looked particularly pathetic without either a tool for his raised, clenched hand to hold or an object to fashion; a two-handled basket for the vendor to carry the wooden sweets that had been left scattered around her feet; and a great many odd garments to replace those that had been worn out. Added to how Dora had washed the place down and straightened it up, the museum was looking refreshed. Ike took some pride in this—it was right that the people should look like people did, even if those people were wax, and a bit creepy by their very nature—and, more important than that, he was pleased that Dora seemed so pleased to have his help.

There was still a long list of pieces she wanted, like the surgeon's implements he'd expected to find in the doctor's office, and still sought. It was not simply a romantic imperative that he should find these things, but a matter of professional pride. A good thief didn't stop trying to steal something just because it wasn't in the first place he trespassed.

With the problem of the surgeon's implements in mind, Ike thought to pay a visit to a horse doctor who, like not a few horse doctors, had a sideline treating the kinds of human ailments that required a strong arm, such as bone-setting, tooth-pulling, and minor amputations. This horse doctor actually operated uptown, at the carriage stables at the Royal Fields, was reputed to be unusually skilled, and, most important for Ike's purposes, was known for the cleanliness of his tools.

"If you ever need your dick cut off real clean and quick, that fella that handles the horses up to the Fields is the one to see. Got a whole rack of silver knives. He's the one took off Groat's pecker for him," Rei liked to remark.

(At this, naturally, Groat was ready with a bushel of the Deadly for anyone who dared to come at his manhood with a knife. Conversation at the Still Crossing tended to proceed in a circular fashion, inevitably coming around to the decrepit man's poisonous fungus.)

There was no one with such clean tools in the Lees; in the Lees, operating tools were tools. Certainly rich folks didn't visit this horse doctor to see about their broken legs and sore mouths, but the people who worked for the rich folks did. If the horse doctor was around, perhaps Ike could make a bargain with him for a pair of spare forceps or something. If he wasn't around, if he'd gone off somewhere, or been taken off somewhere—this possibility, which snagged on the story the fly had told him like a strand on a nail head, Ike did not pause long to consider—he could just claim them.

△

Since it was an hour's walk uptown, Ike opted for the tram. The first to arrive at the So Fair stop was packed from stem to stern. Ike hustled along beside the rolling wheels and hauled himself onto the driver's step. The tram driver told him to go hang from a lamppost. The trammer was sleepy-eyed and grimacing, as if all of his energy had been used up in the production of his mustache, which was florid and black. He wore a bright-blue bowler hat.

Ike said, "Hold on, I only came up here because my sister wants to know how she can marry a trammer. She thinks it's a glamorous way of life and that all you drivers look gentlemanly."

"I don't know about glamor," the driver said. His grimace deepened before he added, at once defensive and hopeful, "It is a sound career." He shifted the tram into second gear and it clattered along rapidly as Ike stood on the step and clung to the door handle. The man's bowler was nifty, Ike thought, too nifty for a mustache that drove a tram. "They can't just get rid of you like with some jobs. These machines don't run themselves. That's what the public doesn't comprehend. You have to be able to mind them and that requires considerable experience. What's your sister like?"

"Do you know the woman lies on the wave curling up in the middle of the fountain in Bracy Square? She looks just like that, but you'd never find her lazing on top of a wave. She's always cooking and sewing. . . ."

For the next mile and a half, Ike regaled the driver about his sister Mary Ann: her experience as an artist's model, the enormous inheritance she was due to receive from a woman for whom she'd cleaned house, and her romantic obsession with tram drivers. "She's amazed by the strength it takes to move that stick in and out the gear."

It was another two miles north to the Royal Fields, but as they drew opposite the No Fair, Ike spotted a pair of callow youngsters carrying rocks in their shirtfronts and felt duty bound to alter his plans.

"There's one thing about my sister, though, that you might not care for," Ike cautioned.

"I don't know if that's true," said the trammer, who in the course of their talking seemed to have become attached to Mary Ann.

"She would never suck a stupid man's cock. Shave your ugly mustache!" Ike darted out a hand, snatched off the driver's blue bowler, and dropped running from the step. He chased after the two youngsters and caught them at the foot of the No.

"I haven't got all day," he announced, and the trio hurried out to the middle of the bridge.

Ike won the first game with a deuce on a scrap of netting. The second game, he gave the pair of little strays double or nothing plus let them play together, and won again, this time by sinking a sheet of newspaper.

"Put that in a frame to admire!" Ike cried. "Hang it up over the mantelpiece and show it to visitors!"

"That's nothing," the boy stray protested, and the girl stray said, "It was already mostly under the water."

"Listen, children, that was a master shot by a master shooter," Ike said. "I know you're frustrated, but you disgrace yourselves with moaning. I'm truly wonderful at this game, one of the very best in the entire town, and you can take pride in losing to me. Now hand me the treasure."

The strays disconsolately forked over their three pennies, a satiny black pincushion bristling with silver needles, and a tiny, jaundiced-looking turtle that, peeking grouchily from under its shell, strikingly resembled Groat.

"What's your names?" Ike asked.

"We got lots of names," the boy said.

"Tell me what to call you, you mysterious little fucker."

"Len," said the boy. Len had black hair and close-set eyes like a gull.

"Zil," said the girl.

"Len and Zil. I'm Ike. What do you know?" Ike asked.

"What's it worth?" replied Zil. Freckles sprayed her face up to her eyebrows.

Ike pointed to the rail of the bridge. "Should we find out if you can swim?"

Though late summer was bending into fall, it was still warm out on the bridge. The river breeze smelled like the horses that pulled the carriages over the bridge and the shit that the horses dropped in their wake. Say what you wanted about the Crown's government, but they had remembered to shovel the shit.

"Why are you wearing a hat on your hat?" Len asked.

Ike had stuck his new blue bowler on top of his old brown cap. "Because I'm the greatest living dribser. I set the fashion and I ask the questions here." He flicked Len's ear. "Now tell me something."

The boy blew out his nose and crossed his arms, making a show of thinking, as if he possessed so much valuable information it was hard to decide which piece to share. "They're giving out bread morning and night at the feeding stations."

"Bread's mostly ashes," Zil said.

"Everyone knows that," Ike said. "What else?"

"Been no cargo ships since yesterday morning. Not a one."

"Interesting. What else? You hear any talk about missing folks?"

The strays exchanged glances, and Ike had his answer. He didn't care for it.

"Nonsense," he said. "Whatever's being said. Fish don't walk on land and boats don't sail on land or in the sky. The Charm's dead, he was murdered by that minister, and it's too bad, but when you're dead, being dead is your job all day. You can't captain a boat and be dead simultaneous. Take it from this Ike, you won't make it out here believing in anything you can't put in your mouth or stick in your pocket."

"Charm's boat isn't a regular boat." Zil jutted her jaw at Ike. "It's magic."

Despite himself, he softened. Tenderness was no favor to a Lees child, he knew it better than anyone, but Ike couldn't help it. "All right. And what kind of magic would that be, that steals people from their homes? Nice magic."

Len piped up. "Maybe he's not stealing them." His smile showed a handful of yellow baby teeth. "Maybe he's rescuing them."

"Maybe," Ike said, surrendering again to his gentler instincts. "Speaking of stealing"—he tapped the pincushion—"one of these things is not like the rest."

Zil was defiant. "So? The door was open and you could tell other people had already been through. I just ran in and snatched the first thing I saw. It's just a pincushion."

"Good for you," Ike said, "but if one of those green armbands shakes you out and finds it, you'll be got and in a cell. Flip it or hide it. Never hold too long. They're stupid, but that's no excuse for you to be stupider. You know the Still Crossing? The bartender there, Rei, she'll give you a reasonable price."

He returned the pennies, the cushion and needles, and the tiny turtle. "We'll mark this one down as a lesson. You'll have to excuse me now. A man can't spend all day teaching children the art of the game. He has to make a living.

"You boil that turtle in clean water for a good long time before you eat it." He took the nifty blue bowler—which was too big for him anyway, and besides he already had the brown bowler to match his brown suit—and jammed it on top of Zil's head and over her eyes, and strode away as she yelled after him.

A block or two from the bridge, he saw people waiting to be fed. He might have stopped—ashy bread was better than no bread—but the line was hours long.

He quit the avenues for the residential streets of the moderately well-to-do, moving north through yards and under trees as much as possible, keeping an eye out for signs of abandonment, houses that he might want to return to visit after dark. Nothing jumped out, however; he heard voices out several open windows, and at one neat yellow house a piano playing from behind an alabaster curtain, some light frolicking tune that gave him a brief vision of himself, in his fine suit, dancing with Miss Dora. In his head, she wore the dress he'd chosen for her and he gracefully led her in between the exhibitions and the wax figures in one of the galleries. The vision ended as he came around the side of the yellow house and saw the splintered knob of the kitchen door, as well as the little spatter of dried blood on the granite step and the wheelbarrow piled with a silver serving set and some folded sheets.

The piano playing ceased and a man's gruff voice drifted out. "We shouldn't fuck around too much longer."

Ike jogged into the stand of trees that divided the yard from the next and continued on to the Royal Fields.

△

When he reached the park, Ike slid down to walk in the culvert that hugged the arterial path. Caution was especially important now; you didn't want to be seen in the vicinity of a place you robbed. And if there were other rough sorts around like those at the yellow house, from the culvert Ike could escape into the woods in three steps. Although it was called the Royal Fields, save for the footpaths and carriage trails, the odd tennis court or set of wooden climbing bars for kids, and the Royal Pond, it was largely forestland. The chatter of the neighborhoods gave way to the creaking of bark and the fizz of afternoon insects. The trees, ancient and tall, made a full green canopy above the arterial, punched through only here and there with pipes of light. He passed no one.

Soon the arterial brought Ike alongside the Royal Pond, which might have been called a lake. It bulged to a span of half a mile at its widest juncture, and it was more than twice as long. There was no one here either: not seated at the spidery wrought iron tables crouched on the stone pavilion, or standing at the rails of the wooden bridge that arced over the pond's waist, or paddling through the lilies that coated the water. A few ducks slid across the water; partially screened by the tall grass at the far bank, a black cat, tucked low, watched them with yellow eyes. A single rowboat, which must have snapped free of its mooring in the boathouse, floated on the pond.

The famous rowboats, each carved to resemble a different king, were available for rent, with or without a boatman to act as pilot. In prior times, on a sunny day like this, even in the middle of the week, Ike might have expected to see half a dozen of them on the water, carrying couples, men in straw hats and women with upraised parasols. The one boat was out near the center of the pond, stirring counterclockwise.

Ike didn't know the name of the king whose face was carved into the prow—probably Zak, or Macon, like the current edition run from town in his gold-plated carriage, that was what most of them were named—but by the style and the weathering he could tell that it was an older one. A gash of rotted black wood marred the king's broad nose and beneath his protuberant glare the tips of his outmoded mustache curlicued like springs. Take away the elaborate whiskers and the gilt-painted diadem above his widow's peak, Ike didn't think the monarch would have looked out of place in Miss Dora's museum. It was as easily the face of a herder or a wheelwright as a king.

Ike's tread shuffled softly through the deadfall in the culvert.

There actually was something wrong. Ike didn't like to admit it, but there was. That was why he'd resisted the story of the Morgue Ship that the flies had told. Everything felt like the path he was walking alongside: big patches of dimness, with just a few spots of bright.

There had been a revolution, but somehow it didn't seem like it. A few buildings had been burned down. Some shots had been fired. A number of people had left. That was it. The city felt unsettled without anything much actually having changed. Now there was this Provisional Government, and they were hanging up posters like there was no tomorrow, and serving up ashy bread, and walking around with green armbands, but it didn't feel quite real. He thought again of Dora's wax people and the way they weren't quite real, the way it was like they were stuck just on the verge of real. What if it turned out that the fighting, in fact, wasn't nearly over out on the Great Highway? What if the real fighting was still to come?

And what if, somehow, someone—not the Charm, of course, that was impossible—was out there, kidnapping people for their own reasons. . . .

Where the footpath curved, there was the sound of snapping branches. At the same moment, the stables that had been Ike's destination came into view beyond the pavilion, and hitched at the posts he glimpsed several horses and a pair of black-and-gold-painted carriages.

In the culvert, he ducked to fold himself behind the octopus screen of a tall tree's exposed roots.

An elderly man, smartly decked in white shoes, a pinstriped suit, and a beautiful white silk scarf, was assisted from the woods and up the side of the culvert to the arterial by a husky man in a checkered suit. A third man, lanky and hollow-cheeked, dressed in a military uniform spangled with medals, stumbled after them—he was looking at a paper as he walked.

"—I know the other door was a good deal more convenient, but we do what we must," the elderly man was saying breathlessly. The sheeny white fabric of his marvelous scarf fully glowed under the shadowy canopy of the trees.

"You won't hear a word of complaint from me, sir," his assistant said.

"I know I won't, Minister. I appreciate that. You've been loyal, very loyal."

Five others, three more well-dressed men and two women in matching seafoam-green gowns, came after them. Like the man in the scarf, all of these individuals were distinctly elderly, white hair sprouting from beneath their various hats, and they exited the woods and managed the valley of the culvert with careful steps. It struck Ike as peculiar, such old and upscale folk taking a gambol in the woods. He squinted and realized the women were twins.

"I was just looking at these orders again, sir," the military man said. "They say to check with you again about the surrender negotiations. . . ." He sounded wearied.

"Listen to him. What a little darling," one of the twins said.

Her sister laughed. "Listen to you. You're a little darling."

"Yes," said the old man wearing the scarf, apparently in charge despite the general's medals. "I believe we can grant the exiles another week to consider the proposals we've made for our diplomatic team. Isn't that what you wrote in your recommendation, General?"

"Oh?" The general peered again at his paper. "Yes, that's right, sir."

Ike shifted and his shoulder bumped the tree roots. A clod of dirt plopped loose into a bed of leaves at the bottom of the culvert with a crackle. He reached for the handle of the razor in his sock; no sooner did he have it in hand than it spurted out of his sweaty fingertips. The blade went crackling into the same bed of leaves.

The twins, walking at the rear of the procession, stopped.

"Sister . . . ," one said.

They both swiveled around, the hems of their seafoam dresses swishing across the packed dirt of the path. At a distance, Ike could see no difference between the two. Both had tight, papery faces and, approaching, seemed less to walk than to slide on well-greased wheels hidden beneath their skirts.

The rest of the group had continued forward, except for the general. He looked after the twins. "Something wrong, my ladies?"

"Only a little wrong," the left sister said.

"If at all," the sister on the right said.

The general grunted and went ahead with the rest of the group in the direction of the stables.

Ike had decided to run, and when the left twin extracted a pearl-gripped pistol from her clutch at the same moment that the right twin extracted a matching pearl-gripped pistol from hers, his good judgment was proven. The women were thirty feet down the path; if he bolted into the woods, it would take a lucky shot.

They passed through a spatter of light that rained through a gap in the canopy and Ike saw them clearly. His legs filled up with water, and instead of running into the woods, he sank lower behind the tree roots.

The Misses Pinter, they were called, and he remembered how the Lodgings head man had lined them all up to be inspected. Great bene-factors to the Juvenile Lodgings were the Misses Pinter, and anyone who shamed the head man by complaining to them about the two excellent meals a day or begging for blankets would experience a form of regret that they would wear on their bodies for the rest of their lives, yes indeed.

The two sisters had gone from child to child, petting their cheeks with calfskin gloves, and softly asking each a question. "Have you ever felt terribly happy?" they asked some of the children. "Do you have nice dreams? Would you tell us one?" they asked some of the children. "What do you love?" they asked some of the children.

One of the Misses Pinter—there was no difference between the two that he could find—asked Ike the question about whether he'd ever felt terribly happy. They'd brought their smiling faces close to his, and the Misses Pinter's breath had smelled like pork and onions, and their hazel eyes, set widely apart on their narrow faces, seemed to tickle his skin like insect legs.

Ike had thought of a visit by a charity group and the gifts they'd brought, and replied, "I got one of the new blankets."

"Let's take the girl who dreams of meeting her parents in heaven," the other sister murmured, even as she smiled and nodded at Ike.

"But you're amusing too," the first sister said to Ike. She pinched his cheek hard before straightening up and announcing to the head man that they'd have Toni, a black-haired girl a bit younger than Ike. They'd take her away that morning. She'd be trained as a maid in their rich house, the lucky girl. But first they'd have her for "a good, big lunch," one of the Misses declared, and the Lodgings head man had clapped for Toni, and so had the rest of them. She'd blushed and waved good-bye and promised to write her friends, and skipped off with the sisters.

No one ever heard from Toni again, though, she hadn't written after all. Perhaps that was to be understood, that she'd want to put the Lodgings behind her, but Ike remembered how one of the sisters had announced to Toni, "We'll have you for a good, big lunch!" and he knew it was just a funny way to put it, they hadn't meant that the girl would be the meal, they meant she would have a meal with them.

He did know that, didn't he?

The twins passed from the light into shadow. They held their pistols at the ready. Ike thought, *No, it wouldn't take a lucky shot to hit me. It would take a good shot, and by the way they level their guns, I believe they're good shots.* He heard the heels of the shoes concealed beneath the bells of their long dresses grinding the path.

Ike closed his eyes, and pictured Dora in her bonnet in the first-floor gallery beside the gears, wearing that cool, keen look of hers. He hoped she'd know he wouldn't just have disappeared on her, not this Ike, not the way he felt for her.

Four shots rang out, and Ike found himself on his knees in the dirt.

△

After the carriages departed, Ike opted to abandon the stables for another day. Dora's wax surgeon could keep. He went in the opposite direction, into the woods, to compose himself.

The shots had shaken him, and the sight of what they had done to the black cat that had been watching the ducks had not helped. In the Lees you saw plenty of dead animals—and, for that matter, dead people on occasion—but it had been bad, the tattered fur and remains of the sacred creature.

A few yards into the trees Ike came upon the ruins of a woodsman's cottage. There were two hip-high walls, a collapsed chimney webbed in lichen, and a large icebox with its door hanging open to show its inside walls. He perched on a pile of chimney stones and listened to the woods and felt his heartbeat.

The Misses Pinter had shot the cat to bits. It was not only awful; it was an invitation to a curse. The talk between the old man and the diffident general had been strange somehow, and that was on top of the peculiarity of such people coming out of the dense woods in the first place. Stronger than before, Ike recognized the shape of something wrong, of an ill thing. He knew, too, that their business didn't concern him, and it would do best to make sure their business never became concerned with him—or any of his friends, for that matter—Dora, his love, most of all. Here was actual danger, not some ghost boat that sailed through the sky.

The shade cooled Ike. His heart was slowing. Flies circled a tacky umber stain on the ground beside the yawning icebox, but their sound was soothing. Around the bottom at the sides of the icebox were countless scratches filled with rust. It looked like the work of years of animals trying to get into it. How disappointed they must have been when someone had left the door open for them to discover that it was empty.

Now that he considered it, the door of the box didn't match the box itself: it was a heavy wood door painted white to match, but the box was metal. It was huge too, tall enough to hang a cow inside, an icebox for a great house, not a cabin. What a lot of work it must have been, dragging it out here. . . .

Ike's thoughts drifted on. The churning buzz of the flies continued to soothe and he felt better. Nothing had to come of what he had seen.

When he rose to leave, his interest in the massive icebox expired, and he left without ever seeing the front of the door, where someone had marked a number of triangles in silver paint.

FROM ACT 1.3 OF
A LITTLE WOLF BOX
BY ALOYSIUS LUMM

Elder Gray leads the mule and the cart to the yard of a decrepit cabin.
Tomas maliciously whacks a stick against the cage. The demon, squashed
inside the small cage, moans.

TOMAS: Ha! You steal souls and sicken the livestock. I don't feel sorry
for you.
DEVIL: Who cares? I feel sorry enough for us both!

Aunt Carina appears at an open window.

AUNT CARINA: What is this?
ELDER GRAY: We've caught a devil. Didn't I tell you I would?
AUNT CARINA: He doesn't look like a devil to me.
DEVIL: She speaks the truth! I'm not! You've got to help me!

Elder Gray points at the red-skinned monstrosity in the cage.

ELDER GRAY: He looks like he was boiled! He has horns! (*Grabs the devil's tail, which lolls between the bars of the cage.*) He has a forked tail!

The Devil hisses and snatches his tail back.

AUNT CARINA: He's probably just got a disease.

DEVIL: I thought you were on my side!

ELDER GRAY: —Listen to me. I placed the cat under the tree where the bandits used to meet, the one with the triangle carved in the wood, and we hid in the brush. Out of the dirt he came slithering, the pig—and went for it! Drawn by the scent, I expect. Does that sound like any sort of man?

TOMAS: Dropped the cage right on him, Auntie!

Tomas chortles and demonstrates with his hands how the trap fell on the Devil.

DEVIL (*aside to the audience*): Let me tell you about me and cats. A long, long time ago, they used to be a part of me, but they crawled out of one side of my mouth while I was telling a very beautiful lie out of the other side to a woman I admired. Now I just want to put them back where they belong, whereas they want to scratch me to death, the little beasts.

AUNT CARINA: Wait . . . cat . . . what cat? Not—

ELDER GRAY: —Shadow, yes. She was already dead.

DEVIL (*aside to the audience*): Indeed, the cat was not as fresh as I might have liked.

Aunt Carina screams and disappears from the window.

TOMAS: Father?

ELDER GRAY: Yes, son?

TOMAS: Well . . .

ELDER GRAY: Ask your question.

TOMAS: What should we do with him, now we've caught him?

The fiddles in the orchestra start to play "The Devil's Theme" and the lights dim above Elder Gray and Tomas, freezing them in silhouette.

DEVIL: Wait, did you think they actually caught me?

The Devil's tail unfurls between the bars to find the lock. The cage door unlocks. The Devil climbs out. He takes a cat bone from the small heap at the back of the cage, brings it to his lips, and begins to play it like a flute. He plays wonderfully. The orchestra soon joins in on a fresh round of "The Devil's Theme."
In the shadows, Elder Gray and Tomas writhe to the music.
The Devil ceases his playing, but the orchestra continues at a lower volume.

DEVIL: It wasn't any bandit who marked that tree. That mark is the entrance to my house. I love it when people bring lunch to my doorstep. Now I'm feeling refreshed. Want to spend the next two acts watching me convince these two yokels to kill each other? I hope so, because there's no refunds now!

He squeezes himself back into the cage and uses his nimble tail to relock it.
The orchestra concludes "The Devil's Theme."
The stage lights come back on, and Elder Gray and Tomas regain their senses.

ELDER GRAY (*as if no time has passed*): What should we do with him? Well . . . I suppose we should skin him?

TOMAS: That makes sense!

DEVIL (*seeming chastened and afraid*): Listen, gentlemen, you've made a mistake. I'm not the Devil! If I was the Devil, my skin would be red—

He waves a red hand to show them.

DEVIL: See? It's not red, is it?

The two men are confounded.

ELDER GRAY: I could have sworn. . . . Does it look red to you?

TOMAS: No, it sure doesn't.

DEVIL (*aside to the audience*): You keep your mouths shut.

Before Entering
the Museum

The museum's first official visitors were a foreign couple stranded by the fighting. They were newly married, each bespectacled, no longer young but not old, dressed in breeches, vests, and boots, the uniform of hikers. Their manner was cheerful, bordering on hysterical. They spoke the language well, but with heavy accents. "A museum for workers!" the husband cried as he stepped through the first-floor gallery. "I hope there's something about academicians!"

D welcomed them and demonstrated the movement of the enormous, interlocking gears. She'd oiled the teeth, and the wheels now turned smoothly, each propelling each in turn.

"It's extraordinary how things go together," the wife said, regarding her husband drolly, and pronouncing "go together" in a tone of reverence. They laughed uproariously.

It was after that the couple volunteered their situation. For D's inspection they displayed two slivers of blue-gray stone. The fragments were chipped from one of the famous monoliths above the Great Highway; it was to take part in this tradition that the couple had traveled to the small country in the first place. Though she had never seen the columns in person, D had seen an illustration in a book: three rectangular rocks set in a diagonal line on a promontory, erected by some ancient folk for who-knew-what-reason. D was also aware of the tradition that held that chips tapped from the stones symbolized eternal devotion.

The rock pieces were thin and jagged, roughly the size of fingernails, and lightly silvered. Even at a touch D felt the density of the mother stone.

"For the rest of our lives, we'll be able to look at these and know where our hearts belong," the husband said.

"And when we do," the wife said, "we'll also be able to cast ourselves back to the time that we crossed the ocean and stumbled into the middle of a civil war so that we could hammer a rock." They laughed at that too, and D joined in.

She might have guessed without being told that her guests were professors. D had encountered enough of them in her service at the university to recognize a commonality in how they spoke, and something professorial in the way they held themselves when they looked at things, frowning and bending awkwardly at the waist to see from this and that angle. She'd cleaned the rooms of plenty of professors too, so there was nothing much to imagine. D knew their small, fragile statues arranged on the edges of the crowded bookshelves, eager to commit suicide on the floor below; their framed degrees that never hung straight; their foyer floors warped where they carelessly let their wet boots and umbrellas drip-dry onto the wood; and their sickly yellowy spider plants.

In the fourth-floor gallery the tourists were drawn to the cedarwood cabinet with the eyepiece that had produced the moving pictures. "Now, what's this?" the wife asked D.

"I was hoping you might be able to tell me, ma'am," she replied, and they all laughed once more.

Later, D found a folded note protruding from the slot of a donation box. It had been left by the couple. The paper said that they were glad to have someplace to go and it was commendable, given the circumstances, that the museum was being kept open. However, it was sad that only one uneducated little maid seemed to be on duty, and annoying that she followed them around everywhere. They understood that the curator couldn't be there to greet every visitor, but someone official ought to be on duty. *And it must be said that the condition of many of the exhibits is terribly shabby. In particular, several of the figures are missing eyes and appear quite sinister!*

Around the galleries the husband's boots had left muddy tracks on the polished floor. Once D had washed up after him, she went to the curator's office and wrote a note of her own to put outside:

PLEASE SCRAPE YOUR FUCKING SHOES
BEFORE ENTERING THE MUSEUM

She hurtled through the building and out to the plot of grass in the back and drank some water straight from the pump. Black night was soaking into the blue of the sky. The reek of rotten eggs from the direction of the former embassy had thickened.

She returned inside and sat again at the desk. She tore up the first note, and wrote a second:

PLEASE SCRAPE YOUR SHOES BEFORE
ENTERING THE MUSEUM

△

But there was no way to hang her note on the museum's wavy, lumpen steel door and no way to hang it on the cement wall beside the door. D considered the problem.

She walked from the museum, down the sidewalk to the ruins of the Society.

In her pique, she ignored the three cats—orange-striped, chocolate brown, patched—spilled around on the lawn in leisurely poses, and the now familiar sight of the Society's red door plunged into the turf. Untended, the grass had grown tall, and the spindly blades licked around the sill of the door and its bottom panel. Through the empty doorway, D could see into the shell all the way to the scorched frame of the magician's closet, "the Vestibule," huddled beneath the few remaining planks of the second floor. Shadows filled the scorched rectangular box. Here was another cat, fluffy and white. It sat beside the closet and sharpened its claws on the blackened wood. The sight tickled at her, but D brushed it off—not now. She needed to get the note down, to get this one rule straight.

D spotted a ball-shaped chunk of burnt masonry in the lengthening grass. She went and picked it up, and turned back to the museum.

Bet was waiting at the bottom of the steps.

The gangly woman held a covered basket at her side and her expression at spotting D was one of slapped disgust. Her free hand found her throat, as if to settle a rising gorge.

"I'm sorry, ma'am," D said. "We're shut for the day." She moved past to set the paper on the steps to the left of the door, and put the fragment on top of it to keep it from being blown away in a breeze.

"Ma'am? You know who I am. And I know you, Dora, and I certainly know what you are. I won't say it, but I know it. Everyone knows. It stinks off of you."

D met the other woman's gaze. Bet appeared even frailer than usual, her narrow slouching shoulders and her bowed torso seeming to be barely held together, as if by rusty clips like the ones that kept the museum figures' heads attached.

But she glared at D like D was something that ought to be covered with a shovelful of dirt before someone ruined their shoe in it. She glared at D like she'd forgotten entirely that it was D who had stopped Pauline and the rest of them teasing about her Gid sleeping with the dogs.

"I am," D said, "the temporary curator of the National Museum for the Worker. Who are you?"

Bet keened. The sound swooped from one end of the avenue to another, and D thought she could sense the windows of the buildings clenching in their frames, and all the quiet hiders inside the buildings clenching too.

"Is my husband in there?" Bet stepped closer. She was visibly quivering and the contents of her basket clinked metallically. "Have you got my Gid in there? Have you had him all this time?"

D met Bet's gaze. "What? No. I've not seen him."

"You're a liar!"

"What are you talking about? Why are you here, Bet?"

"Because the soldier told me!" Bet began to weep and her words were half-spat. "I talked to a soldier and told him my husband kept dogs and he told me that he remembered Gid! 'Oh, the dog man,' he said! 'How could I forget,' he said!

"And he said he sent Gid to an address around the corner over there and that was the last he saw of him!" Bet swung her clinking basket in the direction of the embassy that had belonged to the imperialist ally of the former government, but now had a different purpose. "I was just walking there to ask, and who do I spy down this street? You, Dora, you! What have you done with my Gid? Doesn't he miss me? Doesn't he miss his pups?"

"Stop shouting."

"That fool librarian told everyone that he saw Gid on the quad, climbing into a boat in the sky! I don't believe it! I believe it has something to do with you, Dora!"

D grabbed Bet's thin wrist. "Bet, you have to stop shouting."

"I know you know where he is!" Bet reached her other hand under the cloth that covered the basket and clasped a knife by its handle and started to draw it out, but D caught this wrist too. She pushed it down, forcing the knife back into the basket.

D wanted to shove her away, but it was mercy that made her draw Bet close and whisper the truth in her ear: "If he went into that building around the corner, he's gone. No one who goes in there leaves on their feet. Ever. The people who go into that building are sent there by the new government to be tortured and murdered, and the man who does it for them makes no exceptions. Unless you want him to hurt you, Bet, you should go from this place, and from this street. You should go and you should never come back."

The Metropole:
The Lieutenant

*I*n his capacity as the temporary Volunteer Leader of the Health and Welfare Committee, Lieutenant Barnes was asked to take the floor and report to the leaders of the Provisional Government at a conference being held in the fourth-floor lounge of the luxurious Hotel Metropole. General Crossley was present, but not seated behind the billiards table at the end of the room with the civilian authorities, Mosi and Lionel and Lumm. Silent unless addressed, stiff-backed in a chair against the right wall, he peered straight ahead and, in Robert's opinion, made for a presence that was only slightly more lifelike than the waxworks at Dora's abandoned museum.

Rows of chairs filled the lounge's opposite end, occupied by the meeting's other attendees, various high-ranking soldiers from Crossley's Auxiliary and Volunteer Leaders. In accordance with the Metropole's reputation as the most "artistic" of the three great hotels, the paintings on the walls were of theater and opera scenes, framed flyers for famous productions were propped at intervals on the shelves, and busts of muses with garlanded hair and long, creamy necks were mounted on Doric plinths in the corners. Chardonnay-colored drapes tied back from the windows allowed a view of one of the hotel's competitors, the Lear, which stood directly across the street.

To make his statement, Robert went to stand beside the billiards table. The lieutenant recounted the initial steps that the Volunteers in his command had taken to secure and record the contents of various warehouses of dry goods; and next, to take possession of the properties of the larders, greenhouses, and root cellars attached to the old elite's estates in the city hills and make a similar account. As for the livestock shortage, he shared the opinion that they'd been too slow; common thieves and black marketeers had stolen the animals within a few days of the takeover. Thus far the populace had responded relatively well to the rationed distributions of flour and vegetables, but plainly it wasn't a long-term solution.

"Plainly," Mosi repeated after Robert. The dockman sat at the left corner of the table idly turning a red billiard ball on the felt surface.

"Let him finish, Jonas," Lionel, in the middle chair, said.

In the third chair, at the table's other corner, Lumm had dozed off during Robert's account of the seizure of the warehouses. He snorted in his sleep.

Mosi barked, "I apologize! By all means, go the fuck ahead, Lieutenant Barnes." The dockman pushed the red ball gently down the table.

Robert hesitated.

Lumm continued to sleep.

Lionel propped his elbow on the table and rested his cheek in his hand. "You heard my colleague."

The two conscious directors had been going on like this all afternoon. Robert had the thought that someday there might be a museum to the revolution, and in it the two men's wax figures would be consigned to share an exhibit for eternity. He made a note to himself to share this observation with Dora. Robert owed her a visit; he had been too busy to see her recently, distracted by the obligations of his position, and also—and he felt guilty about this, though he really had no reason to—by the attentions of a patriotic young woman who worked in the kitchen of the very hotel where they were meeting. Willa was lovely, but he missed his clever maid. He also had the troubling—ridiculous—thought that Dora might not miss him.

Robert went on: "My reading is that there's a general dissatisfaction. People aren't sure what life is going to be like. The papers we've printed tell them, and we tell them face-to-face at every opportunity that we'll help them form committees among themselves to elect representatives. And they like the sound of that, of having a say in their own lives for once. At the same time, from their perspective, it hasn't amounted to much, because we're in this in-between period. Four weeks have passed. The committees have formed, and the representatives have been voted in, but they don't have anything to do."

The basic problem had been alluded to by the other Volunteer Directors who had already reported. The city was closed: the dockworkers had nothing to load or unload; there was no wheat for the breweries; all construction had halted because there was no one to pay for it; and so on. Some people had money, but with each passing day there was less to spend it on. Assertions that the old regime's force on the Great Highway was on the verge of surrendering were given short shrift—shorter with every day that passed without a clear handover of power that would reopen trade and allow the economy to start up again. There was a pervasive suspicion that the revolution was less than secure.

△

Though Robert did not mention it, he'd been struck by an interaction the previous day with a woman in a breadline in one of the westside wards of the Lees.

A small group of seven or eight had been listening as Robert described the framework of local committees that would oversee the neighborhoods and, eventually, piece together a shared government with directly elected national representatives. They had been at a corner of a street of knocked-together boardinghouses. The afternoon was hot, and dust floated, fizz-like, over the hungry line that stretched two or three blocks long, and over Robert's tired-eyed audience.

He gave them his usual speech, which he was still proud of, and which he still believed in. It was a variation on what he'd heard Lionel Woodstock say at the first underground meeting he'd attended at the university months before. Lionel had talked about how wealth stagnated, about how a few people got so much of it, by the accident of their birth and the success of some ancestor. The wealth accumulated more wealth, more than they knew what to do with, while the majority had to scrape for their pennies. These circumstances seemed settled, as if some higher power had made them so; but they weren't. If men wanted it another way—so that everyone received a share in goods and property that reflected the wealth that they added to the economy, with humane allowances made for the incapable and the infirm—if they wanted there to be an economy that functioned for the betterment of all people, they could make *that* so.

While Lionel had captured Robert's imagination with his talk, Robert's experience among the men at his father's estate had led him to ground his own pitch in terms that were more specific.

He finished by asking his listeners to imagine a whole staff of people, maids and carpenters, laundresses and woodsmen. "These men and women, they take care of a lovely house and rich fields. They know exactly how to do everything, change the curtains, clean the windows, prune the garden, replace the rotted shingles, whatever arises. They go to bed when it's dark and they get up when it's dark and they go back to work.

"At the end of the day, they go home to their rooms. Six, seven, eight to a room. More. They're so tired they can sleep even though it's stifling from all the bodies and loud from all the breathing. And I bet some of you good folks here, you'd give a lot to have a regular situation like that, wouldn't you?

"And these maids and carpenters and the rest, as they're sleeping, what's happening at the lovely house? Nothing. The halls are empty. The rooms are empty. The blankets are tucked in tight. There's not a soul except for the house cat. Why?

"Because the lord of the place is at one of his other lovely houses. Do you see the shame of it, my friends?"

Except for a few coughs, the group before him was silent, and the little burst of adrenaline he usually felt as he came to the part about the vacant manor quickly dissipated. Over the heads of his audience, Robert saw a man in a yellowed union suit emerge from a structure across the street. The man stopped at the top of the steps and lit a pipe, and as he puffed, he stuck his hand through the flap of his underwear and rearranged his balls.

Robert trailed off lamely, telling his listeners that soon life was going to be much less difficult for everyone, and the main thing to bear in mind was that they would all need to do their part, like the gears of a factory works. "But you won't be treated like gears anymore. You'll be able to take pride in what you do, in the part you play."

He took notice of a woman who stood below his left shoulder. Her face was scorched with dirt and grime, her body layered in rags. She did not seem elderly; she seemed beyond age. Her eyes were unnervingly fixed in her mask of filth, and they bored into Robert.

The lieutenant waited for a few seconds, calmly meeting her gaze, expecting the glaring woman to say something in opposition; he wished, in fact, that she would. If they expressed their concerns, he could explain to them what they were failing to see. The poor weren't bad, not in the slightest; they were just uneducated.

The line shuffled ahead and his audience went with it, sidling politely, so that even as they moved, they continued to face Robert.

He felt the push of desperation, and asked the staring woman, "Doesn't that make you glad to hear, ma'am?"

"Oh, yes, very glad," the woman said. "I love a story. I'll dream on my room in that lovely house for the rest of my life. I'll dress it all up in my head and feel very glad."

Robert suspected he heard amusement in her voice and it irritated him. He was trying to help her. They were trying to help all of them, lift them up, improve their lives, improve society by helping people who would themselves in turn help people.

(It was the same idea that he'd been attempting to get across in the letter to his parents, the letter he kept beginning and throwing out, and that he wouldn't be able to send to them until the Great Highway was cleared, anyway. . . . And after that, well, there was the question of which of their properties they were staying at. They might have gone farther north at the news of the upheaval. . . .)

He wanted to insist, "It's not a dream, it's true," but he didn't want to sound like a child, begging for the grubby ageless woman to believe him.

"But every day's a glad day in the Lees," she said, and then he knew for certain she was mocking him. "No limits to the gladness. Thank you, sir. Good luck to you, sir. I hope a cat smiles on you, sir."

She and the others shuffled away in the line. Robert managed a perfunctory tip of his hat, even as he stared blankly ahead, trying to figure out what it was that he'd said wrong, where he had lost his audience.

"D'ya have a problem?" the ball handler hollered, for it appeared that the lieutenant was staring at him.

Robert shook his head and looked away.

Two urchins, a boy and a girl—the latter wearing an absurdly gaudy blue hat that went over her ears like a helmet—sat at the base of a nearby wall. Each had their own pile of rocks. As Robert watched, the children compared their treasures with grave seriousness, weighing them, testing them with short drops, and conducted a series of trades, stone for stone.

△

"No one is more impatient to resolve the standoff than I am. But we have an opportunity to avoid bloodshed, Your Honors," General Crossley said. "Those were the orders I was given by this Provisional Government: avoid bloodshed. Were they not?" He slipped out a wrinkled piece of paper from the sleeve of his uniform jacket and checked it, as if the aforesaid orders were, indeed, written there.

But Robert, standing near the general, could see that the scrap was covered not in words but in tiny, red-inked symbols—moons, stars, triangles. Military code, he assumed. Robert remembered the general checking red-inked notes at the interview with Westhover. Whatever else, there was no doubting the man's thoroughness—or his preferred ink color.

Mosi began, "Yes, those were our damned orders, but we gave them to you based on the assurance you made to us that those up on the Highway would roll over in a couple of days. Here it is, four weeks later, and we'd like not to lose the support of the populace, which if we did, might also result in bloodshed—"

"Treaties are complex." The general folded up his paper. "You want peace and you want justice. I will get those things for you. I have the greatest confidence in the negotiating committee that I assembled with Mr. Lumm's advice, and they promise me"—he waved his little paper—"right here, that it's a matter of days now until the terms will be fixed."

Mosi grimaced and the gaze he settled on Crossley was withering. The general stared ahead, unperturbed.

Lionel indicated that Robert should once again continue.

The lieutenant went on to touch on the gossip that individuals vaguely connected to the old government were being kidnapped. Some of the other heads had mentioned this too. "I even wrote down a few of the names that people gave me, and I checked them against the indictments at the Emergency Court and against the rolls of the detainees in the holding cells at the Magistrates' Court, but I didn't find any of them. I agree with what's been said before, that it's fair to assume that the missing, loyalists or not, fled the city somehow or other. What concerns me is that I couldn't convince any of the rumormongers that my information was conveyed in good faith."

Lumm abruptly came to; he shook himself upright, smacked his lips, popped his eyes, blinked, and said, "Rumors, no matter how foolish or asinine, often hold an emotional truth, and truth, as we all know, is gem-hard. Bury the truth for a thousand years, dig it up, and it's unchanged. Unchanged. Use truth to score stone. It won't break. It's the same truth. . . ."

The playwright blinked a few times. Robert had the horrible feeling Lumm was trying to remember either where he was, or to whom he was speaking, or both. Over the few weeks of the Provisional Government's reign, the ancient man's thin face had cratered; his cheeks had become so concave that if you had laid him on his side, you could fill them with pennies.

". . . But if you overmind a rumor—or a superstition—if you pick at, dig at—it acts not like a rock, but like a dandelion. The wind blows it and that's bad enough. You don't want to help a dandelion. You want a gardener who acts with the greatest, greatest discernment.

"Emotions are in play at either end. The tender soul can be hood-winked by sentiment. That's what the artist writes toward, paints toward, and acts toward in the stage lights. We want to fool the audience and they want to be fooled.

"So.

"So, we have to control our sympathies without losing our sympathies. And then, gentlemen, you find you must fall back on the truth, on that hard, hard truth. Which is gem."

The playwright clasped his gloved hands and nodded smilingly at Robert, and at the small audience of Volunteers and officers in their seats. A slug of drool shone in the white bristles of Lumm's unshaven chin.

Robert saw Mosi and Lionel share a look. The student leader raised an eyebrow at the union man. Mosi, who in the midst of these meetings usually gave the impression of a prisoner who had all but relinquished hope of escape, covered his mouth and glanced away. In the chair at the wall, Crossley maintained his rectitude.

"You understand my point," Lumm said, the drool slipping down to his throat. There was a faint, pleading note in the playwright's voice.

"Yes, sir," Robert said, but inwardly he found that he could no longer argue that a degree of skepticism on the part of the common people was unwarranted.

The Metropole:
The Sergeant

*T*he men milled around in the hall outside the lounge, and Robert winced at the tracks of mud their boots deposited on the Metropole's sand-colored carpets. The maids would have their work cut out trying to get them clean.

He spotted Sergeant Van Goor lingering by the elevator. The sergeant was staring at the dial above the golden gate, apparently transfixed by its inching progress from the numeral 3 to the numeral 2. Behind the murmur of conversation there was the jingle of the elevator's chains.

"You should try it," Robert said.

Van Goor twitched, laughed. "I don't know, sir. An old soldier like me, a handsome piece of work like that, I'd probably ruin it somehow." He gestured to his mud-caked boots. "For goodness' sake, look at these boots of mine. I should see your lady that fixes them, shouldn't I? Can she give a nice smart polish too?"

Robert felt his cheeks warm. He had not forgotten about the seeming misunderstanding between them that night at the Magistrates' Court, the false notion he'd given Van Goor about Dora's availability; nor, it seemed, had the sergeant. Robert didn't blame the man, who had undoubtedly grown up roughly and didn't know any better. But he needed to rectify the misconception. This was the opportunity.

"You're as good as anyone, Van Goor. Come on, let's wait for it to come back and ride down together."

"Is that an order, Lieutenant?" Van Goor's expression was positively jolly.

"If that's what it takes," Robert said. The sergeant's mention of his rank elicited an unpleasant association with Dora's habit of mentioning it in a very different context.

"All right," he said, "a soldier knows his place."

"But listen," Robert said, "since you mention it, I should tell you, I was mistaken."

"No!" Van Goor grinned. "I don't believe it, Lieutenant! Not you!"

Robert laughed, relaxing. He enjoyed the teasing that went on among the soldiers. "Yes, yes. I was. I'm afraid Dora doesn't know how to repair boots."

The sergeant snapped his fingers in comical exaggeration. "Ah! That's too bad, isn't it?"

In the time it took the elevator dial to tick its way back from the 2 to the 4, the hallway outside the lounge largely cleared. The elevator clanked into position, and the accordion hinges of the gate clattered open to reveal the compartment. Posted inside was the operator, a young woman in a purple suit with a tasseled usher's cap balanced on her springy hair, and whose gap-toothed grin gave no indication that she minded the recent change in the hotel's clientele. Tucked into the corner on the floor was the hotel's cat. It blinked at them sleepily, and rested its chin atop the curl of its abundant white tail.

The men stepped forward. Robert told the operator, all the way down. She yelped, "Excellent, sirs!" and grasped the edge of the gate.

"You'll like this," he said to Van Goor, who was glancing all around the swirling gilt moldings of the ceiling.

"I'm sure I will. I wouldn't doubt you, Lieutenant."

"Is there room for two more?" asked a tremulous voice.

Aloys Lumm and General Crossley appeared at the elevator doors. The hunched playwright gripped the general's elbow for balance. Crossley stood straight and tall and blank-faced.

"Oh—" Lumm said, shoe poised on the threshold. "Look at you."

It took Robert a moment to determine that he was addressing the cat. Lumm grimaced and waved a finger in the animal's direction. "Clever, clever," he said, before shifting his gaze to the humans in the elevator. Lumm's countenance smoothed and he winked at them. "It knows how to ride an elevator. Isn't that wonderful. Saves energy for hunting that way, I'm sure. Looks a little crowded in there, General, and we need the exercise, don't we. Let's take the stairs."

Both Robert and Van Goor moved forward, protesting, offering to move the cat or give up their spots, but Lumm, with Crossley for support, had already turned along the hallway toward the stairs. As they moved off he croaked, "No, no, it's fine, it's fine. . . ."

The two men stepped back into the box. In the corner, the cat, shameless, had closed its eyes. Van Goor shrugged at Robert. "Down in the Lees they love their cats. Some still even have little churches to them, you know. Myself, I never saw the point of them."

His phrasing caused Robert to chuckle. "Oh, I'm not sure animals have a point. We just live, don't we? I remember, when I was younger, there was a groom in our employ, a big, bald, not particularly talkative man. I asked him why he didn't have hair, and he looked at me as if I was mad, and he said, 'Because it didn't grow.' Of course, the other grooms fell over laughing. I felt foolish, but the man—his name was Reuter—he didn't laugh or even smile. Reuter just said, 'Well, it's a fact,' and went back to his work. That's what I think of when I wonder what the point of something is. Do you see what I mean?"

"Yes," Van Goor said. "That's good, Lieutenant, that's really good."

The operator had shut the gate and thrown the lock, and now she told them to get ready. She cranked the control lever. "This is the exciting part, sirs." With a slick, tinkling rattle, the elevator began to descend along its chains.

△

It was the fawning over them, Van Goor had meant, the point of that; of adoring them and keeping them as pets for fancy hotels and leaving scraps for them, such as some people did who didn't even have enough to feed themselves. It wasn't just that the rude schoolboy talked to him like he was stupid, it was that the rude schoolboy was so fucking sure of his own brilliance. First he had made the offensive assumption that Van Goor was illiterate. Then he had decided that Van Goor had never taken an elevator, although he had taken one that very afternoon in order to reach the fourth-floor lounge!

What form would the next insult take? Would he offer to show him his left from his right? Give him tips on using a fork and a knife? Would the young bastard cut right to the chase and propose to teach him how to wipe his own ass?

The sergeant did not need the irritation. As rosily as Crossley had put it to the so-called leaders of the Provisional Government—and a wonderful team that was, a rock-skulled porter, another schoolboy, and a babbling corpse—the situation on the Great Highway was not nearly resolved. That was pure ass-covering on Crossley's part.

Envoys had come down from the Crown's encampment, but from what Van Goor had been told the talks had hardly advanced past the introductory cock-measuring stages—the arguments over who would be speaking for whom, the schedule, the location, the arrangement of the fucking tables and chairs, that sort of bullshit. Contrary to Crossley's description, Van Goor saw no signal that the Crown was ready to wave a white flag. They seemed content to stay where they were, singing the royal anthem behind their fortifications, shooting game, and letting summer change to fall. For Van Goor, this meant that he was at his post by the tiger statue at the Court at nearly all hours, redirecting orders from the command post on the Highway, and answering the stupid questions that stupid people wanted answered. If it wasn't some openmouthed corporal with his fly unbuttoned, too blind to see the mess tent standing in the middle of the square, it was a clerk from the Currency Ministry, or a librarian from the Foreign Ministry, or some other nervous underling—a game-keeper, a milkman, a rich lady's dresser, a magistrate's children's nurse, that stinking fucking dog man, you name them. Every idiot in the city who no longer had a master to tell them what to do since the old masters had run off north urgently required his direction. Van Goor swiftly sent these bewildered inferiors off to Legate Avenue to make their confessions and receive their little slaps on the wrist, but it was exhausting. The sergeant hadn't thought of Barnes since the night of Westhover's interview, and if not for this latest volley of high-handed abuse, it was likely he'd have been blessed never to think of him again.

Enough was enough. He'd been generous to let the first slight go, but Van Goor had his self-worth to maintain. Without self-worth, you were just something for other people to use, a cigarette to smoke up and flick away, a stair to drop a bootheel on as you climbed.

△

Van Goor, as a youngster, had been bound in a provincial town to a wheelwright, a remarkably rude individual named Karnel, who believed he had discovered the key to all wit in his assistant's surname. Van Gunk, Van Cunt, Van Piss, Van Sweeper, Van Shit Shoveler, Van Sloppy, Van Lazy, Van Slow, Van Dumb, Van Poor, Van Whore, Van Please, Van Sorry, Van Weepy, and Van on and Van on. For two years, Van Goor had absorbed the wheelwright's nasty, belittling gibes and his hitching, screeching crow's laugh, *hee-hee-hee, hee-hee-hee.*

One day a soldier brought a military carriage into the wheelwright's barn to have its jumpy wheel tightened. It had been a simple job, but Karnel put on his usual show of pacing around the carriage, sighing and pinching his flabby throat, lamenting the state of the hubs and the rims, and acting in general as if the fix might be impossible. This was all a run-up for him to demand an inflated fee and, following the completion of the task, to smugly declare that "not many other could have managed, but I did!"

The soldier threw him off, though, brusquely asking, "Well? Have I come to the wrong man?"

"No, of course not!" Karnel snapped, and yelled at Van Goor to bring him the second-smallest mallet. When Van Goor brought it, Karnel threw it back at him, hitting his underling in the knee and giving him a bruise. "I told you to get the smallest mallet, Van Shit!" While he went about the business of resetting the wheel, the wheelwright, in a fury at being prodded by the soldier, rained a continuous stream of abuse on Van Goor. "Van Puke, hurry up!" "Van Waste, are you Van Deaf?" and so on.

The soldier, whom Van Goor never did see again, had taken a seat on the bottom step of the stairs to the hayloft. He sprawled with his polished, red-striped black boots stretched out.

Van Goor was accustomed to Karnel's invective, but the presence of the soldier, overhearing it as he relaxed in his shiny boots, made him horribly ashamed of his own scuttling lowness.

When the work was done, the soldier gave the wheel a shake with his hand and a tap with the toe of his boot, and said it was satisfactory. He handed Karnel his money and nodded mildly in Van Goor's direction. "I'm surprised he puts up with you talking to him like that. Rude makes rude, in my experience. Hurts morale."

"He puts up with it and he's grateful," the wheelwright said. "Van Grateful, I call him, *hee-hee-hee*." The scrawny man's neck wattles flapped and wobbled with his cackles. "*Hee-hee-hee!*"

"Maybe," the soldier said, in that way people did when they actually meant, "No," and climbed onto the carriage. He clicked at his horses and drove away, rattling up the long dusty road that led to the main thoroughfare.

The exchange shook something awake in young Van Goor, though.

For some time, he had been supposing, disconsolately, that he would probably have to murder Karnel, or else lose his mind. It wouldn't be hard. Van Goor was young and strong, the wheelwright close on sixty. The problem was that upon killing his master, his own hanging would soon follow.

What the soldier said altered his consideration. His notion of the possibilities turned on the soldier's key word: *rude*. Karnel had been rude to Van Goor, outrageously, ceaselessly rude. And as the soldier said, rude made rude. More than that, Van Goor thought, rude *deserved* rude.

Now, murder—murder was a little more than just rude. It was also letting them off the hook. If you murdered someone, they didn't have to live with the feeling that rudeness put on you, the invisible dirtied feeling that made you feel less than human. Yes, rude deserved rude.

Anything short of murder, however, anything that left the subject alive, would qualify. That left quite a menu of discourtesy for young Van Goor to peruse and contemplate.

The wheelwright's servant lay on his pallet in the hayloft and deliberated on his revenge, and further, mused on the relaxed way that the soldier had draped himself over the steps and stuck out his long, shiny boots. If you wore a uniform and had fine red-striped boots, people must know better than to call you names.

He decided that the next day he would break his contract and enlist. Van Goor was enthusiastic about the idea of the army, where there were standards of behavior, consideration was given to morale, and you received excellent boots.

Before departing, Van Goor, armed with a metal spoke, waited in the gray of the predawn, in the breezeway between the house and the shed. When Karnel emerged, on his way to his morning piss and fumbling with the button of his underwear, Van Goor clubbed the spoke across the back of the wheelwright's skull. He dragged the unconscious man to the barn, roped his arms and legs across a sawhorse, and waited for him to regain his senses.

And when Karnel did, blinking and moaning, he begged to be let go. "I was only teasing, Van Goor!" he cried.

"That's Van God to you," Van Goor had replied, and proceeded to do something terrifically rude to the wheelwright. It was such a rude thing, in fact, that he knew the wheelwright would never go to the authorities about it, or about his servant breaking their contract.

Later, he heard from an acquaintance that Karnel walked with a bad limp. The news made Van Goor laugh, *"Hee-hee-hee!"*

Even in the military, the problem of rudeness cropped up disappointingly often. Rude foreigners waving legal documents written in foreign; rude privates questioning his handling of prisoners; rude saloonkeepers nagging about his bill; rude prostitutes making filthy comments in his ear while he was trying to concentrate; and once, a breathtakingly rude drunk in a saloon in the Lees, who had commented, "What are you, champ, nearly forty? You look nearly forty. And not even a captain yet? What's holding you back? Something about you that the quality-type folks don't appreciate?"

At a certain point, it was out of your hands. You did what was natural. Rude made rude and rude deserved rude, and, when necessary, Van Goor believed he could be ruder than any other man alive.

Δ

The elevator, *clink-clink*ing down its chain, descended from 4 to 3 to 2.

The "lieutenant" returned to the matter of boot-repair. Though Dora, the whore he'd obtained the building for, unfortunately didn't know how to fix boots—simply no use going to see her, sorry about that!—it so happened that "Lieutenant" Barnes had found a man who kept a tidy leatherworks shop on Sable Street. The fellow did a wonderful job with boots and really anything else. Van Goor should visit him. A real craftsman he was, just you wait and see.

"I should," Van Goor said, rubbing one of his emerald cufflinks with his thumb.

The cufflinks' previous owner had been a pigeon-chested, loyalist doctor who kept an office up in the Hills. The doctor had declined to forthrightly hand over his equipment and supplies, so Van Goor had used the doctor's head to unlock a few of the cabinets and, as a further lesson, fined him his handsome cufflinks.

"You were rude," he told the doctor, pushing his boot tip into the doctor's gut as he lay on the office floor, bleeding and crying, "and thusly did you cause me to be rude. I hope you understand now, Doc, that I am not the man to go challenging in a Contest of Rudes."

Well, it seemed to Van Goor that the "lieutenant" had thrown down the fucking handkerchief, or the fucking rose, or the fucking hat, or whatever fucking item it was that schoolboys threw down when they wanted to tell each other they were sore. But Van Goor wasn't going to slap-fight like schoolboys did when they had it out. He was going to assess this schoolboy the beating of a lifetime, and after that he was going to make him watch while he fucked his whore.

Δ

The elevator let them out in the lobby and the sergeant said, "You know, Lieutenant, it's a pleasure to me, who is just an old soldier, to be able to spend time with such a smart and refined gentleman as yourself, and learn from you." His broad grin in his scarred and broken face cheered Robert and gave him hope. Here was someone who wasn't afraid to adopt a positive outlook.

"I'm sure I have just as much to learn from you," he said to Van Goor before parting. The Sergeant appeared doubtful and shook his head, but said, "I can only so hope, Lieutenant."

The Metropole: XVII

Talmadge XVII slipped out behind the two men and crossed the peacock-fanned blue field of the lobby carpet to the Concierge's desk. She hopped onto the desk and folded herself into the outgoing mail tray, and from this position she seemed to monitor the comings and goings through slit eyes. In previous times, wealthy tourists and travelers had paused to fuss over the cat, to stroke her ears and scratch her chin; now the soldiers did. "Bless you, friend," a soldier said, running his thick fingertips through Talmadge's long, feathery fur and along the length of her spine. "Aren't you a glorious one."

It was undeniable: she was glorious. XVII was just the second female Talmadge (after Talmadge III) in the Metropole's history. Among the hotel's long-timers it was widely agreed that she was the cleverest, most beautiful, and most bloodthirsty Talmadge in living memory.

XVII had been delivered, per tradition, to the Metropole during Talmadge XVI's final days. XVII had only just been weaned and XVI had been nearly immobile, hunched on his purple satin pillow in the Manager's office, rawboned with cancer. XVI had hissed at her without rising, but the tiny heiress had simply sat there, neat as a statue, and waited. Even in their sorrow for the dying cat, the hotel staff was impressed by her reserve.

And the next night, XVII had slept upon her own brand-new purple satin pillow.

That was four years ago. She had grown into a luxurious, cloudlike presence, the most perfect symbol yet of the supple rest that guests could expect at the Metropole. She moved freely through the front and back halls, the lobby, the offices, the laundry, the baths, and the basement, and rode up and down in the elevator according to her whim. Whatever was going on at the Metropole, XVII always seemed to be present—nestled in corners, curled in nooks, peering out through the radiator grilles that she squeezed behind. Some of the maids called her Pretty Spy. They joked that if she could have understood words, there wasn't a secret in the hotel that she wouldn't have known.

Other maids called her the Slayer. The whole staff—but the maids, especially—loved XVII for ending the Metropole's vermin problem. Toward the end of XVI's administration a wave of mice and rats, seeming to sense his infirmity, had invaded the great hotel. XVII had put a stop to that. In her earliest days, it had not been uncommon of a morning to find six or seven tattered rodent corpses thoughtfully lined up beside the garbage chute. The staff joked about how glad they were not to get on the wrong side of XVII; imagine what she'd do to someone she really didn't like!

Parallel to XVII's spot in the tray on the Concierge's desk was the lobby sitting area, with armchairs, card tables, broad-leafed potted plants, silver spittoons, and a drinks cabinet attended by a bartender in the Metropole's purple regalia. The section of wall nearest to the area was carved with cubbyholes to display the taxidermied bodies of the "retired" Talmadges. They rested in the massive grid with their majestic white coats frozen in full, bright bloom, and glassy, wide-open eyes. XVI sat in a cubby with XV in the cubby to the left. To his right was an empty slot. Unlike some of the other Talmadges, the Metropole long-timers had observed, XVII was distinctly indifferent to the stuffed bodies of her predecessors; she never jumped up to lick them in their cubbies, never hunched up her back or fluffed her tail at them. Sometimes, however, when she lounged in one of the armchairs, her half-lidded gaze seemed to settle upon the empty cubby to the right of XVI. But it can be hard to tell with cats, when they look like that—it can seem more like they're dreaming than seeing.

"Good kitty," a maid said to her, dusting around the mail tray and scratching XVII's chin, "good kitty. What a Pretty Spy. Bless you, friend."

XVII purred and stretched, but even as she twisted her head for the maid, she kept her eyes on the lobby.

The two men from the elevator crossed through, going in separate directions outside the glass doors.

A minute or two after that the other pair of men, the ones who had opted not to take the elevator, appeared. They paused by the sitting area. The old man turned and studied the grid of Talmadges. His attendant kept a grip on his master's elbow. XVII began to switch her tail back and forth.

The old man rolled up his shoulders as if against a downpour, and moved again toward the door, assisted by his retainer. He cast his gaze in XVII's direction. His blue eyes met her blue eyes, and the old man sneered. He whispered something to the retainer. The retainer nodded and they left.

The cat calmly rose and yawned.

The retainer, hand on the holstered weapon at his hip, reentered the lobby, and approached her. XVII leapt from the Concierge's desk, scattering some letters from the tray. She pattered—briskly but not at a run—through the offices behind the desk. XVII passed to the rear maintenance hall and trotted to the door at the end of it. She meowed at a valet who was leaning against the wall making a cigarette, and he opened it for her. "Bless you, friend." XVII went out, into the city.

Δ

She left the hotel district behind and went south. She traveled by way of the city's backsides, the stable yards and the courtyards, the trash dumps and the cesspits. To get over some fences she climbed hay bales, and pressed her body down into the dirt to scramble under others. In the yards she kept to the shadowy places under eaves, or sneaked behind the garbage piles, or threaded through the thick goosegrass that grew around the cesspits. If a quick boy or a quick girl had observed XVII's progress downtown, they would have had to grant their admiration: the Metropole's fancy cat might look like a powder puff, but didn't she operate.

Except, of course, because the operation was to be invisible, no one did see her.

The two quickers in the alley two blocks down from the Metropole, gloating over the white silk scarf they'd snatched from a rich carriage— they didn't see her.

The coachman had left the carriage door open while he helped his elderly passenger inside the Metropole. "It was so free, Zil," the boy thief crowed, "it hardly counts as stealing!"

The hostler in the stable yard complaining to a coworker about his sheets having been taken by a neighbor—he didn't see her.

"The bastard plucked em right off the line and I seen em on his bed right through the window. No shame. I complained to this green armband and he told me his hands are full and I told him, my problem is, this other bastard's hands are full of my sheets!" You had to have some law, didn't you, the hostler protested.

The scavengers digging through the trash barrels in another yard—they didn't see her either. They were talking about the army, asking what had become of Gildersleeve and them, the real army, not Crossley's mutts and these university boys. "They say everyone's equal, but then they give you a bunch of orders." And what did you know, the ones that had to shovel horseshit were the same ones who had always shoveled horseshit. All that had changed was that now there was no meat and there was no Constabulary to prevent thievery.

Groat certainly didn't notice her. ". . . the ship in the nights, sailing wherever it wants . . . wherever, wherever . . . ," he mumbled thoughtfully to himself, as he leaned on his crutches in back of the Still Crossing and dribbled on the stump.

But the cat—Pretty Spy, Slayer, Talmadge XVII—saw them to avoid them, and she must have heard them too. (Bearing in mind that we can never know what, if anything, a cat makes of the things that humans say.)

△

A retired actress named Lorena Skye was the sole full-time resident of the Goodheart Playhouse, a defunct and ruined theater not two blocks from the Still Crossing. She lived in the only extant opera box, slept on a bed of chair cushions, and used a heavy canvas backdrop of a Riviera scene—villas, streets of khaki-colored stone meandering toward a turquoise harbor—for a blanket. She had been a superb comedic player in her day, but age and an unfair reputation for difficulty had undone her career, plummeting Lorena from the great stages to the country stages, and, finally, below the So Fair to the Goodheart, which had actually been more of a dance hall than a theater, and had anyway been closed since the better part of the roof fell in a few years earlier. Somewhere along the line, an important section of Lorena had collapsed in on itself too, although she remained cheerful. The arrival of the cats did not bother her.

They trickled in through the crater-shaped opening in the roof, jumping from the lolling tongue of shingle to the rafters, and from the rafters to the stage below. There was a striped cat, an orange cat, a patched cat, a stunningly beautiful white cat that reminded her of the cat that used to live at one of the fancy hotels—the name gone from her memory, but the one that served the cinnamon-flavored soda water—and several other fantastic felines. One after another they landed on the stage and proceeded, according to their ritual, to go and piss on a tattered script that lay in a corner.

The cats had been coming for a while, and they always did this: every single cat pissed on the script. It was like a performance. Lorena wondered if it *was* a performance.

The story seemed to be: a group of cats sneak in through the roof of a theater, piss on some paper in the corner of the stage, go to the center of the stage and make a circle, thump their tails back and forth, and stare at each other. The End! Lorena didn't get it, but it was riveting. She was lonely, and they were so gorgeously alive—and so damned organized!

You had to laugh. She hadn't been able to get a sniff at a part for years. Cats were taking all the great roles.

But this time, once the cats finished the pissing scene and made their circle at stage center, the show changed. The one with the patched face stepped into the middle and dropped something. It looked like . . . felt? Black felt? Come to think of it, wasn't there usually a black cat? Where was it?

Lorena picked at the gilt of the opera box's railing as the striped cat entered the circle next and dropped a little piece of paper on the stage.

Imagine that: a cat carrying around a paper! They were so talented! First they'd usurped the actors, and now they were coming for the dogs!

Next it was back to the normal thing, the cats whopping their tails off the planks, staring, whopping their tails, staring, minutes going by, whopping, staring, The End. Exeunt actor cats through the broken roof into the starry night.

Lorena hoisted herself up and clapped, but they did not return to bow. She found that she felt unusually good. Lately her lungs were often heavy, and sometimes her vision darkened strangely. But tonight her body was oddly light.

She wrapped herself in the Riviera canvas and traveled the dusty balcony steps to the ground floor. She dug her way through the maze of moldy curtains in the rear passage to the stage.

Lorena went to inspect the script. *A Little Wolf Box* by Aloysius Lumm, read the yellow, wrinkled cover. Not a play she had heard of, but one thing was for sure: the reviews were withering!

Curious, she freed up a hand, picking up the soggy packet between thumb and index finger. It sloughed apart as she lifted it, leaving her with a single page:

Tomas stabs Elder Gray repeatedly. Elder Gray dies. Tomas works to saw off Elder Gray's head.

*The Devil turns apologetically to the audience, and speaks over the sound
of the blade grinding through gristle and against bone.*

DEVIL: He does this every night and I never get used to it. (*To Tomas:*)
Please stop. You've killed him. This is unpleasant to behold. You are
distressing the audience.

Tomas stops and weeps.

TOMAS: I loved him. He loved her. What happened to us?
DEVIL: I was cruel to you. But here's the good news: you're like me now.
TOMAS: What do you mean?
DEVIL: Once you've taken the blood of your own, you can live forever,
and do whatever you like to whoever you like.
TOMAS: Why would I want that?

The Devil rubs his face in comic frustration.

Lorena dropped the single script page. What a smug prick the Devil
turned out to be. It figured, but what a disappointment. It was fine for
what it was, she supposed; not interesting enough to read on pissy paper,
though.

She went to look at the props the cats had left behind.

The black felt was a piece of meat with some black hair. She recoiled
and lost her grip on the canvas. It rattled down to the stage. Lorena shivered, shaking her head in admiration. The things the prop artists made
these days were incredible.

She bent and picked up the crumpled paper. It was ripped at the
corner, stained with rock dust. Lorena read:

**PLEASE SCRAPE YOUR SHOES BEFORE
ENTERING THE MUSEUM**

So that was it. The cat play was about a museum. That explained all the staring, didn't it? That's what you did at a museum. You stared at the art, and at the other cats who came to stare at the art. You went to the museum and you stayed away from the dead meat place. Simple as that.

Lorena imagined herself in a cat body, sleek and long and young and imperious, and felt herself flick an invisible tail. She could do it, no question—and the absence of the black cat proved they needed an understudy. She resolved to propose it next time.

Lorena turned to retrieve her canvas shawl.

There was a boat in the turquoise water of the Riviera scene that she'd never noticed. It was getting closer. The prop artists were amazing, just amazing! She lowered herself to take a closer look.

"Ahoy, there," she said.

"Lorena!" a man answered from the ship's deck. He called to her that she'd been hiding in the wings for too long. There was a role for her to play.

"Golly," Lorena Skye said. "Say no more." She stepped into the canvas and onto the Morgue Ship, though her body remained in the balcony, where it had stopped breathing a while before.

News

For D's bricklayers Ike brought two pairs of plain brown suspenders. They reeked of alcohol, but were perfect otherwise. He insisted on putting them on the wax figures himself. "Here we are, fellas." D was touched by the assiduous way Ike went about buttoning the suspenders into place, smoothing them down, arranging them over the shoulders just so.

He stepped back, and they stood and looked at them.

The new-old suspenders replaced the makeshift string belts and restored a bit of dignity to the bricklayers, a grinning, gap-toothed pair who exuded affable capability. The two men inhabited a dirt-floored basement room in the Lees, D imagined, a space that couldn't really be cleaned. In their damp and candlelit hole, they shared a bed to save money, and induced each other into fits of wild amusement by drawing filthy pictures on the stone walls with fragments of brick. When they fell into exhausted sleep, they breathed the river basin clay deep into their lungs.

"They're still mutts," Ike judged, "but there's no law against being a mutt. We just can't expect them to apply themselves to their task if their drawers are about to fall down, can we? And most are mutts, anyway. You go out to the Fields and see the rowboats that have the kings on them? Their heads on the fronts. Pretend you don't see the crowns, and they look like any of these ones here. Isn't that funny, Miss Dora, how ugly goes around?"

"Not around to you, Ike. Someone could put you in a frame to admire."

He reddened, and D immediately felt badly for teasing him. She made a point of spying a spot on the glass of the case of plaster hands that was nearby. She walked to it, licked her thumb, and waved it over the nonexistent blemish.

"How is it outside?" she asked over her shoulder.

The question came out dry and cracked. She hadn't slept well. Bet had come, and after that the night had been long. Let me do it, a man had screamed, let me, let me, let me, but D's neighbor had not let him do it. Her neighbor had gone at his own pace.

She cleared her throat, turned with a smile to repeat her question.

"Itchy," Ike said. He'd composed himself. There was just a touch of color on his cheekbones; but now she noticed the shadows under his eyes. It seemed that her quick boy hadn't slept too well either.

"You're better off inside, take it from this Ike. You lock the doors, don't you?"

"I do. There are thieves, apparently. What do you mean by itchy?"

Things weren't right; that was the gist of what Ike told her. With no vessels entering the bay, the docks and factories and breweries were closed. With nothing being made, nothing was being spent, and nothing was being bought. It was a lot of Nothing. People were used to a little. You could survive on a little. But Nothing . . . You started to think, naturally, about what came next. You couldn't feed the entire city on oysters and ash bread indefinitely. If the fighting was over and the old government was beaten and exiled, what was going on? You started to think. This Ike had certainly started to.

". . . And people are being spooky with each other." He scowled.

"Spooky how?"

Ike waved the question off.

"Tell me."

"You know the Morgue Ship?"

She knew enough, which was that bodies had been displayed on the miserable little boat anchored below the So Fair. She'd heard people talk of it, but never given it more than a moment of thought. What was a dead body if not a thing that used to be interesting? It was what happened to what had been inside the body that interested D. (Or maybe, who happened? Whose face?)

Ike related the story in a tone of mock horror. D was familiar with the first part from reading about it in a newspaper: the Morgue Ship, which had been built round about the time the moons split, and was likely held together with a single nail and a daub of glue, had drifted off, and probably sunk somewhere in the Fair.

"But what sense would that make?" Ike asked, making his disgust clear. On the contrary, he continued, word was that it had been stolen by Joven's corpse in league with the boatman. The two of them were sailing up the river and down the river and along alleyways and in mirrors, luring some people, and stealing others.

"There you have it! Your husband or your wife disappears, it isn't because they got sick of your face, or swallowed a bucket of beer, it's because ghosts took them. And a lot of these people no one can find, they worked for the government or for rich families. No way would those sorts want to skip out, right? They've been taken away on the magic boat. All makes sense, Miss Dora, nevermind that the Charm's been good and dead for well over a year."

Ike laughed and stomped his boot. "But isn't it foolish?" The tiredness remained in his eyes, though, and she felt that, at least partly, he was asking for reassurance.

"Yes." The ghost story didn't trouble her. It seemed to her as silly and improbable as Robert's banter about spirits flowing through letter slots. The rest did, though. D knew as well as anyone that things were unsettled, didn't she? The man who lived in the former embassy was taking people sailing every night.

Before she sent Ike on his way with a fresh list of items to get for the museum, D walked him to the cabinet with the eyepiece in the fourth-floor gallery. She wanted to know what he made of it. All D could determine was that it was some variety of camera. She had looked into the lens and seen a picture of a man and a cat, and the cat had moved its tail and the man had turned his head, and there had been a few words of explanation—so not a picture, exactly, but a moving picture. After that there had been other living pictures too, and other titles to explain what was happening, D said, but without going into the details. The moving cat and the moving man seemed mad enough; she thought it was better not to mention the episodes with the saw, the knife, or the doppelgängers.

The process Ike went through was essentially the same one she had gone through herself when the machine stopped. He peered through the dark lens, examined the button with the white triangle printed on it and the scratches on the wood around it, pressed the button, listened at the sides, rapped the wood with his knuckles, managed to rock the heavy cabinet slightly back and forth on its spot. Ike frowned, pointed at the lens. "I'm with you that it has something to do with seeing, but that's as much as I can figure."

△

The quick boy studied her list and decreed that the items would be no trouble. Come to mention it, he already had a quality lead on the surgeon's tools, the prospect just wasn't quite mature yet. D told him to make sure the prospect was fully mature; she didn't want him taking risks. "I mean it, Ike. It's not important enough. It's not really important at all."

Ike ignored her caution and pointed to the top request on her paper. "Now, this one, Miss Dora, about getting some new eyes, that seems key to me. That's been on my mind since the first time I looked around at the place. There's many more one-eyed workers in here than you see in real life. And if you give up and just stick in some odd marbles, that's going to be twice as bad. Your white marble, your black marble, your swirly marble, just imagine that." He bugged his eyes and mimed a choking face. "Any of those'll cause your workers to look devilish and like that.

It's a specialized thing, though, eyes. I'll need to make some inquiries. But if anyone can find them, it's this Ike."

"Is it?"

"Oh, yes." He blew at his hair, evidently irritated that there was any question as to his ability to find glass eyes in a city of a quarter million.

"I know." She touched his forearm, so he'd pay attention. "Really hear me, Ike: I don't want you to get hurt. Understand? And I especially don't want you to get hurt for me."

"I won't get hurt." Ike grinned at her, blushing again, and withdrew his arm from her fingers.

"Don't be foolish." D laughed her annoyance. "Everyone gets hurt. Everyone."

"Sure, but you can't go around thinking you might get hurt," Ike said.

She laughed again. "Yes, you can. That's how you avoid getting hurt, you idiot."

He frowned. "It's not nice to laugh at people, Miss Dora."

"I'm sorry. Have I hurt you, Ike? I thought you weren't going to get hurt."

"Not when I'm careful like I am," he said stubbornly.

And it struck D, as Ike stepped backward from the curator's office, red-faced and grimacing, struck her fully and startled her like a gust of cold rain, that there was nothing more heartbreaking than a young man's confidence.

She stood there, feeling punctured and emptied out, sodden and exhausted. She told herself he would be all right; if anyone would be all right, it would be Ike, this Ike.

He lingered woundedly past the doorway.

"I'm sorry," she said. "I'm just tired. I haven't been sleeping well, and I don't want anything to happen to you, is all."

These words seemed to relieve him. She followed him outside into the bright daylight. D noticed that someone had stolen the sign in front of the door from beneath its rock.

Ike walked into the street. "Can I tell you something, Miss Dora?" he asked her.

"You can tell me anything, Ike," she said.

He inhaled and blew again at the hair on his forehead, and swung abruptly away, breaking into a run. "I just need to make sure I say it right!" he cried.

Ike dashed to the corner and turned left, showing off, bouncing on one foot, skidding and raising tiny clouds of dust and grit, waving his arms in circles as if to keep from falling. He barreled ahead, disappearing around the corner before she could say that she'd see him soon.

Δ

The stench like rotten eggs that wafted from around the back of the building, notably stronger than yesterday, filled D's nostrils. The smell reminded her that if she wasn't waiting for Captain Anthony by the window that night to acknowledge his salute, to receive his shining, black-bearded smile, he would search for her, and find her, and punish her the way he punished people each night. And she would deserve his punishment. If she doubted their crimes, doubted their punishment, and didn't do anything to stop him, then she had to stay and at least protect Robert. Anything less was cowardice, and whatever else D had been in her life, she had never been a coward.

She covered her mouth with the back of her hand to restrain her bile, and retreated into the museum's cool dark.

Brewster

$\mathcal{B}$rewster Uldine, tram driver, bareheaded since the theft of his bowler, was eating his lunch in the tram yard when a Volunteer came walking and provided a suitable object for his bad mood to fixate on. Brewster informed the Volunteer that he wouldn't have any bother. "I can't help with anything right now. You have no authority over me. I'm allowed to have lunch. You're not a constable."

"That's a friendly greeting. What's wrong with you?"

The Volunteer lowered himself with a groan onto a mound of rusty chains a few feet from where perched Brewster with his pickled oysters laid on his lap on a handkerchief. A dowdy man whose patched clothes sagged all over, the Volunteer carefully set out his own victuals, an onion and a roll, and a book, each item on its own ridge of the chain pile, like little monuments on a little hill. The display annoyed Brewster, who was not a reader, but did like onions and rolls, and was sick of eating pickled oysters every day.

"What's wrong with me, you ask? I'll tell you. If you were a constable, you'd have to do something about the ones come around after dark and cut the lines," Brewster said. "That's just one thing. It puts us behind on our routes and enrages the public, and that falls on us drivers. You wouldn't believe the things we have to listen to when people can't get where they need to be on time."

"I don't know anything about that," the Volunteer said. He picked up his roll and bit the bread with a mouth of jumbled teeth. It made a stale-sounding crunch.

"No, you don't know," Brewster said. "Thieves'll take the lid right off your head these days." The Volunteer should have known, though. They claimed to be in charge but took no responsibility, and did nothing about criminality.

Only the other morning Brewster had encountered two venerable, vulnerable grandmothers in touring hats the size of carriage wheels, wandering around in the tram yard, carrying pruning scissors and baskets of wildflowers. It was a tick past dawn, the first mist of autumn shimmery in the early light. He'd been there to wash the seats of his tram preparatory to driving the day's routes. The women had appeared through the mist, youthful in their silhouettes. They clarified as they came closer, wrinkled and wispy-haired in their hats, which were weighted with huge paper blossoms and drooping ribbons. More startling still, they had been identical—a pair of ancient twins.

"What's this, madams?" he had asked.

The dears were giggly as children. They told him they were looking for wildflowers to make bouquets for the orphans in the Lodgings. It was so hard for orphans in the Lodgings even at the best of times, and now things were strange, they must be terribly unhappy.

"Have you seen any wildflowers?" one asked. "Or cats with long pretty tails?" the other asked, and they both croak-laughed at the hilarity.

Brewster told them he was sorry, but they couldn't be there. There were people about, sneaking around and cutting the tram lines and tampering with gearboxes. Whoever it was might well be dangerous. (It momentarily occurred to him that the ladies themselves could be using their pruning scissors on the tram lines, but Brewster cast that thought off quickly: the idea of a pair of elderly rich women—twins, to boot!—performing as saboteurs was too far-fetched.)

The sisters had said, oh dear, the vandalism was terrible, and wished him good day before walking off, arm in arm.

Anything could happen to a person these days and there wasn't a soul to do anything about it. Brewster disregarded the talk he overheard among his passengers about Joven and his ghost boat full of ghosts. It was plain lawlessness. It started with delinquents feeling free to hang on to the sides of the cars and make sport of you and snatch your lid off, and the next thing you knew it was no longer safe for early-risen grandmothers to search for flowers.

"Someone could be harassing old women, and you'd sit there eating bread." Brewster was particularly annoyed about the bread part. He'd had virtually nothing but pickled oysters that week, purchased from his landlady at triple the price.

"Listen to me: I'm going to read my book," the Volunteer said, and added a great, juicy chomp from his onion to the portion of half-masticated roll that was already in his mouth. He chewed as he spoke, rolling his jaw in a donkeyish fashion, and sending flecks of white and brown jumping off his lips. "Let me eat my lunch and read my book and rest my feet. I came over here because I wanted a quiet spot, not because I wanted to give you any trouble. You said you didn't want to be bothered and it's you giving me bother. If there's something I can help you with after I have my lunch, I'll help you. Right now, I'm on break."

The Volunteer flapped open his book. There was a disdainfulness in the way he did it, as if he were shaking snot off the pages. The cover had no illustration, just a title, *The Dissatisfaction: Fifty-Five Poems*, and the surname **RONDEAU** printed in bold beneath.

"I could tell you all you ever wanted to learn about dissatisfaction," Brewster said. "Had plenty."

"Oh, fuck." The Volunteer expelled a mordant sigh, then grabbed up his onion and other things, and took himself away.

△

Alone again, Brewster Uldine pitched oyster shells at the pile of chains, and mourned Mary Ann, the sister of the young bastard who had tormented him and stolen his blue bowler a few afternoons ago, Mary Ann who was fixed to adore him in every way, and be adored by him in every way, and who did not exist. Brewster felt stupid and lonely.

The driver had only purchased the bowler recently, right before the government had fallen. Such a luxury had never occurred to him previously. He'd seen the model on the crown of a shopkeeper who was rocking on his heels outside a haberdashery on Sable Street, a bowler as blue as a jay and worn slightly cocked. The shopkeeper snared Brewster with a wink and asked, "Well, friend, shall we smarten you up?"

The tram driver had long harbored a fantasy of asking a woman to marry him, wherein, after she cried, "Yes!" he'd sweep her up and swing her around and declare that from that point in time, she'd never pay to ride the tram again for the rest of her life. Brewster added the new bowler to his scene; he doffed it before presenting his question. While the delinquent had been telling him about Mary Ann, he had thought to himself that it was really going to happen. He'd even thought, while the young bastard was talking, that the impulsively purchased bowler was the key, the element that had completed the picture of his ultimate happiness, made it possible.

People sometimes did awful things on the tram. Left garbage, wiped rotten stuff all over, dripped blood. They hurried off before a driver could notice. There was something vicious loose in the world. Brewster Uldine had glimpsed its auburn hair, and its laughter and its dashing footsteps rang in his ears, and it made him feel vicious too.

Δ

"I'm sorry I talked to you like that," Brewster said. In a fit of self-recrimination, he had gone to find the Volunteer, discovering him in the cab of a junked tram in a different part of the yard. "I was in a bad mood." Brewster stuck out his hand.

The Volunteer pursed his lips and kept his arms crossed. "You can't be an enflamed asshole for no reason. That's how wars are begun. That's how this war was begun, in fact. You don't need to understand the deeper economics or the political details to see that. The Crown was an enflamed asshole to us all, behaved in a cavalier manner, was greedy, was a bright burning hole that dribbled shit for decades and decades, and what's transpired has resulted in some short-term heartache for the likes of you, but ultimately a better life."

"I am sorry." The casual vituperation of the Volunteer's speech dazed him.

"Naturally I'll accept your apology," the man said. "I know about strong feelings. That's my subject, really, when you get right down to it."

They shook, and Brewster wondered but did not ask, *His subject?*

Brewster gave his name, and the Volunteer gave his as Hob Rondeau, Poet, and magnanimously offered the tram driver the opportunity to buy him a drink.

△

Deviancy was the answer. That was Rondeau's subject. Who felt more strongly than the deviant? "Arsonists, murderers, maniacs—sexual maniacs in particular, the sort who lust for the dead, or who like to hide in the alleys just off busy streets and peek out to see the people walking by, and play with themselves—all those kinds of people intrigue me. I write from the deviant's point of view. I channel them so that they can make their confession. Inhabit them. Like the medium of a séance does for a spirit, although those people are charlatans."

"Oh," Brewster said. "All right."

"This is one of mine." The poet brandished the thin volume he'd been studying with his lunch, *The Dissatisfaction.* "These poems are about a brilliant but oversensitive writer who gets teased by a fat, self-important publisher. In response, the writer makes a vow to slash the Achilles tendons of every single person that the publisher knows."

Where the tram driver had been in a state of aggravation when they first met, he now felt bewildered, and slightly afraid of Rondeau. The poet spoke in a rapid near-monotone, only occasionally pausing to give a bullish snort or take a drink.

Rondeau said, "Every single one. Right down to the old tailor who takes out the fat publisher's huge pants. Uses a straight razor to do it." The poet snorted.

The only response Brewster could find was, "He does?"

"He does." Rondeau drank from his jar of brown beer. Foam clung to the bristles of his patchy beard.

They had retired to a grim corridor of a saloon called the Still Crossing and stood crushed against the bar. Despite the early-afternoon hour, it was crowded and loud with the shouts of a dozen or so alcoholics complaining at once. The tram driver thought, wistfully, of Mary Ann; she was too reserved and respectful to tell her husband where he couldn't go, but if they were married—if she were real—he would never sully her trust and good reputation by entering a foul place like the Still Crossing.

"Wriggles along the ground to get to his victims when they're distracted, whips out the razor, and slices their tendons. That's his method." Rondeau swabbed the foam off his lip with his big gray tongue. "The maligned writer maims them all, leaves them cursing the fat publisher's name, exactly as he planned, but ultimately feels no better. Which is the moral, you see."

"I should get back to work," Brewster said. "My shift starts soon."

"Law is the salve, and there is no other, my man. A law for every human being, not a law of the rich and the royal only. Revenge can never heal. That's what my art seeks to demonstrate in this case. But it's not warm milk to soothe the sick belly of the complacent." He offered a shy grin at Brewster, clearly trying, in his off-putting way, to be friendly. "Come on, let's have another and toast to everyone being friends and having enough. Now everyone rides for free, don't they? You don't have to tell the lame and the poor they can't get on because they don't have any pennies." Rondeau waved for the bartender. "Must be a load off your conscience."

"Yes," Brewster said, although he actually hadn't thought at all of the wider variety of passengers who rode the tram since the Volunteers had torn out the money boxes. He felt unexpectedly chastened.

Rondeau continued, "Tell me what you know about the committees that are being set up. I'm sure you'll want to join and—"

"I'm afraid I have to be on my way, Mr. Rondeau," Brewster interrupted, putting down a coin. He edged a path through the crowd and out the open doorway into the street.

△

Warm, gritty wind tousled Brewster's hair. The Strand lay before him, the river beyond that, and on the opposite riverbank, the city's seaside fortifications, the salt-scarred gun towers with their rows of fifty-pounders pointing at the mouth of the bay. Gulls wove in the sky, murdering the peace with their torn voices. A single sandpiper was picking in the mucky sand at the water's edge. Its plaintive call seemed to bemoan the gulls' racket. A brown cat lazing atop a crumbling rock kiln eyed the sandpiper. The river lapped and mumbled as it made its way into the bay.

Brewster inhaled deeply. As everyone said, with the factories closed, the air was fresher.

The Volunteer's words set Brewster to considering the plight of the poor. He wasn't wealthy, but he had a job, hadn't he? He had food to eat, even if it wasn't what he wanted to eat. He'd even had enough money to buy that fine blue bowler. There were ones, especially who lived down here at the south end of the tramline, who had nothing, who starved. Brewster saw them reflected in his mirror at the front of the tram: no shoes on their feet, dressed in too many clothes, or dressed in too few, and dirty. Why hadn't he thought more of them before this?

At the same time, he was supposed to do his job, drive the tram, and that was even more difficult than it had been before. The normal parts of the city had to function properly, or where were you?

Brewster wasn't a bad man. He didn't mind personally if rough people rode the tram. It was only the vandals and crooks he opposed. He had nothing against anyone, so long as they weren't idlers, and made an honest effort for themselves.

An unaccountable and discomforting thought came to the tram driver, as sharp as the steel zing that tickled his nostrils when he threw the lever and the brakes bit on the rails: But what effort did a king make for himself, or the son of any rich man?

Brewster chewed his thumbnail, which tasted of vinegar from his lunch. If only Mary Ann were real, he'd have liked to talk to her about it.

The water of the Fair was blackly solid in the sunshine.

Two strays, a freckled girl in a man's blue bowler hat that almost covered her eyes and a barefoot boy, ran past. The girl had something clutched under her shirt—a vase, perhaps, by the elongated shape—that she was clearly endeavoring to conceal. This made less of an impression on Brewster, however, than did the bowler.

The driver's ears flamed. It was not his thief—not Mary Ann's hooting auburn-haired creator and annihilator—but it was most definitely his hat!

The children entered the Still Crossing and disappeared into the swarm.

A few seconds later, Hob Rondeau emerged, hipping and assing people out of his way, saying, "Yup—yup—yup," where most would have said, "Pardon." In each hand he carried a jar of beer. He held one out for Brewster. "Thought you had to go. You forgot your beer, brother—" Rondeau paused, reading his expression. "What's this?"

"Right off my fucking head!" Brewster blurted, and took a step toward the saloon.

The Volunteer got in front of him. If he'd been wronged, there was a right way to handle it.

Rondeau guided Brewster a few yards away, and while they drank from their jars Brewster explained about his hat and the thief who'd snatched it, and the stray, wearing the same hat, he'd just seen enter the Still Crossing.

"Funny," Rondeau said, "but I believe I may have encountered your snatcher myself. He was with a young woman when I met him. She was very proper, had a paper that gave her a caretaker position at a museum, but I didn't like the looks of him. Snotty mouth."

Brewster had calmed somewhat, but he was still in an angry state of mind. Right off his fucking head! Something needed to be done.

"We don't want to be rash," Rondeau said, nodding at his own advice. "There's more than one criminal involved, perhaps an entire syndicate. That girl, the one I met with your thief—if he's the same—she might even be in danger, under duress." He suggested they see the man who handled the public's queries, a sergeant in General Crossley's chain of command. This sergeant, a Van Goor, could usually be found at a table near the tiger statue in the Magistrates' Court.

The Fields, Pt. 2

I looked for you everywhere," Robert said when she raised her head from the desk to see him sitting on the opposite side. "I thought you'd run off with one of your wax swains. I don't think they like me, Dora. Especially the clamdigger with her little beach. She reminds me of someone's very formidable mother. It's discouraging. I find this whole place discouraging, but her especially. She looks so pleased and certain of herself, swinging along with that bucket. Dora, she looks victorious. I have this feeling that she's about to tell me that her daughter, who I love, has already agreed to the proposal of a richer man's son. Or maybe to the proposal of one of the wax miners."

Dora blinked her sticky eyes. She had fallen asleep in the curator's office. Her lieutenant regarded her with his elbow propped on the desk and his clean-shaven chin propped on his fist. A groggy dustiness filled the small room.

"Are you throwing me over for one of the miners?"

"No. The telegraph operator. What time is it?"

"Just after noon. Isn't the telegraph operator . . . oh, I remember, the small room by the chemist's laboratory, *Telegraph Service* above the door. The operator wears a white suit? Holds a notepad and a pencil? Portly?"

"Yes."

"He has jowls." Robert used a hand to shape a jowl in the air around his own face. He frowned. "They don't have parts, do they?"

She shook her head. "No, they don't. They're smooth. But the telegraph operator pleases me in other ways, Lieutenant."

"That son of a bitch. I'll have to kill him." He spoke without any conviction whatsoever, leaned back in his chair, and crossed his legs. He nodded at the tintype of the old king on the wall. "You should take that down."

He was right. D stood and grasped the sides of the framed picture of the old king, whose murky eyes were seeded beneath wooly eyebrows. What Ike had said after seeing the kings carved into the rowboats was true; if you took away the medals around his collar, he was a mutt. The old king could have been the brother, in fact, of the nightsoil man on the second floor, who hunched arthritically under the arms of his barrow.

D lifted the picture off the wall and revealed the bright-yellow window of paint beneath.

"You look wretched," Robert said.

D set the picture on the floor against the wall. "The telegraph operator hardly lets me sleep."

"Enough."

"It's funny, but that's what I said to the telegraph operator last night."

Robert said he was taking her somewhere for a few hours, wherever didn't matter, she needed some sunshine, needed to get away from this place.

"It smells awfully ripe too," he said. "Have you looked to see if something crawled into the basement and expired?"

Δ

The park was the obvious place for a walk, and D thought Ike would be happy to know that she'd seen the rowboats he'd mentioned. She made the suggestion and her lieutenant thought it was perfect.

They left Little Heritage Street and headed north. Robert hooked his elbow through hers. As their steps carried them past the former embassy, she averted her eyes.

"All the nice places are on Great Heritage: the National Arts Museum, the National Science Museum, the National Historical Institute. That's where we should have set you up. I should have insisted. All the places on Little Heritage are odd. It should be called Very Little Heritage."

He gave her a piece of chocolate. The chocolate tasted slightly of the wool of his pocket, but mostly like heaven. She moaned at the taste, and he gave her another piece, and that one was even better. They left Legate and walked on a street that smelled like late-summer roses. D felt the sun on her face and hair, and breathed, and felt herself loosening inside her skin.

"I shouldn't have said you looked wretched," Robert said. "You couldn't look wretched if you tried. I meant you looked tired."

"You shouldn't be so kind to me," she said.

"Why not?"

"It'll make me suspicious," she said.

Robert cleared his throat, revealing everything in the three or four seconds too long that it took him to respond. "No more chocolate for you."

D patted his arm. She wasn't mad. "You're a good soldier, Lieutenant." She leaned against him, and felt him relax as he absorbed her weight.

Δ

It had been roughly a year earlier, the evening D saw the same handsome boy who'd run away from the crowd of other boys—ball under his arm, crowing, "Never, never, never!"—go into the university library, and decided to indulge her curiosity.

D went to the circulation desk and informed the notoriously eccentric night librarian that she had been asked to fetch a book for a professor and bring it to him along with his clean sheets.

The librarian looked up from the flyer he had been studying with his tongue sticking out of the corner of his mouth. Though they were upside down, D could read the big words at the top of the paper: *A MORAL CALL FOR THE BETTERMENT OF THE POOR AND THE VOICELESS*. It wasn't the first time she'd seen the pamphlet. It was all over campus.

"Be my guest, girl," the night librarian said, accepting the story without interest. "Look, though: some comedian's been littering in the books!"

Hunched over their work, the students at the long tables in the study hall didn't look up as she moved through, stepping softly, to the stairwells.

D searched for the handsome boy until she found him in the deep stacks of the library basement, crouched between two high shelves, peering at the spines of the books. The newly wired strings of electric lights in the high recesses of the ceiling were weak, doing barely more than warm the highest shelf. At the whisper of her shoes, he glanced without standing.

"Hello, there—?"

"I'm Dora, sir," she said.

"I recognize you. I'm Robert Barnes. I'm afraid you're in the wrong section, Dora. This is the Drama-That-No-One-Has-Read-in-Fifty-Years Section." He gestured down the aisle. "The Sheets Section is over there past the History-Books-That-No-One-Has-Read-in-a-Hundred-Years."

"I recognize you, too, sir. I've seen you playing sports in the field. You're very talented."

"Thank you. That's nice of you to say. Unfortunately, Dora, I'm not quite as talented at the classroom sports. I've missed too many classes of my Dramaturgy Seminar. My professor sent me here to get a book to read for extra credit, but I think his real plan may have been to cause me to ruin my eyesight as punishment."

Robert Barnes smiled a smile of such openness and generosity, it could only belong to a person who had never been hurt by anyone in his whole life. From that look, D couldn't imagine someone not liking him immediately; and she couldn't imagine him imagining someone not liking him. For his rooms, she pictured surfaces polished by maids, rows of shoes polished by bootblacks, and on the hangers in the closet, jackets with sagging pockets of loose, forgotten coins. The shadows seemed to retreat from his clean, handsome face.

"Can I help you look, sir?" D asked. "A fresh pair of eyes can help sometimes."

"By all means. I'd be grateful," he said.

D held out the bundle of sheets for him to take. Robert rose and accepted them. "Thank you, sir." She asked him the name of the author and he told her. D ran a finger along the spines of the shelves, reading her way down to the bottom where the boy had been looking—last names starting with LU. D tucked her skirts under herself and sat.

While she examined the volumes on the bottom shelf, she waited for Robert to say something else. He didn't. He stayed quiet, a pair of trousered legs beside her, smelling like the camphor in the university's laundry's soap.

A miniature symphony played at a barely perceptible volume: the slow, fat, cracking swell of ten thousand leather book covers, the hum-sizzle of the electric bulbs, the murmur of the dust, the tender hurrying of mice. It was nice, to be in the mostly dark with this young man, to have his patience, and the walls all around them that kept everyone else far away. It made D feel less like herself, and she liked that. If she wasn't herself, then she hadn't ever lost anything, and didn't want anything. If she wasn't herself, she was somebody else. And when it came to somebody else, there was nothing—nothing in the world— that they might not do.

Between two thicker books was a skinny one with its spine turned inward, the pages facing out. D wiggled it free: *A Little Wolf Box* by Aloysius Lumm; the book he'd been trying to find. The cover illustration was of a pair of disembodied hands clapping. Oozy musical notes issued from the palms.

— 241 —

D got to her feet. "It was jammed in so you couldn't see the binding."

They went through the operation of exchanging the sheets for the book. When the transfer was finished, she didn't move away, and they stood close, face-to-face in the aisle. D could smell his cigarettes and his hair tonic.

"Thank you, Dora," he said. "That was kind of you. I know you had somewhere you were going and you stopped to help me." The young man's expression turned serious, skin clenching around his soft eyes and long mouth. "I want to tell you: where I grew up, I know the men who work with horses, and the men who plant and tend and harvest, and I consider them my friends. I believe they have value beyond the value our society gives to them. I don't believe it's right that some people should have to do everything while a few other people get to have everything. This fellow I know, Lionel, he started a group that wants to make it all a lot fairer, and I've joined up with it."

D wondered if the men who planted and tended and harvested considered Robert their friend. She thought they probably didn't, but nodded. "All right, sir."

His face relaxed. "Believe it or not, I actually have a rank in the group—like in the military. I'm a lieutenant."

She nodded again; if that was how he wanted it. "All right, Lieutenant."

"I didn't mean for you to"—Robert laughed—"oh, well. I suppose I asked for it, didn't I? I can't believe that old nut of a librarian sleeps here. Where's his hole?"

"He doesn't sleep here."

Her lieutenant angled his head at her. She guessed it had probably occurred to him that she'd come for him, but he was too intelligent to believe it. "What are you doing down here with those sheets, then?"

"I followed you, Lieutenant," she said. "I was only carrying the sheets so no one would notice me. They're not for anybody. But maybe you'd like to have them. Maybe you can find something to do with them. Maybe we can together."

Δ

There were, D thought, a lot of loose boats all of a sudden these days.

The one in the pond, at least, appeared unmanned by ghosts: it ticked counterclockwise out in the middle of the water. It also gave their idyll a purpose: to retrieve it, and restore it to the boathouse and the bosom of its fellow royalty.

Robert insisted that D should have the honor of selecting the vessel for their rescue mission.

She walked the boards of the covered dock that grew from the empty pavilion, inspecting the severe countenances of the ships that were tethered to labeled brass moorings and knocking softly in their individual slots. D settled on Macon XI, who had the gape of a man in the throes of a coronary attack and leaves of whitish-green algae caked around his nostrils.

"Because he's the fiercest and the most putrid?" Robert asked.

"Yes," she said.

"Excellent," he said.

He climbed in and helped her to a seat on the bench opposite. The boat was big enough for four, and the seats were padded with white cushions.

Robert fitted the two oars into the locks, D unknotted the ropes, and they skimmed from the shade of the boathouse into the bright of the open water. The pond's blue-green expanse was glazed and cracked with silver and gold. On the bank, the pavilion's pale-gray flagstones and wrought iron tables looked like they'd be hot to the touch, and the arcing wooden observation bridge was half obscured by the haze that rose off the water.

D shut her eyes against the light. Robert grunted and pulled the oars, sculling them briskly toward the abandoned boat.

"We don't have to hurry, do we?" She didn't want to return to the museum, to the window above the embassy's courtyard, any sooner than was necessary.

"No," Robert said. "There's no hurry."

The oars clicked in their locks as Robert drew them in. She felt the boat ease into a drift. Their little ship creaked. Birds peeped. It smelled even better, purer, out on the water; the marine tang blended with the green warmth of the late summer trees and grasses of the park. D undid the bonnet laces beneath her chin.

Robert cleared his throat and exhaled.

D didn't open her eyes. "What about you, Lieutenant? How are you?"

"I'm a little worn out too, I suppose."

She heard him stretch out, his boots clunking on the bottom of the boat. He struck a match, and she smelled the sulfur, and the smoke of his cigarette.

"People are anxious."

"Should they be?"

"No," Robert said, but he said the word as if the answer were actually more like "Maybe."

They floated. She listened to him smoke, sipping on his cigarette.

D opened one eye. Robert had his elbows propped on the gunwales and his cigarette clamped in the fingers of his right hand. He raised an eyebrow at her.

"I'd like to know about your mother," D said. "Tell me about her."

"My mother's reserved. Gentle. She's very short—shorter than you. She makes beautiful handwork. What else? She reads novels. She writes letters to her sister. Sometimes I think she's melancholy—I hear her sighing on the other side of the door, but if you ask her, 'Are you all right, Mother?' she'll say, 'Am I all right? You mustn't worry about me. As long as you are all right, I am all right.' It's tedious."

"Have you heard from her since—?"

Robert shook his head. "Because of the standoff, the mail's been held up."

They wouldn't forgive him for acting against their interests, against their estate and holdings. He hadn't faced it yet, but it was there if he could bring himself to it. D didn't feel sorry for them, but she felt sorry for her lieutenant—for Bobby, leaning on his elbows, his tie bunched up, ticking his cigarette ash into the glimmering water. D reached out and smoothed his sock where it protruded from his gray trouser leg.

He said, "When I was small, my mother told me that she found me under a mushroom and carried me home in a teacup. She loves to tell people about that. She brings out the teacup she said was the one she used and passes it around."

"Is it true?"

"My mother's not a liar, Dora."

"Do you think she'd like me?" D asked.

Robert blew a smoke ring. Tiny rivers of gold trickled through his oiled curls. "Do we have to tell her that you were in service?"

"I'd rather you didn't."

"We won't. In which case, yes, she'd like you."

"Good. I look forward to meeting her."

"What's inexplicable to me," Robert began, looking past her, "is we had the element of surprise, the people weren't opposed to us, and the enemy didn't have an army. They still don't have any army, just a small group of loyalist guards. I've seen the numbers in the field reports. We could finish them at any time. I know their position is good, and I don't want to see anyone killed, but we're letting them stall. Crossley is. There's no urgency. That's what I can't figure, Dora. We're telling them—we're telling Lionel and Mosi and Lumm—well, I'm not sure poor old Lumm is taking much in at this point—but we're all telling them that people no longer believe what we're saying, and I can see that Lionel and Mosi are concerned. At the same time, Crossley is telling them that he's on the verge of gaining the enemy's surrender, so they're in this bind, they . . ." Robert kept talking, about the uneasy sense he had that they were walking into some kind of headwind, but they couldn't see it stirring or hear it, it was just this invisible thing blocking the path.

D closed her eyes again. The sun painted the insides of her eyelids red. She rested her head against the rail. The rocking of the water traveled down her neck and through her bones. The boat creaked and the oars clicked and the birds *whoop-woo*ed and Robert talked. It felt like they were the only people in the park, in the city, in the world.

D squeezed his ankle. "Robert."

He broke off. "What?"

"Suppose it's just us."

"Hm?"

"Suppose that we only have each other now. There's nobody else. What do we do?"

"No other people anywhere?"

"No other people anywhere."

"Hm. I don't know. What do we do?"

D let one of her hands dip into the water. It was bathwater warm from the sun. "What we're doing now."

"And then?"

"We take his lordship's room at the king's estate. We stay there as long as there are rooms with made beds. We never sleep in the same bed twice. After we've exhausted the king's manor, we move to the foreign minister's manor, and we do the same thing. I'll never make another bed for the rest of my life. Your turn now, Lieutenant."

A few seconds elapsed while he fixed a fresh cigarette. The little tides of the pond licked at the sides of the boat. He lit a match, inhaled, and exhaled. "I'll teach you to drink."

"Excellent." D was relieved he hadn't been obvious and boring and mentioned sex.

"Cocktails in the lounge at the Metropole to begin with. One drink one night, two the next, and so on. After we've cleared out the Metropole's liquor, we'll start on the bar at the Lear. Once that's done, we'll go to the King Macon and really set about ruining ourselves. I'll also need to teach you sports."

"I'll do my best."

"Not with that attitude," he said. "We'll go up to the Bluffs and kick balls into the ocean."

It might be fun, D suggested, to go into people's houses and read their diaries.

If there were still animals, if it was only the people who were gone, he said, they'd have to free them. The horses from the stables, the dodos from the zoo, the pigeons from the rookeries.

There were still animals, D said. There had to be: take away the people, that was one thing, but the city would collapse without its cats.

She was going to drive a tram and he was going to wait at a stop to be picked up, he said. "You have to wear the uniform." She said of course she'd wear the uniform. She'd wear it better than anyone ever had before. Robert said he had no doubt of that. He was of the opinion that she'd take it off better than anyone ever had before too.

Robert said, "It might be fun to light something on fire. How about that damned museum? I know they're your friends, Dora, but I want to melt all those wax men. What do you think?" Dora said if they were destroying things, they should use hammers to break up the anatomically absurd statue of the woman in the fountain in Bracy Square. Robert said he liked that statue, it was great art and she just didn't understand it, but perhaps it was better if they didn't ruin anything. If anything, they should make efforts to preserve such treasures. He was glad she'd mentioned it, though; he would have to carefully scrub the statue on occasion.

"We could burn down the Juvenile Lodgings," D said. "I wouldn't mind that."

"All right," Robert said, and she said, "Good."

Would he take her to see his family's home? D asked.

He should, shouldn't he? On the way, they could climb into the hills, and visit the monoliths, and chisel pieces. He'd always wanted to see them up close.

Their boat drifted in the sun and they grew sleepy. Robert brought her to see the platform some of the men from his father's stables had built for him in a tree in the woods of the estate. He showed her where he'd carved his name in the wood with a fork: BOB. "I was just a Bob," he said. D went to Mrs. Barnes's bedroom, but only to make sure that the doors were closed and locked. Eternal privacy was the only gift she could give to the absent woman.

Robert wondered how long they could keep enjoying themselves with everyone gone, if they would miss people too much.

D put her handkerchief in the water and squeezed it out and rubbed it over her cheeks, which she could feel tightening with sunburn. "Maybe if we wander around enough, we can find someone else. We could take a boat across the ocean to . . . Paris or Constantinople . . . London . . ." But Robert said, "No. They're gone, Dora. It's just us. You'll have to try to be satisfied with me, and I'll have to try to be satisfied with you, and we'll have to try to be satisfied with everything left in the world. Those were your rules." She asked about other worlds—maybe they could go to other worlds, maybe there were magic places, places where you could go through—she used to believe maybe there was magic in the Society building, she got the idea from her br—

"No," Robert interrupted, peevish, "no, you have to accept it, you have to accept that this is it," and she said, "All right . . ."

But eventually they did leave home. There was nothing left to see in their country.

They sailed to France. They visited the pyramids. They drank tea in Bombay. They got old. On a promenade in Yalta, they lounged on blankets as the sun uncorked itself from the Black Sea and muscled into the gap between the two quarter moons, a yolk returning to its shell. They settled into a sweltering foreign palace that was thick with dust and full of books written in a language they couldn't read, and surrounded by rioting gardens.

D and Robert argued listlessly over who would die first and leave the other alone. "But it won't be up to us," she said.

"No," he admitted.

Robert crawled to D's bench at the stern. He sprawled beside her. The boat rocked and his hand found her hand. "I care for you," he said. "You understand that, don't you?"

"Yes," D said, and she thought, *I love you a little too, Robert Barnes.*

"There's not another man under my command that I'd rather have with me," she murmured.

She turned on her side and pressed her hot face into the hair at his temple, and inhaled the anise of his tonic, and his sweat, and the afternoon. They drowsed.

"*Blood is the toll and blood is the key.*"

The Vestibule

*I*t was not quite evening when Robert left her at the museum. He couldn't stay the night; he had to attend to his Health and Welfare Committee. "What about my health and welfare, Lieutenant?" D asked.

He kissed her. "I expect you can take care of yourself, Dora. But I'll see if I can get a few men to come over and open up the sewer at the corner. That's got to be your smell. Something must be broken."

D lifted a hand, but he had turned his back and was walking away. The rot stench had cooked all day in the heat and the atmosphere in the street had worsened. The stink seemed to have substance; she could feel it pick at the neck of her dress with cracked yellow fingertips.

D climbed the stairs to the first-floor gallery in slow, scraping, echoing steps, legs heavy from the day's sun. The sweat-stiff pieces of hair at her nape felt like scabs. She wished Robert had stayed, but she was also relieved he had gone—it was safer for him away from the museum and her neighbor.

On the gallery floor, D made her way toward the back door. The transition from the glare of the evening outdoors to the shade of the vast hall made her slightly faint. They'd had water from a tap at the Fields, but it had been warm and dusty-tasting, and she was still dehydrated. She yearned for a long cold drink from the pump in the garden.

"Good evening," D said to a woman in a gray union suit, who sat in a chair off behind the printing press exhibit, holding a dial. "You can tell everyone I won't be long. I just want some water."

Half a dozen strides more brought D to the door leading out to the garden, where she halted. She could not recall having noticed the woman in the suit before.

Δ

Auburn hair tied in a tight, high bun, the waxwork woman in the chair had straight posture, and her jaw was held taut, informing a focused, humorless expression. The gray union suit she wore was made of a thick fabric that felt incredibly smooth between D's thumb and forefinger. A belted holster cinched her waist and from the holster protruded a thick, rectangular pistol grip. On the breast of the suit was a label, stitched with a name: **Lieutenant Hart**. The woman looked to be about D's own age.

A narrow bed with plain brown blankets pulled smooth and snug, D thought, that was nearly all there would be to this neat, serious, bizarrely dressed young woman's chamber. The walls were bare of decoration and the woman's small case of clothes was pushed into the shadows beneath the bed. The only other thing was a night table, and the black pistol in its holster, laid upon it. Because, somehow, this woman was a soldier—a real soldier, a real lieutenant, not like her Bobby.

D removed the dial from the wax woman's hands.

It wasn't a dial, though; it was two dials, set into the face of a hexagonal plate. The plate was dark blue and as thick as a small book. The dial on the left was marked *HORIZ*, and the dial on the right was marked *VERT*. There were numbers inside the dials, as in a compass, and arrows buried at zero. In the center of the object was a window imprinted with what D recognized as a rifle target. Underneath the target was a small red button. In the middle of the button, drawn in white, was the museum's familiar shape: Δ.

Yes, the shape confirmed: the soldier was in the right place; she belonged to the museum.

Below the button was a compound word D didn't understand, *PAYLOAD*.

The plate felt hard and thin at the same time. D had never touched a material like it. It clicked when she tapped it with her fingernail.

On the floor at the woman's feet was a large green metal box with four small turbines sprouting from its sides. *UNMANNED COMBAT VEHICLE* read the white-painted words on the top of the green box.

D didn't know what to make of the female soldier, or of the two attendant objects, beyond a sense that the smaller one, despite its lack of a connecting wire, somehow controlled the larger one. More than that, she couldn't see how she'd missed the small exhibit—it was so close to the door to the garden through which she'd gone back and forth repeatedly to draw buckets of water and pick vegetables.

She felt certain the woman and her incomprehensible tools had not been there, but that was impossible because they were there now. And they weren't entirely incomprehensible, were they, these tools? The first floor was for *MACHINES AND THEIR OPERATORS*, and the machines that soldiers operated were weapons.

She stared at the controller object that she held in her hands. The button with the triangle—*PAYLOAD*—seemed to radiate with vile implication.

D abruptly dropped it into the wax woman's lap, as if it scalded.

She thought of the other button with a triangle symbol, the button on the box with the pictures. The fluffy cat on the armchair in the moving picture was the twin of the white cat she often saw in the wreckage in the vicinity of the Vestibule, the conjurer's closet. When the conjurer took women inside it, they came back out wearing each other's heads . . . other faces . . .

D breathed across her dry tongue and between her dry lips. After a drink of water, she could think this through.

There was a loud bang, the heavy front doors crashing open.

D felt the tension leave her body. It was over. She had been so afraid, and in a second or two she would be afraid again, but for that instant she felt a blessed and ghastly resignation. It had been inevitable, that her neighbor would come to visit.

"Hello! Is anyone here?" The heights of the gallery's ceiling doubled and tripled the voice. "This is Sergeant Van Goor, from the Provisional Authorities!" Boots scuffed on the steps.

D exhaled. It wasn't her time yet, after all.

"I'm looking for a maid named Dora! A pretty little patriot who's friends with Lieutenant Barnes!" The voice mockingly stretched the word "lieutenant" into five syllables: *loo-ooo-ooo-ten-ant*. "My goodness, Maid Dora, it's ripe outside! We should have someone take a look at the pipes!" His laugh boomed through the gallery.

She remembered that Robert had told her not to deal with Sergeant Van Goor. It hadn't made sense at the time, but it made enough sense now. The way he called her a pretty little patriot and the way he said *loo-ooo-ooo-ten-ant* felt wrong.

He sang out again, "I just need a word with you about a burglary case! It's a serious matter, but nothing for you to worry about, and nothing for Lieutenant"—*Loo-ooo-ooo-ten-ant*—"Barnes to worry about, I shouldn't think! So long as you're honest with me! You haven't done anything wrong, have you? Of course not!" He laughed some more. "Unless being a whore is wrong? Oh, dear, you may be in a bit of trouble after all. Ha-ha! But I'm sure we can find some way for you to make good, Maid Dora. Come on out and let's have a chat!"

Any doubt that the sergeant meant her harm vanished instantly.

A dumb, dazed plan came to her: grab the broom leaning against the wall, go beside the printing press, turn her back to the gallery's center aisle, make herself still, and pose as the wax maid that the previous curators had forgotten to include.

D cast off this doomed idea before panic could set in and force her to attempt it. She stole to the back door. Her skirts brushed against the soldier's chair. The controller she'd dropped slid from the soldier's lap and fell, striking the hard wood of the floor with a hollow, resounding clap.

"Maid Dora?" came the voice. "I think I hear you bustling about! No reason to clean up for me!"

At the far end of the gallery, through the hole of the middle gear, she saw the figure of the sergeant. He lifted his hand and wiggled his fingers hello.

She opened the door and bolted through.

△

The smell slammed into D, hitting her in the eyes, reaching into her open mouth with her inhalation, and grabbing her stomach. She retched and lurched toward the right side of the garden, toward the barrier of boxwoods that separated the museum plot from the Society's side lawn. The bucket that she'd left on the ground tangled her feet, and she stumbled, breaking through the trellis of tomato vines, splintering the wood, sprawling flat and feeling the warm tomatoes burst through her blouse.

She scrabbled to her feet, tore off her bonnet, and flung it in the direction of the stone wall that bordered the embassy. She ran to the boxwoods and began to eke and thread her way through the mazy, ropy limbs. Spiky branches snatched at her hair and apron and skirts, but she yanked herself forward, ripping fabric, tearing hair. The sound of the leaves rattling and the limbs banging had an awful hilarity to it, as if the bushes were cackling at her as she tried to claw her way through them.

D shoved herself through a last loop of branches on her hands and knees. She emerged into the ankle-high grass of the Society side lawn, pushing up to stand and moving dizzily for the broken wall of the burnt building. Blood was loud in her head, but from the other side of the boxwoods, she heard the jiggle of the doorknob and the door clacking open.

D caught herself against the charred wall and hurried alongside it in the direction of the street.

"Maid Dora, what's this about?" said the sergeant from the other side of the boxwoods. "Oh, isn't this a shame? You've gone and trampled your tomatoes. But which way did you go? I see your lovely bonnet over there, but . . ."

Three-quarters down the length of the building's wall, D heard him smashing through the hedge. At the corner of the ruin, she broke left and kept to the wall, hustling away from the museum, heading for the empty frame that had held the Society's front door. The squeak of her breath, like the highest key on some sick organ, made D furious. She ran faster.

Once through the empty doorway, she clambered onto one of the central mounds of rubble. It rose in uneven ridges and waves of broken brick and split timber. Ahead, on the small, jagged platform that was all that remained of the Society's second floor, was the white cat that she had seen before. It was calmly sharpening its claws on the Vestibule's doorframe, leaving pale gouges of raw wood in the charred surface, indifferent to D's plight.

"I know you're just having a joke on me, Maid Dora, I like a good joke as much as anyone, but there's nothing funny about thievery and whoring!" His voice was closer, coming around the museum-side wall. "It's rude to make a man run all over like this when he's trying to look after the public good."

The fragments shifted under D as she scrabbled upward. She reached, grabbed, and a handful of blackened papers crumbled into powder between her fingers. She slid down the mound and immediately pushed up and kept ascending. She wasn't going to let this chuckling pig kill her.

The blackened rectangle of the Vestibule stood on its island of floor a few yards to her right. D stopped climbing and sidestepped on a rim of piled wreckage, making for a valley sunken between sections of the mound. She ducked through the gap and scaled a loose ramp of scree to the bottom of the Vestibule's doorframe. The white cat's unreadable face peered down at her over the edge. D grabbed the section of jutting floor and hoisted herself up. She staggered, brushing past the cat, into the Vestibule's gaping black interior.

△

Pressed to the left wall of Simon the Gentle's Vestibule, she inched toward the rear corner, where she would be hardest to see from her pursuer's eight o'clock angle at the Society's gaping entryway. It was the obvious hiding place, though—the one semi-intact structure inside the collapsed building. Unless she was lucky, he would be coming, and he would find her, and when he did, she'd be trapped in it with him.

"Smart, throwing off your bonnet like that, but I do believe I heard you go through the brush!" The sergeant had entered the building shell; no obstacle dulled his voice now. "Don't be rude, Maid Dora! Come on down here! I'm not mad"—there was clinking, scraping, and a grunt, as he began to make his ascent of the rubble—"but I may get there if this game goes on too long!"

Conjurers' closets had false walls; how else to explain the illusions of disappearance? That was her one hope.

The words of the cheery stranger in the spangly gold vest who had conducted her through the Society fifteen years before recurred freshly to D: "The conjurer tells you an impossible tale and then gives you proof that it's true. . . . Like thievery, but what a conjurer steals is faith, and the man who made tricks on this stage was the most wonderful, wonderful criminal you can imagine." A "funny, funny man," she'd called him, and Ambrose had said, "Quite, quite," and they'd had to smother their laughter to keep from waking up Mother and Father. Only a few weeks later the men had wrapped her beautiful brother in his own bedsheets and taken him away in a wagon to be incinerated. She smoothed her palms over the wood as she moved along the wall. Dust ground softly under her shoes on the closet floor.

The depth of darkness in the Vestibule confused D. The evening light seemed to fizz around the edges of the doorframe, unable to enter, and past the threshold, it was inky night within, so thick that D could not see her hand, let alone the wall she touched.

"Do you think he's coming, your Lieutenant Barnes? He's not. I saw him walking away. Truth be told, I may have hung back and waited for him to walk away."

Her fingers found a raised shape with three sides—a triangle. She jabbed at it, but nothing gave. It wasn't a button, just a carving. Over slightly was another raised triangle, and another, and another. She pushed on them each in turn, and they were solid. Somehow her squeaking breath had found a higher key.

"But I'm sure he'll come around later, and won't that be an amusing surprise for him? See, I do like a good joke, but I'm picky about who gets to make it—"

A light, she needed a light to see which triangle was the button, the button that opened that secret door. D stuck her hand into the pocket of her apron to check for matches, and the fine tip of the tiny drill bit—△ **FOR TAKING SAMPLES FROM SMALL METEORITES** △—that she'd meant to polish stabbed into the flesh between her forefinger and her thumb. D bit her lip and yanked back her hand, the fresh blood spilling hot across her palm, while the breeze from the rear of the Vestibule stirred her torn skirts.

△

D came to the end of the long hall at the back of the Vestibule, and opened a door into a summer's day.

Purple wildflowers covered a series of three hills, each cresting higher than the one before. Clouds like sheared wool were stuck to the blue sky. There was ocean in the air, and a sugary, tattling breeze. She heard, faintly, a meow, a cat scratching at a door.

D glanced over her shoulder. The door she'd come through stood upright in the grass. *Scratch, scratch, scratch, meow.*

What was the story the believers told? There was a tree in the desert, and a black cat . . . and it scratched the tree like the white cat scratched the charred doorframe, and . . . that was how the wanderer found her way. . . .

D took a step to open the door, to let the cat in—or out?—but the breeze whispered through the hairs at the back of her neck and drew her gaze around.

A window hung in the air. D saw her reflection in the glass. It smeared, like paint, and she comprehended that in this place, she could see herself however she wished.

The smear collected into the image of the most beautiful woman she had ever seen, an apple-cheeked actress who had mugged on a theater poster that Nurse pointed out to her when D was a child. "That's Lorena Skye," Nurse had said. "With a name like that, how else could she look?" D saw herself smiling serenely as Lorena's gorgeous twin, but she could feel that she was still breathing hard, and she didn't want someone else's face.

The couple in the moving picture had worn blindfolds with painted eyes. D brushed at her face. She felt something—much lighter and thinner than a blindfold—tear away, and the world changed.

Where the three hills had sloped gently upward, the moons poured a sick and vibrant yellow over three towering columns—large, larger, and largest—and the shadows of the stones warped across a rocky plateau. A pass lit at intervals by illuminated globes led downward.

The window was revealed to be a guillotine. Below its blade was a wicker basket. Beside it, an ancient woman perched upon a stool. Her white hair draped to the ground and she stared at D with sleepy eyes. In her hand she held an oversized, shining needle threaded with a length of black string. Tattooed on her forehead was a dark-red triangle.

The Hard Worker

Look at this poor, shabby steer, Van Goor had thought, taking the measure of the towering, bearded man in the ragged shirt and pants who stood in front of his table by the stone tiger at the plaza in the noon light, holding a hat that was mostly holes pressed against his chest. "Lieutenant Barnes sent you?"

"That's the name he gave me, sir," the man said. "And he said you were the one to talk to about a job. I'm a hard worker, sir. I can do whatever you need, doesn't matter how dirty. I just want to be able to make my bread."

"You know he's not a real lieutenant?" Van Goor credited the young Volunteer for his balls, showing up that morning and requesting an entire building as a present to his favorite fuck, but he was no soldier, whatever they called him. "Those green armbands those university boys wear, those are just pieces of cloth." The sergeant tapped the rank insignia on his breast pocket. "This is the actual."

"Yes, sir." The filthy giant nodded. "I'm a hard worker, sir. I'll outwork anyone."

"So you say, but so far as I can tell, the only thing you're good at is making a lot of shade. What am I supposed to give you to do?"

"I'm a hard worker, sir." He smiled a little red smile, a bright vein amid the black tangle of his beard.

"That's three times you've said that."

The man blinked. He was a cow through and through. That was fine, though. Every army required a large complement of cows.

Van Goor grunted and picked up a sheaf of documents, requests for men at various positions. He flipped through them, glancing occasionally at the looming figure, pondering his considerable magnitude. He asked the man if he had his letters, expecting him to say no. But the man said yes.

He removed a square of paper from his pocket, unfolded it, and passed it to Van Goor. "Here's a poem I wrote."

The sergeant took it. The title at the top was "Soul of the Souls." *You are the soul of the souls now, my darling, the heart of all the hearts, my darling . . .* it began.

Van Goor was favorably impressed. "Handsome." The fellow might look like a great stack of shit, but those were real words. A university boy like Barnes couldn't have made it nicer. The bottom of the paper was signed *Anthony*.

"All right, Anthony, here's what we'll do with you. . . ." The sergeant returned the paper and instructed him to go to the outfitters for a uniform, and after that to proceed to an address on Legate Avenue, a vacated embassy, and set himself up to take notes.

Van Goor would be sending low-level servants and retainers of the previous regime for his examination; they had professionals to interrogate captured prisoners, but they needed someone to interview these minor associates of the Crown and they didn't need any more crowds milling around in the plaza. This particular embassy he was being assigned to belonged to a country that the Provisional Government didn't plan on inviting back anytime soon, so he could make himself comfortable.

"First, you take their names," Van Goor said. "Then you have a little talk. You say sternly, 'Tell me everything you know about the greedies you worked for, plus anything else I might find interesting—all of it.' And you write down what they say. When that's finished, you put them on their way and send a report back on your conclusions. You think you can manage that?"

He said he could, this Anthony. He could give them a little talk. He was a hard worker.

That was three weeks ago.

△

It was night when Van Goor gave up his search. He'd looked for over an hour in the ruin. The maid wasn't there—not behind any of the piles of rubble, not in the burnt closet, not hiding under a layer of ash. He snatched a lump of melted brick and threw it at a white cat perched on the jutting fragment of a second floor, and screamed his frustration. The lump of brick sailed past the cat, disappearing into the dark with a dull thud. For its part, the cat did not even move, just sat idly, regarding him with its shiny blue eyes. The way it stared at him, Van Goor had half an idea that the whore had somehow transformed herself, but that was peasant nonsense. He told the animal it wasn't worth the bullet and stormed out through the empty doorway.

Before coming out into the small garden behind the museum he'd been certain he heard her breaking through the hedge, but the sergeant wondered now about the bonnet on the ground. It had been near the wall that set off the courtyard on the opposite side, which belonged to one of the former embassies on Legate.

Rather than squirt his way back through the foliage again like a fucking garter snake, Van Goor walked through the high grass in front of the ruins to the street and directed himself toward the corner of Little Heritage and Legate. If the maid wasn't in the former embassy with the courtyard, he could use the roto there and call the switchboard at the Magistrates' Court to send for reinforcements. With a half dozen men and a couple of dogs, they'd search the whole block, and find her before dawn.

Van Goor thought out his next steps: he'd take the maid around a corner for questioning; she'd make a move for his weapon, and he'd have to shoot her to protect himself. While it was less satisfying than what he'd planned, it amounted to the same thing, a valuable lesson for the "lieutenant": if you are a rude prick, someone may lose their temper and kill your whore. And who knew? If Barnes absorbed the lesson, perhaps they could leave the matter there.

The fire of his outrage had quickly consumed what energy he had in reserve, leaving him merely surly. He had been tired before, and he was more tired now; not even sure, in retrospect, if he would have been able to give the bitch the kind of treatment he'd intended. While the Lieutenant Barneses of the world fluttered around, men with real responsibilities got no rest; as soon as he dealt with the maid, he needed to be on to the next task. In the morning he was scheduled to go downtown and attend to the thief who had taken this fool tram driver's stupid fucking hat, and as he was at it, clean out all the rats in the black-market rathole in the Lees where said thief apparently lurked.

To the sergeant's way of thinking, it was striking a harder line than was necessary or strictly prudent, with people becoming restless about the blockade that was keeping them out of work and creating shortages—but Crossley was clear he wanted an example made.

"They say they want constables to keep the peace. We'll show them that we can do that. We'll show them how we pay out to ones that take advantage," the general had explained to Van Goor about the order, and added that he was also sending along a couple of reporters to write up the raid for the press, so the news was spread far and wide.

Crossley was a cool one, fish-cool. You couldn't imagine him breathing hard. He was forever looking at his special paper. He kept it in his pocket and checked on it the way that some men checked their watches. Van Goor had been close behind him once when he'd taken it out and he'd got a look at the general's special paper. There was no proper writing on it that Van Goor could recognize, just small drawings of serpents and clocks and triangles, all done in red ink. What was that about? Some kind of lucky charm? Some kind of code? Not that it made Van Goor doubt him, it was just odd.

Van Goor turned right at the corner of Legate. He unbuckled his pistol from its holster in preparation for shooting the lock off the abandoned embassy.

The putrid air around the place was like nothing that Van Goor had ever breathed, meaty and shitty and rotten and acidic. It stung his tears from his eyes. All he could compare it to was the smell of a battlefield, but none of the battlefields Van Goor had been on—and he'd been on several—had ever been so potent.

At the bottom of the embassy steps, Van Goor pulled up short at the sight of the white numbers fastened to the lintel, **76**.

Hold on a moment . . . he knew this address! He'd written it down two dozen times, at least, for various men and women who'd come to his table at the plaza: **76 Legate Avenue**. This was where he'd set up that big lout—Anthony, his name was—to take down information from the Crown's low-level sorts who turned up.

That would certainly make things easier. Anthony could help him look for the woman. Van Goor holstered his pistol.

He climbed the steps and rapped on the lacquered door.

While he waited, Van Goor breathed through his teeth and searched his memory of Anthony. It occurred to him that even as he had been regularly sending on minor officials and staff of the former government for interviews, he had heard nothing in return from Anthony, received no reports.

The door opened, and a gush of air spilled out that was so ripe it made Van Goor gasp and recoil.

Anthony stood barefoot, dressed only in his uniform pants; the pelt of his chest hair glistened with damp. Van Goor supposed the knocking had awakened him from his sleep—too fucking bad.

"Sergeant?"

Van Goor shouldered past the oaf into a small sitting room. "I'm looking for a woman. She's been squatting in the building behind you." The sitting room was illuminated by a single bulb in a sconce, which did little more than render the shapes of a few armchairs, a low table, a hearth, an escritoire, and the door to the next room. "She's a saboteur, very dangerous. I came to bring her in for questioning and she ran. It's possible she came through the back. Have you seen her?"

"No," Anthony said. "I was just there, tidying up. She didn't come through the back, sir."

"You're sure?"

"Yes, sir," Anthony said. "How about some sweet coffee, sir?"

"Where's your roto? What's going on around here? It smells like twelve hundred shits." Van Goor's gaze lit on the escritoire in the corner, situated under a painting of what in the dimness he could only make out as a bird. On the escritoire was a roto.

Van Goor went to it, picked up the mug, and listened. The thick stench made him cough, and he covered his mouth with his sleeve and spoke through the fabric. "We're going to get some men and dogs and find her. Hopefully she'll turn over whoever she's been scheming with in exchange for leniency. I think if I can have a word with her alone I can convince her. What is that smell, man? It's fucking awful."

"How about some sweet coffee, sir?" Anthony asked again.

Van Goor dropped his arm and looked at Anthony, who had shut the front door and moved into the center of the room. His long arms dangled at his sides, and his sweaty ape chest shone. "No, I don't want sweet coffee! I may need a fucking bucket, though. Keep the door open so the air can circulate! Are you stupid? Has the sewer overflowed somewhere? Why haven't you had someone come to fix it? Even if they couldn't fix it right away, they could put some lime down and dull the reek. How can you bear this, can't you smell?"

"You get so you stop noticing," the man said, and asked, "Lime?" in a musing tone.

"Yes, lime! Because it smells like a slaughterhouse in August!" In his memory, the man had seemed able enough—he'd written that impressive poem about the souls—but it was apparent that Van Goor had been mistaken. He was as dumb as a rock. It was enraging. "What have you been doing? Have you been interviewing the people I sent, or do you just stare at them until they go away? Where are the reports you should've sent?"

"Let me get you some sweet coffee, sir," the man said.

Van Goor waved a dismissive arm. It was hopeless. He couldn't talk to the imbecile, pay attention to the roto, and concentrate on not choking on the fumes all at the same time.

There was still no sound from the mug. He bent to peer along the wire running from the back of the roto into the darkness behind the escritoire. Van Goor lifted the wire and found it ended in a clean cut.

△

For security reasons, Anthony—though that was not his name—had used a pair of garden shears to snip it. A young nurse who had worked for the family of a magistrate had surprised him by shaking off the dose in her coffee and going for the roto. The man who was not actually named Anthony had stopped her easily, but it had been a warning that he'd heeded, and he'd cut the wire.

Afterward he'd put her through a particularly thorough interview, during which the nurse had told him everything, every secret she'd ever kept, every hope she'd ever harbored.

"And do you believe that she loved you too?" he'd asked her near the end. They'd long since moved past her knowledge of the magistrate's affairs—in fact, she'd only ever even met him once; he wasn't involved with the younger children, hadn't been able to tell the twins apart—and had been speaking about her deeper self for quite some time. It was to the matter of an affair she'd had with another member of the house staff, a cook, that they had now turned. "Be truthful, ma'am."

The nurse's remaining eyelid had fluttered and she exhaled in a thin whistle. "No . . . I don't believe so. . . ."

She seemed honest, but still, people could be inconstant. If you wanted to get to the bottom of matters, you couldn't just take their word. "You understand, ma'am, that it's quite possible that eventually she'll find herself where you are now, and I'll be able to check with her?"

The nurse's lips had turned up in a tiny smile. "Yes," she said. "Oh, yes . . . I hope so. . . ."

The-man-who-was-not-Anthony hoped so too.

The-man-who-was-not-Anthony had always felt apart. It was inter-esting, getting to know people. They were starting to make sense to him. They were more like him than he'd thought.

Sergeant Van Goor had straightened from the escritoire, and he was holding the limp wire in one hand. He was a small, well-built man with a cranked nose and a swollen sneer. He reminded the-man-who-was-not-Anthony of a fighting dog.

"Why didn't you say it was cut, you fucking fool? This wild bitch is running around and you're wasting my time! Was it like this?"

"Sir—" he began.

"Did you do this, you fucking hairy idiot? Why?" The sergeant cast aside the wire. "What have you been doing here? Is this stench something you've done? Where are my reports?" He stepped forward and slapped his hand into the damp nest of the-man-who-was-not-Anthony's chest hair.

The larger man stared down at the smaller one, while the smaller one stared at his hand, pressed into the curls that the light of the sconce now showed him were soaked in blood.

Van Goor took one backward step, but the-man-who-was-not-Anthony drew the long pliers from the back of his belt and whipped them into the sergeant's left temple. The blow sent the smaller man tumbling into a chair that collapsed under his weight. The sergeant was on his knees a moment later, crawling blind and headfirst right into the wall, *thud*. He flopped sideways and the-man-who-was-not-Anthony saw that the pliers had opened the sergeant's scalp to the bone; the wound looked like a chunk of spidered white tile. Van Goor twisted onto his back. He wore a drunken expression, eyes unfocused, the tip of his tongue sticking from the corner of his mouth. But his right hand had found the butt of the gun at his hip and ripped it free of the holster. The-man-who-was-not-Anthony swung the pliers down again, breaking three of Van Goor's fingers and shattering the gun butt too. The sergeant screamed and reached up with his good left hand and grabbed the-man-who-was-not-Anthony's crotch and squeezed. The-man-who-was-not-Anthony gasped and swung the pliers once more, snapping Van Goor's left forearm into a V, and loosening the hold.

The-man-who-was-not-Anthony staggered and caught himself against the wall. He took one breath and vomited onto the embassy's rug. It had been a long time since someone had hurt him. He didn't mind it. Everything seemed brighter.

On the floor, Van Goor hyperventilated. His ruined limbs were splayed to either side. Somehow a shard of the wooden pistol butt had ended up stuck to the blood and sweat on the sergeant's forehead.

". . . Why?" he asked.

"Because I need to know what you know," the other man said, taking slow breaths, feeling the shard of ice that connected his testicles to his stomach swell and subside. "I can't be done with you until you've told me everything."

And he was as good as his word, though it was a long while before they finished. By the time that Van Goor had told all he knew—of the uncertain Provisional Government, of the stalemate on the Great Highway, of the anxiety of the populace, of the legend of the Morgue Ship that sailed sea and land and in-between, of the young maid with the museum and her lover the lieutenant, of where to obtain large quantities of lime— and by the time he had made a full account of all his many offenses—the violations and the cruelties, the indecencies and the depredations—it was a new morning. Only then did his interlocuter very politely cut the sergeant's throat.

PART III

THE CURATOR

The Charmer was sailing away with doomed souls and the capacity of his vessel was without limit.

Stray Cat

There was a game her brother invented, called Stray Cat. In this game, you waited in a dark place—behind a door, say—and when either Mother or Father or Nurse passed by, you leaped out and pawed at their legs. If they screamed, you were an excellent stray cat.

△

Someone's low-class maid had seen Ambrose in the Lees one afternoon. He denied it, but Mother didn't believe him. Father didn't care. D overheard her parents sniping at each other about it. "So what if he went once? Boys roam around," he said.

Father was a banker. He preferred not to be bothered. The only time he'd ever played with D was a game he made up called Quick Girl.

In Quick Girl, she fetched the newspaper from the front table, gave it to him, and said, "Here you are, sir," and Father pressed his thumb into her open palm, hard, as if he meant to leave an imprint, and said, "There's a good girl, here's your penny." This had been sort of amusing when he first taught it to her, but that was the whole game. Once he had the paper, she was instructed to go away and be a quiet proper girl.

"Let me deliver the paper to someone else now, Father," she proposed once.

"Not unless you give me back my penny," he replied, chuckling behind his upraised paper.

Mother was, in many ways, even more indifferent. She was generally occupied with appointments—shopping, lunches, concerts. Some days D only saw her at bedtime, when she'd give D a light kiss after Nurse tucked her into bed. "There's a girl, you're all set for your dreams now," she'd pronounce and quickly stride out into the hall and shut D's door, leaving a trace of lavender perfume in the dark room.

The rumor about Ambrose disordered Mother, though. It was like the time she'd discerned a wrinkle in the dining room wallpaper. She hadn't been able to eat, her eye kept darting to it. Father finally ordered the serving maid to stand in front of it so she could manage to take a few bites, and a man came in first thing the next morning to redo the paper.

"What was Ambrose doing down there?" She jerked the hairbrush through a snarl in D's hair. For the first time D could recall, Mother had sent Nurse out after bath and come in to attend to her daughter herself.

"He didn't go down there," D said. She actually had a hunch that he probably *had* gone to the Lees—her brother certainly went to the Society in the afternoons, so he might go other places as well—but he hadn't told her so. She hoped that, if she was loyal and denied it, Ambrose would tell her in the future.

"Boys have bad ideas sometimes," Mother said.

Girls had bad ideas too. D had imagined what it was like when her brother beat the mean boys with the ash shovel, and it had not made her feel even a little sad. In fact, it had made her happy. Mother wouldn't understand that. She wanted D to be smooth like wallpaper.

"And if you follow through on a bad idea," Mother continued, "and do something bad, it's like a stain. Some stains come out, but most don't. The Lees are full of people that had bad ideas and got stained. That's why they have to live down there in all their filth." Mother dragged the brush, and D thought she could feel her scalp lifting free of her skull, but she bit her lip and held still. "No one wants a girl with a stain, I can tell you that, Dora."

"Can you see it? The stain?"

"Sometimes," Mother said, voice dropping to a whisper. "But it doesn't look like a stain. It looks like bumps. It makes you sick and everyone can see it."

△

Ambrose was annoyed. D had reported everything to him about Mother's suspicions. It was night and the rest of the house was asleep.

"She thinks I'm going to catch the Pox." He sat on the edge of her bed.

"You do go to the Lees, don't you!"

"My travels take me all over the city."

"Are you going to catch the Pox?"

"No."

"What is the Pox, Ambrose?"

"Just another thing that can kill you. You're better off worrying about being stabbed by a thief or catching cholera."

D knew about cholera. *Glove on the door, walk on some more; taste a dirty drip, you'll take a sailing trip.*

"Most people are gullible," Ambrose said. "It's a survival instinct. Because they aren't strong like we're strong. The thing Mother can't see is that for actually wanting to know, she's one of the stupidest ones, because she's not equipped to know the full truth."

"What about me?" she asked. "Am I equipped to know the full truth?"

It was too dark to see the rabbit grin, but it was in his voice. "For now, maybe just half the truth. There are incredible forces out there, D. Forces that if we could learn to control them, would give us power over everything. Power to stop the wars, power to make enough for everyone. Power to see into the future and avoid whatever pitfalls may await us. Power over death even. Power to save the world. Power to leave this world altogether. I can't say any more. When you're older."

After he said sweet dreams and left, she worried that Ambrose would steal away in the night, and go to live with his friends at the Society for Psykical Research, and read books beneath the giant mobile of the universe and eat his meals beside the great fireplace, and do whatever it was you did when you were trying to learn to control the incredible forces that could save the world—and he would forget about her. D would have to follow him. What scared her, though, was that she might go up the walk to the neat building of cheery red brick and knock on the red door with the silver triangle, and this time no one would come to let her in. That she'd be shut out. But they had to let her in. Wherever he went, she needed to be allowed to go; without her brother, she didn't even have a name.

△

A few days later Ambrose asked if she wanted to come with him on an errand. She did; of course she did.

There was no one to know. Mother was out shopping and Father was at work. Nurse had taken too much medicine and been sick and, just as the funny, funny man who talked to D at the Society for Psykical Research had suggested, Ambrose had given her more medicine. This made Nurse feel better, but she had lain down for a nap and fallen heavily asleep.

They rode the tram to the end, to a stop near the South Fair Bridge. As they traveled farther down the line, the passengers who wore nicer clothes, like their own, got off, and passengers in older, less nice clothes got on. The air that streamed through the open windows became smoky and fishy. D rocked from side to side with the braking and shifting of the tram in her seat on the bench beside Ambrose. The women on the tram held wicker bags, and muddy shoe tips protruded from beneath their muddy skirt hems. An unshaven man with a chapped, blood-crusted lip and a hat with a broken eagle feather dangling from the band winked at D. A trail of red-white blisters started at the corner of his eye and hooked up around his eyebrow. She wanted to stare, but she pulled her gaze away to the passing scenes: a bushy striped cat perched on a windowsill, a man with a shovel spreading dirt, a black cat slinking along the ledge of a roof, a woman beating a rug, a white-bibbed cat curled up in front of a door with a black glove under the knocker—goodness, there were so many pretty cats in this part of town, no one had told her.

At the same time, the feeling of the stranger's wink was like a fly had landed on D's bare arm and there was no way to brush it off. She sensed that he was still watching her.

When they got off the tram, the broken-feather man followed them. He called in a croaky voice, "You there, young scholar, you taking her to sell to someone?"

Ambrose grabbed D's elbow, guiding her farther away.

"Just funning!" the man cried. "I fought alongside Gildersleeve, you know. Penny for an old soldier?"

D's brother leaned close and whispered, "Ignore that rummy. He'll be dead of the Pox in a month or two.

"Now, listen: you've probably wondered if I did something to those boys who were rude that time when I went back out with the ash shovel. I think you've probably decided that I did."

"Yes."

"Good. So you know you're safe with me and you don't have to be afraid."

She was afraid anyway, but she nodded. If she admitted she was afraid, he wouldn't ask her to come next time, and he might go to live at the Society and leave her behind forever.

They went downhill for several blocks and continued into a neighborhood of tightly packed buildings where the street was just a four-wide path of planks. D could tell that they were close to the level of the river; below the planks was scummy brown water that lapped the foundations. Black mold scorched the doors as high as the knobs. The buildings themselves were clapboard, and all shrugged noticeably to the left, as if they were trying to get away from something.

There were, above all, dozens and dozens of cats. They peered from behind windows, from the ledges of roofs, from the sparse branches of the few sun-starved trees, from the tops of jumbled fences, from the stoops, from the irregular gaps between buildings, from perches on broken barrels or broken crates. D sensed more of them—hundreds and hundreds, so many more than she'd seen from the tram—moving through the crooked corridors and rooms of the leaning buildings, warm and quiet and aware.

"They pray to them in these places, the ones that don't know any better," Ambrose said softly, noticing her looking around at the animals. There was a note of disdain in his voice and she sensed that he was reciting something he'd learned, probably from his friends at the Society. She remembered that the cheery man had disapproved of the conjurer's love for the fancy cat that lived in the hotel. "That's why there are so many."

D wanted to ask what was wrong with that—she found the cats so intriguing; it would be interesting just to follow them for a while, to see what they did, where they went; you could tell they had secrets that would be worth knowing—but she had to hurry to keep up with Ambrose's quickening pace as they went deeper into the swampy neighborhood. He ignored the frowns of the other pedestrians, slack-mouthed men in rumpled jackets and tired-faced women in mended dresses.

At a nondescript alleyway he made an abrupt left, taking them along an off-shooting plank pathway. A few steps brought them to a building's side door.

They went inside and ascended a dim stairway. Sawdust squeaked under their steps and the only light came from holes in the exterior walls. Somewhere a woman was singing to a crying baby and a man was hacking. It smelled like sick. D pressed her hand over her nose.

"Come on," Ambrose said.

A woman in a kerchief passed them on her way down. In her hands she carried a wet burlap package tied with twine. D caught a whiff of raw meat. The woman's steps were hurried and her heels kicked up sawdust that flared gold in the small beams that shot through the holes in the walls.

On the second-floor landing there was a small table and some melted-down candles. In the murk, D could make out pieces of broken pottery. She picked up a shard. It was painted with part of a cat's face, a blade of pupil and a yellow eye.

"Don't touch things here, D." Ambrose drew her onward. "We can't linger."

The smell thickened with every riser they climbed. There was a musty, pissy animal fragrance underneath the sick smell.

At the third-floor hallway, they stopped. At the far end of the hall a seated man was silhouetted against a small window. Ambrose approached and D followed. The man's chair was outside the last door, and he was smoking a cigarette and using a serrated knife to shave an enormous corn on the heel of his bare foot.

"Elgin," Ambrose said.

"Hm." The man didn't look up from his task.

They silently observed as the knife blade edged beneath the skin, the metal visible through the translucent uppermost layer of flesh. The corn was the yellow of a lemon rind. Ash dribbled from the cigarette onto the bloodstained apron that covered the man's lap. He breathed through his broad, flat nose.

"It hurts no matter what, but if you're careful, you won't bleed." The corn slowly opened into a flap the size of a dollar coin.

And D saw it, that Ambrose was going to sell her to this terrible man. She pressed her lips down on the scream that wanted to come out. She would be quiet. If that was what he wanted, she would prove to her brother that she could be trusted.

When there was just a little hinge left connecting the skin to the heel, the man sawed it off, and flicked the piece onto the floor.

He sniffed, cocked an unhappy look at them. His skin was pitted, like soft soil that had been drilled by a minute's hard rain, then let to dry. There were red circles under his eyes and red webs in his eyes and yellow snot clinging to one of his nostrils. He smelled like Nurse's medicine, and like vomit.

"You again," he said to Ambrose. "Errand boy." He spoke, in spite of all evidence, as if Ambrose were the disgusting one. D pressed herself against her brother's hip.

"I'm here for the order." Ambrose brought a roll of folded bills from his school jacket and held it up. He wasn't selling anyone or anything. He was buying. "You have them? And they're all clean?"

The butcher Elgin stabbed his knife in the floor and snatched the money. "Sure, they're clean. Spent two days boiling the whole mess.

Almost burned off my fingers for you and your friends. Should think they're clean." He yanked his knife out of the floorboard, stood to go into his room. "I hope you know who you're in bed with, boy," he said, and opened the door and went in, shutting it softly behind him.

Δ

After three stops they got off the tram to switch to a different line. Ambrose carried the sack the butcher had brought out and given him, and the contents clattered as he walked down the tram steps into the small station. The sound was like a basket of knitting needles to D's ears, clacking and sliding against one another, but he said, no, it wasn't knitting needles. D guessed kindling, then croquet balls, then dried apples, then pencils. Ambrose seemed amused initially, telling her that she was "fabulously wrong," and "impressively wrong," and "beautifully incorrect," but a melancholy set came over his jaw, and he said he was tired of the game. She noticed that he held the bag away from himself as they waited at the stop for the next tram.

"Are you all right, Ambrose?" she asked.

"Oh," he said, "it's just that sometimes important tasks can be unpleasant. You know it's for something higher, but you feel badly about what you've had to do."

"Getting that bag for your friends, you mean?"

"That's right."

"You should never feel badly about anything you have to do, Ambrose. You're good."

Her brother smiled his shaded smile at her, but it seemed halfhearted. "You're sweet."

D was suddenly desperate to cheer him. "No, I'm not. I'm going to tell on you. I'm going to tell Mother that you went to the Lees to meet your friend with the nice, beautiful feet."

"You again." Ambrose said this in a deep voice like the butcher's and made a face at her.

"Us!" she shot back at him. "I helped!"

"My friend with the nice, beautiful feet." He snorted, and shook his head.

She laughed and so did he. Ambrose put down the sack and threw his arm around her shoulders and they rocked back and forth.

"I like you best," he said. "You're the good one."

D's laugh fell apart into tears. She pushed her face into her brother's stomach, between the flaps of his jacket into the starched cotton of his shirt. She was eight years old and the rest of her life stretched out like all the tram tracks in the world nailed together. Without him, she'd be alone. "I don't care what's in that stupid bag, Ambrose. I don't care and I'll never tell on you, but just promise you won't ever leave me."

"I promise," he said, gently returning her embrace, "so long as you do too."

△

After they handed the sack to the servant who answered the door at the Society, Ambrose brought D out on the North Fair Bridge and taught her a game called Dribs and Drabs. It was simple: you dropped rocks into the river and tried to hit the trash. When D hit a tin can, Ambrose tipped his hat to her. "Three for the young lady," he said.

D curtsied. She felt better above the water, far away from the half-sunken neighborhood in the Lees. Sunshine sparked off the can as it bobbed off down the Fair.

A boy who'd been watching them said it was wrong. "That's five, fella. Gotta be. Look at the size. That's hot shooting, floater as small as that. Come on, now, don't be cheap." The boy had a terrible ruined ear; it was scarred and clenched like a tiny fist.

"You heard the gentleman, D. It's five."

The boy played a round with them and won by bombing a rock onto the deck of a passing barge.

"That's so simple it oughta *cost* you a point!" a sailor on the barge's deck yelled merrily from below and showed the boy a middle finger, to which the boy replied with two middle fingers.

Ambrose called it a win, but the boy shook his head and refused to accept a penny. "Nah. Just fun now, but I'll sell you some oysters. Fresh and clean." He produced a small hemp bag of oysters and a packet of salt.

"Hungry as I am," Ambrose said, "I'd rather not die."

"I don't blame you. But these aren't Fair oysters, these are from way out. Look how big they are."

D's brother looked into the bag, shook the oysters around. "They are big," he said, and paid him a penny for the food.

While D's brother broke open an oyster and salted the meat, the boy scratched the bare skin above his dead ear. "But tell me, fella, I'm thinking I've seen you go to Elgin's, ain't I?"

D had been about to ask for an oyster, but now her knees went hollow and any thought of eating left her.

As if to demonstrate that the question was of no pressing importance, her brother raised his oyster and tipped it to his lips, letting it slide into his mouth and down his throat. "It'd be quite a trick if I could tell you what you're thinking."

"I'm not about to tell you your business," the boy said. "Probably I didn't see you. But I'm only going to tell you, fella, I wouldn't go eating any of that man's cuts if I could help it. What he calls pig, you and I would call it something different, if you catch my meaning." The boy tugged his dead ear twice and added, quietly from the corner of his mouth, "Listen, fella, it's no accident that's the only building in the Lees where you won't find a single cat."

△

On the walk home from the North Fair, Ambrose seemed moody and lost in himself, worried even. He twisted and untwisted the neck of the hemp bag with the remaining oysters. Twice he asked D if she didn't want an oyster, forgetting that she'd already declined.

The next morning D's brother was too fevered to leave bed. In the afternoon the doctor visited, declared it was cholera, and ordered them to boil all the water they drank until a chemist had tested it. Probably he'd picked up the sickness elsewhere, taken a dirty glass of water that looked clean, you never saw it in good neighborhoods like this that were away from the river, but they would want to be sure.

Ambrose spoke ramblingly of the moons. "The sun stops at the door, but the moons are twice as bright when you get around to the opposite side!" For a while, he insisted that some invisible person return his cap, although it was hanging from the post of his bed. "It's part of my school uniform, you cretin! Do I need to go get my ash shovel?"

He moaned, crying for his mother, for his father, for his sister, where was his good little sister? Ambrose couldn't seem to see them, and they couldn't go to him.

Despite the doctor's saying that it was all right to be near him and hold his hand, that it was reasonably agreed upon now that you couldn't catch cholera from another person like that, D's parents ordered Nurse to draw a line at the edge of the room, well beyond Ambrose's reach, past which no one was allowed to cross. "I'm here," D said, "I'm here," even as his eyes slid blindly over his family on the other side of the chalked line. Mother held D's shoulder so tight the girl knew it would leave a bruise. "There's nothing we can do," Mother said. "It's up to him. We can only pray for his strength."

Nurse brought chairs from the sitting room for D's parents and placed them behind the chalk. In his delirium, Ambrose scratched the air, and giggled about cats' paws. "Move your paw with my paw!" He sobbed. "It's not right, it's not right—they hurt too, they hurt, they hurt—how can it be right to do that to them? What are all the bones for?" He slept for periods of an hour or two, before convulsing awake.

During the second day, Ambrose announced that he was waiting for someone. "He's meeting me by these rocks." Drool trickled from the corners of his mouth. "You can see my mark, the triangle. It's tattooed behind my knee." His eyes had turned pink and his face had turned gray. "Yes, the president," he said, as if it ought to be obvious. "Who else?"

Despite the ventilation of the open window, the smell of Ambrose's evacuations became oppressive.

D's father lit a cigarette and waved at the smoke to spread it around. "Come on, boy," he said between his teeth, leaning forward in his chair. "Let go or pull yourself through."

D looked at Father. He returned the gaze with a raised eyebrow. "Hm?"

When she did not reply, he made his own interpretation. Father flapped his hand through the smoke, brushing it toward her. "Breathe that, see if it helps."

"What do you say, darling, let's take you away for a little rest." Nurse plucked D's sleeve. But instead, D slumped lower on the floor, her knees against the chalk.

"Back's tired, long day, ready for cold milk," Ambrose whispered. "Cold milk for everyone. Everything for everyone. No more suffering." They used a pole to push a bucket of water with a cup floating in it up to the bedside, but he didn't reach for it.

"Yes, I see you," D's brother said, and he sounded suddenly astonished. "Your . . . face," and his last exhalation whistled through the gap between his two front teeth.

△

After she watched through the green glass and saw the men leave with Ambrose's body, D went upstairs and eavesdropped outside the drawing room with her hand resting on the brass doorknob.

"I thought he was stronger than that," she heard Father say.

"I thought he was smarter than that," Mother replied. "I can't believe he brought it into our house."

He asked if she wanted a cigarette and she said yes. A match snapped. D smelled the sweet fragrance of Father's tobacco.

"Do you want to have another?" Father asked.

Mother laughed nastily. "What a question."

They talked about urns: nothing gaudy. They talked about friends with dead children. They talked about supper. They weren't hungry, but they needed to eat. It wouldn't do any good, not eating.

"Maybe we could try, Eddie," Mother said. "I know you want there to be a boy." Her tone had become weary. "Maybe in the spring we could try again." Father gave a solemn grunt. "But it's a sad day, isn't it," he said. Mother said she needed a drink. Father said, "Make it two."

Mother opened the door, and D leaped in front of her, hissing, hands clenched into claws.

Mother gasped, and slapped D, who staggered back against the wall.

"He wasn't stupid, he was saving the world," D said. "He told me. He was helping his friends save the world. He might not even be dead. He might just have gone to another world. He could come back for me."

Mother stared at her with an expression of disgusted astonishment, and slammed the door shut.

"I thought you were going to get us drinks," came Father's voice, muffled by the wood.

In D's bedroom, Nurse was asleep in the rocker. Her bonnet was askew and her soft cheeks twitched, and her eyes rolled beneath the lids.

D crouched at the windowsill and gazed out. The section of cobbles below was where the wagon had parked before taking Ambrose away. A few yards farther on was a broken spot filled with dirty water. The pillow lay half in and half out of the puddle.

Lorena Skye, Aboard
the Morgue Ship

"Where are we going?" she asked.

At the rail beside Lorena was the man she'd been told was the first mate. He had a slack face and ancient, quilted skin.

"We mean to go home," he said.

Stars Lorena did not recognize cast their reflections on the surface of the black sea. Mildly warm air tickled against her cheeks.

"What about our current whereabouts? Are we lost?" She wasn't afraid if they were. She was already dead, and death had not only been painless, but downright interesting. Lorena had just crawled through the canvas. Who knew? Honestly, if someone had told her, she'd have done it sooner.

"No, it's just over there." He gestured vaguely at the darkness. "But we can't land without a dock."

"I don't see anything, but I'll take your word for it, Mr. . . . ?"

"Zanes."

"Mr. Zanes. I'm Lorena Skye. You can call me Lorena or Ms. Skye, whichever you like. It was kind of you to invite me aboard. I hope you won't take offense, but why did you?"

Lorena had made the acquaintance of many of the other passengers. There were several household workers on the ship, some lower-level government employees, and even a man who made his living by caring for dogs, but so far as she could tell, no other veterans of the theater.

"We pick up anyone that's been cheated. Ever since we set sail, we've done that."

"Cheated of what, my dear?"

"Their rightful portion in life."

"Can you be more specific?"

The first mate gazed steadily into the starry darkness. "We are crewed mostly by the murdered, but we also welcome aboard the luckless and the ill-treated."

Ah, Lorena thought, that made sense. She certainly checked box three.

"The next phase can't begin unless we land," Zanes said.

"And what will that be? The next phase, when we land?"

"*If* we land," he said. "Captain makes no guarantees. Says we'll need luck. It takes blood. Blood and a door. Blood is the toll and blood is the key."

Mr. Zanes reminded her of certain pessimistic stagehands she had known. Men who made no promises, and subsisted on tobacco and vexation, but supposed they might possibly be able to rig a smoke pot or figure out a way to add some hinges to the backdrop, and inevitably did.

"Well, I'm sure it will work out," she said. "Presuming we do land, what happens?"

"We'll have our revenge."

"On whom?"

"The oppressors, the wicked, the greedy. Any that would harm a cat."

Lorena could find no argument with this choice of enemies. Not even oppressive, wicked, greedy people liked other oppressive, wicked, greedy people. Down with them all! And only monsters would harm a cat.

"Splendid," she said.

He dug at his eyelid. She asked him if it hurt. Zanes shrugged. Lorena asked him if he liked shows.

"I do not."

"You just haven't seen the right one yet," Lorena assured him.

She asked him what he thought of the captain. "A hard man," Zanes said.

"We wouldn't want a soft one," Lorena said.

She glanced to the wheelhouse. The captain was visible through the warped window, frowning, his four or five hairs plastered to his otherwise bare skull, hands gripping the ship's wheel. They said he'd been in the pottery business. Not an obvious transition, pottery to seagoing, but he looked exactly right at the ship's wheel, ready to face down any storm or wave. Lorena thought she'd never seen a more determined-seeming man.

△

Before the night the cat had come onto the Morgue Ship and awakened Joven, sticking its claws into his bare and bloodless chest, his soul had been stranded in a muddy corridor. The mud had been as high as his ankles. The corridor had been plain, dimly lit, and long—but he had not cared about that. Joven had not tried to find his way out. Instead, he stayed put, feverishly compelled to make one solid thing.

But no matter how he squeezed the globs between his palms, the stuff dripped through his fingers. For what seemed like years Joven had kept trying to mold the loose mud. He knew he was dead, knew that the thieving minister had murdered him; and he somehow knew that if he stopped bending over and picking up the patties of mud and trying to mold them, he'd begin to sink into the morass, and that it would envelop him entirely, and feel good and cool.

Except Joven didn't want to feel good and cool. He wanted to get the fucking mud to cooperate, and let him find its shape, let him transform it into a cup or a finger bowl or even a single shitty clay marble. If the mud thought it could frustrate him into giving up, it was wrong. The idea infuriated Joven, infuriated him to his outraged core. It made him squeeze harder on the mud.

They had called him the Charmer as a joke on his unfeelingness. What they never understood was that it was the reverse—Joven felt it all. His life had been shot through with other people's doubts: doubts about his ability to fulfill orders, doubts about his ability to pay loans, doubts about the quality of his wares, doubts about his background, doubts about his word as a man. They hurt him, the doubting ones. Their smug grins of skepticism dragged him with needles. The reason Joven had never taken a wife, had lived as a bachelor in his echoing manor in the Hills, was that he had not wanted another person to hear how he sobbed wildly in his sleep, raging at the figures in his dreams who exiled him from their doorsteps with arrogant fluttering waves.

He took not a bit of satisfaction from his life's work. The thousands of thick, glazy plates and platters and bowls, decorated with elegant scenes of the natural world and fine-lined symbols of esteemed heritages, stocking the oaken cabinets of some of the wealthiest estates not only in his own country but on the Continent and beyond, brought him no joy, either in their crafting or by their existence. His pleasure—grim, and always short-lasting—came only in the defying of those who would discount him, of anyone who ever supposed that he wasn't up to it.

A logical accounting showed that he had proved his mettle: he had demonstrated to the minister and to the world that the only way to get rid of him was by killing him, and by killing him, the minister had proved him right.

But Joven didn't feel like he'd won.

The mudman reached into the mud, and stirred and stirred for something his hand could keep.

Joven found that his place in the long corridor had somehow come to a door. The mud was gone. A black-and-white cat was twining at his feet, knocking its big head against the doorsill each time it curled around, causing the door to clack in its frame. It seemed obvious to Joven that the cat had brought him to the door. He resented the interruption.

"I was doing something," he said to the animal, and showed it his muddy palms. "I was making. Put back the mud."

The cat ceased twining and started to scratch at the doorframe. Its claws tore splinters from the soft wood.

"You shouldn't do that, it's destructive," Joven told the cat. He reached for the knob anyway, to let the creature through, thinking that the sooner he placated it, the sooner he could get to searching for his mud—but the knob didn't turn. On balance, this struck Joven as just. If the cat was going to make a habit of setting its heart on getting to the other side of closed doors, it ought to get itself hands, or else learn to accept disappointment.

"Too bad," he said. "You'll have to find another door, and another doorman. Now, return me to the hall with the mud."

The black-and-white cat rose on its hind legs, stretching so that its eyes were nearly level with the keyhole beneath the knob. He sensed that it wanted him to look. He thought of the worshippers in the Lees, the ones who left perfectly good food out for feral cats in the hopes that the animals would reward them with a vision. Joven had not requested a vision, however, didn't want one, and resented the animal's prodding; he had mud to tame.

"I'm not accustomed to taking orders from someone that licks their own asshole," he said to the cat, and the cat gave a long, wounded meow. It twisted its head at Joven and blinked its beautiful green eyes that shone like glaze at him. What a glorious tone it was, bright, shallow, and vast. You only ever saw that color in the early morning, when the light struck at the boggy edge of the Fair just perfect. He wished he were alive and had his paints.

To Joven's surprise, he felt tears at his eyes.

The cat meowed again.

He bent to the keyhole.

Through the aperture he saw a grand dining table, heavy with dishes, platters of lamb and trays of whole fish, tureens of steaming soup and bread that glistened with honey. Seated around the table like men were a dozen or more wolves. They were decrepit, their scooped-out shanks trembling on their velvet-padded chairs, their gray and black fur scraggly, flaking pink skin showing in patches. Joven blinked in shock, and between that blink and the next, the diseased old wolves were men in suits and jackets; and one of them was that cheating, murdering shit Westhover! After the second blink, they remained wolves, but Joven knew them for the greedy rich men they were in life.

The animals snapped and dug at the banquet, slavering as they devoured and destroyed the meal, their snouts and jaws covered in sauces and bits of food. The plates and bowls clacked against each other, and several crashed to the floor.

Joven gasped: they were his plates! The plates he'd designed for his own home! He recognized the riverside scene that he had inked himself, the stripe of Fair beach that was his earliest memory.

The rabid bastards were eating off his personal fucking service!

He stepped back and delivered a ferocious kick to the door. "Open up! Open up!" From the other side of the door came a fanfare of cackling howls. Joven kicked the door again and again, but it did not so much as shiver in the frame. He kicked until he was bent breathless.

The black-and-white cat sat neatly, staring at him green-eyed; he knew somehow that it had been waiting for him to wear himself out.

"Well?" he asked the animal. "Go ahead. I can tell you want to tell me something."

And damn if the cat didn't smile at him.

And in its green eyes was a green vision of just revenge: of a mound of slaughtered wolves, a goodly flyblown hill of them.

"Yes," Joven said.

The cat purred in agreement and licked its chops, and Joven opened his eyes in the tub of ice.

△

The late factory owner had climbed up to the deck with the amazed boatman, Zanes. The ship was combing through black waters, far beyond the city and the Fair.

"What's happening?" the boatman asked.

"We are sailing," Joven said.

"To where?" Zanes asked.

"Perhaps to those lights," Joven said, and pointed to a red glimmer on the distant water, and demanded that the boatman find him some pants.

The red light was not, however, a landing. It was a stranger, and yet this stranger's name came naturally to Joven's tongue. They brought the refugee aboard, and then another, and another, and another, expanding their crew.

Joven didn't know how he knew them all, but he did. It was the cat's doing, undoubtedly, and that was fine. The cat had wanted what Joven wanted, and the refugees they brought aboard wanted it too: to have justice; to skin the human wolves who'd stolen their lives. He trusted that, when the time was right, the cat would do as the believers said and show them the way, bring them to land to enact their vengeance. It had smiled at him, after all.

In the meantime, they sailed, and found the lost.

Δ

Lorena looked from the captain back to the sea. Starboard, a cluster of reddish lights appeared on the surface of the water. There was a liveliness about them that was quite apart from everything else about the night world: they pulsed and they fizzed. The glow they cast made long red slashes on the swells.

"What's that?" Lorena asked the boatman.

"More like us," Zanes said. "New crew."

Still Crossing

The quick boy dropped from his attic, set a satchel on the bar, and asked Rei, "What would you say if a fella asked you where he could get a glass eye?"

"If he had two good eyes already? I'd say he was asking for trouble," Rei said offhandedly. "You know, Ikey, Groaty was a hell of a fighter. He could whop em. Believe me."

The saloonkeeper leaned against her shelf of bottles and, with a faint smile on her face, looked at Groat sitting at his table, blinking at the light muddling through the dirty street-side window. The individual strands of his tufty hair shone.

"I don't doubt it," Ike said, wanting to get back to the business of the glass eyes. There was no time to waste on historical matters. It had troubled him, how worn Dora had seemed yesterday, how unhappy and worrying, how small and alone she'd looked in the dark doorway of the huge building. He had decided to ask her today to be his wife. She'd said he was fit for a frame—like he said, because that was what all the sharp ones said, the cardplayers and the numbers men at the tracks—and it had given Ike the reddest feeling he'd ever felt.

Through the night, Ike, stretched on his pallet in the attic above the bar, had practiced his speech on the slanted ceiling. "Do you know that, since the day I met you on the bridge, when you looked so lovely, and you beat me fair and square, do you know I never stopped thinking of you, Miss Dora? And I never will be able to stop thinking of you. And I never would want to, Miss Dora, which is why I would like you to be my wife. Will you be?"

Folded neat in the satchel was the fine brown suit and hat, the smart blue shirt, the polished brogues, the blue dress with the white ribbons, and the big-ticket ring with the circle of pink diamonds. On the way from the Still, he could find a tie, and it might not be perfect, but the rest of his ensemble could carry it. If, as a tribute, he also brought along a few glass eyes to fix up Dora's wax friends, Ike didn't see how he could miss.

"But what about glass eyes, Rei?" Ike asked.

Rei ignored the question. She was still on her husband's boxing career. "Groaty'd get in on em, low, let them have the back of his skull where it's hardest, and while they banged away on that, he'd put it in their ribs, *boom-boom-boom*! Crack their ribs and they'd lose their breath."

The saloonkeeper ran her hands through her great mane, exposing the liver spots at her temples and wrinkles high on her forehead. She was younger than Groat because everyone was younger than Groat, but Rei was no kitten herself. A melancholy thought came to Ike: someday that rotten stump covered in piss moss would be around and Groat and Rei would both be gone. He vowed to himself they'd be remembered. He'd tell his own kids about them. "Children," he'd say, "listen here to the story of the saloon where I sprouted up, and the good old barwoman who fenced my odds and ends, and was only a little greedy, and her husband, who lived on beer and pickled oysters, and threatened to make people eat the sickening weeds that he did his drizzles upon, but never actually did make anyone munch them, or hurt anyone in any way, so long as I knew him."

"You think you could still whop em, Groaty?" she called over.

"Any snapping dog—" Groat strained. "Ahem."

He cleared his throat and spat on the floor, then recommended without shifting his eyes from the muted glow of the window, "Any snapping dog came close enough, I'd put a bushel of Deadly Salad in their jaws and push it right down into the bottom of their bellies. And if necessary, I would hold it there, till it was digested."

"Damn right, Groat!" Ike hoped this salute would win favor from Rei.

The saloonkeeper gave Ike a suspicious look. All the time they had been speaking, Elgin and Marl had been asleep on their stools with their foreheads on the bar's sticky wood. She probed her teeth with a finger, examined what she'd found, and flicked it at Marl. The passed-out fly was unperturbed.

"Glass eyes, eh? You think I should know about such peculiar things?"

"If anyone did."

"True. I like those two quickies you sent along, Ike. They seem like up-and-comers. Spirited."

"Nevermind those two strays. They've got a lot to learn. If you're going to be sugary, be sugary with your loyal Ike, who brings you presents and enlivens your everyday and is like a son to you. Now, where can I get glass eyes, Rei? What's the word?"

"The word is . . ." Rei brought over a lit candle from the shelf of bottles and dripped wax into Marl's hair, and into Elgin's hair. The flies did not stir.

". . . Charmer," the saloonkeeper finished.

△

"Charmer? What do you mean?"

Got a blind friend, do you, Ike? Is she pretty? Rei thought to ask, but it was obvious enough in the way that he was fidgeting.

Funny to imagine, their own Ike with a sweetheart; their own Ike, who'd come into the Still looking for shelter, ten if he was a day, and begged to be taken in. "I'm young, but I can help, miss," he'd said, and Rei had seen the tearstains on his dirty little chipmunk's face, and told him he could have the attic—"But if the rats eat you, I won't mourn for long."

"Hurrah!" Ike had cried. Instead of running out, he'd passed her test, shown that he might actually be able to survive in the Lees, and Rei could allow herself to become fond of him. You'd never seen such a happy boy!

Ike had shot right up, hadn't he? He'd become a good-looking young man and a nifty crook. It was no surprise that he'd find someone, now that she thought about it, but it did make Rei feel nostalgic for her own youthful romance.

"Joven is what I mean. The Charm." She told Ike he ought to make a visit to the little store at Joven's former factory. The Charmer used to permit his employees to sell things they made themselves in their off-hours. She recalled there were marbles in the shop, but not just regular marbles—some of them were painted as eyes.

Ike hopped off his stool. "Owe you, Rei."

"Nah," she said. "This one's free, boy."

Ike laughed in disbelief—"Sure it is, Rei"—and left the saloon.

Though it stung a little, his summary discounting of her generosity, she supposed it was just as well. Tenderly though she felt toward Ike, what good would he ever be to a woman if he lost his edge?

Rei glanced again at her husband. Groat looked like a meal that had been eaten twice, it was true. But even now, in the jut of his lower lip, she could see the young boxer who'd told her she was the only one had ever knocked him out cold.

"What's the word, Rei?" Groat asked abruptly, as if he'd heard her thoughts. He swung his head around at her. He grinned a broken-toothed grin.

"*Fortunate*," she said. "That's the word. Would you get me glass eyes if I wanted, darling?"

"Yup," he said.

"I know you would, Groaty," Rei said, her heart feeling big the way only Groat could make it.

The saloonkeeper went happily about arranging some cups, giving a spit-shine here and there.

Elgin woke in a panic. "Ah! Ah!" He dug at the wax clotted in his hair. The drunk's eyes twitched around, and it was clear that he was greatly unnerved. He wept. "I hate the things that come into my brains when I'm asleep!"

"You don't have any brains left, Elgin," Rei said, not unkindly, and poured him a beer, and herself a finger of whiskey. When she lifted her glass, she made a private toast to Ike's darling, this impetuous girl who demanded in tribute some eyes that were made of glass. Rei liked her spirit; she could hardly wait until he brought her home.

△

Elgin's sniffling roused Marl, who had lately come to fear that his old drinking partner was losing his wits, and Elgin had not been oversupplied with them to begin with. He saw that tears were trickling over his pal's cheeks as he drank. There was also a bird-shit spatter of wax in the poor bastard's hair. It was sad to see. If you swam for too long, though, you got deep wet.

"I'll have one too, Rei," Marl said.

"You will, will you," the saloonkeeper said, but brought him a cup of beer. He drank.

Groat got to his feet and poked toward the back door, crutch tips popping oyster shells. Rei asked if he needed a hand. "Nah," Groat grunted.

"My poor brains . . ." Elgin heaved a shivering sigh. *"Eh-eh-eh."*

Marl clapped Elgin on the back. "You're just parcht, pal." He asked Rei, "Do you remember Miss Alphabet?" Miss Alphabet had been like Elgin was now, a truly pathetic case.

"Not if I can help it," Rei said.

Fifteen years or so it must have been, that was when the madwoman had used to beg on the waterfront. Miss Alphabet would cry and call for her "Dee-Dee-Dee," her "good little shadow, Dee-Dee-Dee," and accost strangers to ask if they'd seen her, seen "tiny Dee." Quite a few found it funny. The woman had washed out her mind drinking headache tonics that could double as silver polish, and misplaced the fourth letter of the alphabet in the process. That was why they called her Miss Alphabet, because she was missing a part of it. When they laughed at her, she usually laughed back, which made the comedy roll around again.

Marl didn't think it was funny. He had felt sorry for her. She wore a bonnet, like proper maids and nurses did, and maybe she had been such a one; but she'd tumbled all the way down to the street. Miss Alphabet smiled even when she was weeping for her letter. That was what stuck with him, the jolly face she kept up behind the tears.

It was gossiped that she used to loiter outside the Juvenile Lodgings, begging for her letter, but a master had come outside and whipped her unconscious. From this, Marl made a deduction: Miss A had made a B with some Mister C, named it D, and somehow or other had ended up surrendering the child to the Lodgings. Poor gal.

In those days, he'd been employed at the duty office. A few times, when it was rainy and cold, he had retrieved Miss Alphabet from a spot out in the open and brought her to the roofed alley of the duty office to sleep. His only requirement was that she not tell anyone. "If you start yelling and fussing about that letter, others'll show up, and I'll be in the street along with you," Marl reminded the madwoman whenever he helped her.

"Dee is the baddest kitten, but the goodest girl. Picks up, listens, helps her sick Nurse when her Nurse is sick. Just gives me a jump sometimes, and I laugh anyway." The madwoman had waved her bottle of curative and laughed. Her bonnet was gray from sweat; she smelled as rancid as the Fair at low tide. "Bless you, sir, and thank you, sir. I'll be quiet and find tiny Dee tomorrow."

Inevitably, though, there had been a wet January night when neither Marl nor anyone else had offered her refuge. Miss Alphabet was found sitting stiff and dead on one of the wharfs, open-eyed and slack-mouthed with blue lips. When they lifted her up there was a pool of blood underneath her seat.

Poor gal. People could be cruel. Marl wished he had a penny; he'd buy a chicken liver and go to the temple, the one at the Point folks claimed still had some magic, and leave it for the cats, and ask them to smile on Miss Alphabet.

Marl drank off his new cup. Mosi and those university boys had promised the revolution would make things better and fairer, and yet here he was, broke as ever. Not that he gave a loose shit for the weasels that had been knocked off their horses, the king and the assembly and the ministers. It was a sweet surprise to see them get a half dose of the treatment they'd given to the Charmer.

But as good as better and fairer sounded, if you lived long enough you realized it would never happen. Though the faces changed, there was always a slick one at the top, holding all the cards.

"Go aheadt and cry if you're feeling woundet," Marl said to Elgin. "It's your right."

He signaled to Rei, and she must have been feeling indulgent because she gave him another, and Marl felt a little guilty about how he'd planned to use the penny he didn't have, when by rights he owed it to the saloon-keeper for his tab.

"Thank you, Rei. I will pay you back one of these days." He lifted his cup. "To Miss Alphabet's little letter."

△

In his nightmares, it went opposite from the way it had happened in real life: in Elgin's nightmares, it was the cats that butchered people and boiled them for their bones; and richer cats in gold collars showed up with wads of money held in their teeth, and bought the white bones for their special club. The butcher cats didn't seem to suffer from guilt the way that Elgin had, though, in his butchering days. All the cats were huge in Elgin's nightmares, the size of elephants. They briskly carried the human arms and legs and heads to boiling pots and dropped them in, *plop!* Once the pieces were tender, the cats scooped them out of the pot, held them up, and the remaining meat slid from the bones, *plop!* again, making red piles on the ground. Elgin ran around his nightmare screaming, feeling his brains in his ears, and yelling that he was sorry, the man in the gold vest had made him do it.

When the man in the gold vest had come to him with the first order, Elgin had refused. It wasn't a matter of money. Cats were special. Cats had magic. Rich or poor, ugly or beautiful, if you were a friend to a cat, they'd be a friend to you. They might even show you the way like they did the girl who was lost in the desert.

It was sick, what the gold vest man wanted: to butcher them and boil them for their bones.

The gold vest man had asked Elgin, "My friend, my friend, do you know what my name is?" and before Elgin could reply, the man had told him his name, and it was true. Elgin could see it must be true.

It scared Elgin, so he took the money, and did what the money was for, catching and killing and cooking, and handing off bags of little bones to the gold vest man's agents. All the while he hoped one of the scratches the poor creatures gave him would get infected and he would die, but instead it had been the cholera that had got him—except unlike most people, he hadn't died. However, as he was burning up from fever in his rooms behind the glove on the door, the man in the gold vest forgot about him, or more likely, found someone else to perform his horrible sacrilege.

Elgin did his best to keep drunk, but it was an imperfect solution. Your crimes had long legs; they kept pace no matter how you ran and weaved. Whenever you sobered, they were right there beside you.

"He told me his name before I could stop him!" Elgin blurted to Marl. "And now my brains aren't right."

"No, they are not," Marl commiserated. "Elgin, your brains are fuckt, but you are among friends."

"In my head, they never put me in their pots. I just see em put others' pieces." He hunched over the bar and rubbed his face. "I'd be relieved to go in! Put me in!"

"You'll get your chance," Marl said. "Everyone gets chosent for everything in the eventuality. Drink up. You'll feel better."

△

In the backyard of the Still Crossing, Groat perched on his crutches above the stump, and waited for his water to arrive. The Deadly looked particularly lush in the dawn gleam that found its way through the patchwork of overhanging roofs that surrounded the saloon. Its fuzzy carpet was vivid with all the shades of bruise, purple and yellow and green. It could use some silver, though, some of that sweet silver that had trickled into sweet Rei's black hair over the years. He had thought the black of her hair was fine when she was young, but the silver of her years was finer.

There was a thud. Groat crooked his head and saw that a portion of the fence had opened. A stubby, bald man swaggered through. Groat recognized the crocker on sight. It was none other than Joven himself, the Charmer, the insolent mudman.

"Put away your cock, Groat," Joven said.

"What do you want, Charmer?" Groat demanded. He had known him for forty years, since Joven was a boy going door-to-door with his Fair mud plates and refusing to bargain. Groat had threatened to feed him the Deadly on more occasions than he could count.

"It's time to sail." Joven indicated the boat ramp that had extended down behind him. Above the fence, hovering in the air, Groat could see the prow of the Morgue Ship.

"Are you sure?" asked Groat.

"Yes," said Joven. "Do you know what that means?"

Groat said, "I know. You fucker. You've no right to sail boats into people's yards. You bald, superior fucker. You've a big, important mouth for a dead man. Too big and too important. I bet I could fit the whole fucking salad in there."

"Eh. Probably you could," Joven admitted. The mudman crossed his arms over his jutting little gut. "But we need you on board, Davey. If we can get ashore, we're going to need a fella who knows what his fists are for."

David Groat had not heard his first name in a long time. Groat wondered how that fool of a minister had ever got it in his head that he could trim so much as a penny on the likes of Joven.

"Very well," Groat said. "I just need to make my farewells."

Joven shook his head.

Δ

Outside the saloon, Sergeant Redmond, who had been promoted after Van Goor's apparent desertion of his post, told the three men he'd chosen for the raid on the black marketers to stand down a moment. He went to the two female journalists with whom General Crossley had saddled him. If that wasn't unusual enough, they were also elderly, and twins, dressed to match in flounced purple gowns and touring hats. He had been tempted to ask the general if he should consider attaching dancing bears to the action as well. In Redmond's mind, he had dubbed them Bag One and Bag Two, but their proper names were the Misses Pinter.

The twins stood in the middle of the trash-strewn, riverside lane with sunny, ingenuous expressions.

"This is thrilling," Bag One said as he approached, and Bag Two echoed, "Simply stirring, Sergeant."

"My ladies," Redmond said, "for your safety, I'll ask you to wait here with Murad until we bring the criminals out. If you want to ask them some questions before we pack them up, you can do so at that time."

"You know best, Sergeant," Bag One said.

"Our readers will appreciate this," Bag Two said.

"So important to paint a full picture for our readers," Bag One said. "Now, if you apprehend one of the children that these criminals have exploited, we'd particularly like to speak to them."

"Our readers are very interested in the plight of the children." Bag Two wiped at the corner of her eye. "Maybe we could borrow the child, and talk to him or her at greater length?"

Redmond had no intention of loaning out any juvenile delinquents so he ignored this proposal, but promised he'd do what he could to provide them with the access they wanted.

It was a cool, gray morning, and the Fair was slashed with whitecaps. Gulls were screaming in the air over the river. Redmond was a soldier through and through, had fought for Gildersleeve before transferring to the Auxiliary, and he'd follow orders, even if that meant doing constable work like arresting lowlifes and naughty kids for stealing hats, but he didn't like it. He didn't like any of it, not the raid, not the old newspaper ladies, not even the dawn promotion that had raised him from corporal to sergeant. When a wretch like Van Goor—known far and wide as a plunderer and a vicious bastard—skipped out, you could be sure that something was wrong. Not that it wasn't obvious, besides that: Crossley's Auxiliary Garrison had five thousand men, yet for more than a month he had been pursuing a settlement with a force of three hundred. And here they were about to put some small-time robbers in irons. It made no sense.

A vagrant boy of perhaps five, dressed in a pair of patched pants, was the only local spectator at this early hour. He leaned against a hitching post in the manner of a sport, absently picking at his bellybutton with a grimy finger as he watched the assembly of soldiers in front of the Still Crossing.

"Are you fairy godmothers?" he called to the Misses Pinter.

"Yes!" they replied in unison, and their laughter sounded like two rusty bells being shaken. The boy ran off, disappearing up an alley.

Redmond signaled to Corporal Murad to stay, and he went ahead to the door of the saloon followed by his other two men.

△

Edna Pinter, firstborn of the twins and distinguishable from her sister Bertha by a fleck of black in her left eye's hazel, removed her tiny bronze watch from her purse. "One hundred twenty should do." Redmond and his two soldiers had just gone inside.

"Yes," Bertha said.

Murad, their guard, noted the watch. It had a design of interlocking triangles engraved on the lid. "Isn't that a cunning piece of work," he remarked.

"I'm quite sentimental about it." Edna held the watch close to her flecked eye to monitor the ticking down of the seconds. "The case was made from one of our father's greaves."

"Killed during the Sack of Rome, poor man," Bertha said.

"My condolences, mistresses," Corporal Murad said. He had not known that Rome had been sacked in living memory.

"It was more than four centuries ago," Edna said, "but thank you."

"Yes, thank you," Bertha said.

Murad knew from his schooling that a century was a hundred years. But that couldn't be right. "Four centuries?" he checked.

"There we are," Edna said. She returned her cunning watch to her purse.

Bertha extracted a revolver from her own purse and jammed it into Murad's stomach. He laughed at the bizarre joke and Bertha laughed back, pulling the trigger. Murad's midsection muffled the report.

The young soldier slumped down to the broken cobbles and hiccupped blood onto his chin.

△

"There's no farewells," Joven said, "not for the likes of us."

"There's what I say there is," Groat said.

A vein had risen on Joven's bald head. "Get on that boat, you! Right now!"

"It's a wonder no one killed you sooner. You were a disagreeable boy and a disagreeable man, and now you are a disagreeable corpse. You make a fair plate, I'll grant you that, but your manners are disgraceful."

"I make a fair plate, do I? Find one better!"

"Wouldn't give you the Deadly, Charmer! You'd like it too much! Now, I'll have my farewells!"

"What you'll do is you'll get on that boat, you stinking old pisser!" Joven pointed at the ship.

"I fucking will—" Groat began.

Joven exhaled.

"—soon's I have my farewells."

△

Redmond put out a hand to the saloonkeeper with the black-and-silver hair. When he'd announced that everyone was under arrest on suspicion of dealing in stolen goods, the two flies at the counter had gone right ahead with their beers, but the keeper had rushed around at him with a nasty piece of stick that had two nails poked through. The newly promoted sergeant had stuck her in the belly with the butt of his rifle and she'd hit the floor of crushed and broken oyster shells.

It was a miserable hole. The air was fuggy, the light was dim, the shells on the floor made it wobbly underfoot, and the ceiling was so low it nearly scraped the sergeant's head. The two flies, fat as frogs and twice as ugly, looked as if they would have to be poured into receptacles before they could be transported from the premises. They had turned around on their stools to observe the scene with bleary gazes, beer cups perched on their guts. Redmond was loath even to speculate on how they both had come to have puddles of wax in their hair.

"You all right, miss?" Redmond asked.

"Of course I'm all right," the saloonkeeper said, and slapped at Redmond's extended hand. "You surprised me, is all. I wouldn't have expected a man in uniform to be so craven." She was a small woman with a thin, proud face.

"Come on, miss," Redmond said. "You could be my mother, and I could be your son."

"You should get a head start and leave now." She gave him a smug smile like he was the one on the ground and she was the one with the rifle. "Soon's Groat's back, it'll be lights out for you! He will give your mouth something it won't like, my boy, and he will see it chewed."

One of the flies rose from his stool and waved a grand, drunken arm. "Groat isn't such an individual to be triflet with, gentlemen. He is possesst of a fiery temper." A second after this, the fly's pants, lacking both belt and suspenders, slipped from his hips and fell down around his ankles, exposing his gray drawers and bare legs.

The other fly moaned, as if the very name Groat caused him excruciating pain.

Both of Redmond's soldiers glanced toward their sergeant, discomfited by the foreboding reputation of this Groat, not to be triflet with.

"Who the shit is Groat?" asked Redmond, a little unnerved himself now. "If he gives me any trouble at all, I will shove this rifle in his ear and decorate the place with his sorry head."

The door from the street opened behind him, and Redmond turned to see the old women enter. Oysters popped and cracked under their boot toes. "Ladies," he said, exasperated to suddenly have to deal with an additional dose of nonsense, and wishing eternal damnation on Van Goor for dropping the senseless errand in his lap, "if you could abide with Murad a few moments longer—"

△

Edna aimed her pistol. The first bullet struck Redmond under his right eye and her second buried itself in his sternum, and he unraveled to the floor.

As this was happening, Bertha killed her second man of the day, targeting a soldier standing an arm's reach from the flies. Her bullet caught the man at the top of his spine and he banged loosely off the bar, spun, and landed with his head in the hammock of Marl's pants.

The remaining soldier attempted to hoist himself over the bar, but both women shot him before he could make it to cover, riddling him with slugs that passed through his torso and shattered several of the bottles on the shelf. He slammed into the shelf and it followed him to the floor, shattering the rest of the bottles.

Bertha set her purse on Groat's table by the window and began to reload. Edna pointed her gun at Marl.

"Not like this," Marl said. He gestured with both hands to his ragged skivvies, and the dead man lying on his pants between his legs, but Edna shot him anyway, putting her last round into his heart.

△

Joven told Groat he was ugly, his moldy bones were held together only by stubbornness, he was so rank and filthy in his habits that farts couldn't bear to be around him, he was so irritating that he'd missed his true calling as the blister on a publican's asshole, and saying all that, Joven was gilding the lily beyond reason. Groat was worse still, and not by a small margin.

"I have my flaws, and I never claimed otherwise," Groat conceded.

△

A small pink flag dangled off of the sergeant's lip. A part of his tongue that he'd bitten off, Rei realized. He was lying on his back a couple of feet away, head twisted, empty eyes seemingly fixed on her.

"Stay there, slattern," said the hag who'd killed him, pointing her pistol at Rei. Her twin was at Groat's table, reloading. Elgin was still seated on his stool, goggling at Marl's corpse by his feet.

The woman pointing the gun at Rei had a face like a pastry that had hardened in a confectioner's window, soft and chiseled at the same time. Except for the blood spots on her purple dress and purple gloves, she might have been just another of the "concerned citizens" in the "Humanity Expeditions" that undertook to explore the Lees every season or so, to gawk at how dirty and drunk and shameful people were. The barrel of the hag's pistol was only inches from Rei's face, looking big enough to climb into.

But she was an idiot. Rei might be dirty and drunk and shameful, but she could count.

"You're out of bullets," she said, and snatched up her thumper from where it lay among the oyster shells.

The saloonkeeper whipped the club into the woman's gun hand. The two nails punched through the meat of her palm. The hag shrieked and lost her gun. Rei yanked the thumper free, tearing it out from between thumb and forefinger.

Rei got to her feet and chopped the thumper into the staggering woman's crown. The two nails sank through the flowered hat, and into the hag's skull with a sound slightly denser than that of an oyster being separated. She went cross-eyed and tipped over, nails buried in her brain, hat nailed to her head. Her legs kicked up when she hit the floor and her skirts flipped back to reveal the satiny petticoats beneath.

"Deserved it, too," Rei said, and redirected her attention to the hag's twin.

The second hag had finished reloading her pistol and put it on Rei. "You killed Edna."

"I did." Rei raised her hand. "But we can call it even now and you can go, or I can turn Groaty loose on you. Your choice."

The hag cocked the hammer of the pistol.

△

There was a ringing blast, a second of incredible pain, and Rei was back on the ground. Once again the hardened pastry face of a hag hung above her. It was a different hag, and this time Rei could not feel her legs, but the situation was annoyingly similar.

"My only sister," the hag said, and drew a stiletto from among the cloth flowers on her huge, hideous hat.

That was how she intended to finish her, Rei saw, with the dagger. Rei wasn't too afraid. It would hurt, but what didn't? Groat wasn't the only one in the family who could take a whipping. Good old Groaty. He'd have a fit over this mess.

But also:

"Fuck your sister . . . and fuck you. . . ."

The hag roared and raised the stiletto.

With a bang, the door to the backyard flew open and crashed against the wall. The old woman's arm froze, and she looked up to see Groat swinging toward her on his crutches with the rigid and relentless forward motion of a wind-up toy, popping and pulverizing oyster shells under the tips.

"I'll give you the Deadly for hurting my sweetie!" he cried, and launched himself, tackling her to the ground, and at the same time biting her nose.

She stabbed the stiletto slantwise into his neck. Blood fountained from Groat's punctured artery. He gnawed and shook at the woman's nose, ripping off a chunk. He chomped again, above her eye on the ridge of the socket, and it was only once he had crushed the bone between his teeth that he died.

△

When the echoes of the shots began to fade, Elgin managed, with assistance from the bar, to gain his watery legs. He stepped over the tangle of Marl and the soldier. On the other side of the bar, the dead soldier who had sought cover was facedown, his body blanketed in glass.

Elgin dared to glance in the direction of his other friends. Rei was splayed beside the soldier with the officer's stripes. Oyster shell fragments littered her black-and-silver hair. Her eyes were open, and her mouth was frozen in a bloody leer, and more blood soaked the belly of her dress. Groat lay atop an old woman in a purple dress, his teeth clamped on her face. A stiletto protruded from his neck. Blood continued to squirt from the wound in thin spurts, but Elgin could tell he was another corpse. Beneath Groat, the old woman spasmed, and what was left of her breath came in harsh whispers. The woman's twin was nearer the door. Rei's thumper was stuck in her skull and pointing straight upward, like a marker in a garden to show where the peas were planted. That made seven dead and number eight with the wick nearly burned.

The room smelled familiar; it smelled like Elgin's butcher shop in the old days, only worse, because it was spiced with cordite and the cloying smell of rose perfume, of oysters and vinegar, and of the Fair River across the road.

There would be a boat outside, he knew, and Joven at the bow, demanding he serve. It was impossible that he had lived and that Marl, Groat, Rei, and the three soldiers and the two rich ladies in purple dresses had not. He'd be the ninth. He had surely earned his sentence; it was a fair punishment for what he'd done to those animals, and for whom he had done it.

He shoved off from the bar and stepped around the old woman with the nailed stick in her skull to get to the door that was slightly ajar. Elgin slid out into the street.

A young boy squatted close by the corpse of another soldier, observing the puddle of blood drying around the body.

The boy looked blankly at Elgin. "What you crying for?"

Elgin touched his wet cheeks.

He looked right and left. He scanned the river. There was not a boat in sight. He let instinct take him, and fifteen minutes later he was in the Quenched Thirst, where he successfully begged a cup on credit.

Ike

At a widening of the river, Ike stood on a pebbly stretch of beach. Joven's ceramic works rose up a hundred yards ahead, a brick-built structure horned with numerous chimneys and backed up against a knuckle of riverbank rock. A network of angled troughs and pipes protruded from the factory's riverside wall and extended over the water. Seabirds roosted atop the stilled chimneys.

A high wooden fence surrounded the works. The front gate was fastened with a massive chain and padlock. Ike had walked the sides, testing a few boards, but it was driven in solid and fitted tight; the Charmer hadn't skimped on security. He could find an ax somewhere and hack a hole, but he didn't like to make a mess that might draw attention if someone happened to come along. Even green armbands were liable to notice a bunch of chopped kindling.

On the rear side of the works the fence ran along a ledge of riverside rock, which descended in rough shelves into the sliding green Fair. The troughs and pipes, sunburned white, punched out through holes in the boards. In normal times, exhaust water poured from these conduits and into the river, but like the chimneys, they were stilled.

Ike figured that was the way.

There was a small altar on the high ground of the beach. Ike tucked the satchel out of sight behind the shrine, which had only a few fish bone offerings placed at its foot, and whose idol was so wind-worn that only the shepherd's crook of its tail made it discernible from a chunk of flotsam.

While Ike sat on the pebbles to unlace his boots, he idly pondered the chances of someone coming along to pray and claiming his fine clothes. It seemed unlikely; the devout were few and far between outside of the Lees; in these parts, most went to church. But once he'd had the thought, he couldn't ignore it. Ike took the diamond ring from the satchel and turned it snug on his pinkie.

△

With his boots tied around his neck by their laces, Ike wiggled from the interior mouth of a trough and dropped onto the top of an industrial-sized oven. He shucked his clothes, which were mucky from the gunk that had collected in the trough, wrung them out, and spread them to dry on the convenient surface of the oven, but put on his boots.

A cursory inspection of the main floor revealed other pipes and troughs jutting from the ceilings and walls, more ovens, vats, vents, and wheels. Curtains of dust motes cycled down. The indolence of people astonished Ike; how could a place like this be allowed to go unrobbed for so long? It was a sad puzzle.

He strolled ahead in his altogether, feeling confident that he'd soon have all the glass peepers that any girl could ever wish to possess.

Off the factory floor, he found a storage room. Here, dozens of tall shelves, clearly the holding place for Joven's stock, were empty, each and every one. Bare circles in the dust marked where stacks of plates had been. Ike's heart fell, even as his opinion of his fellow man was somewhat restored. An enterpriser—probably one with a key—had cleaned the area of everything but the dirt. You had to tip your hat.

A door leading from the storage room brought Ike to the factory's front room, where Rei had said the workers kept a small store to sell their baubles.

This front area held a counter, whose several empty drawers had been yanked out and chucked aside, more bare shelves, the broken glass of smashed jars spread across the floor, and nothing else to speak of. Now Ike was less inclined to tip his hat. There was an unspoken principle: if you could put your hands on a thing, by all means do so, but don't be a messy bastard about it. Jars were easy enough to open. Ike kicked around some of the glass.

In the corner was another door, slightly ajar. There was no sense in bothering, Ike knew it. The tree was well picked and he was starting to get cold wandering around the gloomy building with his flowers and frolics exposed.

He left and went back through the storage room to the factory floor— and stopped. For there was another principle to consider:

If he was going to tell his wife that he'd looked everywhere, it needed to be true.

"I've never lied to you, Dora, and I never will," he proclaimed aloud, and returned to the ransacked shop, went through the slightly open door, and climbed the short flight of stairs that lay behind it.

△

At the top of the stairs was an office with a window that looked out onto the factory floor. A drafting table in the middle of the room was covered in papers, and more papers were scattered across the hardwood.

Ike picked up one of the papers. It was a letter, addressed to a supplier of raw metals, and signed *Henry Joven*. There were faint, blackish fingerprints at the paper's edge, surely Joven's. Well! There he was, dressed in his boots alone, in the Charmer's very own office, holding the Charmer's very own letter. Put that in a frame to admire!

It fascinated the quick boy that Joven had been born to the same streets as himself. It seemed amazing to Ike that you could become so rich, the master of a massive factory like this; only to become so dead, first packed in a tub of ice for folks to peek on, and second as an infamous ghost to scare the gullible, supposedly conscripting souls for his cursed ship.

Ike had wanted to see Joven's corpse, but the quarter admission charge had offended his sensibilities. He regretted that lost opportunity now.

Mostly, people had remarked on the size of the dead man; he looked small, they said.

When he set his own fingers over the fingerprints at the edge of the letter, everything seemed possible. He saw a great house in the Hills like Joven had owned, and inside it a long table covered in a whole army of shining silver salt and pepper shakers, and at the opposite end was his wife, Dora, smiling at him. Ike imagined taking her for a carriage ride, and halfway across the South Fair telling the driver, hold it up here, friend. Dressed in their finery, they would climb out and play a game of Dribs and Drabs, and all the sports and quicks and strays and bums would stop in their crossings, and remove their hats out of respect for Dora's beauty and Ike's class.

Ike shook his head clear of the fantasy; he needed to finish his business so he could go and see the real Dora before he caught pneumonia.

Built-in cabinets were set into the walls of the office, but they contained only ledgers and more papers. Here and there he tapped for hollow spots, without any luck.

The closet initially seemed to be empty too; nothing hung on the rack, nothing on the floor. Ike felt around on the storage shelf at the top of the closet and his hand touched something soft. What he pulled down was a small cotton pouch. Its contents clicked. He undid the cord and looked into the pouch: it was full of glass eyes.

A small note inside read:

SPECIAL ORDER
CURATOR
THE NATIONAL MUSEUM OF THE WORKER
LITTLE HERITAGE STREET

Ike shouted in triumph, then began to laugh. A door banged downstairs. He clapped a hand over his mouth.

△

"You hear anything, Zil?"

"I might have heard a dead man, if he doesn't show himself this second."

Ike stepped through the door from the stairway into the little factory shop. "Have you come to apply for a job? I'm sorry, there's no position available for a pair of useless little vandals!" He kicked some of the shards of broken glass in the direction of the two strays, Len and Zil, who jumped away.

"Calm down, Ike!" cried Len. "We didn't do this! This is the first time we've been here. We just liked the looks of the place. Look at what we found behind an altar down on the sand a way. It's got a dress and some twit's opera rags, I figure." He patted Ike's satchel, which he had under his arm. "We can split it up."

"Why don't I just take all of it," Ike said, "seeing as that's my stuff." He stepped forward, ripped the bag from Len's hands, and retreated around behind the counter.

Zil had shaded her eyes. "Do you always go wandering around naked in empty factories wearing nothing but boots and a diamond ring on your finger?"

"Yes, I do," said Ike from behind the counter, kicking off his boots and taking his fine clothes from the bag. "How did you get in here? The place is cleaned out already, but if you chopped a big hole in the fence everything but the foundation'll be gone by tomorrow night."

"We used a ladder," Len said.

"That won't draw any attention." There was no hope for the youth. It made Ike feel exhausted. He pulled on his suit pants.

"We pulled it up after ourselves with a rope, of course," Zil said.

"Wise," he granted. Perhaps there was a little hope.

"Thanks. What's in here?" She picked up the pouch from where he'd set it on the counter and looked into it. "Oooh! Glass eyes! It's funny, right, Len? This one is running around in his skin and boots with a diamond ring and a bunch of glass eyes."

"Put it in a frame to admire," Len said.

— 317 —

"Hide it in the closet where the neighbors can't see," Zil said.

Ike pried the pouch from the girl and placed it farther away along the counter. "I've never liked children and this is why."

"Can I have the dress?" she asked.

"Nope," he said.

"You going to sell it to Rei?" Len asked. "You think she'll take the eyes? Who would want such a thing? We sold her some things. You're right, she's fairer than most."

Zil said, "We asked about you to give our regards, and she said you were out somewhere pretending that you were important."

This was not worthy of a response. Ike carefully buttoned the silk shirt from the doctor's office and tucked it in. He drew his leather belt through the trouser loops and sat on a stool to put on the matching brogues. Next was the brown bowler, which he surveyed carefully, picking off two or three bits of lint, before setting it squarely on his crown. Last was the jacket.

Predictably, the strays lost interest in nipping at his heels and nattered on about the various thefts they'd pulled—small-bore, all of it, letter openers and sugar bowls—as well as the hard bargains they'd made with Rei, where in every instance, Ike silently noted, the saloonkeeper had shorted them. From there it was the latest versions of the old stories of the breadlines (longer for less), the Charmer's magic vessel (spied over the rooftops of the Magistrates' Court), and the rising discontent ("Provisionals so much as kick dust on the wrong man's shoes, folks are delighted for an excuse to fight rather than eat a single bite more of ash bread," Len proclaimed).

Ike only gave it half an ear. He used a pocket mirror to examine himself, and with a rag dabbed off the specks of dirt that had got on his face when he crawled through the trough. He mouthed his words to himself, "Do you know, since that day I met you on the bridge . . ."

Ike shoved the mirror into the satchel and stood. The other two had stopped talking.

The arrangement, the strays on their side of the counter, amid the broken glass and dust, and he on his side, in his duds, like the fellow who ran the place, impressed itself on Ike. It gave him a fulsome sense of adulthood and, to his surprise, a touch of mournfulness. He had been like them not long ago, but he never would be again.

Zil's dirty, freckled face had taken on some color. "You look awfully nice like that, Ike."

"Those rags do suit you." Len added a grunt to convey the manliness of the compliment.

"Thank you." Ike felt compelled by his new maturity to leave them with some words of counsel. "I know I probably seem hard to you, but—"

"He needs something for his neck, though, Len!" Zil interrupted. "What about that silk you lifted from that old fart's coach outside the Metropole?"

Len snapped his fingers. "Oh, yeah!" He reached under his shirt, patted around, and slid out a white silk scarf. He offered it to Ike. "Good as a tie."

△

Ike felt like he was wearing a snake around his neck, an icy-smooth, alabaster snake. It was a wonderful sensation, and the pure luck of the scarf coming into his possession seemed like fate. He'd admired the old man's style that day in the Fields, and if this wasn't the same scarf he'd worn, it was its twin, a five-foot length of white silk with a design of golden triangles stitched at the ends. He wore it in three overlapping loops and let one end dangle down the back of his left shoulder and the other down his front.

"I wouldn't gamble against you, looking like that," Len said, "but I'd ante up for your tips."

The strays brought him across the factory courtyard to the place where their ladder leaned against the inside of the fence.

Ike climbed to the top and paused. He had the satchel containing Dora's dress and the pouch with the eyes draped over his shoulder. They were gazing up at him, smiling at how smart he looked. "I owe you for the silk, and this Ike pays off."

"That was nothin." Len said this in the tone of a boy who stole so many silk scarves that, quite honestly, it was a relief to be rid of one.

"If you're looking for me, I probably won't be around the Still much going ahead," Ike said. He gave them the address of the National Museum of the Worker, described the massive building with flaking green shutters, and told them it was more likely they could find him there. "Give me a few days and I'll have some coins for you, or some item of fair trade, and I'll throw in a few Dribs pointers on the house."

He tapped his hat brim and hoisted himself over the fence. They heard Ike land on the other side and his shoes trotting across the turf to the street.

Zil, who had drawn the correct conclusion from the combination of the fancy clothes, the dress, and the diamond on the quick boy's pinkie finger, burst out, "I pray she says yes!"

△

To Ike's disappointment, none of the handful of pedestrians with whom he crossed paths on his walk from Joven's factory to the National Museum of the Worker seemed to notice his attire. Most were heading south, in the direction of the So Fair and the Lees, several at a run. A red-and-white-striped hospital carriage passed by Ike, horses at a gallop, the second man on the box whacking his bell with a hammer and screaming, "People hurt! Clear out-the-way! People hurt! Clear out-the-way!"

At one stage of his short journey, a woman was weeping in the arms of a friend in the middle of a narrow sidewalk. Ike had to press close to a wall to get by and actually brushed the hem of the distressed woman's skirts, but she didn't react.

"All dead," she was saying through sobs to her friend, "every soul in the place. Slaughtered. Blood everywhere." Her friend immediately blamed "that son-of-a-bitch dockman Mosi"; he had vouched for them university rich boys and for Crossley's soldiers, and it had resulted in butchery.

It was worrisome talk, to be sure. Since that day in the Fields, when he'd spied the old bones in his scarf and the horrible Misses Pinter and the soldier with all his high-ranking badges, Ike had sensed something was amiss in the state of things. He'd mused on it some: it was the waiting.

The waiting for an official peace, for new rules, for new constables. That was why the revolution didn't feel real.

When Ike had been a little fellow fresh from the Lodgings, he'd made a penny one morning lugging a bucket for a clamdigger with a bad back. After the digger paid him, Ike squatted in a court and spun his penny on the stones, just taking pleasure in the shine of it. A lady had come over.

The lady told him she could get him a bag of sugar drops from her sister's house for half a penny and he gave her the coin eagerly. She promised to be right back with the candy and his change. Ike kept to the spot, waiting until dark for the lady to return with the treats and his halfpenny, before he finally went home to the Still and, crying, told Rei.

A dockman at the bar overheard, laughed, and bellowed, "Lovers' Promises!"

Rei had tousled Ike's hair and pinched his cheek and cheerfully observed, "You'll never get robbed that way again, now will you, Ikey?"

It was like that, how it felt: like the moment before you came around to realizing you'd been done a nasty cheat.

If the Provisional Government collapsed, he and Dora would have to be careful. That was all right. Ike knew how to be careful, and he had an idea that she did too.

He didn't stop to inquire for specifics about the nature of the current crisis. If it was as big as it sounded, the news would soon be everywhere, and the details clearer.

His current mission lay elsewhere—and he looked damn smart too! Even if everyone was in too much of an uproar to pay him any mind.

∆

Ike let himself in the unlocked door of the museum and called out for Dora. There was no answer, and his stomach, which he hadn't realized was triple-knotted, relaxed. She must be out fetching supplies. In the future, Ike resolved, she'd be able to stay put because he'd bring whatever they needed.

He took the dress from his satchel, concerned that it was getting wrinkled, and smoothed it across the desk in the small office. Beside it, he set down the pouch of glass eyes.

There was nothing else to do but have a look around.

He pushed the oversized gears. The way they turned each other was very satisfying, and he stepped back and forth through the central gear.

On the second floor, while studying the wax baker, he had an idea. Ike got down on his hands and knees to peek under the baker's skirts to see what it looked like between her legs, but an attack of embarrassment overcame him, and he jumped to his feet. Ike apologized to the statue and told her he was just looking for something he thought he'd dropped. "Not that you care, because you're wax," he said, walking away and not looking back at the figure.

At a window, he viewed the ruins of the building that had burned. Three or four cats were climbing on the mounds of brick, and another three or four were slinking amid the high grass out front. He couldn't see Dora as a worshipper, but he'd make vows at an altar if she wanted. Ike enjoyed the little critters—how could you not?—he just didn't think they protected people from evil.

Up on the fourth floor, he fiddled with the wooden box with the lens and had no more success than on the previous occasion. "It's really busted, fella," he informed the snake-eyed wax man who was supposed to be in charge of it.

When his exploration finally brought him to the fifth floor, he stopped for a couple of minutes to contemplate a peculiar mining exhibit he'd somehow overlooked on previous visits. A miner in a white suit carrying a pickax stood on one side of a barrel filled with bright-yellow sand, and a wax lady in a startlingly tight skirt stood on the other. What sort of strange sand had the miner dug up? What was the lady's role here? The woman in the tight dress appeared positively gleeful. Was she buying the stuff? What did her husband think about those clothes she was wearing? Ike could see how maybe he'd like them, the wax woman's husband, but also how maybe he wouldn't, at least when other men were around.

Ike could not decode the scene at all, and he wished Dora were there to help him understand.

More than an hour had passed. He hoped she would not be much longer. He felt anxious again. It was such an enormous space that it almost seemed like the building was bigger inside than it was outside, though that was nonsense; and the wax people, the way they stood there in the corner of your eye, you had to fight the urge to glance in one direction and look back suddenly to catch them moving, which was obviously nonsense too. Ike declared to himself that he wasn't afraid, just "antsy." At the thought of that word, the bare skin at the backs of his hands felt ticklish and he had to wipe at them.

"I don't know how you sleep alone here, Dora," Ike said aloud, and the sound of his voice made him feel better.

Some of the yellow sand had escaped the barrel and lay scattered across a glass stream. Footsteps were tracked in the sand. Ike followed them to where a wax prospector in a raggy hat was fixed into the glass water, pawing through a metal screen full of shiny rocks. The prospector's wife was hanging raggy clothes on a line. This exhibit he did recall.

Ike doffed his hat to the prospectors. "Good day, country folk. I'm Ike, Dora's future husband."

The clothesline stretched from a shack. The shack had a pair of cane chairs out front. Its door was closed.

He thought Dora might be sleeping in the shack—maybe it had a bed—so he knocked on the closed door. "Dora?" There was no sound from within. Ike put his hand on the latch, but hesitated. She might be shaking off a drowse. He did not want to be intrusive and catch her half awake and undressed.

What if he opened the door and she told him to get out, screamed at him to get out?

What if she rejected his proposal?

What if she laughed?

You can't cry, he told himself. *You can't cry, you can't cry, you can't cry.*

His lifted his fingers from the latch. He stroked the cool silk of the white scarf. He was just winding himself up: How could she say no? He had brought her everything she'd asked for.

Ike steeled himself with the thought that if she did say no, he would still serve her. He would serve her for as long as it took to win her. He would serve her until he fell, if that was what it came to.

"Dora?" he asked. "It's me, Ike. May I come in?"

△

The man who lived in the embassy and who was not named Anthony was awakened by Ike's voice greeting the wax prospectors. He quietly sat up from his nap in the bed inside the shack and crept barefoot through the curtain that served as the shack's fourth wall. Each small, soft step made an ache that went from his crotch through his torso and into his tongue, but he swallowed the pain that Sergeant Van Goor had given him as easily as a raw egg.

"Dora? It's me, Ike. May I come in?" the young man asked as the man from the embassy slipped along the outside of the shack's wall. He was well-spoken. It was a mark in the young rascal's favor.

The-man-who-was-not-Anthony circled around behind the young man, who was prettily dressed too. What to make of it? Her husband-to-be, he called himself!

The-man-who-was-not-Anthony had been up for hours with Van Goor and had only taken a short rest, but his curiosity was freshly piqued. A thorough interview would be necessary.

He surveyed the near figures—the prospector, the prospector's wife, the fruit picker, the miner, the miner's happy friend, the farmer, the farmer's dog—to see their reactions. But all were turned away, as if by not looking they could maintain their innocence.

The young rascal, this Ike, stiffened. He had felt breath on the back of his neck.

"I'm sorry," said the-man-who-was-not-Anthony into Ike's ear. "She's away somewhere. You've got me, though. Perhaps I can help you."

A Dream of Three Days

*S*he emerged from the Vestibule into a hot, overcast afternoon. Inching her way between the banks of wreckage and blinking at the brightness of the muted sky, D stepped through the empty doorway to the expanse of the overgrown Society lawn. Across the street the dark-blue manse of the Archives for the Study of Nautical Exploration and Oceanic Depth squatted sullenly, the frayed gold rigging on the door like a big loosened bow tie.

D moved forward. The uncut grass swished around her skirts and a yellow poplar leaf, tangled in the grass, caught in a fold of the fabric. She brushed it away. D felt refreshed, but dazed.

In the Vestibule, she had fallen asleep and had a night of wild, vivid dreams:

There had been sweet hills, a great blue sky, and a window that made it possible to change her face, to transform herself into the most beautiful woman imaginable. But D had realized that she was blindfolded, and she took the blindfold off. With her real eyes she saw it was night, the moons glowing with an infected shine, and the hills were actually the famous columns on the plateau above the Great Highway. She'd walked to a mountain pass. Plinths lining the path held globes and a few of the globes contained lights. D looked closely into one and saw a tiny man burning, skin puckering and bubbling, even as he stared at himself in a tiny glass, wherein the same man wore a blissful expression and was unharmed. Imprisoned in the other lit globes were other hypnotized men and women in flames, but the majority of the globes contained only cinders, as if their tiny inhabitants had burnt away. Throughout all this, D's comprehension was muffled; she had felt gauzily obliged to explore; and at one dark globe, where the remains of someone's soul lay in ashes, a powerful awareness of Ambrose came to her, a certainty that he was nearby. Part of the gauze around her mind tore. At last! He was so close! She became desperate for help. At the bottom of the path, in a natural bowl formed between ridges, there had been a massive open-air temple with a hundred or so stone chairs. In perhaps a dozen of the chairs, elderly men and women lolled, asleep, dressed in golden robes, their long gray hair spooling onto the rocky ground. More fiery globes burned on ledges that encircled the temple, and cast their lights on the sleepers. D had retraced her steps to a tattooed crone who was seated on a stool close to the door she'd come through, revealed by her true eyes as a triangular portal.

D frantically told the crone that near a globe of ashes she had sensed her brother's closeness; a teenage boy with a cap pulled low and a toothy smile, had madam seen anyone of that description?

"Do you need your face changed?" the crone asked, and with a humongous sewing needle—as large as a carving knife—pointed to a guillotine.

D said no; she was looking for her brother, Ambrose. Hadn't madam seen him?

"Your eyes are cleared, woman. If he came here, and he's not one of them, and he's not burning, you can see for yourself what's become of him. They soaked themselves in his light. They drank him up. You should have kept your eyes covered if you didn't want to know. Do you want a face or not?"

When D hadn't replied, the old woman had snarled and jabbed the needle in D's direction, and D had staggered away through the portal.

△

"Ah! There you are!"

She saw a driver in white-dusted work clothes standing in the street beside a wagon that was stopped in front of the museum. He was waving his wide-brimmed hat to her. The two horses yoked to the wagon were nibbling the weeds that grew in the gaps between the street cobbles.

"I've got your lime!" he called. "I apologize for the delay!" The man flapped the hat in front of his face. "Not a minute too soon, I can tell! Potentl Latrine, is it?"

The driver had soft middle-aged features that seemed made to smile, swelling cheeks, a broad mouth, and a bulbous nose. There was nothing dangerous about him. His room was a thatched hovel, D saw. A sunken mattress and a kettle and a rocking chair to relax in, its runners squeaking happily in the accumulated carpet of dust that had accompanied him home from his lime pit, that was enough for him. But the driver had come to the wrong place.

"I didn't order any lime, sir. I'm sorry."

He tilted his chin in a demonstration of perplexity. "But the feller that made the order said to bring it to the corner of Little Heritage and Legate, and I was under the impression Legate's all empty now. I took the order myself. Tall feller, a military man."

On the other side of Little Heritage, in front of the offices of the Association of the Brotherhood of Tram Workers, a scatter of maroon in an oak tree caught D's eye. She glanced back at the Society wreckage: thin veins of yellow leaves twisted through the poplars' green bells.

There hadn't been any autumn colors when Robert had walked her home from the pond. She'd been sunstruck and wanted a drink, and she'd gone into the museum and . . . there had been a new exhibit—no, not new, obviously, but one she hadn't noticed before. It had been a soldier . . . a female soldier with a weapon that D couldn't understand.

. . . And she had gone to sleep in the ruins of the Society, and dreamed.

D looked at her skirts, torn from crawling through the hedge and climbing the piles of shattered masonry, and stained black from the ashy debris of the building—where she had run to hide from the sergeant, who had come to hurt her. There was a dirty, scabbed cut between her thumb and forefinger from the drill bit.

"Maybe no one told you. Is your master here?" the driver asked.

"She doesn't have a master."

Her neighbor had appeared a few feet behind the driver, dressed in his full uniform. Captain Anthony's hands were pressed palm-to-palm before him and he was bent slightly with his shoulders turned up. In the daylight, there was something shy and apologetic in his bearing; the reflexive embarrassment of a giant in a human world. He indicated D's building. "She's the one that keeps that place there, the museum. I'm on Legate at the corner."

"Oh," the driver said, and his expression was confused as he glanced again at D in her soiled clothing. "What do you know? Legate's not empty. Beg your pardon, miss."

"If you lay the bags out front there on the sidewalk at the corner, I'll bring them through to the back," Captain Anthony said to the driver.

"Are you sure? That's a lot of lifting for one feller. I wouldn't want you to strain yourself." There were at least a dozen dusty sacks piled in the wagon bed. "What have you got, anyhow? Latrine overflow? It's rotten, I'll tell you."

"A mess," D's neighbor said.

The amiable driver seemed to expect more, but after a moment the bearded man's grinning silence defeated him and he nodded. "Right, right, I'll lay them out for you, you know how you want them," and started to unload the sacks of lime from the wagon, stacking them on the sidewalk.

D remained at the door of the museum. It had not occurred to her to go inside. She'd been fixed. To see him was like seeing a stone gargoyle lift off its cornice at the top of a building and smoothly flap down to the ground. To see him was like seeing all the wrecks at the bottom of the Fair burst up from the water as one to float once more, a mucky, coruscating ghost armada, bound for the open sea. To see him was like seeing a gore-caked wolf standing on its hind legs and dressed in a soldier's uniform to receive a large supply of lime to cover the scent of the festering corpses of the people he'd tortured to death and stored in the stables behind his lair.

Captain Anthony approached her. His head was angled so that he seemed to address her left elbow, and he moved with a new, noticeable limp, his left leg dragging after the right. "Captain Anthony, miss." Her neighbor bowed to her. "I'm sorry I haven't been by to introduce myself earlier. As you know, I've been busy with my work." His eyes flickered up to her and the corners of his contrite smile turned down, indicating the sadness and the disruptiveness of it, of his nightly labor murdering human beings. She supposed that she had already known that he must be mad, but she saw it in his expression then. His lips were like a pair of red worms in the black brush of his beard.

She curtsied. "Dora, sir."

He redirected to her elbow. "I was worried about you." He spoke in a gentle, stroking voice. "You've been away for three nights. I thought something might have happened to you."

"I fell asleep in the ruins of the Society building," D said. She couldn't imagine lying to him.

"In those ruins there?" Captain Anthony gestured at the wreckage with an expression of amusement. "That was a funny thing for you to do."

"Yes, sir," D said, and the full implication of his words settled on her. "Did you say three days, sir?"

"Indeed. You must have been terribly tired, to sleep for so long."

D thought it had to be more than tiredness, but she agreed. "Yes, sir."

He seemed willing to let the matter pass. "I looked after your museum for you. Checked in every day. It's quite a place, Dora. A great tribute to the working folk. It reminds you what a righteous thing it is, that we should all have our own little duties. The miner breaks our coal, the apple picker gets us our sweet fruit, the sailor brings us our fish, the lady teacher helps our children learn their numbers and their letters. I liked to see them all, even the ones toiling away at trades I don't know anything about, but hard at them, and good for those folks.

"Myself, I've been at all kinds of work. I wasn't always a soldier. It turned me around to see all my old jobs! Field hand, mudman, grave-digger, they were all there. I was tickled to see it! I thought, 'Look at all you've done, me!'" Her neighbor made a noise of gratification.

"But some of the folk"—he darted a narrowed glance at D—"quite a few, really, they looked worse for wear. Shabby clothes, no shoes. Filthy words scratched on the teacher's lesson board. Some had missing eyes."

"I know, sir. I've been making repairs."

"It's a shame. Imagine if you visited and saw your kind of person there laboring, dressed in scraps. I know folks sometimes do look that way, rough-lived and all. Maybe they mostly do. I've been that way myself. And it's a shame. It seems like, in a grand place, we should be shown at our best."

"Yes, sir."

"I'm glad we agree. As you keep at it, know I'm rooting for you."

"Thank you, sir."

"I was worried about you, Dora. I didn't want to believe that you'd abandoned your post."

"I wouldn't do that, sir."

He lowered his voice: "That Sergeant Van Goor that was looking for you, I spoke to him at length. I sounded him out, and he's all settled. So, you can be at ease there. You can focus on your duties."

"Thank you," D said, her voice catching. "Sir."

Her neighbor waved her appreciation away with a sweep of one big hand.

"We ought to talk at some point as well. Just to sort out some matters related to what the sergeant told me. Make sure it's all clear, and we know everything we need to know. Then you can let go of the teasing and tell me more about where you actually were the last three days." The skin around his eyes crinkled with amusement.

Up close like this, she could see the scuffed quality of this band of exposed flesh, and the fine webs imprinted underneath his eyes. D thought that he'd rarely had a room, at least not until recently. He'd spent most of his life under the open sky. When she had first tried to imagine the place he kept, she had seen only darkness, and that had been right: night dark. This time she envisioned it and heard sounds: birds crying, rodents clawing bark, insects droning, a well chain squeaking, a goat sorting through some straw, and the voices of a family coming from the open windows of their farmhouse, unaware of the man in the yard below, the wayfaring stranger who stretched out with his head resting on a bundle and listened, smiling, to their bedtime prayers.

As he raised a grime-packed thumbnail to his mouth and gave it a gnaw, his beard shifted into a frown. "Really, Dora, I shouldn't have said 'ought.' To keep things proper, we do need to talk. No wiggle. Have to speak with that Lieutenant Barnes too. It happens he came up in my conversation with the sergeant as well. Have to sit you both down, I'm afraid."

Bile flooded the bottom of D's throat, and she swallowed it down. He must have known she was afraid, but she wouldn't let him see it, wouldn't let him have that without doing the work that it was clear he took so much pride in.

"When?" she asked.

"That's the trouble of it. I'm not sure," he said. "I know that's no help to you and I am sorry about that. I know you have your own duties to consider, but my ledger, it seems to fill up as fast as I can turn the pages.

"But as soon as I can, you have my word. I'll just come over and make a knock on your door, and we can have our talk, all right?"

"Of course, sir," D said.

He bowed, glancing up to meet D's gaze in that servile manner again. It made her think of street vendors, the ones that sold the cheapest items, wilted greens and pieces of string—as though the death he brought were but a meager product.

"Good day, Dora," he said. "See to your charges. I'll look for you in your window tonight."

△

Even as the memory of her encounter with the sergeant rematerialized in full, it took on an abstract quality. Van Goor had intended to murder her, seemingly because of some slight committed by Robert, and she had eluded him; for his part, Van Goor had not eluded her neighbor. Van Goor had been a dangerous man and D was glad that he was dead, and not sorry he had suffered. There was also no time to linger on it. Soon, her neighbor had promised, he would come to see her for their talk.

D focused instead on her dream in the Vestibule, her dream of three days. The minutes that had passed in there had been hours here. She thought of the moons that looked like boils; she thought of the globes with the happy burning figures, mesmerized by their own reflections, who did not seem to realize that they were engulfed; she thought of the globes that had contained only ashes, where the figures must have burned out, like the one where she had sensed her brother; she thought of the ancient sleepers in their golden robes, bathing in the light of the flames; and she thought of the blindfold and the old woman with the long needle who sat beside the guillotine and asked if D wanted her face changed.

On the fourth floor, D went to the box with the lens, drawn to it, thinking of how the old woman with her guillotine and needle was very much like the webby woman who had a saw and a needle in the moving pictures. She wished it wasn't broken, and she could watch the pictures again. The guardian of the viewing box, the wax man with the fez and the lizard's gaze, gestured toward it.

The direction of his hand brought her eyes to some scarring at the bottom of the box. She bent and ran her fingers over a half dozen fresh scratches. D recalled the cat outside the Vestibule, working its claws into the charred wood—because it wanted her to go there.

And, at some point while she was gone, it had slipped into the museum and made these marks, because it wanted her to go here.

D put her eye to the lens, and pressed the button with the white triangle. She thought maybe, for some reason, it would work again.

With a click and a shudder, the light turned on at the bottom of the lens, and the magisterial cat with the jeweled collar appeared sitting on the arm of the chair, staring at her, flicking its tail back and forth.

△

The story was the same one that the cheery man in the gold vest, her brother's friend, had told D in her girlhood, but different—or perhaps, not exactly different, but with details the cheery man had, along with his name, left out.

In the moving pictures, the suave man in the outmoded clothes with the beautiful cat that looked so much like the one she kept seeing and with the ace of diamonds in his hand—the conjurer, surely, Simon the Gentle—was blindfolded when he emerged on the other side of his closet with his dance partner ("THE CONJURER WAS ARROGANT. HE BELIEVED HIS MASTERY OF ILLUSION PROTECTED HIM. HE WAS BLIND."), and did not understand the true nature of the magic, which was the webby woman's saw and needle ("FOR EVERY TRICK IS THE TRICK OF ANOTHER . . ."); D could not see the owner of the gnarled hands that gave the knife to the frantic man ("HIS HANDS EXTENDED A KNIFE FOR THE CUCKOLD TO TAKE!"); and in the last scene, the central figure was mutable, taking the faces of his victims to convince them to kill themselves ("BEGUILED BY THE MONSTER'S DECEIT, THEY SACRIFICE THEM-SELVES!").

The night librarian at the university library had once shown her a very old book. "Come here, girl!" he'd called from the circulation desk, demanding that she come away from the study table where she had been bent polishing fingerprints off the brass lampshades. D was tired at the end of a long day of cleaning up after rich young men, but she tucked her rag into the pocket of her apron and went anyway. There was no one else around.

"See?"

Laid open beneath the librarian's lamp was a tome of vellum pages, its leaves covered in a tightly written hand.

"Now, look to the gaps," he said. The night librarian slid his index finger under a page and raised it slightly, so the light could pour through the material. Other lines of text rose up faintly between the darker lines, hazy shapes emerging in mist.

"Do you see it?" the night librarian had asked. "Do you see the dirty secrets the writer put down so soft there in the leading for his dirty secret friends to read?"

The version of Simon the Gentle's story that she watched through the lens was like the softly written words in the leading of the night librarian's book, a dirty secret that was intended only for someone's dirty secret friends to know.

But it extended beyond the moving pictures in the wooden box; there was a sense of something furtive and sly and marginal pervading everything, both inside and outside the walls of the museum.

△

D made a circuit of the museum. She found that she was not surprised to discover three more exhibits like the ones on the first and fourth floors, which she had not noted during her earlier explorations of the building.

On the second floor, where Hand Work was celebrated, an odd, long table had appeared near the loom exhibit. This table was strapped with a belt, and laid on the belt were various pieces of machinery, clips and bolts and screws, and chunks of gray clay and metal beads. Three wax builders, two women and a man, bent over the machine parts at intervals along the table. Their heads were encased in helmets with transparent masks of heavy glass. At the end of the table was an example of the product of their labors: a thick, rectangular green plate that stood on short metal legs. A length of wire connected the back of the plate to a steel handle with a button. On the face side of the plate was written △ **FRONT TOWARD ENEMY** △.

A singular metal wagon was now parked at the end of the row of train engines on the third floor. Boxy, painted in waves of olive and brown, the wagon sat on fat black wheels that were tacky to the touch, like shellac. It was manned by two wax soldiers in uniforms like the one the woman soldier—"Lieutenant Hart"—wore on the first floor. Their faces were painted in the same olive and brown tones as the wagon. One man perched on a leather seat with his hands on the driving wheel; the other stood through a hole in the vehicle's roof, and commanded a bristling rifle. Rectangular metal tags bolted to the wagon's bumpers were labeled with white triangles.

On the fifth floor was an exhibit of a miner and a rich woman.

D could tell that the one figure was a miner because he carried a pickax, though it differed notably from the curved, wooden-handled pickaxes that the other miners of the fifth floor wielded. This pickax was made entirely of a silvery steel that was so polished it showed D's reflection. His puffy, full-body white suit and the big glasses that were locked around his eyes were coated in dust, like the man who had brought the sacks of lime, but this dust was yellow.

Even though the formfitting style of the woman figure's blue skirt and jacket were alien to D, she knew that the woman was rich by the supple leather purse drawn over her shoulder. Like the miner, she wore large glasses and puffy white gloves. Between them was an open barrel. He gestured to the contents; she leaned forward with an unguarded smile, as if to make the acquaintance of a charming toddler. The barrel was filled to the brim with a yellow sand whose brightness seemed unnatural even before D registered the distinctly ominous symbol on the barrel's side: a circle overlaid with three pincer-like shapes and captured inside a triangle.

D tried to envision the rooms that belonged to the miner in the puffy suit and the woman in the tight, luxurious clothes but could not get very far. What did come to mind was the white-tiled ice closet at the university, where the chefs hung sides of beef on hooks and blocks of ice were stacked to keep the meat cold. In D's imagination, she saw the white-tiled ice closet, but instead of meat hanging from hooks, there were more puffy white suits.

This last exhibit was located on the floor between the prospector's plot and the fruit picker's trees, a space that D crossed multiple times each day. There was no possibility she could have failed to notice it. Seemingly windblown, a scattering of the yellow sand had escaped the barrel, flecking the large cloth leaves of the nearby fruit trees and scumming the glass of the prospector's stream.

D understood these exhibits without knowing what to call them. They had to do with seeing, with communicating, with traveling, with powering, and, above all else, with killing. They had to do with some wicked future work.

△

It was early evening. The deliveryman was gone, and her neighbor had removed the sacks from the sidewalk. They had leaked, though, and a trail of lime grains curled around the corner.

D walked away from this path toward the ruins.

A dozen or so cats of various colors and patterns roamed the high grass of the lawn, dragging their long evening shadows. Others perched on the tops of the broken walls and slapped their tails on the brick. The bushy white cat was there too, sprawled in front of the door stuck in the ground, chin resting on its paws, watching her with slitted, unfriendly eyes. It did not look as if it possessed supernatural powers. It looked like it had a full belly.

D went to the wall of the museum that faced the ruins, which was blackly stained with the ashes of its neighbor. The stains surged above the museum's fifth-floor windows, all the way to the roof.

By turning the point of her drill bit—△ **FOR TAKING SAMPLES FROM SMALL METEORITES** △—against one of the museum's cement blocks, D was able to gouge a small hole. She used the bit to chip the hole wider and continued to dig the point in deeper. Twilight fell as D twisted the drill bit, carving into the museum's sullied wall.

Once her efforts had created a crater that was an inch deep and wide, she stopped, and retreated a step to contemplate the results. Instead of unblemished cement beneath, the jagged gash was as black as the surrounding surface. The smoke and ash of the Society for Psykical Research had seeped into the museum's very walls.

The Previous Curator

The sounds were different that night: instead of screams, a dense tide of banging and shouting.

D had not been sleeping anyway. She had been thinking of the Vestibule. It seemed to D that she had been right all along, that there was some other place. If you removed your blindfold, you saw it was the same world, just a little different. The conjurer, Simon the Gentle, had fallen for an illusion of that second world, and D thought that Ambrose had too. The moving pictures in the wooden box had showed how it worked and her own experience had echoed them. When D had gone through the door, the window had showed her a face of her fantasies; the people in the burning globes had stared, enthralled, at reflections of their own faces—or maybe what they thought they saw was not their own faces. "Yes, I see you," Ambrose had said. "Your . . . face." Maybe it was a face they took for God's. Whatever it was, it made them so happy they didn't notice they were burning alive.

What of the box with the pictures itself, though, and the war machines, and the barrel filled with yellow sand and painted on its side with the foreboding symbol? Those things had come from a world with engineering that was advanced far beyond the engineering in her world. They seemed distinctive, too, from the place with the path and the globes and the crone with the guillotine and the sewing needle. Maybe the burning of the Society building and the Vestibule had opened the way to more than one other place. Or, if not opened the way, created a fissure in some barrier that allowed a bit of another different world to seep through.

What came to D's mind was the front door of her childhood home. On either side of the door there had been decorative rectangular windows made up of pieces of green and yellow stained glass, trapezoids and rhomboids and triangles. Whichever fragment of glass you looked through, you saw the world changed, saw it bent in a particular way. There might be as many worlds as there were fragments of glass built into those long, rectangular windows. The Vestibule had poked out one glass shape entirely; the fire had cracked another.

What would happen if the cracked shard fell out and the inhabitants of the world of the war machines could come through unfiltered? The box with the moving pictures did not seem inherently evil, but that was the exception, one she could only attribute to the cat. It was the note on a black gift box. What would happen if all the shards fell out, and all the worlds were unlocked? This prospect was something that she could not fully master—it was too vast—but it scared her. As bad as the war machines were, what was there to say that there were not even more terrible worlds with even more terrible weapons?

Outside, the sounds of commotion seemed to be growing louder.

△

She left the prospector's cabin and went downstairs to the street. Once outside, she immediately noticed that the awful sick stench was gone. There was, in its place, a tingling acridness.

The lime, D surmised. He'd used it to cover the bodies.

At the corner of Little Heritage and Legate, she looked toward the intersection of National Boulevard and saw crowds. Lamps and torches bobbed, light glinting off rifle barrels, knife points, shovel blades, hammers, and pans. "Open it up! Open up the Highway! Open up the port! Open it up!" the crowd chanted.

"Can't blame them." A couple of yards on, her neighbor, a large, square-shouldered shape in the darkness, sat on his steps. Glowing white insects floated around his head. "You can only tell yourself that ash and chalk is flour for so long before you get tired of spitting."

"Good evening, sir."

"Good evening, Dora."

"They're marching to reopen the city," D said.

"That's right," he said.

"What does the Provisional Government say, sir?"

"'Any day,' they say."

"Do you think so, sir?"

"I don't know anything, really. I just attend to the men and women they send me. Examine their stories. But it does seem like the public has exhausted its patience." He made a clicking noise with his tongue. "You aren't aware because you were away. It's not just the short supplies and the bad bread and the waiting. Three days ago, there was an incident in the Lees. Ugly. A beer room full of dead sousers and dead soldiers, and no one to hang for it. Killers must have escaped, and there's no Constabulary to find them because they all got fired.

"Those armbands that Crossley vouched for and put up on the box, the dockman and the other two, they seem to have lost the handle. They're making promises, but they've been making promises all along. Folks seem to be feeling like it may have been safer the way it used to be."

Amid the crowd, a woman on a horse waved a flaming broom. Sparks gusted from the burning straw and snowed on the ranks behind her.

D wondered if Robert was safe. At least she knew Sergeant Van Goor had not got to him. She worried about Ike too, but reassured herself that he was too slippery to be caught. "Sir . . . the lieutenant who appointed me to this post, did he visit while I was away?"

"No," her neighbor said. "Didn't see Lieutenant Barnes."

She exhaled.

"If I do see him and he asks, I'll have to tell him you were absent from your duties for three days. You understand, Dora."

"Yes, sir," D said.

"You know, a couple of times, I thought those figures of yours were about to scamper on me. Off to the side, I'd catch one, seeming to lean"—she watched him lift his hand in the dark and tilt it—"just a little, like they were waiting for me to turn, so they could make their move."

D did not immediately respond to this statement. There was something nearly hilarious about standing out in the dark, talking to him like an actual neighbor—but only nearly. He was insane and, she was certain, had definite plans to murder her when his schedule opened up.

"Yes, sir," she said nonetheless, because he wasn't a person with whom you disagreed. "They do look real sometimes."

The lights of the torches flowed upward with the slope of the avenue, like the lights of the mountain pass that she'd seen on the other side of the door.

"Can I tell you something?" she asked without thinking. There was a hideous intimacy between them. It was like a sore that her finger wandered off to test without her permission.

"Oh, heavens, yes. Anything," he said. "That's what I'm here for."

"I've been looking for my brother for years, sir," D said, "even though he died of cholera when I was young. I had this dream that he was too beautiful and good and special to really be gone, that he loved me too much to really be gone, and that he must have only traveled to some other place, and if I searched, I could find him there. I don't know if I really believed it, but I think I did find him, and it was another place, but I don't believe he lasted after he made it. I believe he is all gone. I think a cat had been trying to tell me, but then I saw for myself. My brother was tricked by a monster: the monster showed my brother an illusion of what he wanted most and while he stared on that illusion, the monster burned my brother's soul for fuel. I think I saw his ashes. They were in a lamp. A woman told me that if I didn't want to know, I shouldn't have uncovered my eyes. That's what she meant. That my brother burned."

Her neighbor frowned thoughtfully. The white insects danced around his head. The parade, thinning, chanted, "Open it up! Open up the Highway! Open up the port! Open it up!"

"That's quite a story, Dora," he said. "The part about the cat especially. People say they come from the devil, from some part of him. Here's something I've mused on: the same people who say they've come from the devil worship them because they're holy, but if they came from the devil, wouldn't they be unholy?" He winked at her and tapped his nose. "It's probably all the same. In any case, a story like that, it makes sense they'd be involved."

The words had needed to be spoken for her to truly know them, but now D wished she could take them back. "A fancy, that's all, sir."

"But I could be convinced," he said. "I'd need to hear it again, check it from over here and from over there, so we had all the facts neat. But I could be convinced."

Her neighbor wished her good night and, carefully pulling his bad leg after himself, went inside the former embassy, leaving the street to D.

△

D returned to the museum.

She closed the steel door behind her, and drew the bolt. The oil in the lamp was low, so she went into the small office to refill it from a can that she had left there.

There was a dress spread on the desk, and a cloth pouch was set there too. These items had not been there the last time she had been in the office, the day Robert had taken her to the Royal Fields. D guessed that Ike had come to check on her during the three days that elapsed while she was in the Vestibule, and had the luck to avoid her neighbor.

D put the lamp on the seat of the desk chair. She saw no note.

She lifted the dress by its shoulders, shifting it close to the light to see the details. It was navy blue with velvet flowers at the shoulders and white ribbons at the waist. "My own Ike," she said, pleased in spite of everything. It would look lovely on the wax teacher in the classroom exhibit.

D put the dress down and turned her attention to the pouch. She undid the cord that cinched the neck. The contents glistened faintly. When she put her hand in, her fingertips felt cool, rounded glass—marbles! D picked one out and examined it. The marble was painted as a pale-green eye with a perfect black pupil.

She laughed aloud at the boy's ingenuity. "How many blind men did you have to rob for these?" she planned to tease him. She slid her hand in again, letting the glass eyes run between her fingers and over her palm.

A ringing cry caused D to flinch, and a handful of glass eyes jumped from her hand and went scattering along the floorboards. "Ho! Ho!" the voice cried. It sounded like he was trying to hail a carriage. The carriage wouldn't stop, though, and the voice continued to bellow. "Ho! Ho!"

She lowered herself to her knees and searched for the glass eyes. The wails of the man who was being tortured next door carried on. D wondered what sound she would make when it was her turn. She tried to steady herself, but each scream made her twitch, and she dropped the eyes she'd picked up. They went rolling again, glass twinkling in the guttering light of the lamp.

By the time she found them all, D was sweating heavily, and the man's howls of pain had grown further apart and lost some of their volume. She wobbled from her knees, blinking at spots, using the wall for support. Her shoulder brushed against the ragged tweedside jacket hung on the coat hook, the one that presumably belonged to her predecessor, the museum's previous curator. The jacket slipped and fell with a soft rustle. This revealed, beneath, still hanging from the hook, a brilliant gold satin vest.

At the sight of it, D recalled the cheery man who had been so kind and attentive to her that day at the Society while she waited for her brother. He had told her the story of the legendary conjurer—"Canny, canny business"—and showed the exhibit of the conjurer's implements and the stain on the rug from where he had bled to death, but she had never learned his name or anything about him. He'd worn a gold vest.

The glass eyes dropped from her hand again, but she did not move to pick them up.

A Collection of Cards

*I*n the pocket of the gold vest was a collection of cards:

A. Lumm, Curator, National Museum of the Worker,
   1 Little Heritage Street

A. Lumm, Senior Librarian, The Horological Institute,
   2 Little Heritage Street

A. Lumm, President of the Society for Psykical Research,
   3 Little Heritage Street

A. Lumm, Head Scholar, Archives for the Study of Nautical
   Exploration and Oceanic Depth, *4 Little Heritage Street*

A. Lumm, Choreographer Emeritus, The Madame
   Curtiz Academy of Dance and the Human Shape,
   5 Little Heritage Street

A. Lumm, Chairman of the Board, The Museum of Dollhouses
   and Exquisite Miniatures, *6 Little Heritage Street*

A. Lumm, Chief Warden of the Association of the Brotherhood
   of Tram Workers, *7 Little Heritage Street*

Mr. Aloys Lumm, *131 National Boulevard, Apartment 3B,*
   Lear Hotel

△

Before the sun rose, D washed herself in the garden, dressed in the smart navy dress that Ike had left, and plaited her hair in the clear side mirror of the boxy gun wagon driven by the soldiers with the painted faces.

It was graying when she set out. Across the street, at the same second-floor window where she'd seen him before, she glimpsed the vulturous man who roosted in the Archives for the Study of Nautical Exploration and Oceanic Depth, observing her. Their eyes met for a second, and his curtains jerked shut.

The cards had confirmed that this stranger—and the other strangers she had spotted in some of the buildings on Little Heritage Street—were interlopers like herself. The previous Curator of the National Museum of the Worker (or the previous Head Scholar of the Archives for the Study of Nautical Exploration and Oceanic Depth) was busy elsewhere, functioning as acting premier of the Provisional Government.

The former curator was the same cheerful man she'd met that long-ago day in the Grand Hall of the Society for Psykical Research, her brother's friend who'd told her the story of Simon the Gentle and wore a shiny gold vest; and he had a name: Aloys Lumm.

Aloys Lumm must be very old now. In his stories about the Provisional Government's meetings, Robert made it seem that the playwright was half-senile. D remembered how Robert had been assigned to read one of Lumm's plays for a class, but only she had.

Their first night together in his rooms, unable to sleep but not wishing to leave yet, D had picked the library copy off the side table. In service there was scant opportunity to read, and the university masters disapproved of their domestics doing so, holding that it would only confuse and distract them.

While Robert slept beside her, she read the whole thing, a story of a devil tricking a father into murdering his sister, and the father's son into murdering the father. The men thought they'd trapped the beast, but he had let himself be caught. After the son committed suicide, the devil excused himself, stepped off stage left, and reemerged from stage right as a young man in the costume of an impresario. Thus changed, he invited a "Beautiful Young Woman" onstage. He asked her if she'd drink the blood of foolish people if it meant she could live forever. "Really?" the Beautiful Young Woman replied, and the devil said, "Truly!" and she had mused—*smiles coyly*, the stage directions instructed—before starting, "Since we're being honest—" just as the curtain dropped and the orchestra reprised the play's theme.

When Robert woke, she'd told him the play was about two hunters who thought they'd snared a devil, but really it was the other way around. D thought she might better have described the play as an elaborate recounting of some executions. The devil was never in any real danger, and planned every event with complete success. She had not liked it; it had seemed mean to her. What was the fun if the characters never had a chance?

Not that she planned to engage Aloys Lumm on the interpretation of his literary output.

She only wanted to ask him, "What happened to my brother, Ambrose? Why is a horrible future bleeding out of your magic box and into the walls of my museum?"

And, ultimately, "Why should I let you live?"

There was smoke in the air from the previous night's fires, but it was also chill and damp. Knee-high autumn mists spread over the streets. D had borrowed the purse from the wax woman in the yellow sand mining exhibit. It was an odd purse, made from a slightly shimmery, slightly sticky material, with an interior of turquoise silk. The name **GUCCI** was printed on a tag on the inside, presumably the woman's name. At a glance, though—especially a man's glance—it would not seem out-of-the-ordinary. D had put the pouch of glass eyes into it, along with the peculiar, blocky stage pistol that had been fastened in the female soldier's holster. The stage pistol was metal, like a real pistol, but not as heavy as its shape suggested. It would only be useful to gain a moment's distraction. Anyone with the wherewithal to look closely at the gun would quickly realize it was fake; the smooth grip flowed up to the barrel with no cylinder in between: there was nowhere to put bullets. Also, the trigger was frozen.

On Legate Avenue, D quickly left the former embassy behind. She also thought of the morning that Nurse had got sick, and she had done exactly as she'd promised Ambrose, and traveled alone to fetch him.

She thought of the morning that Robert had accompanied her to take possession of the Society for Psykical Research, and how they'd joked about souls being incinerated.

Those previous mornings seemed impossibly close to this morning, as close as the other world had been to the charred Vestibule all along—just a step. D half-expected to meet her earlier self, approaching from the opposite direction.

Her heels clicked lightly on the sidewalk. She was aware of the dress's unfamiliar bustle behind her.

D was aware, too, that she was being followed. At the edges of her vision, she noticed the cats, darting soundlessly, small shadows slinking inside the fog that clung to the foundations of buildings. As one dropped off, another picked up the trail.

Their company did not frighten D. Not that she supposed that they regarded her with any special affection. What she sensed, above all, was their insistence. D's feeling was that they had their own particular aims, and those aims somehow aligned with hers—to this point, at least.

Events Leading to the Overthrow of the Overthrow of the Provisional Government, Pt. 1

*T*he grind of Jonas's snores informed Lionel that his lover had been awake worrying most of the night before fatigue finally pulled him under. Once they'd agreed to give General Crossley the ultimatum to either clear the Great Highway—by receiving the immediate surrender of the government holdouts, or by launching a full-on assault—or else relinquish his command, Lionel had fallen asleep easily. As things had worsened, as the public's discontent had swollen and the peace negotiations had stalled and the standoff extended, as Crossley had become more impenetrable and Lumm more confused, Lionel, conversely, felt growing within himself an odd, capricious assurance. Problems were always difficult—until they were solved. They were on the verge of it.

"It's bound to go right eventually," he'd explained to Jonas, and Jonas had said that was not at all true, damn it. Jonas had called him a sweet fool.

"You'll see," Lionel had said and kissed him, and Jonas kissed him back, and said in a clenched voice, "Griffin's Eggs!" which was some sort of dockman's slang.

Lionel was careful not to wake him as he dressed. He paused in the doorway to fondly regard his dockman. Jonas's tension lines loosened in sleep, stripping twenty years from his face and giving him an expression of ingenuousness that Lionel thought reflected the man's true character. It was not the flinty dockworker who had taken a courageous stand on behalf of the poor and the indigent, and for law and fairness; that man had seen too much to believe in a new order. It was some deeper, younger part of him that had answered the call.

His thick arm, atop the sheets, was tattooed with a rope that wound from his wrist to his elbow. Lionel loved to trace the rope with his finger. It looped around on itself, so that it had no visible ends.

"That's right, fella," Jonas said, which was what he had taken to calling him, to Lionel's delight. "That's because I tied the knot where you can't see it." He'd winked and flashed one of his rare gap-toothed smiles.

Lionel was Jonas Mosi's fella. How could everything not turn out for the best, when that had?

Once, when Jonas thought he was asleep, Lionel heard his lover pray. "Strike your paw down on the things that would hurt us, and hunt the wickedness back in its hole," he murmured. His belief moved Lionel. Jonas was so proud, and yet he asked for help, humbled himself before the invisible.

Lionel had an urge to go and sit beside Jonas and slide his finger along the tattooed rope again, and whisper to him that there was nothing to worry about, they could never go wrong, not if they were together. But dawn was burning along the lower slats.

"See you at breakfast, Jonas," Lionel said to the sleeping man, and went out into the hall, shutting the door softly behind himself.

△

Mosi dreamed of Lionel.

Lionel was at the rail of a ship's stern. He removed his hat and put it over his breast and looked solemnly upon Mosi, who was back on shore. There were dozens of other men and women on either side of Lionel at the rail. One of these passengers he recognized as the little saloonkeeper of the Still Crossing, who had a sideline as a fence. Another was Joven, short, bald, and sour-mouthed.

The condition of the ship appalled Mosi: violent green barnacles muscled up to the gunwales, and the deckhouse looked like a clapboard shanty. He called to Lionel, "Fella, be ready to swim!"

Δ

Since the days immediately after the uprising, Lionel and Mosi had been installed in rooms at the Metropole. This made it easier for Crossley's security to protect them. (Lumm had steadfastly refused to be dislodged from his own apartment across the street at the Lear.)

The luxury of the great hotel embarrassed Lionel, but he could not deny the convenience of the situation. Though no one who knew either man well would ever doubt their integrity, both were acutely aware that it was not strictly appropriate for two of the three leaders of a democratic undertaking to be involved in a romantic relationship with one another; however, this housing arrangement made it easy for them to move between each other's rooms undetected. Jonas's room was on the third floor and Lionel's was on the fifth. Their guard detail was stationed in the lobby, and the domestic staff was closely monitored, allowed to tidy the rooms only in the afternoons when the men were at meetings or other business, and under protection. The simple key, therefore, was to avoid the elevators, where the operator might take note of Lionel leaving Jonas's floor at the odd hour of six in the morning, and stick to the stairs.

As was usual for the early hour, Lionel stepped out to find that the elevator door was closed and the entire span of the third-floor hall was empty—except for the latest incarnation of the King Macon's mascot, Arista, at the door to the back stairs. Like all of her predecessors, she was a chocolate-colored Siamese.

Arista stood and trotted along the red-and-gold-patterned carpet runner to meet him, and twined her lithe body between Lionel's legs.

"Good morning, ma'am," he said to the animal, and petted her between the ears. Lionel forgot if this Arista was XXII or XXIII. She was also in the wrong hotel. The Metropole belonged to Talmadge. "I'm glad to see you, but you're supposed to stay at the Macon. If Talmadge sees you, I'm afraid there'll be trouble."

Arista purred softly. "Are you smiling at me, little thing? I'll make it worth your while if you do. Come see me at breakfast and I'll give you a piece of bacon, and I'll bet that my fella gives you two pieces."

Lionel continued down the hall. The cat darted after him and shot between his legs, which caused Lionel to stumble, but he caught himself against the wall. His palms made a soft *thump*, and he looked back to make sure that no one opened their door. No one did.

He returned his attention to Arista. The cat had reset herself in front of the door to the stairs. Her amber eyes focused on him steadily as she meowed.

He put a finger to his lips. "I understand," he whispered, although he didn't, and moved around the cat. It meowed yet again. "I'll give you bacon," he said quietly over his shoulder.

△

The Provisional Government's youngest leader opened the door and went through.

"Sir," said a soldier in an auxiliary uniform sitting on the steps to the fourth floor. He had a tonsure of gray hair and raw cheeks. Set across his knees was a rifle.

"What is it?" Lionel asked. He didn't have time to be frightened before the second soldier, the one who had been on the right side of the doorway, put a bayonet through his back. He sank sideways, and a third soldier, stepping around the closing door, caught him and hoisted him up. Huge waters crashed around inside Lionel's head, and it felt like most of his body disintegrated. He could only feel his toes jammed into his shoe tips and the damp hand clamped over his mouth.

His killer drove the blade into his belly, yanked it free, and stabbed it in again. The old soldier on the steps did not rise from his seated position.

He scratched his scalded cheek and met Lionel's eyes with an expression that might have been faintly apologetic.

Lionel thought, *I just wanted to help people.*

He thought, *I should have listened to that cat.*

He thought, *I hope that Jonas knows I loved—*

On the Tram

*B*rewster didn't give the large, bushy white cat a second glance. Cats wandered onto the trams all the time. This one climbed the stairs at the north stop of the Legate–National Boulevard Station, trailing a woman in a neat blue dress. Brewster picked her for a teacher, or a member of one of those charity societies. The animal hopped onto a seat and set to cleaning its leg. The woman sat across from it.

The driver threw the tram into gear and it began to trundle ahead.

It was quiet following the clamor of the previous night's march. Only a half dozen passengers sat in the linked tram cars, a combination of drunks and morning-shift workers, most of them half-dozing. Brewster was tired himself. He had not slept since he'd heard about the killings at that saloon in the Lees. Thoughts of the dead bodies and the lost lives and the anger it had kindled, of what he had set in motion with that damned Hob Rondeau by going to see that sergeant about his stolen bowler, would not stop rolling around in his head.

Brewster swore to himself that he'd never wear a hat again so long as he breathed. He wanted to punch the haberdasher who had lured him into the shop and sold him the gaudy bowler. He wanted to punch Hob Rondeau. Above all else, he wanted someone to explain himself to, someone who loved him and thought the best of him, and who would tell him that he wasn't to blame. But there was no one like that. For a few minutes that other morning, with the quick boy hanging onto the side of his cab, the tram driver had believed there could be, but Mary Ann had only been a tease. Those people at that saloon were dead. He'd caused it, him, Brewster Uldine.

In the overhead mirror at the top of the tram's windscreen he searched for a distraction, and found the reflection of the woman in the neat blue dress. "And where are you headed today, miss?" he asked.

"The Lear Hotel," she said.

△

Robert rubbed his cheek where Willa had slapped him after he told her he didn't want to meet with her anymore. He guessed he'd deserved it, but it had felt perfunctory; she hadn't really cared for him either. He hoped that Dora did care for him. It had never seemed important before, but suddenly it was. The revolution was sagging, there had been a massacre in the Lees, and the people were marching for relief. She was the only thing that seemed solid.

The lieutenant needed Dora to care for him—the maid of no family, the Lodgings girl who could not play piano, or draw, or dance, or do anything beautiful. He felt she did care for him, and it wasn't because he came from money, or because he was intelligent, or because he did things for her. Money wasn't important to her; she was smart enough on her own; and there would be no shortage of other men who would do things for her if she wanted one.

"Don't just stand there dreaming," Willa said, "get the fuck gone. That's what it means when a woman slaps you. It means get the fuck gone."

He left through the Metropole kitchens. When he got to the foot of the alley that separated the King Macon and the Metropole, Robert lit a cigarette.

Wagons and carriages were clattering in both directions. Across the street, in front of the Lear, a man was shoveling shit into a barrel.

An old auxiliary soldier leaned on the wall of the King Macon on the opposite corner of the alley. Robert saluted him. The soldier's gray hair fell down from under his cap and puddled in curls on his thin shoulders. He gripped a cane in one hand, and he had a hunch too. Robert was disheartened. What was a man like this supposed to fight, a bowl of oatmeal?

The soldier saluted in return and hacked a few times into his elbow. "Just waiting for some friends, sir." There was a tattoo of a triangle on the back of his wrinkled hand.

"Wonderful," Robert said.

△

The tram driver had a drained look. D imagined an apartment of cheap furniture, crumbs of a lunch made by the landlady on the table, a newspaper covered in fingerprints after already being read twice, and on a shelf some insipid luxury object, some small totem of male pride to pour his love into: a schooner in a bottle to polish, or a loud-colored hat to brush.

"What do you think of the news about those murders down in the Lees?" he asked, and she sensed that her destination was irrelevant, and he had just been seeking an undefended ear for the real subject of his interest. "I think it's a terrible tragedy, but things like that seem to happen down in those parts. It seems wrong to throw around blame." His tone was defensive, as if he expected to be challenged.

"I'm sorry, but I don't know anything about it," she said.

△

The new sergeant at the table in the Magistrates' Court told Rondeau he couldn't help him, he didn't know where Sergeant Van Goor could be found.

Rondeau informed the man that he was wrong.

"You can help me, and you will help me. I need a word with Sergeant Van Goor. I need him to explain to me this dear fucking mess that's he allowed to come to pass in the Lees that has endangered the entire project of this society we're trying to build where not everything that's dismal and rotten and sick is piled on the backs of the poor, and the fat ones eat clotted cream and drink champagne and merrily rub their cocks on silk for the fun of it. You can help me, and you will help me."

The sergeant who absorbed this diatribe felt as though he'd been ambushed by a thunderstorm out of a clear sky.

"Listen, I just took over here," he said. "I mean—" He ruffled through some papers that Van Goor had crabbed with his blocky print. There was one with a list of twenty or so names, and an address—**76 Legate Avenue**.

"Seventy-six Legate Avenue!" he cried, seizing on it as the quickest means of diverting the intemperate Volunteer. "That's where you should go. That's where he is, I bet."

△

"I'm sure if the people there'd behaved themselves, no one'd been hurt. What happened, it proves how dangerous they were, that's what I think. If you've ever heard of that saloon, you know it's a rathole of thieves and cheat artists. That's well known."

The tram driver's opinion of a saloon where some murders had apparently occurred was of no interest to D. She was thinking about what she had to do. She was thinking about how Ambrose had trusted Aloys Lumm.

The tram rattled past the rows of theaters, all of which were shuttered, the framed posters on the walls outside advertising plays that had last been performed the night before the government fled. The white cat finished its bath and curled up in the canvas pocket of its seat.

D reached forward to examine the cat's collar. The cat regarded her with a half-lidded eye, but did not otherwise shift. *Talmadge XVII— Resident of the Metropole Hotel*, read the collar's small silver tag. D brushed the top of its head once lightly, not making too much of the creature—it did not present as the kind of cat that appreciated cosseting—and leaned back into her own seat.

The cat's eye closed, and though its whole body trembled with the motion of the tram, it appeared to fall into a sound sleep.

△

It's impossible to know what XVII may have been thinking, or if she dreamed as she went to sleep on the tram seat; whether she missed her home at the Metropole Hotel where the staff had become increasingly worried about her absence of the last few days, especially in light of all the trouble that the Lear had gone through in recent times with its cats disappearing; how she might have reacted to an Arista in one of her hallways; whether she was comfortable in the small, rocky dugout that she had chosen for her new home amid the ruins of the Society; what had compelled her to twice sneak into the museum to sharpen her claws upon the wooden box with the lens; if XVII understood anything at all, or if she was entirely driven by instinct.

But she did purr in her sleep. Her stomach was digesting the mouse that she had feasted on in the ruins at dawn. She had crushed it in one pounce, pinned it between her paws, and batted it around for a while before she slit its guts and ate.

△

Elgin tottered his way across the So Fair. He was so drunk he didn't know if he was going east or west. He was so drunk he forgot a promise he'd made to himself, and let his gaze drift over the railing to the river, where he feared he'd see Joven and the Morgue Ship and his dead friends from the Still Crossing.

There was nothing but the water, though. The Fair was a gray-green wrinkled sheet in the fog. Elgin exhaled. The sun, muted by banks of cloud, sat on the horizon somewhere past the bay. He was all right.

A hand touched his shoulder.

"Don't be afraidt, brother," Marl said, stepping forward to stand beside him.

The drunkard's corpse went unnoticed for quite some time. Sprawled on the ground beside the bridge's railing, he only looked to be sleeping.

△

The knife Bet used to cut her wrists, one of the carvers that she'd taken from the university kitchen, fell from her fingers and stuck its tip in a floorboard. She sat in Gid's chair by the hearth with her arms flung out. The blood was hot on her skin. She heard it pattering faintly. Someone had murdered her Gid, and so she had murdered herself.

Cruel as life had been, Bet harbored no expectations for an afterlife. She did not anticipate that the Mother Cat would carry her to a warm place; or that she would meet the mother and father who had left her to grow up, disparaged and abused, in the Lodgings; or to be reunited with Gid. She expected more cruelty. Her best hope was for nothingness.

Bet's head tipped to the side. She stared at the knife stuck in the floor. Blood was pooled around it, and more blood was falling, falling out of her. Bet listened to it patter, and other noises grew up behind the patter, clanking chains, lapping waves, a man bellowing to send out the dinghy and fetch that poor woman.

△

Although they'd never know, Len and Zil had only missed D by an hour. They had come to make a "Social Call," an activity that Zil had wanted to try out ever since she had heard a rich lady say it on the street outside the theaters once. But no one answered their knocks on the doors of the museum.

"Do you think she said yes to his proposal?" Zil asked. "He looked sharp."

"Maybe. He looked all right." Not only was Len skeptical of the concept of the "Social Call," which ritual Zil had insisted required him to wait in line at a pump and wash his face in ice-cold water beforehand, but his opinion of Ike had peaked at the factory, and been on the decline ever since. The older boy carried himself too big, that was Len's view: "That Ike isn't so good a dribser as he talks. It's tiresome."

Len nodded at the wreck of the Society building. "Would you look at that pile."

Zil knew this was his way of saying that he wanted to go play in the filthy ruins.

"Do you want to go play in it?" She knew he'd never admit it.

"Play in it?" he scoffed. "No! I was just observing."

"Let's go then."

Len grunted and kicked at nothing. He had, in fact, wished to play in the filthy ruins. "Social Calls are a lot of shit," he said vengefully.

Zil ignored his sulking. She was disappointed not to learn how Ike's proposal had turned out, and she was intensely curious to meet his intended; but at the same time, she had been nervous about how he might be taking the news of the gruesome murders at the Still Crossing. The quick girl had got the idea that he was quite fond of Rei and them that had died.

She was a step behind Len at the corner of Legate when Len blurted, "Back it up," and grabbed her arm. "Green armband coming."

They hustled past the museum, and ran through the empty doorframe of the shattered building to hide.

On the second floor of the former embassy, the man who inhabited that place happened to spy the ragged boy and girl before they disappeared from the corner. He was fond of children, especially the mischievous sort, which he himself had been. He hoped they stayed in the neighborhood. He would like to meet them.

The clack of the embassy's knocker echoed from below. He limped downstairs and invited Hob Rondeau inside.

Δ

With a twanging screech, the tram halted at the station in the center of the National Boulevard that was set between the Metropole and the King Macon on the eastern half of the thoroughfare, and the Lear on the western.

"May a cat smile on you," the tired-looking tram driver said to D as she rose to leave.

Events Leading to the Overthrow of the Overthrow of the Provisional Government, Pt. 2

The scratching and whining woke Mosi.

A cat was clawing at the door. He lay on his side and blinked in the light that filtered between the slats of the street-facing blinds. He sensed without looking that Lionel had left the bed.

Mosi sat up, feeling like his whole body had collapsed into his stomach, and that his body was made of stone. If Crossley refused to follow their orders, if he refused to give the command to move his forces on the loyalist position on the Great Highway and finish this thing, they were going to have to relieve him and issue the order themselves. If Crossley's auxiliary soldiers didn't like the order, they were dead.

Lionel said they couldn't fail. Mosi had come to love Lionel, had found in the younger man someone he could laugh with like he had never laughed with anyone else, and he had come to understand that he was totally sincere, that there was nothing he wanted more than to make life better and fairer and less sick. For such a smart person, however, he was maddeningly optimistic. *Oh, sweet fella! Of course they could fail!*

A key fitted in the lock, *click*. Which was unusual, because Lionel didn't have a key. Their arrangement was for Mosi to leave the door ever-so-slightly unlatched. The maids had a key, but it was too early.

Mosi, wearing nothing but his drawers, stood as the lock turned over, and swept the blanket off the bed.

A baldheaded auxiliary soldier with scraped cheeks came in after the opening door with his rifle and bayonet pointed. Two more red-cheeked auxiliary soldiers crowded after him. Mosi threw the blanket over the first man, and the soldier fired, blasting a hole in the cotton.

A dozen tiny teeth bit Mosi's bare chest and neck as he roared forward. He caught the blanketed soldier around the neck and hurled him into the men who were following. The collision of bodies sent the rearmost man banging into the hall's opposite wall, and his rifle went off, blasting the weapon's single round into the ceiling. Plaster spattered the rug. The second man fell on the floor with a croaky gasp and dropped his rifle. The soldier covered in the blanket went twisting, trying to stab his way free of the blanket with his bayonet.

Mosi poured out into the hall. The soldier on the floor had something of the grasshopper about him: he was long-limbed and bug-eyed and had a jutting Adam's apple. To judge by the gray hair sticking out from under his cap, he was also old enough to be a grandfather. Mosi stomped his bare foot on the geezer's crotch and felt something important to the man pop under his heel. The soldier screamed, the scream turning into a raspy wheeze.

The one who had shot into the ceiling crouched against the wall, gaping, clutching his rifle. The dockman ripped the gun from his hands. This man was old too. A single wild white eyebrow bristled with dandruff above his close-set eyes, and when Mosi whipped the bayonet across the old soldier's face, it opened a bone river between his eyebrows and his eyes. Blood splashed across Mosi's neck and face. The man collapsed.

He reset his attention to the first one, the baldy who'd led the charge. The remaining auxiliary soldier was a few feet away. He'd got the blanket off and was regarding Mosi coolly. He was not so elderly as the other two, perhaps only four or five years older than Mosi himself, and had a muscular build. While the soldier watched Mosi, he patted his bandolier, feeling for a bullet.

The attacker Mosi'd stepped on was making a noise like he had a chicken bone stuck in his throat and clawing halfheartedly at the butt of his rifle beside him. The other soldier was convulsing, soaking the rug with his blood. Down by the door to the stairwell hunkered a brown Siamese cat, observing it all.

None of the doors opened and there were no other sounds. Mosi figured they'd cleared the place out to do the assassination—smart. His skin was on fire where the bullet fragments had hit him.

"You killed him, didn't you? You killed my fella."

The bald soldier had found a cartridge and taken it out but made no move to load. It must have dawned on him there wouldn't be time. If he tried to prime another shot, Mosi would be on him before he could get it off. They were going to finish up with the bayonets. The soldier slotted the cartridge back into his bandolier.

"We did," he said.

"Did you make it quick?"

The soldier nodded.

Mosi rubbed a fist across his wet eyes. "Thank you. Did Crossley send you?"

"Don't be ridiculous." The soldier laughed. "We're with Lumm."

"Really?" said Mosi, and he wondered if they had been very stupid, or if Lumm had been very clever.

The soldier twisted his neck and rubbed one of his scraped-looking cheeks against his shoulder. As he did so, his other cheek showed, and Mosi discerned that it wasn't scraped—it was tattooed: wavy red lines broken by a red triangle. They all had tattoos like that, all three of them.

"You're old for a soldier."

For some reason this drew a chuckle from the soldier. "Not in my particular army."

"I suppose you thought tattooing your face couldn't make you more unsightly," Mosi said. "You were wrong."

"That so?" the soldier asked.

"It is." The dockman wasn't in the condition he'd been in in his younger years, he was wounded and half-naked, and the soldier looked to be made of firmer stuff than his companions—but it would make no difference.

"I'm going to kill you," Mosi told him.

"No," the soldier said, and his posture relaxed. He lowered his rifle to his side.

This irritated Mosi. "I don't accept your surrender—" he began, unaware that the man on the floor had at last got hold of the dropped rifle.

The prone man pulled the trigger with a burble of rage. The bullet sheared through the dockman's torso, and bits of his stomach and ribs painted the wallpaper, and that was how the second-youngest leader of the Provisional Government died.

The Lear

The white cat debarked ahead of D, but instead of staying with her or running ahead to scratch something, it went underneath the tram stop's bench. Once there, Talmadge XVII curled her paws beneath herself and stared from the shadows, not at D but at the front of the Lear Hotel across the avenue.

It seemed that D's escort had concluded. She could only assume this meant that, as far as XVII was concerned, she was on the right track.

D crossed the street.

Δ

"You hear that, sir?" the doorman of the Lear, in his gray uniform with black piping and black rope at the shoulders, asked a guest in a cream-colored suit for whom he had been about to open the door. There had been two pops in the distance.

(The first pop was the bullet that shot through the blanket and peppered Mosi's bare neck and chest; and the second was the shot that went into the Metropole hall's ceiling.)

D was stepping up onto the curb a few feet away. She hesitated, making some business of adjusting her sleeve, and keeping a sidelong eye on the two men in front of the Lear's doors.

There was a third pop. (This was the shot that killed Jonas Mosi.)

"I think I did hear something," the gentleman in the suit said, and yet another sound, more distant but bigger, a pillowy boom, punctuated his assent.

Δ

(This larger, farther-off sound belonged to Gildersleeve's artillery; they had opened fire on the encampment of Crossley's Auxiliary on the Great Highway.

The general had landed on the northeastern tip of the country four days previous and, in nightly groupings, moved his army on foot to gather in the forest a mile behind the Crown's encampment. His engineers had dismantled three of their big guns and, using handcarts with greased wheels, quietly rolled the pieces up the steep footpaths to the plateau. At the top, by lamplight, the cannon teams had reassembled the guns, concealed behind the famed stone monoliths. Loads of lead and smoke shot had been brought.

Gildersleeve ordered his infantry commanders, meanwhile, to convey to their squads that anyone in their path or in their sight should be treated as an enemy fighter.

"And when we reach the city limits, sir?" a captain had asked.

His stomach pain had reduced Gildersleeve to making his preparations and directives from a flat position on a hammock in his tent. No longer could the general keep down even water-thinned cottage cheese.

He checked his letter with the red symbols, folded it away. "Captain, we have intelligence that they've dressed many of the traitors from the Auxiliary in civilian clothes, even disguised them to masquerade as women. Shoot anyone that shows themselves."

"Yes, sir," the captain said.

When King Macon XXIV visited, General Gildersleeve apologized for his inability to rise. "There's an evil sickness in my belly, my lord."

The king graciously excused him, and asked if they were ready.

Gildersleeve said, "If it pleases you, my lord." It did please the king, and His Highness issued the order to begin the attack. Gildersleeve—who despite his physical incapacitation still wore his uniform, one of the new ones with the triangular shoulder patches that his letter had told him to add to the army's regalia—drifted into his deathsleep as the surprise shelling on Crossley's position began.

Later in the morning, by the time his army overran the remainder of the single unit of Crossley's Auxiliary on the Great Highway, and began to reorganize and draw up the larger body of the cannons for the assault on the city proper, the general's flesh would be good and cold, his soul rather warmer.)

△

"There's another," the doorman said after another distant boom. He leaned out to gaze up the street in the direction of the city limits, and with his hand on the long brass handle of the door, pulled it wide.

D saw this, and stepped for the door.

"Definitely something," remarked the man in the cream-colored suit.

D slid around him and, drawing her skirts close and keeping her head low, swiftly moved into the Lear Hotel, unnoticed and unquestioned.

△

The central feature of the Lear's lobby was a parallel row of black-potted, red-leaved Japanese maple trees. They formed a runway to the grand staircase, and divided the lobby into two sections. To the right was the hotel saloon and the Concierge's desk; to the left was the reception area. The elevator, a later addition to the original structure, was behind and to the left of the grand staircase. Its gold door was pulled aside, and the elevator operator was visible, slouched on her stool inside the box. There was an auxiliary soldier stationed at attention at the bottom of the grand staircase, and another right outside the elevator door.

As D entered, nearly everyone in the massive room—auxiliary soldiers, hotel workers in the Lear's gray and black livery, a few young men with Volunteer bands tied around their arms—was reacting to the sounds, looking up from their places at the mahogany counters of the reception area and their seats in the ivy-patterned armchairs around the hearth in the saloon toward the Lear's wide plate-glass windows to see if there was something going on in the street. Beside the hearth, a violinist in tails continued to play a sunny melody.

"That's cannon," a gruff voice pronounced from the saloon side.

From this point, there was no way to make herself small enough to avoid being noticed. D let her skirts unfurl and slowed, forcing herself to keep her steps moderately paced. She tilted her chin. A woman of status, a woman who belonged in the lobby of the Lear Hotel, did not rush. The deep carpet sank under her steps. She had Gucci's purse tucked in her armpit, where it seemed to contain her heartbeat.

There were murmurs of concern as the gruff voice went on: "Heard it enough times in the Ottomans with Sleevey."

A Volunteer in a green armband, a university boy whom D recognized from her time in service, came running down the grand staircase. His name was Dakin, she remembered, and he had been very specific about how to starch his collars and used to leave notes for the laundresses that said things like, *I don't consider it too great a request to ask you to do things right.*

She looked past him and didn't break stride. Dakin hurried by, sparing her just a short, puzzled glance.

"Get ahold of Lionel!" she heard him call to someone. D was halfway across the lobby.

Ahead, a member of the hotel staff stepped out from between two pots on the right, about to cross the lane of trees to the left side, but paused, noticing D's approach. This man, full-faced with an immaculately combed beard of gray-blond hair, had an insignia on his breast that identified him as a manager of the hotel. His rooms, she guessed, were pin-clean: three mugs on three hooks, sheets turned down, windowsills dusted, a sealed letter in the top drawer of the bedside table detailing how his affairs should be dispatched if he died unexpectedly.

He gave D a measuring look, and she thought, *It's still too far to run.*

But that was all right. Why would she run? She was a valued guest.

Before the manager could decide whether to move on or to greet her, D quickened her steps and flicked a hand at him, mimicking the gesture of irritable toleration that she had seen the rector's wife use on the mornings that the domestic staff cleaned the rector's residence and had to pass through her sitting room, disturbing her breakfast.

"Sir," she said.

He bowed, training taking precedence over the extraordinary circumstances. "Good morning, madam. Are you finding the Lear to your satisfaction?"

D counted to four before answering. "It's fine," she said, indicating clearly by the interval that it was the opposite.

"Excellent, Madam—?" The manager frowned as he tried to place her name, which he should already have known. All the manager really needed to remember was that her husband was the kind of man who could still afford the rates even in these turbulent days, and that there were other hotels glad to take their money.

"There's a girl out front begging," D said sharply. "I've never experienced anything like it. They don't allow things like that to go on at the Metropole, I can promise you."

He clicked his heels and bowed again. "Madam, I apologize on behalf of the Lear. I'll have the doorman see to it immediately."

"Thank you," D said. "The creature scattered when I shooed it away, but I expect she's lurking around somewhere in the vicinity."

"Trust in me, madam. You won't be bothered again." The manager swiveled off his original course and moved toward the hotel entrance.

Another soft boom caused the red leaves of the potted trees to flutter lightly. The violinist playing ceased with a sharp squeak.

D went on; at the end of the lane of trees, she nodded to the auxiliary soldier at the foot of the grand staircase—"Ma'am"—and curled around the left newel post. She walked to the second auxiliary soldier by the elevator.

"Officer," she said.

"Ma'am." He had a black mustache waxed into jolly points, a few broken capillaries beneath his eyes, a patch of glossy pink scar tissue at the right line of his jaw, and a wide, benevolent smile that seemed to invite you to share a laugh and a few sips too, if you had the time. D thought his rooms were jumbled and full of family: sons, daughters, and a wife who also enjoyed a laugh and a drink.

"I just need to see your key," the friendly soldier said.

She reached into Gucci's purse, brushing her hand over the strange pistol, and found the pouch containing the glass eyes.

△

What had worked with the manager would not work with a soldier. She removed the pouch and gave it to him. "I'm not a guest, actually. I'm supposed to deliver these to Mr. Lumm on the third floor."

The soldier undid the cord and looked into the pouch. "Are those—?" He barked a laugh. "Isn't that just like our Mr. Lumm? If it's not books he's getting, it's something else—big crates of tea from Russia, special black wood for his fireplace. He had a statue come of a man with an octopus for a head that'd give you nightmares, and so heavy it needed to be pulled up the side of the hotel and in through his window with block and tackle. What a quiz he is! Course he'd need a supply of glass eyeballs. Good old Mr. Lumm!"

The soldier stirred his finger in the pouch of glass eyes. They tinkled against each other. He shook his head, laughed again, redid the cord, and handed the pouch back to D.

"Thank you," D said, smiling lightly in return.

She returned the pouch to her purse and took a step—before the soldier's arm intruded between her and the elevator. "I apologize, ma'am. I know a lovely thing like you would never hurt anyone, but we've got to check with Mr. Lumm first."

There was another soft boom, and another tide of worried voices from the lobby.

"Of course," D said. She stepped back.

"Vanessa, can you ring Mr. Lumm and tell him there's some glass eyeballs for him?"

The elevator operator, a middle-aged woman with loose brown hair and half-spectacles who had been morosely observing their interaction, climbed from her stool. "Yuh." She unhooked the bell of the house roto that hung on a wall of the elevator, stuck it over her ear, and spoke into the com. "3B."

"We'll get you right up, ma'am," the soldier assured her. D smelled his mustache wax.

Another cottony boom resounded. The soldier's smile wavered, but he took a deep breath and pulled it back together. "No need to panic," he said, and rubbed his scar with a thumb.

D thought he was talking more to himself than to her.

"Good morning, sir," the elevator operator said, keeping her ear pressed to the bell. "This is the lobby. Sergeant Gaspar has a young lady with a delivery for you. She comes from—" The woman glanced at D. "Ma'am?"

"I'm employed by the manufacturer. It's for the National Museum of the Worker. Mr. Lumm is the museum curator."

"It's for the National Museum of the Worker. The delivery is some glass eyeballs."

The operator listened, nodding. She looked to D again. "And your name, ma'am?"

Sergeant Gaspar smiled down on D with his glistening mustache tips.

A fresh boom interrupted them, which gave D long enough to calculate that, as well as she'd done to get this far without raising an alarm, she couldn't get around Sergeant Gaspar and Vanessa; even if she drew Gucci's gun on them, an alarm would be raised, and someone would stop her on the third floor before she ever got to Lumm's suite; she was going to have to run, after all; she wasn't going to be fast enough and she was going to be arrested; and, on that other morning years before, Lumm had told her all he would ever tell her—about the conjurer, Simon the Gentle, "the most wonderful, wonderful criminal you can imagine"—and she would never know for certain what had happened to her brother.

The echo of the cannon receded. "Ma'am?" A wrinkle appeared between the sergeant's eyebrows and he angled his head at her. "Your name, ma'am?"

It occurred to D that, actually, she did have one trick left:

"Simona Gentle," she said. "My name is Simona Gentle."

Events Leading to the Overthrow of the Provisional Government, Pt. 3

*G*eneral Crossley hesitated at the open door of Lumm's suite. "Tell me again how it will go, Mr. Lumm?"

Lumm was at the table, soaking his poor hands in a bowl of hot water.

"Check your paper, dear," he said to Crossley, observing as the general took from a pocket the small piece of paper that had been his closest companion over the last several months.

When they had decided that they were ready to acquire a military man, Westhover had written the Red Letter in the traditional way—using the fibula of a cat as his pen and some of his own blood as ink—and mailed it to the general. This method of control was taxing to prepare and only worked on the weak-minded or the very sick, but they had chosen well in their selection of Crossley. The paper was creased and feather-soft from handling, the red drawings and markings blurred.

"What's it say?" Lumm asked.

"*My soul becomes a light*," the general read. His expression relaxed. "Right. That will be good."

"And you'll have a nice glass house. Marvelous, marvelous views." This was a simplification. The glass house was actually more of a lantern globe, and Crossley's very thin soul would not become light so much as it would be burnt to make light, and the true benefit would accrue to Lumm and his friends, who bathed in the light of souls like lizards, and were rejuvenated by it, made young again—but there was no reason to bewilder the general with details.

A soft thud echoed from the north: Gildersleeve's cannons.

"What will happen to my men?" With Crossley it often came back to this tedious question. Lumm liked how helplessly sad the general was—sadness was a big part of why souls burned so well, he suspected—but the last living member of the Provisional Government was close to done in, and they had to get on with things. Lumm needed to be reborn.

"They'll be fine. Those new shoulder patches we had made for their uniforms, the ones with the triangles on them, will keep them safe. Their souls will turn into lights too, pretty little lights. Now, hurry off to your room, dear."

Westhover, who had been quietly contemplating the ember of his cigarette, left his place beside Lumm and moved to usher out the general. "Farewell, you numb turd." He clapped him cheerfully on the shoulder, shoved him out into the hall, and shut the door.

△

General Crossley shuffled to the door of his room, 3F, and went in without bothering to shut it behind himself. He checked his paper. It now read: *Cut a triangle onto your hand.*

He tucked away the paper and took out his pocketknife. Crossley unfolded the knife as he walked. He stretched out his left hand and cut three lines onto the back, forming a triangle. There was no pain. Blood pooled up from the incisions and dripped down around his hand and his wrist.

Crossley wiped the blade against his hip, closed it, and put it away. He took out his paper. Now it read: *Climb on the chair.*

There was a chair already set up in the middle of the small sitting room. A noose dangled from a pipe above it. Earlier on the paper had told him to make these preparations.

He walked to the chair, and stepped up on it.

Though the general's next task seemed fairly evident, he scrutinized his paper just in case. *Put on noose, step off*, the words now read.

The latest in a series of large booms thundered from the north, and Crossley was reminded of his men. He looked at his paper again. There were his men, drawn in red ink, and protected by lines of red light that repulsed the shelling. They wheeled out cannons of their own, which were also red, and enormous. The general did not remember inspecting these mighty red cannons, but he was glad to have them.

He folded his paper and tucked it away. He put his neck through the noose.

The Curator

"Ready when you are," Currency Minister Westhover said after showing out the general. The minister's costume could not quite obscure the man's essential vulgarity: black-tinted spectacles, a full yellow beard held on by spirit gum, and a dark, ready-made suit. Westhover was supposed to look like an apprentice bank clerk or a stenographer, someone harmless, but instead he looked as if he might sell you pornographic drawings. A truer indication of the man's character, Lumm thought. It was temporary, though, and Westhover had played his part well, sticking around to be arrested and giving Lionel and Mosi and the rest of them plenty of testimony to be sanctimoniously outraged about over the last few weeks, distracting them with legal issues and financial forensics while the actual conflict remained unsettled.

Once the Crown and the government were reinstalled, Westhover could reclaim his position and continue his work as the Society for Psykical Research's key political representative. Crossley had used some excuses about "security risks" to keep the currency minister out of confinement at the Magistrates' Court and under house arrest at the Lear, but until the revolutionaries had been fully routed, it was important that he keep a low profile.

Lumm looked at his hands. Like clockwork, every time he got into his sixties, they started to jaundice and flake. In his seventies, the skin grayed and peeled. Now he was eighty again and his hands were dead again, a bloodless blue crossed with empty black veins. The only way he could get any feeling was to soak them in nearly boiling water.

This thing with his hands, he didn't know why it happened. There was, in fact, a great deal that he didn't know. Lumm enjoyed giving people the impression that he was the devil, but in reality, he was just a literary man of three hundred or so odd years, and the duly elected president of the Society for Psykical Research.

His predecessor in that office, Frieda, had claimed that the story about the city's founding stonecutter being surprised to death in his castle was essentially true, except the invading beggars were not people, but cats. Frieda held that the stonecutter's angry ghost had made the first door to the Twilight Place, and that the Society had been originated by an adventurous girl who spotted it in some brambles and risked her skin to test it.

"Well then, who is that woman with the sewing basket and the guillotine who changes our faces for us?" Lumm had asked her.

Frieda had confessed her ignorance on that point. "She was there when I started. I can't even get the old bitch to cough up her name. But she's dedicated to the task."

The conjurer Simon the Gentle (real name: Dick Gennity) had believed the Twilight Place was a mistake. "It's like a worn spot on a shirt, Aloys, my dove. A minuscule tear at the armpit or the collar, and someone put their fat finger in there and widened it out, and got more than they bargained for."

Simon had discovered the Twilight Place on his own and used the place's powers of mutability in his act. He smugly refused to reveal how he'd learned of it, or explain what materials he'd used to construct his portal—the Vestibule—or even if he had constructed it. He stuck to his childish insistence that a cat had taught him all his magic. "I told you, Aloys, my dove, it was a big white cat that gave me my tricks. Like in the tales, it scratched them down on a piece of bark."

A majestically irritating individual, low-class from the first, a sticky sleight-of-hand artist and a cat worshipper, a Dick Gennity through and through. The conjurer never actually understood the Twilight Place. In all of his performances, he never recognized the glamour that veiled the other side of the door, and neither did his volunteers. They just went through to use the mirror that changed their faces. Dumb Dick had assumed the mirror was the whole thing!

Lumm had written a Red Letter and given it to the suggestible husband of a woman who went into the Vestibule during a performance, and that had been that for Simon the Gentle né Dick Gennity. *Die slowly on the floor, my dove.*

The Twilight Place, the crone with the thread and the guillotine, what the Society did to stay young, the techniques they'd learned from parchments and tablets recovered on archaeological expeditions and then refined: Lumm liked to believe it had all come about for no other reason than the universe had decided that they were deserving. He liked to believe that the universe had realized that charming, interesting people shouldn't die as easily as charmless, uninteresting people. It would not have been charming to say that, obviously—charm lay as much, if not more, in the unsaid as it did in the said—but it was one of the lessons that he hoped his work for the stage demonstrated. Few things made Lumm happier than the notion of some artless fellow wandering into a theater and seeing one of his plays and, in seeing it, realizing that he was best off being cautious and respectful in his behavior, not fussing or drawing attention to his artless self, and that he should be grateful for the luck that allowed him even a single existence in the shadows cast by his betters.

What was a certainty was that every few generations it was necessary to freshen up the stage, and resecure the authority of the right people—front men like Westhover—so the Society could operate freely, perform its experiments, and continue to advance its studies.

A year or so earlier, the urban peasantry's whining—about the pollution that kept cholera and other diseases circulating year after year, and their low wages, and the army's losses—had grown distractingly incessant. Westhover had lost his temper and executed that booger of a mudman in full view of an audience. The university radicals started publishing their pamphlets and the volume of the moaning increased.

Lumm grasped the situation early on. A revolutionary fervor had been born, the kind that, if allowed to simmer long enough untended, could bring about an uncooperative, impertinent, and expensive new government. His solution, which everyone had agreed was ingenious—"Sly as ever!" Edna (R.I.P.) had crowed, and "Slyer than ever!" Bertha (R.I.P.) had contended—was to quicken it up, to birth the hideous thing ahead of its natural schedule, and suffocate it in its crib.

He had made entreaties to lure out the rabble-rousing cretins like the dockman Jonas Mosi, and the romantics like the student Lionel Woodstock. Once he had been accepted as a fellow by the mutineers, he brought in Crossley, and it had seemed to the revolutionaries as if they had everything they needed.

Crossley and his Auxiliary Garrison seized the city, and the Crown retreated, and—that was it. Nothing was resolved. The public was left to stew in the promises of an impotent Provisional Government at the mercy of its stubborn general, and in the interval Gildersleeve received a Red Letter and sailed home with the regular army. In addition, a demonstration to show the Provisional Government's complete lack of command had been orchestrated: the massacre in that grotty beer hall in the Lees. The popular support for the revolutionaries, such as it was, had been profoundly undermined.

While the loss of his two best assassins was not a part of the design, it was really not a bad corollary. The Pinters had been forever giggling, but he couldn't remember a single witty thing either one of them had said. As gung-ho as Edna and Bertha had been, they were also rabid, and Lumm would have needed to dispose of them in the next life or two, in any case.

It was the irregularity of their deaths, if anything, that nagged. Lumm preferred a strictly scripted performance.

But Gildersleeve had returned. His forces would mop up Crossley's garrison, the rabble-rousers, and the radicals. They would have free rein to perform a bloodletting among whoever else showed their faces, which would act as a warning to never again fail to rise to the defense of the Crown. The soldiers who died would be recycled. All the complaints would cease for a good long while.

Beneath the surface of the water, his poor hands looked like islands of bare volcanic rock.

Now, the talk about the Morgue Ship and Joven and the missing people, which had reached even the third floor of the Lear Hotel, that was a mystifying business. Lumm didn't know what to make of it. The idea of a boat sailing through the air, or through walls, or down alleyways, was less outlandish to Aloys Lumm than to most people. Still, it was probably nonsense.

His only real remaining concern was the cats; he couldn't know what the cats might be planning.

△

On the subject of cats, Aloys Lumm took a hard line.

Some members of the Society regarded his beliefs as pure superstition, and felt that hunting them was the organization's hoariest and most futile tradition, the flip side of the foolishness preached by the old-time believers who prayed for the little monsters to bestow good fortune and provide direction. These members, for instance, argued that it was nothing more than an affectation to use cat bones for the composition of Red Letters, that it was proven the magic worked just as well if the symbols were written with a nib.

Credit where it was due: Edna and Bertha had taken the matter seriously. Where cats were concerned, they had not fucked about.

One reason that Lumm had taken residence in the Lear was because of its central location; living there put him closer to what was going on, and made him seem more accessible. That said, he could have found accommodations in the center of the city that didn't house one of those pampered ass-lickers. Lumm had done so with the purpose of letting the beasts know that he could go wherever he liked. He was speaking their language, pissing in their territory, warning them off.

The others could think what they liked; cats knew that the members of the Society wore different faces. They really, really did. They looked at you differently than they looked at regular people. Their eyes widened and their bodies tensed and you could feel them already burying pieces of you for later.

That's just how cats look at everyone! the doubters protested.

Fine, fine. Suppose you allowed that cats came by their unpleasant, ravenous, inspecting gazes naturally. How did you explain their fascination with the original door in the Fields? Why were they always lurking around the place, no matter how many of them were killed, waiting for an opportunity to scratch at the icebox? Wasn't it obvious? They wanted in. They wanted someone to open it and let them into the Twilight Place.

The doubters laughed and cried out, *Cats hate all closed doors!*

Very well, very well. The Society's stories about the danger of cats were myths, and the way they looked was the way they looked, and their obsession with closed doors was a matter of simple animal instinct. Lumm might have given the skeptical all of that.

But there was something else he knew, something that he had seen.

△

Frieda let herself get too old.

This was two Macons, two Zaks, a Bertrand, and a Xan ago, in the days of catapults, leeches, and widespread public agreement about the flatness of the world. In many ways, a better age.

The Society and its members had arrived at the usual point where a restart had become advisable, but Frieda had wanted to wait for the Keyhole, the tredecennial aligning of the moons. In the Society's library an extraordinarily fragile scroll of intriguing provenance—a pyramidal crypt on the outskirts of Alexandria—had turned up. The parchment was written in an unrecognizable language that, after years of study, she had translated. It was a recipe for the grinding of a lens, which, if pointed at the Keyhole, would reveal the location of a new door to yet another new world, one that was richer and more clement than what they called the Twilight Place. Many in the Society had theorized the likelihood of such a possibility. If there were two worlds, it seemed as likely as not there were countless more—worlds of infinite riches, worlds of unknown powers to be tapped.

A good restorative Nap lasted a year or two, and Frieda had not liked the prospect of having to wait another thirteen to place her eye to the lens. So, while the rest of the Society limped through the door on their arthritic hips, Frieda stayed behind, and her aide, Aloys Lumm, remained with her.

"You know," she said conspiratorially, "Aloysius, as my most loyal factotum, you'd be the second to step through to the new place." Frieda was like that; she acted as if she'd rescued him from cannibals or something. (In fact, he'd been part of a handsome traveling show when they met, making a fair living performing ghost stories for peasants.)

The scroll, however, was a forgery of Lumm's own creation, and once it was just the two of them, he only had to wait. On a crisp spring morning when she suggested a ride to the Bluffs in her gig to "taste the salt," his opportunity arrived.

At that hour there was no one else about. They had inched out onto one of the balconies—in those days, constructed of raw logs—on their old legs, propped by their canes, until they reached the rail. In front of them, the ocean, ruffling gray-blue, spanned to the horizon, touching against a white-blue sky. The seabirds floated above the water on invisible drafts.

Frieda, holding her gold shawl pinched beneath her chin, closed her eyes and smiled beatifically in the full light. "Isn't the sun good, Aloysius?"

Lumm said, "Frieda, I feel dreadful about this."

"What do you mean?" she asked without opening her eyes or turning her face to him.

He let go of his cane, grabbed her by the waist, and hoisted her over the railing.

She plummeted, skirts fluttering, screaming. When her frail body struck the wet rocks, it seemed to crack apart like a bundle of sticks.

The effort of throwing her badly strained Lumm's back, but he was joyous nonetheless. He hung over the railing, spine burning, blood rushing up into his head, and laughed at her smashed body so far below, the tide already snatching at it. No one would believe that it was an accident, but no one would mind. The occurrence, in and of itself, proved her unfitness. She had grown cavalier, and Aloys was the obvious candidate to replace her. It was too bad that he would never be able to tell anyone the best part: the scroll had been made from the hide of a donkey.

He righted himself with a grunt of pain and staggered backward. As Lumm caught his breath, his blood pressure gradually slowed, and his vision cleared. There was still no one else in sight.

Once he had carefully lowered himself to pick up his cane, Lumm poked to the railing for a last look. He wanted to remember Frieda this way, as bits of meat and jelly spread across rocks.

A flicker to his right drew his gaze. Lumm gaped as the ocean breeze hurled salt into his mouth.

The broken ledges that lined the bluffs were too narrow for human feet—but not for cats.

Twenty cats, thirty cats, forty cats, who knew how many, it was hard to count them as they slipped along the ledges, zigzagging downward in a mottled caravan of white and black and orange and brown and gray. The cats trickled down the face of the bluff to the tumult of sea-washed stones below. When they reached the field of wet and jagged rocks, the lead cat—black as an empty night sky—seemed to instinctively detect a path, and jumped and darted from one dry protrusion of stone to another.

The cat's direction drew Lumm's eyes and he leaned over the railing—and that was when he saw her move. It wasn't much, just a slight twist of her head, or rather, of the vaguely headlike splotch that was what remained of it.

The black cat crouched over the splotch, obscuring it, and a second cat crouched over the bloody chest of her gown, and then the swarm covered her entirely in a furry, twitchy, patched blanket. Before he pulled himself away, two sounds rose above the tide: a broken scream, and the wet and clicky burr of eager gobbling.

The Society had uncovered many wonders, but Lumm did not dare to share this incredible story. Frieda had suffered an accident and the waves had washed her into the ocean; that was all that had happened. He was elected president of the Society for Psykical Research, and after his Nap, the crone sewed him a new face, and he began his long and fruitful reign.

But he hadn't forgotten what he'd witnessed. Lumm knew what the cats really wanted to eat, and it wasn't fish heads.

△

You couldn't just kill them, either. Well, you could kill cats singly, and Lumm had. (Most recently, it had been his pleasure to execute a half dozen Celandines.) But there was no way to combat them *en masse*. Not only were there too many—they bred like rodents—but the commoners loved them and nurtured them. There were thousands of them in the Lees, maybe hundreds of thousands. It was dangerous enough to go down there into the slums where so much sickness lurked, endlessly pruning the human population even as the furry shits proliferated. If the people in the Lees caught you exterminating cats, you'd being getting off easy if they merely stabbed you to death. The Society's membership was exclusive, they didn't have the manpower to risk.

So he held his ground at the Lear, and hoped that the message he sent with each new Celandine was received.

More than once lately, Lumm had wished he could retreat to his study at the Society, and attempt again to translate the oldest books—not forgeries, but true texts written on the coarse skins of animals that no living person had ever seen—and learn what they could tell him about such things. He regretted the decision to burn the building and its secrets, and to abandon their quiet street. He had been afraid that one of the others—Edna or Bertha, probably, or Edna-and-Bertha—might attempt to take his place at the head of the Society, the way he had done to Frieda during a different period of change. With the building gone, so much of its contents existed only in Society President Aloys Lumm's wise head, making him indispensable. It had seemed like a worthwhile insurance policy, but in retrospect all he'd achieved was inconvenience: the arson had also destroyed Dick Gennity's conveniently located Vestibule. These days whenever he needed to go through, Lumm had to go to the middle of the Fields, and tromp into the woods to the original portal.

His mood was turning sulky. He needed his Nap.

After he had his Nap, Lumm thought he might ask the crone to make him a woman this time. He thought that might be fun, to be a very plain woman that people would either ignore or underestimate.

△

"That's enough," announced Lumm, and he lifted his hands from the water.

Westhover brought a towel. He lightly patted Lumm's hands dry. "Better?"

"Some." The feeling that the hot water had brought back to his fingers and knuckles was needly and painful. Each time he got old, it hurt more. Westhover had just helped him slide his calfskin gloves on when the roto rang. "Answer it," he said. "It's probably Lovering to let us know he finished with the student and the cretin."

The currency minister went to the roto on the wall, unhooked the bell, and listened. "All right, hold on." He covered the com with his palm and peered at Lumm over the tops of his shaded lenses. "It's a delivery for the National Museum of the Worker? Some glass eyeballs?"

Lumm was perplexed. He hadn't thought much about any of his properties on Little Heritage Street over the last few months. That was their purpose, really, to be the kinds of places that discouraged attention. But the National Museum of the Worker was his favorite of the bunch, and although he sometimes purchased so many things that he forgot buying them in the first place, he did remember ordering the glass eyes.

"Who is this person?"

The currency minister asked for a name, nodded when he got it, and covered the com again. "Simona Gentle," he said.

Lumm considered. "Better send her up."

Not Who He Believed
Himself to Be

To one side of the dining room's long, polished oak table was a crowded sideboard, laden with plates and bowls and decanters, as well as a vase sprouting peacock feathers, a gaping plaster mask, a vessel of cloudy liquid with a preserved pig fetus floating inside, and a stack of leather-bound books. Above that was a mirrored mantelpiece dominated by a domed clock, which was surrounded by an assortment of small, pure-white animal bones. On the other side, linen-draped windows overlooked the street.

The playwright's assistant put D in a chair at the end of the table that was nearest the door to the hall, and opposite Lumm. In the corner to the playwright's left was the statue the sergeant had mentioned, a muscular male nude with an octopus for a head, its tentacles frozen in midwrithe. An entryway to a drawing room showed shelves filled with more books and oddities—miniature figures, taxidermies, more bones—as well as a multitude of dead and ailing plants, their limbs drooping with yellow leaves; there was a triangular fireplace beneath a painting of a hunting scene.

The assistant took a seat in the corner across from the statue and lit a cigarette and smoked, holding an ashtray in his lap and smiling at her between puffs, eyes concealed by his dark glasses. They had sent away the auxiliary soldier who had attended her to the third floor.

Lumm also smiled at her. He was a much-diminished version of the cheery man she had met that day in the Grand Hall of the Society for Psykical Research. His shoulders were coiled with age, and he hunched doggishly over his end of the table. A greasy bare spot showed amid his white hair.

There was another distant boom, and noises from the street: people yelling to one another, soldiers shouting orders, wagons clattering.

The men continued to smile at her.

Sweat gathered under D's collar. She did her best to ignore the itch it created between her skin and the fabric. Her toes wanted to wriggle inside her shoes, and her fingers wanted to squeeze the mouth of the purse that she had placed on the surface of the table before her, but she refused to let them.

Lumm didn't know what D knew, or what she didn't know. That was her advantage. D had already waited fifteen years for answers. She could wait a little longer.

The old man broke the silence. "Good morning, Ms. Gentle. I believe you have some eyes for me."

Δ

She took the pouch out of Gucci's bag and the assistant came and fetched it. He conveyed it to Lumm for his inspection, and returned to his corner seat.

"Oh, these are beautiful." Lumm removed an eye, and held it between a gloved finger and thumb. There was a gingerliness to the movement. "I ordered these from that man Joven. Marvelous craftsman. No fun to dicker with, but a marvelous, marvelous craftsman."

From the corner, Lumm's assistant grunted in agreement.

"Other concerns have taken me away from my responsibilities at the National Museum of the Worker, and from my responsibilities at a number of other organizations where I hold the honor of office, but I couldn't be more fond of that great, grand building and its evocations of the nation's extraordinary laborers. Have you ever visited?"

"Yes, sir," D said.

"One day I noticed that several of the mannequins were going blind. I thought it would be nice to freshen them up. What do you think?"

"I agree, sir," she said.

"You're a modest-seeming girl," Lumm said.

There was a boom, still far, but closer than the previous ones. The glass dome of the mantel clock rattled lightly.

"If you say so, sir," D said.

"You know, your name, it's quite a coincidence. Many years ago, there was a Simon the Gentle. He was a member of another one of my organizations, the Society for Psykical Research."

He gave her a sly glance from beneath the wiry bunches of his eyebrows, and returned his attention to the eye clasped between his thumb and finger. It was a yellow eye. "Simon was naughty, though. I don't want to shock you, but apparently he tampered with a married woman. A jealous husband shot him in the groin and he bled to death."

"Someone mesmerized the husband into doing it."

Lumm abruptly dropped the glass eye back into the open mouth of the pouch. "Where did you hear that? That's a remarkable theory."

So the moving picture was true. "There's an exhibit about it at the museum."

He shook his head. "No, there's not. You're being facetious, and this is an odd, odd time for that. I'm sure you don't know any better, but it's a little bit tacky. What's this really about, my dear? Have we met?"

"Yes," she said. "I'm sure you wouldn't remember. We had a mutual friend. A young man named Ambrose who visited the Society for Psykical Research."

"Oh." Lumm squinted at her. "Yes. Ambrose. I do remember him. Curious mind. Knocked on our door one day and asked what it was we did. I liked that, so frank. Tragic. He had potential, tremendous potential. Cholera, that terrible plague. And how did you know him?"

"He told me he was helping you save the world."

"Hah," the man in the corner blurted.

"Be quiet," Lumm said to him, and the man said, "Apologies," and smiled some more at D, and tapped ash from his cigarette into the ashtray in his lap.

"He gave us too much credit. Sweet boy. The Society's scholarly pursuits have incalculable potential, but I'm sorry to say that there is much we don't yet understand."

"You betrayed him." D was surprised at how easily the words emerged. They spread out as easily as a tablecloth.

"I beg your pardon, girl?" Lumm's mouth pinched.

"You sent him on an errand to pick up cat bones from a butcher for some grotesque ritual," D said, "and then he got sick, and when he died, he went somewhere, a secret place that you and some friends of yours keep for yourself. I used to fantasize I could find him again. It was all I wanted. But he died again in that place. He thought he would get to be like you and your friends, get to change his face, but you put him inside some kind of lamp, and somehow made him see what he wanted to see, and while that was happening you burned him up. Didn't you?"

"That's quite an accusation, quite a hell of an accusation." Lumm wiped spit from the corner of his mouth with his wrist. Robert had described him as doddering, drifting in his speech, but now he spoke rapidly, peevishly. "You've been through. What's your real name? How did you get these eyes? Have you been squatting at the museum? If there's been any damage to the premises, it would be a serious, serious matter, a criminal matter—"

Another boom tinkled the beads of the chandelier that hung above the table.

Lumm settled back in his chair. The look he leveled on her was one of bald distaste. "How did you know how to go through the door, you presumptuous bitch?"

The sudden realization came to D that this man was not what he believed himself to be. It was in the petulant, trembling clench of Lumm's chin as he sank down into himself, a display that was merely off-putting and unpleasant when it intended to be imperious. It was in his rooms too: the jumble of objects spoke not of great knowledge but of a grasping urge to acquire and hoard. He was not the wizard of darkness that she had half expected; he was just an arrogant, sour man who was used to having his way. D thought he did not even know what real darkness looked like; she thought it would surprise him. Real darkness looked like a black-bearded giant with red, red lips, and it did not need to trick or intimidate, it only needed to hurt.

"Did you use Ambrose up?" she asked again. "I want to know. I deserve to know."

"You're quite ugly. I wouldn't look twice at you. I wouldn't let you usher."

The insult meant nothing to her. D would have her answer. "Did you take Ambrose to your secret place and burn him up?"

"He was a servant! He had an accident and he died, and he was granted the honor of providing a little more service! He thought he was in heaven, probably! Most people would be grateful for even a glimpse of it! The only pain he felt was at the very end!" The old man waved a gloved hand. "That's enough of her."

The undertakers had carried Ambrose away, wrapped in his sheets, and left her to live alone with their parents. Ambrose, who had beaten those boys to defend her. Her brother had cared for her in that cold house where Father jabbed his thumb into her palm to make her not bother him, and where Mother warned her not to get stained because nobody wanted stained girls. Ambrose had a special smile for her, for only her. He had been more than her brother. He had been her first, truest friend. She had needed him in the Juvenile Lodgings #8 when the mistress slapped her, and she had needed him when the sergeant had chased her. She had needed Ambrose so many times, and he was not there because Lumm had taken him. The last D would ever see of her brother, he'd been rolled up like a rug.

She didn't love him any less for being a servant. D had been a servant too, had mopped up tobacco juice, stripped sheets dirty with sex, scrubbed shit from toilets.

Now she would do something in service of herself. She meant to find something in this room to kill this hideous old monster who had murdered Ambrose.

The assistant set his ashtray on the floor. He got up and stepped toward D. There was a boom, and the whole room twitched. The noise in the street had grown into a roar.

"I read one of your plays," D said, "and I thought it was a stupid thing that wanted to be smart." She brought the strange, square-edged stage gun out of the purse and pointed it at Lumm. "Tell him to sit."

"Sit," Lumm said, suddenly sedate, to his assistant.

The assistant resumed his chair, crossing his leg over his knee. He was still smoking, but he didn't bother picking the ashtray up again. To D his blond beard looked fake.

"You didn't understand the play. Which one was it?" Lumm asked. "Nevermind, I don't care. You're an imbecile. Where did you get that pistol?"

D glanced around for something real and heavy to crack the bastard's skull. A few feet from the domed clock, at the end of the mantel, there was a tall brass candleholder.

She wanted to keep him talking and sitting, so she said the first thing that came to mind—the truth. "I found it in the museum." She pushed out her chair from the table and stood. D concentrated on keeping the gun still, but it juddered in her grip anyway.

"I've never seen a pistol like that, have you, Westhover?"

"Can't say that I have," the man in the corner said. "Awfully square."

"I know that museum top to bottom. There's an iron forge exhibit, but no gunsmith."

D sidled toward the mantel. "The museum's growing. Something of what burned in the Society building blew into the walls in the ash and smoke, and it's growing, and one of the things it grew is this."

"Really?" Inquisitiveness inflected Lumm's tone. "What other things did it grow?"

"Things to kill people with. Things that exist in some other place. Things that are better off not existing."

"That sounds fascinating," Lumm said. "Quite fascinating."

"When I'm done here, I'm going to destroy the door. That place you go, the place that those things in the museum came from, it's dangerous. They're sick things from a sick place." D grabbed the candleholder. It was as long as her forearm. She pointed the gun at the assistant. "Go into the drawing room."

"Shan't," he said, and rose again. The assistant withdrew a pistol of his own from his jacket pocket and settled the barrel on D. "Lay down that candleholder, and put down that absurd toy gun."

The Hanging Man

The blond-bearded man in the tinted glasses disarmed D and kept his gun on her while the old man shrugged on a traveling cloak.

"Not in here. I'll be sending someone to pack up my possessions later to send to my new home and I don't want any mess spread around. Take her to Crossley's room. I'm sure he left his door open."

"Happy to," the assistant said. As he held his gun on D, he examined the square stage pistol with half an eye, turning it over in his other hand. He had found a slotted nodule on the side and thumbed it along its groove. "Hm," he murmured. "Bizarre toy."

"Remember to put the mark on her," Lumm said.

"Certainly." He pressed the flat side of the stage gun experimentally against the skin of his temple. "Hm, feels like metal."

"I'll take the carriage to the Fields and send it back for you." Lumm paddled his way around the table, clutching the backs of chairs and steadying himself against the wall.

"Now it's you that's almost used up," D said. "You might die before you get there."

"You were clever to get in here. I'll credit you that," Lumm said, heaving breaths. "Nasty tramp." The booms had become consistent, the approaching steps of slow, enormous feet. "But clever is not wise." He left.

The assistant pocketed the stage pistol, went to a drawer, and took out a grease pencil. He tossed it to D. "Draw a triangle on the back of your hand."

A deep memory resurfaced in D's mind: Ambrose saying, in those delirious final hours, that he had tattooed a triangle behind his knee.

"Now," the assistant reminded her.

She did as she was told. If there was going to be a moment, it hadn't come yet. "Why?"

"So we can see you again in the Twilight Place," he said.

"So you can use me up, the way they used Ambrose up," she said.

"That's right. Out into the hall and take a left. We're going to 3F."

She started toward the door, thinking she could snatch the vase with the peacock feathers off the sideboard and break it over his head, but he was digging the gun barrel into her spine. "You'll just make it easier for me if you try to run."

The metal point pushed her away from the sideboard, with its clutter of potential weapons, to the doorway, and out into the hall, heading left. "Don't worry, I don't have time to do anything except shoot you."

Everything about the hall seemed unusually vivid: the gray carpet that was the color of the bay on a stormy day, the white wallpaper with the raised pattern of silvery seagulls in flight, the window at the foot of the corridor that showed sky and the face of the Metropole Hotel across the street. D thought, *I slipped away from the sergeant, but I can't slip away from this man's bullet.*

The assistant nattered on. "You won't believe me, but Lumm's more fun than he seems. The pressure makes him cranky. It takes an enormous amount of planning to pull something like this off. You have to get all the slow-witted people herded in the correct direction. It's a damned task."

They came to the half-open door, and D thought to stall him. "Pull what off? What's going to happen?"

"Gildersleeve and the army are going to kill all the traitors, and all the people who helped the traitors, and anyone else they're not sure about."

"I don't understand," she said, as he reached around her and nudged the door wide.

"You don't have to." A boot slammed into her bustle with a wiry crunch. D stumbled and banged into a pair of limp ankles, knocked against a chair, and sprawled onto the rug.

"Oh, golly, Crossy." A peeling laugh came from the assistant. "Look at you. You know when you finally let yourself choke, you're going to shit yourself?"

D stared up from the floor at the man in the military uniform hanging from the noose. His face was a violent purple and his tongue protruded from his lips like a piece of liver from an overstuffed sandwich. Blood dripped over his fingers from a triangle cut into the skin at the back of his hand. He was still breathing, though, making a sound like a rusty wheel, and his eyes were partly open, showing half-moons of red sclera; the very tips of his shoes touched the seat of the chair.

Her collision with his legs had jarred the hanging man, causing the shoe tips to drag over the chair's seat. The pipe that held the rope moaned.

She pulled herself up with the back of the chair. The assistant still had the gun angled in her direction, but he was regarding the hanging man. He looked delighted. "Crossy, Crossy, Crossy. You're going to die and take a very large shit in your pants. You know when you ordered that plate of chipped beef at breakfast, I thought to myself, *Gosh will it stink—*"

The moaning of the pipe lengthened to a whine.

This was the moment. D grasped the dangling legs by the calves. "Hhhhh," gasped the hanging man, inhaling more air, and his hands jumped from his sides to dig at the noose. D shoved as hard as she could, and he swung, twisting, at the assistant.

The assistant shouted as the hanging man's body flew at him. He fired a wild shot and a window shattered. The hung man's shoes and ankles clasped around the assistant's neck; one of the shoe heels cracked the assistant's dark glasses and scraped off a large patch of his yellow beard. As the hung man rode the assistant's shoulders, the assistant shot again, this time into the ceiling.

D scrambled for the open door. The pipe broke with a pop, and a glittering spout of clear water gushed down. The two men crashed to the floor in a soaked tangle. A gun lay on the rug, and D scooped it up by the barrel as she ran into the hall.

The door to the stairs opened and Robert came through. His expression was bemused. "Dora! I just bumped into Dakin—do you remember Dakin? He said he saw you and—"

"Robert, he's coming! We need to go!" she cried.

"Dora, why are you holding a gun?"

Two reports exploded deafeningly from inside the room. D looked down at the pistol that she was clutching by the barrel. She was extending the weapon out toward Robert, as if she meant for him to have it.

It was the fake gun.

Robert, responding to the gesture, reached out and took it. "Dora, what's happening here, why do you have a—"

There was a splashing of footsteps. D glanced back to see the assistant emerge from the room. His glasses were gone, there was blood on his forehead, and his blond beard was torn off and caught in his collar like a filthy napkin. In his hand he was holding the real pistol.

Robert stepped past D with the stage gun raised, and before D could warn him that it didn't have bullets, he needed to draw his own sidearm from its holster, her lieutenant pulled the trigger—unlocked since Westhover had switched the safety—and fired. The currency minister flew backward with a smoldering hole in his chest that was as big as a dessert plate, and skidded along the gray carpet, dead before he stopped.

Robert

Robert led the way out, taking the stairs to the ice room that he knew from his first trip to the Lear, the night they'd had the meeting in Lumm's apartment with the dockmen. The hatch from the ice room let them into the alleyway beside the hotel. As they hustled toward the street, Robert tore off his green armband and dropped it on the ground.

The Boulevard was overrun. Groups of Volunteers and auxiliary soldiers from Crossley's garrison, unaware that their general was dead in a pool of water on the third floor of the Lear Hotel, were erecting makeshift barriers from wagons and sandbags. Women dragged their crying children, riders drove their horses through the crowds, and scores of people hurried in all directions; everyone trying to get somewhere before the fighting arrived on the city streets. Someone screamed that Mosi was dead! "They murdered Mosi, they murdered Mosi!"

At an intersection, a tram wire had snapped and the carriages were frozen on the track. The tram's driver was asking over and over if some strong men would help him push the tram to the intersection so he could reconnect it; no one stopped.

Amid the back-and-forth of bodies, Robert even saw several cats, all wisely darting in the same southwest direction, away from the growing tumult. The smell of cordite drifted on the air, blown from the cannon blasts on the Highway.

△

When Dakin had come outside and spotted Robert in front of the Metropole, he had rushed to him and grabbed him by both shoulders, and excitedly told him two things: first, "Bobby, the soldiers are saying those are Gildersleeve's guns out on the Highway," and second, "I just saw your girl in the lobby of the Lear, walking to the elevator." Dakin had let go, grinning and looking like he was about to cry at the same time, and added, "Make sure you have plenty of ammo!" before hurrying inside the Metropole.

The encounter had started Robert thinking about certain things, mainly about dying, and the pain of dying, and never seeing his mother or father again. He crossed the street in a daze, hardly feeling the people who jostled against him.

Inside the Lear, the sergeant guarding the elevator told him that a young woman had gone up to deliver a pouch of glass eyeballs to Mr. Lumm, but while that fine old gentleman had just departed, he hadn't seen the young woman come down. Rather than wait for the elevator, Robert had taken the stairs, his existential considerations briefly shunted aside to wonder why Dora was bringing glass eyeballs to Aloys Lumm. No sooner had he shot and killed the ex–currency minister with Dora's bizarre gun, however, than his new misgivings resurfaced, and coalesced. Robert wanted to live, and it seemed like the best way to do that was to disassociate himself from the revolution, take refuge, and take stock.

On the streets, when they approached the rising fortifications, he tilted his hat to keep from being recognized by comrades or acquaintances. Dora seemed to instinctively understand, for she slipped in front of him, grabbing his hand and plunging them through the throngs. "Let us by, let us by," she repeated.

Observing her in the blue dress he'd never seen before, and the new brusqueness of her manner, he had the scattered, buoyant thought that it really might be possible to bring her home to his family. Nothing gave her away, revealed that she had ever crouched on her knees to scrub floors.

If they concocted a smart enough story, she could pass for a dead officer's daughter, someone with a solidly obscure pedigree. An officer's daughter's manners could be rough around the edges and no one would look askance.

Robert marveled to think that he had started his day getting slapped by Willa. He had killed a man, quit his commission, and now was thinking of marriage; it was not quite noon yet.

She flashed a questioning look at him as he lent her a hand to negotiate the obstacle of a carriage that had tried to detour onto the sidewalk and become stuck. The rolling reports of the cannons had been joined by the coughing sound of rifle volleys.

"What?" he asked, raising his voice to be heard.

"You looked so contented for a moment," she said.

△

It was afternoon when they reached the museum. Robert immediately bolted the door. He dragged a bench from the first-floor gallery, and brought it clattering down the stairs to further brace the door.

Dora sat on another bench in the gallery. She'd unbuttoned her bustle and it rested on the floor at her feet, incongruous, looking like a tattered gift. Her face shone clean from wiping it with a handkerchief, which she passed to him wordlessly.

"What were you doing there, Dora? At the Lear?" His voice caught in his throat. It wasn't until he'd spoken that he realized he was afraid of the answer, afraid that she had another lover.

Dora responded blandly: "Lumm was the curator of this place. I supposed that he still was. There was a delivery for him, it had his name on it. So I went to see what I should do with it."

"Is that right?" Another question occurred to him. "Where did you get that gun?" He had stuck it in his jacket pocket.

"The gun was the man's. He had two guns. I didn't think that one was real."

"Yes." Robert, relieved, looked around as if for confirmation. Nearby, a wax man with a bald head and a scope wedged into an eye socket toiled at a table with some springs and gears. His shirtsleeves were rolled, and he held a pin in each hand. His face was a mask of testy concentration.

"He's a clockmaker," Dora said. "Or maybe he only fixes them. I don't know."

"Oh." Robert walked over, cooling his neck with pats of the cloth. He fished out his own watch and set it down in front of the clockmaker. "There. That's better."

"Thank you, Robert," she said.

There were other questions, though. "But why was that other man after you? Did you know that was Westhover? I recognized him. What was going on in that room?"

"Lumm left me with him. Lumm called him his assistant. I'd never seen him before. He told me to come with him to that room and there was another man there, a soldier. The men fought, and I grabbed the gun, escaped, and you were there in the hall."

She said this all in the same steady voice, but it didn't make sense. "What was Westhover doing with Lumm?"

"I don't know," she said. "I told you, I didn't even know that was Westhover."

He turned to her. There was a shiny black purse in her lap that, like the dress, he'd never seen until that day. A tendril of hair had come loose of its pin and stuck to her cheek in a lovely corkscrew. Robert didn't want her to be lying to him.

"Maybe Westhover fooled Lumm somehow," he suggested, reluctant to speak the other possibility aloud, the one that made more sense in light of what Dora had told them—that Lumm had betrayed them and been in league with the ex–currency minister.

"Maybe." As Dora brought her clear gaze up to meet his, she picked at the arm of the bench, tracing a triangle that was raised in the iron.

"It's done, I think," he said. "Everything, I mean."

"I'm sorry."

He wandered to a window. It looked onto the ruins of the building next door, the one Dora had wanted in the first place. Probably two dozen cats were rooting amid the debris. One of them resembled the big fluffy beast he'd seen in the elevator at the Metropole, though it was too far from the hotel to be the same. It was quite a gathering. He wondered what they'd uncovered. Some old store of food, he supposed. The sound of the cannons was muffled by the museum's thick walls, but they brought Robert back to the present. He walked to Dora's bench.

"If we keep our heads low, wait, there could be an opportunity to get out of the city in the next few days. We could go to my parents' estate. I'm sure we won't be the only ones leaving. Lots of traffic. We'll blend in." The plan made itself as he spoke it, but he thought it wasn't bad.

"All right," Dora said.

"If someone identifies me, you say you don't know me." He almost added, "Just don't say anything about what happened in the hotel," but he couldn't speak the words.

"You shouldn't feel bad about it." Dora had seemed to sense what he was thinking. She reached out a hand to him. "You had to shoot him."

"Yes." Robert squeezed her hand.

He suddenly felt very heavy, and sat beside Dora, still holding her hand.

Robert had never been sure he could kill someone. The ex–currency minister was a bad man, a murderer. Westhover would never hurt anyone else now, but he would also never be kind to anyone again, or laugh again, or order a steak again, or open a door for someone again. If Westhover had been reading a book in his free time, he would never learn the ending of it.

"You feel sick about it, because you aren't someone who likes to harm people. That's the goodness in you that makes you feel sick about it. I promise you'll feel better after a while. The awfulness of it will fade, and you'll feel better."

He couldn't see how Dora could know that. He wanted her to be right, though.

She gently rubbed his thumb with hers. "I wish we could spend another afternoon on the pond. Don't you, Robert?"

"Yes."

What if they escaped the city in a crowd, made it all the way home, and his parents turned them away? Robert felt heat behind his eyes, and closed the lids against it.

"What is it you like about me, Dora?"

The quickness of her response surprised him. "I've thought about that a lot," she said. "I like your nose. I like the way you move. I like the way you shot that man who was going to take my life."

"That was decent of me. . . ." With his free hand, he thumbed off the tear that had escaped from the corner of his eye.

Dora went on, "It's fun to talk to you. I like to think about you getting old, and a little fat, and of all the interesting things you'll accomplish. I like ordering you around. I like having you as my second-in-command. You have nice brown eyes. I like how your friends call you Bobby.

"Sometimes I think, *My Bobby*, and it gives me a happy feeling."

Robert felt more water behind his eyes, and he was glad that she wasn't looking at him. "We could tell my parents that your father was an officer. That he was my friend and that he was killed. They don't have to know anything about your background. They'll understand, and they'll help us. They'll help us get abroad if that's what it takes. We could go to Switzerland."

"I'd like that, darling," she said.

He took a deep breath and leaned against Dora and smelled her hair that was tinged with cordite.

Δ

Evening arrived, and D brought Robert upstairs to the prospector's shack.

When they passed the exhibit with the miner and the woman and the canister of yellow sand, he took no notice, even as his shoes crunched through the light trail of the sand on the glass stream. She sat him on the bed and even bent to remove his shoes for him—something she had never done for him before—with the thought that she never would a second time. Once he fell asleep, she was going to go next door and enter the Vestibule; she was going to find Lumm, and this time she was going to kill him, and if she could, she was going to close the door, forever.

Robert lay down without a word, quickly drifting off.

D sat at the prospector's small table and wrote him a letter.

Dear Robert,

The man in the embassy, Captain Anthony, is dangerous. It won't be safe to stay here after tonight. You need to leave. He'll kill you if you don't. You must believe me.

Here is what I want you to do: go down to the second-floor gallery. Take the clothes off the red-haired bricklayer, he's about your size. Put them on and go. Get as far south as you can. Once you're below the South Fair Bridge, ask where to find the Still Crossing. It's a saloon, and there's a boy there named Ike. Tell him I sent you, and that I wanted him to hide you, and then to help you escape the city. Tell him that I told you there was no other Ike I'd trust.

Robert, I am grateful to you for so many things. When you are married, and your children are playing, and your wife is playing the piano, and your thoughts wander to me, if you ever recall my name, I'd consider it a great compliment.

Do not linger. Do not go to Captain Anthony. Leave.

That's an order, Lieutenant.

Yours Always,

Dora

She folded the paper and tucked it into the cigarette case in his jacket that was slung over the back of the chair. In the morning he would find her note when he went to have a smoke.

It wasn't full night, but it was dark enough that D intended to light the lamp on the table and take it with her when she left. She turned in the chair to look at her lover before departing. The way the shadows removed the definition from Robert's face conveyed a hallowedness, as if he were made of marble.

D felt compelled to reach out and touch his face to make sure of the warm flesh.

He opened his eyes. Apparently he hadn't been asleep, or not very deeply. "Won't you lie down with me?" Robert asked.

"Of course," she said, grateful to put the world off for a few minutes longer.

And D was tired, too. The distance from the prospector's shack to the Vestibule was only a walk of five minutes, but it felt much farther. A short rest would do no harm. It might help. D took off the blue dress and slipped in beside him under the sheets of the narrow bed.

"You looked sad just now."

"Did I?" Robert's body was warm and solid against her hip.

"Will you miss your museum? And all your wax friends?"

"I will, and that's why, wherever we go, you'll have to find me a new museum. . . ."

"That's just the thing I was going to suggest. Are you sure everything is all right, Dora? You don't have to be afraid. I promise I'm going to take care of you."

"I know, Robert. I know. . . . Maybe I was just thinking about my brother. . . . He's been on my mind so much lately. . . ."

"You never told me you had a brother," Robert said, but she did not respond. He listened to her sleeping breath, and felt her heartbeat where their bodies pressed. He closed his own eyes.

△

Robert was on the deck of a ship, peering down to the darkened first-floor gallery below. Triangular constellations of stars twinkled among the crouching shadows of the exhibits. He couldn't figure out the up and down and in-between of it, the sky that seemed to be in the floor, the boat floating above it.

Somewhere in the night sky, a horse had broken its leg. A horse broke its leg when he was a boy. He'd heard it all the way up in his bedroom, and he'd fled to his father, who had told him what happened. "You know, Bob," his father had comforted him, "it's not the pain that makes the animal carry on that way. It's just the fear."

The screams made Robert's stomach rise, and he lost his balance on the deck. Vertigo overcame him and he plummeted, the starry triangles rushing to meet him.

He jerked upright in the prospector's bed.

The museum was dark and Dora was fast asleep beside him. Robert's heart rate started to slow, but the horse's next scream—a torn and gurgling howl—sent it tripping ahead.

"Dora," he said, "did you hear that?"

She stirred a little, but her breathing resumed its soft rhythm.

The building vibrated with the thud of a cannon blast. The shelling was starting again and it was close; on the outskirts of the city, he guessed. No other scream came. He was entirely awake, though, hot from sharing the close bed, and shaky from the dream and the piercing cry and the shelling. A smoke would be good.

He eased around Dora and went to the chair where his jacket was hanging. Instead of putting it on, he fished out his cigarette case and his matches. He took the lamp from the table, lit it low, and left the shack through the rear curtain, to keep from disturbing Dora.

As he crossed the fifth-floor gallery to the stairs, trying to convince himself that it must have been an owl that had made the scream, or some other hunting bird, he looked out a window and saw the glow of a light at the former embassy next door. The auxiliary soldier there—Captain Anthony, Robert remembered his name was, with a great black beard— must have been awake, too.

He could go knock on the door of the embassy, renew acquaintances with the man—who had been quite friendly—and find out what reports he had. He could ask Anthony if he'd heard that awful scream.

Near the window was the wax fellow in overalls with the bag of fruit who stood under a tree, and had an empty socket where one of his eyes was missing. It was a shame that Dora had not taken one from Lumm's delivery to fix his sight for him.

Why hadn't she ever told him she had a brother? If he was going to be her Bobby, he needed to know everything about her. Except, as he pictured Dora's dark gaze, he realized that he never could. There was too much to her, and it was too deep. This comprehension amused Robert, and saddened him, and relieved him as well. A great deal of what he loved about Dora—and he did love her, he thought—was that she would never burden him. It could only ever be the other way around. Behind those dark eyes was a set of coolly inviting rooms, rooms and rooms, and he thought he could spend the rest of his life exploring them and never find the secret one where she devised all her plans.

Three more cannon blasts broke the air, gigantic punches delivered into a gigantic bag of flour. He wasn't worried. Robert imagined the great hulk of the museum building taking a direct hit and, when the dust cleared, standing undamaged, responding with a small belch, like a man stretching after a full dinner.

He gave the fruit picker a nod and a pat on the shoulder, walked on to the stairwell, went through the door, and headed below.

A Lot of Dead
People to Bury

*W*eeks earlier, on the day of the revolution, he was paid a dollar to dig a grave in a little family cemetery. He had been wandering the midday streets, listening to people talking about the unrest and the strikes, about the pamphlets that said the king and the government were robbing them all, and about the army that was lost on the other side of the ocean. The particulars were of no interest to him, but the unease was exhilarating. It felt like something remarkable and terrible might happen. He hoped he would be close when it did.

"You, there," a man called to him. "What's your name?"

"Hubert," he said, plucking a name that he'd seen on a discarded oats box in a gutter and that had adhered to his mind. He never got too attached to any name.

The man who addressed him wore a vest with a prominent watch chain and had an important manner. He said that his mother was being prepared for burial in the family cemetery, but the gravedigger had not arrived. "You look strong enough to dig a hole, Hubert. I'll give you a dollar. What do you say?"

The-man-who-was-calling-himself-Hubert said, "Yes, sir. I'm a hard worker."

"That's fine."

The-man-who-was-calling-himself-Hubert followed the watch-chain man from the street to a large, handsome house. Behind the house was a neat cemetery bordered with a wrought iron fence. Every stone bore the name Bello.

△

The gravedigger opened the required hole at the foot of the newest stone and retreated to the shadows of the trees behind the small family cemetery. No one had paid him. He didn't care about that anyway. Money was even less important than a name. He leaned on the shovel he'd been given and watched. It was late afternoon when the coffin came.

A churchman spoke a few words, and waved around a cross. The family members in their black suits and black dresses bowed their heads and prayed. A sniffling scarecrow tossed a piece of paper into the hole, and the watch-chain man led the scarecrow—his father, presumably, the husband of the deceased mother—away from the gravesite back to the house. The other mourners followed, leaving only a round-faced young man.

The round-faced man rested a flank against one of the stones. He removed a bottle from a pocket of his black suit.

The gravedigger emerged from the trees and doffed his hat. "My condolences, sir." He nodded to the open grave. "Is it all right?"

"By all means," the young fellow said, and took a drink from his bottle.

Though it was a mild night, the young fellow had a moist, sweaty look, like worked clay. The gravedigger surmised that the bottle he was sipping was not the first he'd sampled that afternoon.

The-man-who-was-calling-himself-Hubert went to the pile of earth beside the new stone—**CAMILA MARIA BELLO, WIFE OF ANTHONY**—and plunged his blade.

"Granny's lucky, I think, to be missing this foolishness," the young fellow said. "This riffraff carping on when we already give them everything so they can sit in their trash piles and be drunk all day. It's grotesque. It's not our fault they can't clean up after themselves and catch cholera.

You feel you can't even breathe for the stink of their filth." He tipped his bottle at the gravedigger and winked. "You're pretty ripe yourself, my friend."

"Sorry, sir," the gravedigger said.

"That's a hell of a big beard you have, isn't it? Think you might have a few spare nibbles stuck in there that you're saving for later? Yummy, yummy."

"No, sir."

"Kidding you!" He winked again. "I was at the university before they shut it down. I won't go back. It's radicals and fools, the whole place."

The-man-who-was-calling-himself-Hubert pitched a blade of dirt into the grave. It made a gritty splash on the coffin lid.

The young fellow drank, gasped as he lowered the bottle, and shook himself. "Poor Granny . . .

"I saw that Joven before the Morgue Ship floated off. Now, there was a smell. Stuffed my nose with cotton and I still wanted to puke. Westhover was generous to put him down as quick as he did. Slow hanging would have been more appropriate. What do you think of that?"

"I don't know anything about it, sir."

"No, you don't. You don't know anything whatsoever. It's a credit to you that you see that. Pet a cat, thank the furry little crapper, thank the king, do your work, don't bitch about your betters, be happy. That's the correct attitude. What do you think of the protests?"

"I don't know anything about that either, sir, I just do my work."

"The king needs to be firm. He ought to order that Crossley who's in charge of the Auxiliary Garrison to shoot them all. What do you think about that?"

The shadows had swelled and grown long from the trees, smoothing the small cemetery in gloom and leaving only a few scratches of sunset brightness on the lawn. Pots and pans were banging around in the house, the cooks preparing dinner for the mourners. The gravedigger could no longer restrain the smile that was rising up inside him.

"That would be a lot of dead people to bury," he said.

"Yes, it would!" The round-faced grandson of Camila Bello chortled and threw back his head to drink some more.

The gravedigger glanced at the house: not a face in any of the windows. He stepped forward and drove the blade of the shovel into the laughing man's guts.

Young Bello made a sound— *"Hllk!"*—and was draped over the shovel, speared on the tip of the blade. His bottle fell on the ground and emptied itself into the grass. Blood came up over his lips. He scrabbled at the handle, blinking at the gravedigger with hurt eyes. *"Hllk! Hllk!"*

"Hllk!" the gravedigger said back to him. *"Hllk! Hllk!"*

He dragged Young Bello, spiked on the shovel blade, around to the open grave, and kicked him off into it, where he landed with a thump on the coffin top. The-man-who-was-calling-himself-Hubert cast the shovel aside and jumped in after him, boots clomping onto the wood.

"Hllk!" Bello cried once more, louder this time, before the gravedigger put his hands on his throat. He squeezed until the man's eyes rolled up in his skull.

The-man-who-was-calling-himself-Hubert lifted his head above the grave. The gravestones stood around him at eye level, and the lawn rolled darkly away. There was still no one. From the house, the pots and pans banged some more.

He stared down at Young Bello. Blood soaked his shirt and streaked over the sides of the waxed oak coffin. He was breathing, hand fluttering at his side, fat ruby thumb ring tapping the wood. The gravedigger had no use for jewels, but he was interested in the piece of paper lying on the wood by the prone man's shoes—the paper the scarecrow had thrown in. Over the course of the-man-who-was-calling-himself-Hubert's life, he'd noticed that people often wrote things that they didn't dare say out loud.

He picked up the paper, opened it, squinting to read in the dimness. "Soul of the Souls," he made out, the title at the top of the page. *You are the soul of the souls now, my darling, the heart of all the hearts, my darling,* the poem began, but the reading tired his eyes. The-man-who-was-calling-himself-Hubert tucked the paper away to study later.

The gravedigger climbed from the hole. He picked up his shovel and shifted the remaining dirt into the hole, burying the unconscious man and the coffin containing the unconscious man's grandmother both.

Shots rang out, and a commotion started in the street, horses and yelling. Some sort of attack was taking place. Chaos was triggered in the house, with all of the inhabitants rushing to load some wagons with luggage in preparation for taking flight. "Where's Tom?" a woman cried, but they wouldn't find him.

The gravedigger removed his hat before the turned soil, and bowed his head out of respect for the dead.

The racket in the street grew louder. In the morning he would look for a new job. Whatever change came, there was always a place for a hard worker.

△

"I met someone else who had a ring like that, Lieutenant."

The-man-who-was-not-Anthony nodded at the hand Robert cupped around the mug he'd given him. When the lieutenant had knocked on the door, he'd invited him inside for some sweet coffee in the former embassy's sitting room.

"It's a university ring," the lieutenant said, and smacked his lips. He sat in one of the armchairs. The-man-who-was-not-Anthony sat opposite. "I'm actually not anymore, though. A lieutenant. That's something to tell you that I should." He smacked his lips again, and flexed his jaw. "Something I should tell you, I mean. I'm just Robert now. Just call me Robert."

"Oh?"

"I resigned," he said.

"And what about the young lady? Does she still hold her position at the museum?"

"Dora . . . ?"

"Yes, Dora," the-man-who-was-not-Anthony said. "The young lady was absent for a few days recently. I looked after the museum while she was gone. I happened to come across this." He held a paper for Robert to see—it was the declaration that gave Dora authority over the museum. "This says *Society for Psykical Research*, but that's been crossed out and replaced with *National Museum of the Worker*. Now, prior to finding this document, I had a talk with Sergeant Van Goor. We covered a number of topics, but in the course of our conversation he had mentioned that it was his recollection that the young lady was only ever given authority over the Society building. My fear is that she may have altered this paper without permission."

A sorrowful expression played across Robert's drooping face and he sighed a huge shoulder-lifting sigh. "The coffee . . ."

The-man-who-was-not-Anthony asked, "You don't remember me, do you?"

"Hmm . . . ?"

"That's all right. You must meet a lot of people. It's just that it was you who directed me into this service. I called to you that I was looking for work, and you sent me on my way to Sergeant Van Goor, who hired me. Do you remember now? I want you to know how grateful I am, and I hope, in spite of the circumstances, you can feel good in yourself about having done a stranger a fair turn."

Robert's head fell against the chair back. His mouth lolled and his eyes seemed to settle on the flag that hung from the eagle-headed gold standard in the corner. When the-man-who-was-not-Anthony had first moved in, every room in the embassy had been outfitted with one—the pattern of red and white stripes and a dark-blue window with a scatter of stars—and a lucky thing too. He had run out of rugs and canvases to shroud the bodies, and fallen back on using the flags.

"I don't know why they make it look like that," he told Robert, "the meaning of the symbols, but I've developed a fondness for it."

Outside

A blast of thunder spilled a wash of snow down on the interior of the shack and woke D. It had been weeks since she'd had such a long, deep, and unbroken sleep. She sat up and took a sharp, startled breath and swallowed a lungful of dust, and fell off the bed to the floor, hacking. There was another crash, and another sheet of dust and grit hissed down from the rafters.

Robert's jacket was hanging on the chair, but he wasn't in the room.

She went out to the fifth-floor gallery in her underthings, coughing and calling for him. Another nearby blast reverberated through the building and made the trail of yellow sand on the glass stream jump and spread. She sensed that it was early morning, but the light through the windows was mustard-colored, varnishing the figures and the exhibits with an acid sheen. Between the blasts, bells were ringing, tower bells and ambulance bells and fire bells. There were cracks, too: bullets shooting, an irregular rain of them, too many to count.

It was happening: fighting in the city.

Robert, she needed to find Robert.

D returned to the shack, and hurriedly dressed in her work dress and apron. She grabbed the square pistol from the lieutenant's jacket.

△

The front door was closed, but the bench Robert had put there as a brace had been dragged away. He'd gone out to see what was happening, the fool. It was obvious what was happening: a war.

D pushed outside into a thick smoke, sharper and thicker than earlier, a fuzzy, undulating brown curtain that hovered on top of a solid, waist-high mist. Above, the sun was a flake of dull quartz.

She held her skirt in one hand and the gun in the other, and moved in the direction of the corner. She couldn't see the ground under her feet or the buildings on the other side of the street. "Robert!" D called.

Rifle fire crackled. There were more bells, bonging and dinging, and panicked voices, squeezed and warped by the filtering air, seeming remote and near at the same time. It smelled like a wet fireplace had vomited its ashes across the city.

She came to the corner. She could tell it was the corner because the embassy building had emerged faintly visible in the brown haze to her right. Hooves clattered, and the leathery flank of a riderless horse smashed the smog half a foot from where D stood. Without realizing she had walked a little past the sidewalk onto the street; two more steps and she would have been trampled.

D retreated to the sidewalk. "Robert!" she called.

"They're shooting everyone! They're shooting everyone!" someone yelled, as if in response. They were running past, but D wasn't sure if it was from the direction of the river or the direction of the city center. "Stay inside! They're shooting us!"

She edged past the embassy onto Legate, stumbled on something, and nearly dropped the gun, but kept it and stayed on her feet. Broken glass tinkled. A red bush bloomed in the smoke where the street had to be. D saw it was a carriage on fire. "Oh, my head," someone said mildly.

The rifle shots sounded like popping oyster shells. D had seen quick boys do that: they bet each other on who could stomp an oyster shell and make the biggest pop; she bet Ike had done it. D called for Robert. She advanced as carefully as she could. Someone bumped her shoulder, and she caught a whiff of peppermint-scented perfume.

A cannon blast shook everything. She heard the gigantic *oof* of a building collapsing, the roar of tons of masonry sliding. D yelled, "Robert! Robert!"

△

How far had she gone? Four blocks? Five? More? She only knew she was still on Legate somewhere. She had been searching and calling for Robert for at least an hour. Salt stung her lips from the tears the smoke made her cry.

A girl appeared. Or maybe she was an old woman, D couldn't tell; she was small and female. A black stole was wrapped over her mouth. The stranger was weeping too, but there was a disturbing lack of alarm in her bloodshot eyes.

"Boat was docked outside the milkwoman's."

"What?" asked D.

"The boat was outside the milkwoman's. Where the second floor was on fire. Vin and his family climbed out up the ladder. They're safe now, I think. The Charmer saved them."

"I'm looking for a tall man with dark hair. He would have been coming from the same direction as me. Have you seen him?" D inhaled too much of the bad air and started coughing. When she had recovered her breath, the woman was gone.

"Robert!" D called. She went forward once more, and tripped over a low barrier. Metal points tore her skirt, and she fell into thin tree branches that snapped and ripped at her hair, and ended up with her spine against a narrow tree trunk. It was a fenced maple. She'd drifted left and toppled over the ankle-high iron fence; another near miss, a branch point could have speared her eye and made her a match for the fruit picker. Oysters popped, hard shoes clapped on cobbles, a woman screamed, "No! No!"

D pulled her hair free of the branches. Her scalp stung. She gripped the column of the tree and took shallow breaths, trying to compose herself, focusing on the bark under her fingertips.

If Robert was out here, she couldn't find him. He could only find his own way back to the museum. She had to return and wait for him. If enough time passed and he didn't return, she would go on to the Vestibule and do what she had to do. She couldn't accept that he was dead, though. Robert was too bright, too much a Bobby, flying past the other boys for the far side of the quad, to be lying on the ground somewhere unseen, seeping his blood into the stones.

D negotiated the low iron fence and stepped back to the sidewalk. Another blast momentarily broke the fog and smoke; D saw the silver lines of the perpendicular tram wires on the National Boulevard. She was at the crossing exactly six blocks up Legate.

She grasped her skirt again and turned in the direction of the museum. She moved slowly, concentrating on keeping a straight track, and listening for the sudden steps of someone who might bowl her over.

The burning carriage reappeared. A ragged susurration emanated from the burning wood along with ruffles of white smoke that melted into the brown smoke. Cat shadows circled around it, projected hugely by the flames, made as big as the tiger statue that stood outside the Magistrates' Court. D thought of Ike, cat of a boy that he was, and hoped he was watching out for tigers.

"Robert!" she called. She hadn't given up hope of finding him. She couldn't.

People were still yelling somewhere, everywhere. The cannonballs whistled and the ground quaked. The different bells clanged and bonged. It was as if they were on the river, all of them, every man and woman and child in the city, and they were floating out from under the shelter of the No or the So, and the artillerymen were the dribsers, and the bells were ringing the points they scored.

The air was toxic: burning wood, burning brick, burning oil, burning everything. Her steps had begun to scuffle, but she knew she was close to the corner of Little Heritage. Each time the blasts tore windows in the smoke, D glimpsed a familiar building, each one nearer to her neighbor's embassy and the corner of Little Heritage.

Ambrose had told her that she could make the world disappear, their special magic; but he'd been wrong. The world waited for you, on one side of the door or the other, and the world had a bellyful of patience; and it wasn't even the only world. She forgave him the lie. He had believed it himself, and he had paid for it.

She'd been walking for a long time, more than fifteen years. If she stopped now, D told herself, her body would harden into wax. They'd put her in the museum and fit a duster in her hand, and set her wherever there was an empty spot. The place would finally have a maid.

D thought, *I'd rather melt.*

The smoke expelled the shadow of a man, and she said, "Robert?" only realizing after a second that it was the hitching post a few feet from the corner of Little Heritage and Legate.

"You," the hitching post whined.

From the vapor, D's neighbor—her other neighbor, the one who squatted in the Archives for the Study of Nautical Exploration and Oceanic Depth—stepped from behind the hitching post. His gray-black hair fell around his face like roots. He wielded a fireplace poker. "Why are you always looking at me in my window?"

D envisioned the walls of his room scrawled with gibberish, the blanket pile in the corner, the tin bowl containing the broken pieces of a cup that, when shaken, rattled urgent truths only his cursed ears could perceive.

"Don't come near me," she said. D pointed the wax soldier woman's gun at him, half surprised to find that she still had it.

"You come and you go through the lumpy door across the street." Smoke and mist raked across him in tendrils and whorls. It made it seem as if the air had made him, and was unmaking and remaking him continuously. "It's not like any door I've ever seen. It's oozy."

"Back away from me," she said.

"I came here to rest," the squatter said. "It'd been a long time since I had a place of my own, but it's not been good for me. The voices got out of my head. Have you heard at night?"

"I'm just looking for my friend. Leave me alone."

The squatter from the Archives spoke through gritted teeth, which gave his speech a pitchy, strangled quality. "The noise, the screaming and the crying and begging. They used to be in me, in my brains." He scraped the poker along the side of his scalp, showing where the noises had been previously. "I didn't mean to let them escape."

D loosened her finger on the trigger. He was mad, there was no doubt about that, but he didn't seem to want to hurt her. "Of course you didn't. You should go back to your building where it's safe."

He shook his head. "I mean to kill the noises." The squatter clanked his poker against the ground. "It's smoky. I can sneak up on them."

"I'm certain you're better off inside," D said.

"There's old books about things from the bottom of the sea in my new house. I read them when I can't sleep. Leviathans, Roman galleons, fish that don't have names. No one knows how many fathoms the ocean goes."

Another cannon blast reverberated. The mist gave a snaky wriggle.

"Wait! Wait!" His eyebrows jumped up, and his face twisted with dismay as he shuffled a step toward her, lank hair swinging. "Is it you?"

D squeezed the trigger of the pistol partway, thinking that it wouldn't work, she'd miss.

His hands were clenching around the poker. The handle was a rusty fish tail. "Is it you that were them, the voices of the pain?"

"Yes," she said. "I am the voices of the pain in your head."

The squatter screamed in fright, dropping his poker on the cobbles, and was suddenly enfolded by a billow of mist and smoke. D darted left into a mass of gray.

She heard his shoes scraping, his hyperventilating, his bare hands slapping on the cobbles. "Ah!" he cried, and there was a scrape of metal that must have been his picking up the poker. D tripped over her feet that she couldn't see and fell. Rough stone slashed through her skirt to the skin of her knee, opening the callus there. The pistol clattered away. She bit her lip to keep from yelling at the hurt, and inhaled, the mist searing the inside of her nostrils.

The poker smashed against the ground close by.

She crawled through the mist, her knee sending stinging pulses into her thigh, pebbles digging into her palms. D knew that the embassy was near. If she could get to the embassy wall, she could use it as a guide to get back to the museum.

She sensed the squatter feeling around with his poker like a blind man with a walking stick. The poker tip made harsh scraping sounds on the stone. "You should have stayed in me!" the squatter crowed. "You should have—"

The speech was interrupted by a collision of bodies, someone running into the squatter. The poker hit the ground again.

"What in heaven's name are you doing?" a stranger's voice asked. "Let go of me!"

"I'm hunting!" the squatter replied.

There was a heavy thump and a rustle of punches being exchanged.

D scrabbled to her feet, put her palms out flat, and in a half dozen steps came to the wall. She felt her way to a corner and slipped along the perpendicular side. The sounds of the fight receded.

△

D followed the slate passage between the embassy and the stone wall that fenced off the museum, and the smoke and the mist loosened. She could see ahead, murkily, a distance of a few feet.

Arms of wisteria hugged the side of the embassy, adding to the sense that she had escaped the chaos and was now on a safe route that led to some peaceful clearing. Her knee was stiffening where she'd cut it and she let her other leg lead, stepping, then drawing the other after.

Though the air was visibly clearer here, it smelled worse. Underneath the smoke and the damp and the burn was a sweet, moldering scent. D thought of the piece of fruit that appeared good and new until you picked it up and your thumb sank into a bruised dimple on the underside. The walls had dulled the sounds of the fighting, but there was a buzzing echo that seemed to swell. D studied her foot as she let it drag over a slate. She followed her fingers, watching as she pinched a wisteria leaf, and pulled it from a branch. The buzzing deafened her to the sound of her shoe sole on the stone and the snap of the branch as it surrendered its leaf. D halted.

The slates disappeared into obscurity on their way around to the rear of the embassy, but she knew the space. She had looked upon it many times from the fifth floor of the museum. The slates widened into a courtyard, and at one end was the back door of the embassy, and at the other were the rectangular stables, overhung by a steeply pitched roof.

In the stables were the people he had killed.

They were in the darkness, swaddled in rugs and blankets, and snowed with lime that could only do so much. That was what she smelled, and that explained the buzzing. It was the flies, a storm of them, so many that she would have to wade through them, like floodwater.

The darkness of the stables was just out of sight behind the smoke, mountain-tall and rising.

How he must hate her, D thought, how Captain Anthony must hate her, to have saved her for so long, to have made her live for the longest with the knowledge of what he had done, and with her powerlessness to stop him.

Ahead not much farther was the place where the museum's barrier wall lowered. She could climb over it and through the hedge to the garden, but she could not move. She could not.

△

A sudden slash of pain bloomed at her calf, and D turned to see the white cat with the jeweled collar hissing at her. Soot peppered its fur and its hackles were raised. The cat's pupils were arrow slits in its turquoise eyes. Talmadge XVII flicked out with a paw, carving at the air between them.

It seemed like it was challenging her to fight.

△

Seduced by cats' beauty, by their seamless movements and their immodest freedom from gravity's law, believers tended to romanticize them. When a cat abruptly broke its aloof posture, trotted over, and allowed them to brush a hand between its ears, they felt befriended, loved. In cats' large and coruscating eyes, believers saw the measureless depth of a wise and placid god's eyes. To their children, they told fanciful stories about the Mother Cat, who would care for them in the afterlife.

In so doing, all but the most unsentimental—like Gid's gran—lost sight of the oldest story: that the first cat came from the devil, that it had separated itself from his very body as he slept. Believers who romanticized them forgot whose descendants they worshipped.

Cats were killers, and they liked killing. Cats were survivors. When the winters were cruel, they ate their young. The sun might adore them in all their patterns and colors, but it was the shadows that gave them their strength, and it was in the shadows that they flourished. Cats were warm because they were full of blood.

△

The horror of the bodies buzzed in D's ears and in her skull, and it sent runners up her nostrils and between her lips, through her mouth and down her throat. She had not been innocent for so long, perhaps not since Ambrose had left the house with the ash shovel, and certainly not since she'd looked through the green glass in the door to see the pillowcase soaking in the puddle.

But there were others—Robert and Ike, the tram driver and the woman with the stole covering her mouth, mothers who would never see their daughters as stained and fathers who would cry if their sons died, mysterious brothers and loyal sisters, stinking bricklayers and wild-haired clamdiggers and drunken nurses, and all the maids, all the girls like her and Bet, who scrubbed their lives away to shine up after everyone else's shit and filth—there was a whole city of others. Lumm cheated death by burning them like lamp oil, and fancied himself a great devil and a great artist.

D didn't know if, by killing Lumm, she could do what Ambrose had hoped to do and save the world. This world already seemed lost.

There was the future to think about, though.

The white cat hissed, and its eyes contained no love, only challenge.

D rolled her shoulders up and drew in a breath. She continued down the path.

Are You Bad?

*S*he hoisted herself over the wall, inched and wove her way through the branches of the hedge, and emerged into the museum's small garden. D crouched at the water pump and worked the lever. She caught the cold water that flooded from the spout, spat and drank, spat and drank, trying to get the smoke off her tongue.

D splashed water around her face and neck. Soot leaked off her onto the ground. She sat against the pump. Her skirt was blackened where it wasn't torn.

The white cat had followed her into the garden. While sounds of carnage went on, XVII strolled the little plot and sniffed at the carrot tops and prodded the folds of a lettuce head experimentally.

"Come here," she croaked at Talmadge XVII.

XVII approached along a garden row, stopping just beyond D's reach, and regarded her for a couple of unblinking seconds. The cat sat and chewed on a claw.

"I would have loved you when I was a girl," D said. "I know you don't give a damn, but once I figured it out, I think I would have loved that about you too. That you didn't give a damn. My parents didn't approve of cats."

The cat went from one claw to the next, making snuffling noises as it ground at them.

"You're beautiful, do you know that? I suppose I don't mind that you sneak into my museum and scratch things up. I know that was you. Even covered in soot, you're beautiful. I wish you could tell me what this is about for you. I'll call you Seventeen, all right? I know it's not much of a name, but neither is Talmadge."

D lifted her skirt to inspect the bloody wound on her knee. The callus, the one she'd built over years of washing floors, had split into ragged wings of skin. "Whatever happens, I'm going to be off my knees for the foreseeable future, aren't I, Seventeen?"

The damp ground around the pump was soaking through the back of her skirt to her bottom, and she knew there was no excuse to put off her mission, but she didn't want to move. The mist tangled in the hedges and the tomato trellis. She pressed her scraped palms into the cool grass. The whole world sounded like one shelf of fragile things falling after another, but knowing that she would be done soon, she felt oddly relaxed.

"Is it more foolish to talk to a cat, or to myself?"

Talmadge XVII had finished tending to her claws. She hunched and stared at D.

"To you, I think," she said to XVII.

D used the pump to get to her feet. XVII uncoiled from her crouch, crossed the garden, and vanished into the hedge that bordered the Society's plot.

△

D limped along the center lane of the first-floor gallery. "Robert? Are you here? You're lucky you resigned, or I'd have to court-martial you for this."

A whining creak drew her eyes to the placard that hung from the ceiling, ***MACHINES AND THEIR OPERATORS***. It swung, still captured by the momentum of the blasts that had, for the moment, subsided. Strings of dust trickled from the beams, spattering her polished floor. The atmosphere of the hall was grainy and gray.

D thought she'd better get something she could use as a weapon. On the fifth floor the farmer had a mattock and the woodcutter a rusted ax. Better still, perhaps, was the shiny pick that the future miner held.

Robert would be in bed in the prospector's shack. The sequence of events revealed itself to her in hilarious lucidity:

He had got up to relieve himself, gone downstairs, and blithely started out the front door with a plan to use the nearest bush, changed his mind when he noticed the world was burning, turned around, and gone down to the little basement toilet. Half asleep, in a hurry to go, Robert had not bothered to shut the front door properly. D had only been a minute or so behind him. No sooner did she step out the front door than he'd reappeared from the basement. He'd proceeded upstairs and thoughtlessly dropped into bed without wondering after her whereabouts. While she'd searched for him, terrified to trip over his dead body in the smog, he'd been dreaming contentedly.

D made her way to the front of the gallery and, sure enough, down the short flight into the entry, the door was shut, the bench replaced beneath the handle. On his way back through, Robert had realized his carelessness, refixing the door and the bench again.

He was lucky she did not have a bucket of cold water or else she'd have been tempted to pour it on him. It was better, though, to let him stay in his dreams. She'd just poke her head inside the shack to see him breathing, and leave without disturbing him. She'd pry the pick from the miner's wax hands and go to the Vestibule. D retraced her steps toward the opposite end of the first-floor gallery and the stairwells.

The placard's hinges crooned and dust whispered down onto the oversized gears. The face of the printer bore an expression of eager attentiveness; she seemed enthralled with her mostly blank reel of paper. D moved slowly, wincing at the pulse in her torn knee. Once she was upstairs, she could unpin one of the rags from the prospector's wife's clothesline and use it as a bandage—

The printer's hair was brown and long. She was the bicyclist. Or, rather, the bicyclist's head sat upon the printer's shoulders, above his shirt with the red sleeve garters. A few feet away, the man who ran the sawmill had been changed too; the head that had belonged to the printer rested on his shoulders.

Perhaps because she was distracted, or because of the relative dimness, on her way to the front of the gallery she'd walked obliviously past. Robert had changed the heads. As a joke, he'd unclipped the heads of the printer and the sawmill man, and swapped them.

D's gaze fell on the clockmaker's exhibit that was set behind the printing display. On the clockmaker's neck was the head of the female soldier. It was angled to the side, so the soldier seemed to peek at D, even as the clockmaker's hands held the pins.

She walked on.

At the next exhibit, one of the two engineers who operated the steam engine now wore the head of the sawmill operator. His gaze was likewise twisted in D's direction. The small ballpeen hammer in his fist, which an engineer might use to fix a valve, seemed instead like a warning not to come too close. His partner's head had been exchanged for that of the clockmaker, arranged so that it also seemed to look at her, the scope still wedged in the eye socket.

It should have been funny, the mismatched heads, and in the abstract it was: the ease and possibility and silliness of swapping them. Instead, the effect was eerie. The figures had always felt something like the echoes of people. It was as if the echo had reversed, suddenly grown louder instead of diminishing. D had the nightmare sensation that she had stumbled unwelcome into the real lives of these imaginary people.

She moved more quickly, but in a half dozen steps she saw Robert, and stopped again.

Δ

He was not looking at her; he was squatting, attending to the bicycle wheel. The black hair at the back of his head was mussed slightly. He might have just run his hand through it, irritated or bemused, wondering how she could have just walked by him like that. The blood from his severed neck soaked the shoulders of the bicycle mechanic's jacket. A metal point stuck up from the top of his crown, the end of the spike that had been driven through his skull and down into the body of the wax figure in order to hold it in place.

It had not been Robert who closed the doors, or played the trick with the figures. "Where are you?" D managed.

Captain Anthony cleared his throat. Shirtless, in his uniform pants and boots, he stood at the doorway to the stairs, with a pair of large rusted pliers cradled across his forearms.

"Miss Dora."

D knew what was about to happen, and as much as she hated him, she supposed that perhaps the punishment that awaited her was deserved. Robert hadn't deserved what the monster had done to him, though. Injustice was hardly abnormal in this world, or in her life, but it still had the power to squeeze the air out of her chest, to make her scream inside herself.

His white teeth shone in the gray shadows. "I bumped into one of your folks, when I was looking after the place in your absence. Head popped right off, *thumpity thumpity thumpity* it goes across the floor! You should have seen me running after it, Miss Dora! I bet I looked an order of foolish. But it gave me a wicked thought. 'When the time is right, I'm going to pull one over on her, give her a spook. She'll think they're about to get her.'" Anthony limped from the doorway, making his way in her direction between some display cases. "Did I spook you?"

"Yes," she said.

"Oh, good! I've never been much of a joker, but I know people enjoy a laugh. I'm trying to learn."

A few feet off, he halted. He gave what must have been his best approximation of a sympathetic look. The grimace was right, but his eyes lacked something. When D met those eyes, it was like seeing a fat fly knocking against the other side of a window. Her neighbor was the fly, and the world was behind the glass, insensibly, greedily fascinating to him.

"I would have liked to talk to Mr. Barnes longer, but still, I believe we covered what was essential. I see why you cared for him, Miss Dora. He told me you were blameless, that it was him who insisted you take this place, and falsified the document. He was probably the most convincing of all the people I've had the pleasure of treating with." Anthony shook his head in another repugnant display of commiseration. "The pleasure and the sorrow. I admired the way that he fessed up, I'll tell you that."

"Document?" D had no idea what he was referring to. She had no idea how she was still standing on her shaking legs.

"Document that gave you authority over the Society for Psykical Research. It was altered to give you authority over the National Museum of the Worker. I found it while you were away and I was looking after things for you."

The memory of that day at the plaza of the Magistrates' Court returned. Robert had written the paper himself, and the sergeant called it handsome and signed it. They'd changed the declaration after discovering that the Society had burned and the museum was unoccupied.

"And you know, Miss Dora, I did suspect that was the case," he continued. "I couldn't imagine you crossing against the law. Little you, toiling day and night to sort this barn out and make it presentable, give the everyday person a look at themself. I try to keep an even hand, not let myself be pulled by affection. But living beside you these weeks, well, I hope you don't mind me admitting that I've grown fond of you. I've felt, at times, as if we were almost colleagues. So it was a relief to speak with your Mr. Barnes, because he secured the verdict and took the guilt of the crime on himself, most manfully."

He tapped the pliers on his arm. "I knew you were blameless, Miss Dora. Maybe the only blameless person in the whole world, never causing offense to anyone."

D stared at him. "Blameless." She looked to the back of Robert's head, his ruffled hair; he might have run his hand through it, or else she might have, lying in his embrace. "Blameless."

"That's right, and let me tell you, in this business I'm in, you start to wonder, is there a person that hasn't ever gone about it the wrong way? You've restored my faith, Miss Dora." Her neighbor looked pleased enough to break out into a jig.

"And before we settled up, I did read him your letter."

"The letter . . ." She took a deep breath and caught the smell of him; her stomach rolled. He smelled like blood—Robert's blood.

"I don't believe Mr. Barnes would mind my telling you that he wept to hear it. I nearly did myself. It was very sweet and heartfelt, Miss Dora. And I can't hold it against you for putting that I was dangerous." He smiled and scratched his chest with the pliers. "Because that's just true, isn't it?

"I've got to be on the road. I do apologize for fooling around with your people here and not staying to help put them correct again, but circumstances as they are, I can't linger. I have one more interview I need to conduct and the subject won't be coming to see me. I'll have to go find this Ike myself. Thank goodness I know where to find him from what you wrote. I appreciate that."

"Ike . . ."

"That's right, that's the name," he said. "While you were gone there was a young fella here who announced himself by that title. He trespassed in the museum and, I don't mean to shock you, Miss Dora, but I believe he had designs on you."

Ike, she thought. *My very own Ike.*

"I thought I had a grip on him, and he stomped on my foot and made a sprint! Didn't expect that! Scarf he was wearing came right off in my hand! How do you like that? He beat it to the stairs and left me holding his scarf.

"Brave boy, and perhaps it was just fear that made him run, but I do need to speak with him. People that run often have something to hide. Anyway, I deduced from your letter that you'd had dealings with the young fella. I can see by your expression that I was right about that. Do you want to say anything on his behalf?"

"You can't," she said. "Please."

Her neighbor recoiled slightly. The buzzing insect behind his eyes slung itself confusedly against the glass that separated it from humanity. "Pardon?"

"You can't go to Ike," she said. "He didn't trespass. I invited him here. He's a friend."

"Miss Dora," he said, "I have to. You're an unmarried woman. It doesn't matter if an unmarried woman invites you to her residence. You don't come inside without permission. That's just proper. You know that. Someone that would do that, who knows what else he might be capable of."

"I would rather die than let you," D said.

"I wish you wouldn't say that."

She wrenched the ballpeen hammer out of the engineer–sawmill operator's hand. The figure, jarred, tipped onto the floor with a hollow bang that echoed in the vast gallery.

"Miss Dora . . ." Anthony frowned and squeezed the handle of the pliers. The fly was rubbing its arms together, trying to understand, never understanding. "Are you bad too?"

D ran at him, raising the ballpeen hammer high, thinking this was her best chance to save Ike. If she startled him, maybe she could strike him down; that was the only hope.

If it didn't work, he'd have her. Once he had her, she'd be dead, but she would try to convince him that Ike was somewhere other than the Still Crossing. But D had heard the people screaming in the night. Their mothers had never come, nor their gods. Once the monster began his work on her, there was nothing, in the end, that he would allow her to keep to herself. She would only be able to waylay him for so long, and when he finished with her, he would go on to do to Ike what he had done to her.

He batted her wrist with one hand, sending the ballpeen hammer flying, and with his other hand swung the pliers in a flat arc that snapped D's nose at the bridge.

Some seconds later, the fire in the middle of her face woke her. D gasped, tasting blood in her mouth, feeling it on her chin. Black snow sheeted her eyes, blocking out almost everything. She looked into her lap, and her vision cleared somewhat: the clockmaker's head lay in her lap. She'd crashed into the clockmaker-engineer. The scope jutted at her from the wax head's eye socket.

"Here, Miss Dora." Her neighbor's hand extended into her vision. "Let's go upstairs. This isn't a proper area for a talk."

D took his hand. He bent, putting an arm around her back, and gently raised her to her feet. The wax head clattered from her lap onto the floor.

Once she was upright, he remained crouched over her, supporting her weight. Though his beard scraped her face, she could not smell him with her shattered nose. "Are you steady?"

"Just a second, please." The words didn't sound like anything more than a mumble to D, but he understood.

"Of course," he said.

D felt in the pocket of the apron. Her fingers closed on the drill bit— △ **FOR TAKING SAMPLES FROM SMALL METEORITES** △. She drew it out, and raised her hand, and drove it into the softness of his temple above his left eye.

Do You See Me?
Do You See My Face?

They lay together on the floor for a while.

D thought she might have slept some. Blood from her broken nose had dried on her face; she felt it crack when she moved her mouth.

She rolled on her side. He sprawled perpendicular to her. Stretched out and staring at the ceiling, he looked calm. His breathing was shallow. His left eye was wrong, the pupil half buried under the lower lid. The blood from his temple had made a pool on the boards. One of the triangular nail head patterns, submerged in the dark red, glowed dully. His right eye blinked at the ceiling.

D put her hands on either side of his head, and turned him to her. She whispered, "Do you see me? Do you see my face?"

His right eye blinked some more, and his breath continued in sipping inhalations and tiny exhalations.

△

"When it was night, and Nurse was snoring, and my parents were asleep, I went to Ambrose's room. His jacket was in his closet, and the bag of raw oysters was in the pocket.

"Ambrose was my brother. He loved me and I loved him, and when some boys laughed at me, he beat them with an ash shovel. I knew, as long as he was alive, I'd be protected. But he'd got involved with some people—with one man in particular—who told him they were going to save the world, and who invited him to join them. But it was a lie. They were greedy, nasty people who wanted to live forever, and didn't care who got hurt or suffered. Ambrose got sick because he was running a filthy errand for them. He got sick and he died. His soul went somewhere else and he thought he was seeing God, but the greedy people were murdering him all over again, and they burnt him to nothing.

"But then, I just knew he was gone. I was left alone, and no one loved me. My mother could tell I was going to stain myself. My father tried to hurt me so I wouldn't bother him. Nurse was a drunk.

"So, I took the bag of oysters, and I brought it to my parents' bedroom. They didn't wake. He was on his side, and she was on her side. I went to his night table and I dropped an oyster in his water glass, and I went to her night table, and I dropped an oyster in her water glass.

"It was from the oysters that Ambrose got sick. You don't eat raw oysters from the Fair. The water's polluted. Everyone knows that. That's why they pickle them. But a boy told Ambrose the oysters were from the ocean, so they were all right. They weren't all right, though. They gave him cholera.

"I sat at my mother's dresser and let the oysters soak. Then I picked them out, and brought them to the garbage. I washed my hands, got back into bed, and I had easy, easy dreams.

"A couple of days later, they sickened. Everyone assumed it was from Ambrose, but that's not how cholera spreads, and they wouldn't go near him after he'd become ill anyway. It was from the water glasses by their bed, the drinks they took first thing in the morning. They suffered the way Ambrose had suffered, crazed with fever, and they died, one right after the other. Some men had to come and wrap them up and take them away too. . . .

"I was angry, and sad, and they didn't love me. I murdered them. I dropped oysters in their waters and I rang their bells."

A long rumbling sound came from the bottom of her neighbor's throat. His bright-red lips made guppy snatches at the air.

D heard a sudden burst of rain, rushing down onto hard wood. A gruff voice ordered, "Pick yourselves up, damn it!"

"I would take it back if I could. But I'm not blameless. You were wrong about that. I haven't been blameless for a long time. And I'm sorry for killing them.

"Not for killing you, though. You were a devil."

New People

The Morgue Ship had abruptly passed from the night sea into a long, high gallery.

Its keel screeched along the floor, and as the vessel settled, it tilted groaningly rightward and came to rest against a wall, shattering shutters and windows. As the deck slanted, Lorena lost her footing, but the first mate, Zanes, caught her arm and saved her from falling. A sign, severed from its wires by the chimney, fell beside them and broke into two pieces:

MACHINES AN
D THEIR OPERATORS

"You all right, Ms. Skye?" he asked.

The sudden transition had rattled Lorena, but she was well trained in improvisation. She exhaled. "I'm fine, Mr. Zanes, thank you, but on first glance I believe we've run aground at a museum."

The door of the wheelhouse opened and the captain, Joven, picked his way up the tilted deck to grab the rail. He looped an elbow under it and swung around to address them. "Pick yourselves up, damn it!" he bellowed. "This is the time! This is the time, damn it!"

The members of the crew helped each other to their feet and braced themselves as best they could.

"Good!" Joven cried. "Now, listen to me: we're going out into the streets, and we're going to fight for our fellows. You've already died, so whatever happens from here on is gravy. Are you with me?"

"Oh, yes, Captain! I'm with you!" Lorena piped up, and clapped her hands. She had always wanted to be in a play where she got to partake in a battle. "What do we do?"

Joven pointed over the railing. "First you disembark"—down below, red stars were twinkling in the museum floor—"and then you find yourself a body, and climb into it."

△

D sat up, but otherwise stayed where she was, listening to them gather: their rigid footsteps in their different shoes and slippers and boots, their coarse pants swishing, their patched skirts rustling.

She listened, and she stared at the pool of blood from the dead man and the triangular pattern of nail heads. They had become lustrous under the red. The wood of the museum floor beneath her palm felt unnaturally warm and she could feel something flowing along the grains of the boards. It was as if the life that had departed her neighbor's body had been absorbed by the triangular symbol, and the symbol had redirected it into a new body—the floors and walls and beams of the museum.

A stiff hand touched her shoulder.

She inhaled and looked around.

Robert's severed head rested on the mechanic's wax neck, above the gore-coated shoulders of the mechanic's jacket, and atop the mechanic's body, but he was still, immediately and distinctly, himself.

His mouth parted into a full-toothed smile.

"Hello, Lieutenant," D said.

He placed his wax hand against her cheek. The fingers crackled as they bent, flaking bits of wax skin. Despite being animated, the hand seemed even less lifelike than it had been. The wax felt as if it had hardened into something stony. There was no warmth at all in it, of course, not like real skin.

D sobbed. "Bobby, Bobby, Bobby . . ."

He put the wax hands under her arms, and gently lifted her to her feet, and held her with the bloodless body.

Crowded around them in a circle was the population of the museum: the sawmill operator–engineer, the soldier-clockmaker, the bicyclist-printer, the bricklayers, the sailors, the clamdigger, the farmer and his dog, the engineman, the fireman, the telegraph operator, the wheelwright, the future miner, the woman Gucci, the surgeon, the surgeon's patient, the skinners, the fruit picker, and all the other workers, in their ragged but clean clothes, glossy-faced, some one-eyed, some carrying their tools. Their countenances ranged from sober to melancholy to joyful, but a confidence radiated from all of them, a solidity, a strange and authoritative goodness. They were awesome, but she was not afraid of them.

Beyond the crowd, she saw Joven's vessel. The Morgue Ship had beached itself at the foot of the gallery, where it lolled against the wall. It fit comfortably in the high-ceilinged room. Water streamed from its sides to the floor.

The stories had been true: the ship had not sunk, but continued to sail. Now, it seemed that the souls that had been aboard it had found new bodies—the wax bodies of the workers of the National Museum of the Worker.

From a floor somewhere higher in the building there was a grinding rumble, wood and glass breaking, the peeling moan of metal on metal, like train wheels on train tracks. D thought she knew what it must be.

"What will you do?" D asked Robert.

His cracked lips slowly shaped three words. He repeated them for D, and repeated them again.

"'We will protect,'" she said.

He nodded.

"The people, you mean?" D asked. "Out there?"

He nodded again.

The rumble that had begun somewhere above was louder, the crushing of wheels reverberating through the shaft of the stairwell.

"Be careful, darling," D said.

Robert winked.

△

The wax army swung around, and shuffled from the museum.

Behind them, the metal wagon drove from the third floor, thundering its way down the stairs. It smashed through the doorway to the first floor in an explosion of brick and lath. The wagon rolled the length of the gallery in a humming crackle, plowing through exhibits and benches, knocking some aside and demolishing others beneath its huge wheels, and shedding clouds of debris. As it passed her, the soldier with the painted face who manned the huge gun atop the machine swiveled toward D, his uniform coated in plaster dust, and saluted.

It drove on, spraying fans of water where the Morgue Ship had drenched the floor, and went jouncing down the last flight of stairs. D heard it bash its way out into the street.

Friends

"I'll slay you in one step." Zil wagged a shard of jagged glass at the figure that loomed in the smoky entryway of the ruins.

Len jumped from a pile of rubble with a shout of war and hurled his shoe at the threatening silhouette. The figure yelled in pain.

Ike emerged out of the smoke with a bloody lip, and grabbed Len around the neck. Zil was immediately pained to see that Ike's wonderful brown suit was torn at both knees.

"I thought you were someone trying to get us!" Len fought Ike's grasp, but Ike didn't let go.

"You hit me in the face with your shoe!" Ike ground his knuckles into Len's skull, and rubbed them back and forth.

"Ah! I got a hurt foot!" Len hopped on one leg, keeping his bare foot off the ground.

Never one to miss an opportunity to point out the lesson in a situation—especially when it came to Len, who had an obstinate streak—Zil remarked, "There's throwing rocks laying around everywhere and this one chucks his shoe."

"What are you rotten stupid children doing in this place?" Ike released the boy.

"We came to make a Social Call!" Len said angrily.

"That's the truth," Zil said.

Ike was nonplussed. "What the bright shiny fuck is a Social Call?"

"It's what people do, Ike." Len rubbed a tear from his eye and sniffed. "It's custom."

"That doesn't explain why you're here. I told you I'd be at the museum."

"There was a Volunteer coming up the street," Zil said, "and we had to hide out. We made ourselves a spot and laid low. Once we started thinking about being off, the bombing and the shooting started up."

"And there's all these cats. If you believe in all that, that means it's safe." Len gestured toward what was, indeed, a remarkable number of cats. There might have been two dozen just in the vicinity of the ruined building's empty front doorway. They crouched and lolled, statuesque, on the stones, on the broken walls, on the odd juts of scorched wood. Not one seemed even mildly indisposed as the smoke and mist licked around them.

Along with the damage to Ike's suit, Zil noted that he no longer wore the pretty white scarf they'd given him. Along with the blood on his lip, there was also something disconsolate in his face, a careworn quality that was different from the shrewd poise that he had exuded in previous meetings.

"What's happened to you, Ike?" she asked.

A terrible thought occurred to Zil that made her grow emotional. "She had another man, didn't she, Ike? She had another man and he gave you a beating. Oh, I'm so sorry, Ike." Zil threw her arms around him before he could respond. "You'll find someone else."

Δ

It was far easier to let Zil believe that Dora had thrown him over than to explain the truth, that he'd run from the terrifying man who'd surprised him in the museum. He'd run and left Dora to him.

"But you'll have to tell me a few things first," the man had said in Ike's ear, and Ike, as calm as could be, as calm as if he were waiting for a piece of flotsam to come drifting out from the shadows of the No, calmer than he'd ever thought he could be, had said, "I'll tell you whatever you want, mister. I don't want any trouble."

This earned a chuckle from his ambusher, and Ike sensed an

infinitesimal relaxation in the body that was pressed up against him. He dropped a hard heel on the man's bare foot and ran. The scarf burned across his neck as the man snatched it, but Ike escaped. At the stairs, he'd thrown a look back and seen the man full-on, big as a statue, black beard like a nettle bush, grinning and holding the scarf.

"I'll have my interview, Ike!" he'd called.

Ike had fled home to the Lees, only to learn that his friends were dead. Good old Rei and good old Groat, the closest to parents he'd ever had, and Marl too. Though they'd only been murdered that morning, they'd already been dragged out, shrouded, and given to the Fair to take away. He'd never see them again.

To allow Ike into the Still, the soldier on guard had demanded the diamond ring off Ike's finger, the one that was meant for Dora, and he'd given it. Blood was everywhere, and all of it crawling with bugs. The smell in the air was of iron and loosened bowels and alcohol. Ike had rushed outside without going up to the crawl space to fetch his things, and puked in the street.

The soldier on guard laughed. "Rich, ain't it?"

Since then, Ike had kept moving. He had no idea if the enormous, bearded intruder at the museum was somehow connected to what had happened at the Still—he couldn't see how that was possible—and he didn't know what, if anything, the murders might have to do with himself. To wait around, though, was plainly dangerous. The man knew his name.

Nights he'd spent under the bridges. Days he'd spent wandering the Bluffs, halfway contemplating leaping off to the rocks below. Every second Ike felt breathless, felt trapped inside himself. His cowardice nagged him, clawed at him with the wind on the cliffs, sniffed at him with the noses of the rats that scurried up beside him in his sleeping places under the bridges. Ike felt that he had been gravely mistaken about himself.

Dora could take care of herself, but she was no match for the man who had nearly got Ike. He had never stopped thinking of her, not since he'd met her, but he wished he could. In his mind, the man with the black beard choked her until she turned dead-blue.

It was only once the cannons and the fusillades of rifle fire had commenced that he had summoned the courage to return to the museum. The churning noise—not just of the fighting, but of the people fleeing and screaming and shouting—had seemed to block out his own castigations, and he finally felt strong again.

His progress uptown to Little Heritage was slow and disorienting. The city was phantasmic, smeared by the smoke and the mist. It seemed as if one wrong turn might take him into a whole other city altogether, one that shared certain traits with his own, alleys and saloons and museums and theaters and folks who had a lot and folks who had none, with the Fields and the Fair but by other names, where Ike would be a stranger to everyone, the sole speaker of his language.

As he came to the city center, the roar of the cannon blasts became louder, there were crowds, and people knocked against him. Ike kept on, telling himself that maybe Dora was all right, maybe the bearded man had not harmed her at all, or maybe he was keeping her prisoner. He fantasized about killing him and freeing her. He eventually found his way to the museum, its bland soaring face materializing through wisps of smoke.

It was only when he pressed his hands to the jutting hammerheads of the front door that his nerve failed him again. How could he defeat a man like that?

Ike scratched at his wrists with his nails, bit at his hand, punched his own shoulder, attempting to batter himself into trying the door latch. *It will probably be locked, and you can go away*, he bargained with himself.

Even that was too much of a chance, too much of a risk to his sorry, cowardly life. He'd retreated, screaming inside at his own weakness—and spotted the flicker of a silhouette in the empty doorway of the neighboring ruins.

△

The young ones were relieved when he told them he'd lead them back to the Lees, well away from the fighting. Ike didn't have the heart to tell them that if the fighting made its way downtown, there'd be nowhere to go after that but the bay.

They held hands as they picked their way across the smoky lawn to the street. Ike held Zil's and Zil held Len's. Zil's hand was sweaty.

"Why do kids always have such greasy damn hands?" Ike asked.

"I don't know why for other kids," Zil said, "but for me, it's because I rub them around in piles of shit."

"That's why for me too," Len said.

Ike said, "I want you to know that I won't let anyone harm you two. That's a privilege I'm reserving for my own self."

A stiff clomping, a marching cadence, gathered somewhere behind the fog. Ike hissed. They halted, clustered together, somewhere near the corner of Legate. Bolts of smoke unraveled around them. There was the lump of a corpse on the ground a few feet away, a poker sticking up straight from its torso.

"Are we gonna be all right?" whispered Len.

"Yeah," Ike said. "But be ready to run."

A human shape appeared. It had a flowing mane. There was a familiarity in the imposing curl of the shoulders.

He almost laughed. "Rei? How the—"

The clamdigger from the museum cocked her head at Ike. The shadows had shortened her to Rei's height, but she was as tall as ever, and her ferocious smile, molded and painted onto her face, was framed by pure white hair, not Rei's black-and-silver.

One of her wax hands dropped onto Ike's head and ruffled his hair.

His breath had caught when he saw her clearly, but now he let it go—for there was nothing to be afraid of. The feel of her hand was cold and inhuman, but it was familiar too.

"Rei," he said, because it was her. Ike knew it. She was the closest thing to a mother he'd ever had, or would have. He'd know her anywhere.

The clamdigger—Rei in a new form—nodded, shoved him ungently aside, and disappeared into the smoke. Zil and Len hid behind Ike. Other figures from the museum passed by, emerging from the smoke, swinging their rigid arms, rocking on their jointless legs, before being swallowed.

A hunched wax figure with the head of a woman and the body of a roly-poly man appeared. Their expression was humorless. Ike had never noticed them in the museum before, but the figure's hunch belonged to Groat.

"Groat?"

The figure gave Ike a not entirely friendly thump of acknowledgment in the chest. No sooner had this new embodiment of Groat vanished into the smoke than there came a bellowing crash of metal, and the grinding of rubble being reduced to powder. A wagon-sized box of green steel rolled out of the smoke on shining black wheels. Brick fragments and wood shards were littered over the machine's front. A wax man in a green uniform stood through a hole in the roof, wielding a rifle that was as long as a cannon. The smoke sucked the massive vehicle into itself after a second, but Ike could still hear its mighty wheels as it swung onto Legate and headed for midtown.

Len had buried his face in Ike's jacket and was crying.

"What do we do?" Zil asked.

"Take it easy now," Ike said. "We're just going to go in the opposite direction. I don't think we'll have any problem from those ones, anyway. I'm friends with some of these people."

△

A cordon of Gildersleeve's infantry had rounded up a trio of suspects and put them against a wall by the crossing of National Boulevard and Legate. They leveled their rifles upon them. "For the crime of disloyalty," the commanding officer said.

A teenaged girl in the suspect group screamed that she wasn't anybody. "I'm just trying to get home!" Another of the suspects, an older woman, slumped down to the ground in a puddle of skirts. "Oh, fuck all of you, you fucking bootlickers," said the third suspect, Brewster Uldine. His tram had broken down and he'd stayed with it, like a driver was supposed to, and Gildersleeve's men had yanked him off and put him under arrest.

He announced, "I'm not a revolutionary, but if you're going to kill me, then consider me joined!" and gave them the finger.

The clatter of hundreds of hollow footsteps echoed from amid the clouds of smoke that obscured Legate.

"Redirect!" ordered the commanding officer, and his line of a dozen men swiveled to aim their rifles into the smoke that swathed Legate.

As the marching steps came closer, the smoke seemed to vibrate. "Fire!" cried the officer, losing his nerve and breaking the protocol against engagement before making visual contact. The soldiers unleashed a full volley into the smoke.

The clattering footsteps continued, unaffected, and the veil of smoke billowed open to reveal a formation of civilians, glossy-faced and glass-eyed, propelled by stiff limbs. Several bore bullet holes from the volley, but none were bleeding.

"Those aren't people," said one soldier, and threw aside his rifle, and fled.

"Halt!" the commanding officer ordered the oncoming figures as they overwhelmed his men, but they did not heed him.

While this was happening, Brewster guided the other two suspects to a doorway, and into a building.

"Who are those that showed up with the weird faces?" asked the girl who had only been trying to get home. The tram driver looked back and saw the huge green wagon rip out of the gloom, spitting fire from the rifle on top, and Gildersleeve's men dancing as the bullets shredded their bodies. He screamed over the deafening chatter to just keep going, keep going and don't stop.

The Hunt

*W*hen they had gone, the wax people with their human souls, walked and driven out the museum's front door and into the city, D gripped the head of the drill bit where it protruded from her neighbor's temple and yanked. It came out glistening blackly with whatever had been inside the monster's skull. She wiped the bit on her filthy skirt and returned it to her apron pocket for just in case. She lifted the pliers from her neighbor's dead grasp.

D made her way through the gallery. Her shoes splashed in the water that had rained from the barnacle-snarled sides of the Morgue Ship.

The wagon had destroyed the wide doorframe and dragged the front doors made of melted hammers into the street.

D stepped out into the gloom. She felt something soft and warm twine impatiently around her ankles, and she followed it to the left, in the direction of the Society's ruins.

△

Inside the Vestibule, D scraped her hand over the triangles etched in the wood, feeling her way through the dark to the deep dark. There was no need to cut herself this time; blood from her broken nose was all over her face.

The white cat was with her, and so were dozens of others. The Society ruins had been riddled with them, perched on the broken stones, waiting for her. Now their animal bodies stirred around her shoes and she heard them licking their chops, purring against each other. D had been around enough cats in her years in service to decipher this behavior. It was what they did when they were excited to be let outdoors to hunt.

That was what they had wanted the whole time, she understood, for her to open the door for them. The secret of the Vestibule was in the way the Gentle had pricked the fingers of his volunteers: a human's fresh blood opened its portal. That was why they had needed her.

While D used one hand on the wall to guide her, with the other she prodded the emptiness with the long pliers. A hot, gritty breeze lifted her hair, and at the end of a dark hall a yellow fold opened. It opened wider and wider.

Δ

One after the other, the dark globes on the path to the temple blazed to life. Lumm shuffled along the path, pausing at points to observe as the spirits of the dead soldiers appeared in the flames, and were immediately hypnotized by their own reflections in the tiny mirrors. It had been Westhover's idea to add the patches with the triangular symbol to both the Auxiliary Garrison's and the regular army's livery and, Lumm had to concede, a brilliant innovation it had been. In the past, in order to obtain the adequate number of souls required to power the lights that rejuvenated the bodies of the Society's membership, they had needed to send out a great raft of Red Letters compelling people to mark themselves with the triangle and commit suicide. But as the soldiers who wore the patches with the symbol died, their souls were promptly delivered to the globes. It was very, very efficient: the soldiers obliterated the agitators, and what casualties the army suffered were delivered to the Twilight Place, to provide succor for their betters.

Where was Westhover, though? He had promised to cross over after dispatching the nasty little bitch with the bizarre vendetta. Lumm maintained no affection for the man, but he was useful.

For that matter, where was the nasty little bitch? Crossley had appeared in one of the globes, and that was delightful and just, but Westhover had put the mark on her too, so she ought to have appeared by now as well. Westhover must have decided to take his time with her. Well, that was all right.

The playwright tried to get his mind around the idea of her enmity. What could that Ambrose, who Lumm doubted he would have remembered if not for the young man's buckteeth, possibly have meant to her? Whatever it was, it wasn't worth it. These distorting attachments that women suffered were, he thought, quite tragic. Look at Frieda, and the blithe way she had gone traipsing around a cliff with an unscrupulous individual like himself, just because they had been friends for a few hundred years.

" 'These Distorting Attachments,' " he said, addressing the soldier who had materialized in the fires of the nearest globe, and who was staring at his own reflection with narcotic reverence even as his body was consumed. "What do you think about that for the title of a play?" Lumm thought it was an excellent, evocative title. He suddenly felt inspired.

The president of the Society for Psykical Research doddered farther up the path in the direction of the plateau and the portal, wanting to see if Westhover had arrived. The first tendrils of a narrative spun out in his mind: an obsessive girl; a brilliant playwright of whom she is jealous; a harm she attempts to do him; and the definitive justice he furnishes in response. Lumm's new muse distracted him from the pain of the arthritis in his legs, from the dumb weight of his dead hands. Near the trailhead, there was a white flowering in his peripheral vision—what could only be in this stony world of muted colors a grain in his eye—and he blinked at it. The obsessive girl's hatred for the brilliant playwright is brought about by his gentle rebuke of her facile attempts at art. She has written an insipid play about . . . cats!

Lumm giggled to himself. He had a vision of the girl's stupid play within the play, of actors costumed as cats, crawling around and wistfully saying things like "I do so hope that some sweet child will make me her pet!"

The white flowering grew. Lumm halted, and looked.

A white cat was running at him, running so fast that its legs seemed not to touch the ground; rather, it seemed to flash toward him, to approach in great, imperceptible jumps. Behind the animal, more cats emptied from the portal; too many to count. The white cat flickered nearer and nearer, and Lumm thought of the conjurer, that low-class rascal who never deigned to reveal how he'd learned a bit of real magic, promising his audience that he had a full menu of delights in store for them, and riffling a deck of cards between his hands with such speed that fifty-two merged into one.

The cat sprang, and Lumm cried, "Who let you in here?" It flew at his face, tiny sharp teeth and tiny sharp claws and eyes of blue glass. "Who the hell—"

△

This time, D saw everything clear and true—her blindfold was gone.

The cats surged ahead of her, bathed in the rancid moonlight. XVII was first, and they followed her in a tide, black and white and orange and brown, solid and striped and patched, navigating the barren plateau with the purpose of running water. They crossed through the shadows of the columns, and rushed to the pass lined with burning globes.

There was a single figure at the trailhead. He was bent and crooked, and wore sparkling golden robes. *Lumm*, she thought. The robed figure shouted once—a frail cry of terror—before XVII and the rest of the cats covered him, and he seemed to melt beneath their weight. More and more cats emerged from the portal, eager to join in the feast.

She let the pliers slip from her hand. They hit the ground with a dull thud.

In her chair by the guillotine, the tattooed crone in the chair snorted dryly. "I knew those cats would get back in here eventually."

She glanced at D's face and scowled. "I hope you killed the son of a bitch who did that to your nose."

"I did," D said. "Who are you?"

The crone scratched a nostril with one of her needles. "Don't know. Forgot. I cut the necks and put on the faces. Who are you?"

"I'm D. I was the curator of the National Museum of the Worker. I'm not anything now."

D shielded her eyes from the glare of the yolky moons. She felt that if she shifted in any direction she would collapse.

"Do you want my job?" the crone asked. There was some hope in her voice.

"No," D said, "I'm sorry."

The crone snorted. This concluded their conversation. The old woman closed her eyes and dropped her chin against her chest.

XVII trotted from the trailhead with a gray thumb in her mouth. She ignored D and disappeared back into the portal with her meal.

D thought the crone had the right idea. She made her legs take her to a stone seat a few feet away. She sank onto it and closed her own eyes.

A little girl appeared to her. The girl did not look like her, was not her child. She had pigtails and an air of mirth. Her grin seemed to contain a half dozen extra teeth. "What are we doing today, Nurse?" she asked.

"I'm going to teach you Dribs and Drabs," D said, "so you can beat all the boys."

They met Ike on the No Fair. He had fully matured into manhood, was handsome enough that he didn't need to steal anything anymore—women would just let him borrow. But despite his fuller face and thicker shoulders, he wore the same sporting cap in the same sporting way, high on his crown. "Oh, look at this! Someone get me a frame," he said when he saw them.

D pictured her rooms: the neat kitchen, the drawing room with its fireplace, and the bedroom with her single bed, and a window beside it, and violet twilight in the trees. It was all very clean, and there was a glorious, polished new lock on the door. She didn't have to let anyone she didn't like inside.

Winter

Amid the repulsion of the Crown's army, the brokering of the new peace, and the elections, three months passed. The new interim government was led by a university student known as Barnes—or whoever the individual was who had the wax body of a bicycle mechanic and the severed head of the Volunteer. During the fighting, the appearance of the bloodless warriors had routed and scattered the Crown's forces. When Barnes, who had sneaked behind the lines, appeared on the heights above the Great Highway, holding in his arms the corpse of King Macon XXIV, and cast it over the edge, Gildersleeve's successor had waved the white flag and surrendered.

While the election slates for the new legislature were being arranged, Barnes and three other wax figures, the two soldiers with brown-and-green-painted faces and a potter, had maintained offices in the chambers of the chief magistrate. The Four, as they quickly came to be called, conveyed their wishes in writing to a unique committee of twenty-one flesh-and-blood members that was, according to design, composed of one representative each from several vocations. A student filled one seat on the committee and a lawyer filled another, but there was also a tram driver and a glazier, a baker and a dockman, and so on. The committee included women too, such as a kitchen maid who had once cleaned pots and pans at the Metropole.

While the political business was handled by the Four, their wax fellows dedicated themselves to clearing debris from the streets and to interring the dead.

△

In the wake of the elections, the Four had disbanded.

Barnes departed, leaving nothing except for a few spots of blood and wax on the chief magistrate's desk. Though people were grateful to Barnes, his presence—the grisly neck that wept fresh blood and the face of living flesh—was disconcerting in a way that the others were not, and there had been relief at the news of his disappearance. He was last seen walking on the Great Highway toward the farmlands of the north.

As for the other temporary leaders, the wax potter had relocated to the Lees, and immediately begun crafting icons out of Fair mud and firing them in the public kilns. He worked at this, so far as anyone could tell, unceasingly, day and night.

The two wax soldiers had driven their machine into the river, and taken a quiet retirement in a suite on the third floor of the Metropole. Though they were rarely seen, the hotel workers reported that they were exemplary guests. They made no mess and hardly any noise, and Talmadge XVII adored them. She was always climbing onto the elevator and riding up to visit her wax friends. She'd scratch and scratch at the door until they allowed her into their rooms.

△

It was around this time that Ike left the Still Crossing for good.

One morning he dropped from the ceiling with a case containing his possessions. The clamdigger was behind the bar, smiling in that wild way that was painted on her face, and with her white hair flowing around her shoulders. No matter how she looked, though, she was Rei, through and through.

After the peace, they'd all come home to the Still in their new bodies. Rei the clamdigger had gone right back behind the bar, and Elgin and Marl, for it could be no others, had retaken their stools in the bodies of those wax bricklayers who wore their old suspenders. The wax figure with the old man's body and the hard-faced woman's head had gone to Groat's seat at the table by the dirty window. At some stage of the combat, a shrapnel blast had torn away a large chunk of the hard-faced woman's head, leaving a gruesome, charred wax crater. This disfigurement suited Groat perfectly.

But it was quiet. These versions of his friends no longer bickered, or told stories, or threatened to feed anyone the Deadly. The one that was Groat sometimes wandered out to the rear yard to stand over the stump, but of course never urinated on it anymore. The glasses of beer that the wax clamdigger Rei had served the wax bricklayers Elgin and Marl were as full as the day she'd poured them. Likewise, the plate of pickled oysters that sat on Groat's table went untouched.

Ike had heard of similar things occurring all over the city. Wax folks had returned to the places their souls knew, and generally been received by their loved ones with acceptance. They had been busy at first, making things how they liked, but save for a few exceptions like the determined potter—whom everyone believed to be inhabited by the spirit of the Charmer himself, just as they believed that the wax soldiers must be Jonas Mosi and Lionel Woodstock—most had soon slowed, and become almost like statues again. Ike had the thought that one day they would probably cease moving altogether. People would keep taking care of them, though. They might need to be reawakened someday.

Ike went to the door, crunching through the oyster shells, and turned to say farewell. "I'll be around to visit."

The clamdigger raised her stiff wax hand, and he raised his in return, and left.

It was only once he'd departed that a couple of tears escaped her glass eyes.

△

The decision to relocate was made easier, of course, because Ike had a place to go.

"Why? There's a disgusting boat stuck in the first floor," Len had said when Ike told him of his plan to take up residence in the National Museum of the Worker. "You can do better."

Zil hadn't liked it either, albeit for different reasons. "You need to get over her, Ike."

Ike would never admit it, but he had come to care about his strays. He was pleased they had taken to attending the new public schools, and were learning to read, write, and calculate numbers. "I appreciate your concern," he said to them, "and I will always follow your progress and keep my eye on you. I plan to be a mentor and an inspiration to you hapless little shits for years to come. You can be assured of that."

"Thank you, Ike." Len, visibly moved by this heartfelt promise, had thrown his arms around him.

Ike clapped his back. "I'll just be a little uptown, that's all, and you can visit anytime."

But there was no way to distract Zil from her conviction. "I don't want you to die of a broken heart, Ike."

She frowned at him, and he noticed that her freckles had faded some. Zil's real face was surfacing, and quite a pretty face it would be, shining out with her sharp wits. Ike imagined her a grown woman, and the boys slouching after her, just hoping for one chance to lose to her at Dribs and Drabs. They'd want to put her in a frame to admire, but he didn't believe that Zil would ever let them.

Something about the look on his face made her furious. "Why are you smiling?" Zil demanded.

"Because," he said, "the only thing that could ever break this old Ike's heart would be if something ever happened to you two."

Δ

At the foot of the No Fair, Ike spied the one-eyed fruit picker who had been stationed beneath the tree on the museum's fifth-floor gallery. The wax man loitered by a railing, unmoving except for his single eye, which slid back and forth as it monitored the traffic that exited off the bridge.

Along with the fruit picker's bag that was slung over his shoulders, he held a stick at his side. The late-autumn cold had printed sparkles of frost on his wax skin.

The stick gave Ike a notion. He approached the fruit picker. "Beat Your Dust?"

The fruit picker nodded and clacked his stick against the railing.

"You suppose if I brought you a couple of things, could you knock em clean for me?"

The fruit picker banged the stick a couple more times against the railing.

"Good man," Ike said. "I'll see you soon."

Farther on he paused to pet a black cat sprawled on the cobbles. The animal's great, bulging stomach was irresistible. "And what have you been eating?" he asked, and the cat purred.

"I've never seen so many fat cats," a passing woman remarked. "Well, it's got to be lucky, is my opinion."

Ike tipped his hat to her and said it must be so.

Winter's first snow was falling by the time he reached the museum.

∆

The new curator spent most of his first day sweeping the first-floor gallery. Propped against the wall, the wreck of the Morgue Ship had dried, and so had the river water it had shed on the floor. Its coating of barnacles had summarily perished, and great masses of them had crumbled to the boards below to create an ashy carpet. Ike swept the detritus into some empty lime sacks that he'd found and carried them one at a time to dump in the ruins next door, where he had found the strays that night.

As he labored, more snow arrived, and softened the heaps of broken bricks and jagged beams. There had, for a while, been a single scorched doorframe in a corner of the wreckage huddled beneath a small wing of ceiling, but Ike noticed that it had either collapsed in on itself or been knocked apart by vandals. Where it had stood there was only a pile of burnt wood. Snow covered this too.

When night fell, Ike laid aside his broom and drew his coat tight around himself against the draft that poured through the broken windows beside the crashed ship. He had already scavenged some planking for the broken front of the building, but the windows would need to be blocked up too. After that he would chop up the rotten ship. It might take all winter, but he had the time.

He went upstairs, carrying a lamp to see, passing through the galleries on his way. No one drove the trains, or sat around the black-painted stones of the skinners' fire, or tended the baker's oven, or stood beside the wooden box with the lens. Without their people, the remaining exhibits seemed small underneath the high ceilings, but Ike thought it might be better. When people came to visit, they could climb up into the trains, or wander behind the baker's counter. Instead of seeing the figures at their work, they could imagine it was themselves doing the driving or the baking.

At the door of the prospector's shack, Ike hesitated, remembering how the man had sneaked up on him. There was nothing to fear, though: the man was dead. On an earlier visit he'd seen with his own eyes two wax figures drag his massive, ugly corpse out the door of the museum.

Ike went in, put his lamp on the table, and turned it down. He climbed into the narrow bed.

The new curator lay and heard footsteps that he knew were not real. He smelled soap on the silk pillowcase, the powdered soap that Dora used, with its faint tinge of lemon. It surprised him that the scent lingered after all these weeks. But Dora was like that, wasn't she? Never what you expected. What kind of prospector had a silk pillowcase? She'd stolen it for sure.

Ike ran his hand over his cheek and pretended it was her hand. He fantasized that the imaginary footsteps were hers, that she had come home to him.

Soon after that, Ike slept, deeply and comfortably.

The very real woman who had been watching him from the darkness stole from the museum.

△

The door in the Fields had been dismantled as well, obliterated with an ax. Not that anyone noticed.

△

Off the Great Highway, not far from the bottom of the path below the monolithic structure, Robert Barnes waited in a cave.

The cave's mouth was screened by a curtain of roots and partially obstructed by brush. He waited, and looked through the gap in the roots, watching the nights chew up the moons and then spit them up. He waited, and spiders crawled over his wax hands, and rodents crept in to sniff at the blood that leaked from the unhealing wound of his severed neck, and he waited some more. On a few occasions, a lean, tawny, striped cat skulked through the brush and nestled beside his wax hip and worked its claws through the material of the mechanic's pants and into the wax beneath, and purred; and they waited together. Snow fell, and he waited, and he waited—until the night that the lone silhouette of a woman appeared on the Highway.

"Robert Barnes!" she called. "Bobby!" She raised a lamp and shone it around. "Lieutenant! Lieutenant!"

He swept aside the roots and the brush, and walked to her across a winter field.

At the sound of his shoes, clomping and cracking through the icy grass, she turned. "We can use this to chip pieces from the stones," Dora said, and drew a tiny bit from the pocket of her coat, and raised it for her darling to see.

"We can use this to chip pieces from the stones," Dora said.

A Note

Douglas Starr's brilliant true crime study *The Killer of Little Shepherds* (Knopf, 2010) taught me about how civilians visited the Paris Morgue as a diversion, and also provided the inspiration for the Morgue Ship. Starr writes of an actual "floating morgue," which blighted the Rhône River in Lyon for decades, until it was swept away in a storm and destroyed.

Acknowledgments

First of all, this novel wouldn't exist if Brian James Freeman hadn't asked me to contribute the short story that inspired it to his *Detours* anthology. Brian, I owe you one.

I'm also grateful to Gavin Grant and Kelly Link for publishing that original story in *Lady Churchill's Rosebud Wristlet*.

Timothy Bracy, Kelly Braffet, Andrew Ervin, Joshua Ferris, Jennifer Krazit, Charles Lambert, Elizabeth Nelson, Mark Jude Poirier, and Stacey Richter read the manuscript in an earlier draft and offered criticism, insights, and encouragement that dramatically improved the story. They all belong in frames to admire.

I've been lucky to have Amy Williams as my agent for twenty years. Amy, thank you for all that you do.

Thanks are due as well to my foreign rights agent, Jenny Meyer.

I'm indebted to everyone at Scribner: Sabrina Pyun, Stuart Smith, Clare Maurer, Ashley Gilliam, Mark Galaritta, Jaya Miceli, Kyle Kabel, Annie Craig, Laura Wise, and especially the ceaselessly encouraging Nan Graham. It was Nan who had the brilliant idea to lure the brilliant Joe Monti away from his responsibilities at Saga Press to edit *The Curator*. Joe really understood the book, understood what it needed, and it was a pleasure to work with him. Joe, let's do this again sometime!

ACKNOWLEDGMENTS

Kathleen Jennings's illustrations are so wonderful, I can't imagine the book without them.

Joal Hetherington's copyedits were extraordinarily helpful.

The short story "The Curator" was dedicated to one of my heroes, Peter Straub. He is greatly missed.

I also want to recognize the following cool cats for various acts of generosity and camaraderie: Mark Amodio, Greg Baglia, Jim Baker, Tom Bissell, Jim Braffet, Theresa Braffet, Michael Cendejas, Richard Chizmar, Christine Cohen, Lauren DePoala, Sal DePoala, Nathan Hensley, Jesse Kellerman, Josh Kesselman, Joe Lansdale, Mark Levenfus, Rhett Miller, Rob Neyer, Elizabeth Nogrady, Greg Olear, Heidi Pitlor, Lynn Pleshette, Jerry Rocha, Karen Russell, and Paul Russell.

Thank you, of course, to my dad, my brother, my sister, and most of all my mother, who was so enthusiastic about the story.

Finally, none of this would be any fun at all without my family. *K & Z, this book is for you.*

About the Author

Owen King is the author of the novel *Double Feature* and *We're All in This Together: A Novella and Stories*. He is the coauthor of *Sleeping Beauties* and *Intro to Alien Invasion* and the coeditor of *Who Can Save Us Now? Brand-New Superheroes and Their Amazing (Short) Stories*. He lives in Upstate New York with his family.